*Dedicated to MARK DEASEY
my dear and remarkable friend.
With thanks to David Greagg,
Richard Revill, Jean Greenwood, Tim Daly
and Dennis Pryor.*

Out of the Black Land

Books by Kerry Greenwood

Out of the Black Land

The Phryne Fisher Series

Cocaine Blues
Flying Too High
Murder on the Ballarat Train
Death at Victoria Dock
The Green Mill Murder
Blood and Circuses
Ruddy Gore
Urn Burial
Raisins and Almonds
Death Before Wicket
Away With the Fairies
Murder in Montparnasse
The Castlemaine Murders
Queen of the Flowers
Death by Water
Murder in the Dark
Murder on a Midsummer Night
Dead Man's Chest
Unnatural Habits

The Corinna Chapman Series

Earthly Delights
Heavenly Pleasures
Devil's Food
Trick or Treat
Forbidden Fruit
Cooking the Books

Short Story Anthology
A Question of Death:
An Illustrated Phryne Fisher Anthology

Out of the Black Land

Kerry Greenwood

Poisoned Pen Press

Poisoned Pen Press
6962 E. First Ave., Ste. 103
Scottsdale, AZ 85251
www.poisonedpenpress.com
info@poisonedpenpress.com

Printed in the United States of America

FEB 19 2013

Contents

The Cast

Scribes

Ptah-hotep	Great Royal Scribe
Kheperren	Army Scribe
Khety	Scribe
Hanufer	Scribe
Bakhenmut	supervisor, married to Henutmire
Ammemmes	Master of Scribes
Mentu	second Scribe
Snefru	the antiquarian
Menna	an old scribe, expert in cuneiform
Harmose	an old scribe, expert in foreign languages
Pashed	the spy

Royal Household of Thebes

Amenhotep	Amenhotep III, the wise Pharaoh
Tiye	Amenhotep's Great Royal Wife and Queen
Sitamen	Tiye and Amenhotep's daughter and Great Royal Wife
Smenkhare	son of Tiye, later King
Tutankhaten	son of Tiye, later King Tutankhamen
Bekhetaten	daughter of Tiye, died young
Sahte	chief maidservant to Tiye
Horemheb	General, later Pharaoh

Tey — Great Royal Nurse, later Queen, step mother of Nefertiti

Ay — Divine Father, later Pharaoh, father of Nefertiti

Mutnodjme — daughter of Tey and Ay, wife of Horemheb, later Queen

Asen — nurse to Mutnodjme

Merope — Great Royal Wife to Amenhotep

Khons — their teacher

Duammerset — Singer of Isis

Userkhepesh — High Priest of Amen-Re at Karnak

Royal Household of Amarna

Akhnaten — Pharaoh, formerly Akhnamen/Amenhotep IV, son of Amenhotep III

Nefertiti — Nefertiti Neferneferuamen, later Neferneferuaten, Akhnaten's wife

Mekhetaten — 1st daughter of Nefertiti, later Great Royal Wife to her 'father' Akhnaten

Meritaten — 2nd daughter, later Great Royal Wife, died young

Ankhesenpaaten — 3rd daughter of Nefertiti, later wife of Akhnaten, then Tutankhamen, then Ay; renamed Ankhesenamen

Neferneferauten — 4th daughter of Nefertiti, died as an infant

Neferneferure — 5th daughter of Nefertiti, died as an infant

Setepenre — 6th and last daughter of Nefertiti, died as an infant

Imhotep — the architect of Amarna

Huy — advisor to Akhnaten

Pannefer — advisor to Akhnaten

Aapahte — chief of the Sekmet Guard of Queen Tiye

Ptah-hotep's Household

Meryt	Ptah-hotep's chief slave, housekeeper and concubine
Tani	Nubian slave
Hani	Nubian slave
Teti	Nubian slave
Anubis	the guard dog

Household of Mutnodjme

Takhar	the cook
Kasa	the small boy
Ipuy	the old soldier
Bukentef	the butler
Ankherhau	servant
Wab	little girl
Ii	maid
Nebnakht	a guard
Khaemdua	General of the Hermotybies.
Khety-tashery	'little' Khety, son of Khety the Scribe

Book One

The Hawk
in the Horizon

Chapter One

Mutnodjme

In the name of Ptah, in the name of his consort Mut after whom I was called and his son Khons who is the moon and time, in the hope that my heart will weigh heavily against the feather and I may live and die in Maat which is truth, I declare that my name is Mutnodjme and my sister is the most beautiful woman in the world.

I was born when she was seven. Her dying mother, the concubine, gave her into the arms of the formidable woman, my mother, Tey wife of Ay. I do not remember the concubine who bore Nefertiti. They say that she was beautiful, pale and silvery and sad, and she died young. Her child was kept apart from Tey's household, and I did not see her when I was a baby. Tey is a small woman, dark of skin and eye; and those things I have inherited from her.

I am small, measured against Nefertiti's length of limb; I am dark against her glowing Theban fairness. I am ugly against her almost divine beauty, and I am miserable against her happiness, for they have just told her that she is to marry Pharaoh Akhnamen, and become Great Royal Wife. She is his; no longer mine.

We have pleated the linen garments for her; and I am sitting on the marble floor of the palace of Divine Father Ay in the great city of Thebes—with the sellers of dates and dried fish calling his trade outside, women's voices, shrill and constant—making wreaths of moonflowers and lotus. I am uncomfortable and cramped, because I have no skill in my fingers for this delicate work, and the flowers will not lie peaceably along the wire frame for me as do those of the other maidens. They are refractory and shed their petals if I force them.

This is the third time that I have had to start again.

When did I first know her, my half-sister Neferiti Neferneferu-amen, whose name means 'The Beautiful One Who Is Come'?

It must have been the river.

I knew that I was being very naughty.

My wet-nurse had been called away on some deep matter involving herbs and childbirth—both female mysteries from which I was excluded—and the servant-girl who was supposed to watch me was flirting with the guard. I was sitting in the garden in Ay's palace, watching the little boats being dragged ashore as the flood filled the Nile and the banks crumbled.

'Egypt,' said Asen my nurse, 'is called the Black Land, because of the rich soil deposited by the river. Our land is the gift of the Nile,' she said, stroking my curly dark hair, 'as you are, daughter, as we all are. And Pharaoh is our Lord and the Gods are above and beneath us, the land our father Geb and the sky our mother Nut, so go to sleep, little daughter. We are cradled in the Nile, nursed by the river,' she said, and went away to tend a woman who was groaning in the next room.

I tried to follow, but an old woman grabbed me by the arm and hauled me from the door.

'Not yet, daughter of Ay,' she grinned toothlessly at me.

I was nettled at being excluded and wandered back to the window, where fascinating debris was being swept down the swollen river. The placid water foamed like honey from Asun. I waited until the girl was entirely engrossed in her guard and slipped quietly out of the window and onto the paved place outside the palace.

The air was full of people crying out and giving orders that no one was listening to. The flood had come down suddenly this year, my sixth in Maat, and early. Little houses which had been made by herdsmen to be dismantled later were being dismantled early by the water, running faster than a running horse. No one noticed me as I wandered through the crowd. Of all the children of Ay I most resembled the common people and apart from the fineness of my amulet and the gold rings in my ears there was nothing to set me apart. A woman leading a mother-goat and carrying a kid almost stood on me and cursed me out of her path in the name of Set, a serious curse. I threaded my way through the people to the edge.

Fascinating. People like ants scurried away from the water, carrying hay and sacks and terracotta pots. A solemn priest of Basht bore away a sacred cat from a grain storehouse which had been inundated. It was soaking wet, spitting and furious, and it scored his smooth pale shoulders with long angry lines, which he did not even seem to notice.

I was so interested in the movement and the voices, crying on a variety of Gods to allow them to get to safety before the water enveloped them, that I did not notice that the water had eaten away the spit of sand which I was standing on and was about to eat me.

I must have screamed as I fell. It was cold water, terribly strong, and I saw the flash of a reptilian tail as a crocodile was swept helplessly past, turning belly-up as it struggled to regain its balance. Ivory teeth flashed in the gaping mouth. I was seized by the Nile, pummelled and thumped. There was no air. A red mist rose in front of my eyes. I struggled to surface, striving against the current, gained the air and gulped, then the fists of the water thrust me under again, and the scales of another crocodile scraped my legs.

I struggled again, twisting all my slight weight, grabbed at something, and was hauled bodily out by strong hands. I came up red-faced, gasping, soaking wet, into strong arms which squeezed the Nile out of my lungs and shook me bodily.

It was the young man Horemheb, double my age and destined to be a soldier. He was tall and good looking, with long hair as black as ink and the most considering dark eyes. His hair was plaited in locks, each one tipped with a blue faience bead, which bobbed across his bare shoulders as he moved. He tucked me under one arm as though I was baggage and climbed the bank. I did not struggle against this humiliation, because I was still breathless and suddenly conscious of being in very deep trouble.

'You ran away from your nurse, Mutnodjme,' he said solemnly, setting me down on wobbly feet. I grasped at him as I felt myself falling and he picked me up again. His body was warm and his arms secure and I relaxed a little.

'Where is Asen?'

'Tending to a woman in childbirth,' I said. 'Put me down, I can walk.'

He did so, and took my long side-lock in his hands, wringing it to spill out the water. He surveyed me. I was a mess. My skin was stained with black mud, my feet and hands filthy, and blood was flowing from the crocodile scrapes along my legs. He wiped at the grazes with a hard hand.

'Doesn't this hurt?' he asked.

'Of course.' I winced as he blotted at the blood with his palm.

'But you haven't cried,' 'Nodjme,' he commented.

'There is no point in crying, Lord.'

He smiled then. Horemheb rarely smiled. It lit up his broad face like Re Exalted who is the sun at noon and I smiled back.

'We can't just steal back into the palace as though nothing has happened,' said my rescuer. 'I know. Nefertiti will help. Come along, little sister. Climb on my back, we have to hurry.'

Thus I saw her for the first time, the beautiful one.

'Now, how are we to get you out of this?' he asked himself, mounting the next bank and striding towards the palace of Ay.

'Now, how are we to get you out of this?' he asked himself, mounting the next bank and striding towards the palace of Ay.

'Doesn't this hurt?' he asked.

Horemheb skirted the palace walls, walked carefully through the first hall, then dived through a curtained door into the Princess' courtyard. I never thought to wonder how he knew the way. A woman was bathing in a pond full of fragrant water. I smelt lotus and jasmine. The air was heavy with scent like spring.

'Lady, I bring you a little sister in distress,' he said, putting me down. 'She was eaten by the river, and faces a beating for being drawn to the Great Mystery of the River, enchanted perhaps by Hapi, God of the Nile.'

There was an odd tone in his voice, which worried me. Hesitancy, from so sure a person as Horemheb? But I forgot all about him as soon as the lady turned and held out her arms to me.

Oh, beautiful, lovely beyond belief, my half-sister Nefertiti. Her skin was as smooth as marble, her features all perfect; long nose, high cheekbones, eyes like almonds, liquid and soft. But it was her gentleness which glowed, which shone. I walked straight into her embrace as she gathered me, mud and weed and all, into her milky pool and I lay on her smooth, rounded breasts as though I had been fostered there.

'You have done well,' she told Horemheb, and he bowed and went away.

I had fallen in love with my sister. She washed all the mud off me with her own hands, heedless of the blood in the water, then called her women. She called her own nurse to treat the grazes on my legs, and then dried me and dressed me, for concealment, in a woman's cloth.

When Asen came to find me, my wounds were carefully hidden under a too-big gown and I was sitting like a good little girl, while my most beautiful sister plaited flowers into my hair.

'Is she not my sister, daughter of my father?' she asked Asen, who bustled in full of outrage and threatening a beating. 'Should she not come to me? Let her come again,' said Nefertiti in a voice like flowing gold, and Asen melted right away in front of my eyes.

So I first saw her, the beautiful one who is come, the Great Royal Wife. And so I first saw Horemheb the young soldier, who rescued me from the Nile.

Ptah-hotep

I cannot remember not being able to read and write.

When I was five years old in Maat who is truth, my father Imhotep sent me to the palace of the Temple of Amen-Re at Karnak to become as he is. I had taken his stylus and made squiggly attempts at letters all over the whitewashed inner wall of the house, using cooking-pot soot for ink, because I had seen him writing and wanted to imitate it. My mother raised a hand to slap me, because she valued her clean walls, but my father had put her aside, saying 'Here is a scribe and son of a scribe, should he not practice his father's profession?'

And the woman my mother had agreed, while I was still naked, while I wore nothing but the amulet and sidelock of childhood.

And here I am now many years later, my legs crossed under me, immaculate fine linen cloth uncreased, the plaster-board laid across my lap, my own palette beside me on the floor. My brushes and styli are carefully selected and meticulously kept and my ink is of the finest, solid black and bright scarlet. I compound and grind my own ink, which I dilute with water if I am writing on papyrus and with painter's size derived from boiled hoofs if I am inscribing a wall. Beside me are a pile of limestone shards and broken pottery, the ostraca for notes and random thoughts, and my master is reading out the *Building Inscription of Amenhotep II*, which the whole class is copying, miserably or obediently.

I am bored almost to extinction. Cruel father, to condemn me to this endless toil! Better I had been such as the young men who work in the fields, who care for oxen and fish in the river. Better even to be a slave carrying water or grinding corn, better to be a weaver in his little house or a laundryman beating filthy clothes in the shallows, a messenger on a fast horse, a soldier in danger of death on the border of Egypt, where the vile Kush lurk in ambush.

Better anything than this: the heat of noon, heavy on the eyelids. The glare outside of sun on marble. The silence except for the droning of a fly, the heavy sigh of some overburdened scholar, the scratching of styli on plaster, the scrubbing of someone rubbing out a mistake with a ball of cloth, the endless, endless droning voice and the never-ending *Building Inscription of Amenhotep II*, the grandfather of the present Pharaoh who lives, Amenhotep III. And my master goes on, and on:

Live the Horus: Mighty Bull, great in Strength: Favourite of the Two Goddesses: Mighty in Opulence: Made to Shine in Thebes: Golden Horus: Seizing by his Might in all Lands, Good God, Likeness of Re, Splendid Ray of Atum, begotten Son whom he made to shine in Karnak.

He appointed him to be king of all living, to do that which his ka did: his avenger, seeking excellent things, great in marvels, creative in knowledge, wise in execution, skilful-hearted like Ptah; king of Kings, ruler of rulers, valiant, without his equal, lord of terror amongst the southern lands, great in fear at the end of the north. Every land comes to him bowing down...'

My fingers know their way. My ears hear the words and write them down. I do not need to pay attention and I find myself wondering, what would it be like, to stand guard outside the palace or to work at one's own trade and lie down in one's own bed at night with nothing more to worry about but tomorrow's labour? All my life I have written other men's words, made permanent their thoughts.

I began by copying the *Maxims of Ptah-hotep*, my namesake, and continued through the *Story of Sinuhe*, who was a man, and the *Contendings of Horus and Set*, who are Gods.

I have written down accounts of journeys and ventures, of wars and conquests. I have written endless lists of grave goods and marriage contracts and all manner of documents by which men regulate their lives and record their words, and I have done nothing at all for myself.

I have married no wife, begotten no children, though I am fourteen years old and a man, with a man's seed to give. I have built nothing, made nothing, repaired nothing, created nothing. If I was to write the inscription for my own tomb now, I could say nothing but 'Ptah-hotep knew all words and three scripts and wrote a clear hand'.

The blow from the master's staff stings across my shoulders. He is standing over me, and he is angry. He must have spoken my name and gone unanswered.

'Show me,' he growls. I hand him my board and rub the weal which is forming across my back. He likes hurting, this Priest of Amen-Re. He has come here to give us instruction in the high script, which only priests use. I can see, turning in my place, the wet lip of the man who relishes pain and I blink hard, determined that he shall not see me weep and drink my tears for his pleasure.

I have written, I observe, most of the chapter of the inscription which he has been dictating. My characters are well formed and flowing and I assume that they are correct, for he drops the board back into my lap and says nothing else, only resumes the droning chant:

He assigned to me all that is with him, which the eye of his uraeus illuminates, all lands, all countries, every road, the circle of water Oceanos, they come to me in submission to my majesty: Son of Re, Amenhotep, Divine Ruler of Thebes, living forever, only vigilant one, begotten of the gods.'

The staff comes down hard on the shoulders of my friend Kheperren, and he gratifies the master's taste for wailing, so he repeats the blow. I wince for him as I would not for myself.

Who will free me of this misery?

Freedom comes in unlikely guises, says the sage Ptah-hotep, and so it came to me. We were bathing in the sacred lake, washing ourselves free of impurity for the evening prayer. I sluiced cool water over my wounded back, still angry and resentful at my fate. The priests were at their meal, the masters were in their rooms with their wives, and for a little while there was no one watching us. My friend Kheperren embraced me in the water.

'I hurt,' he complained, and I stroked the raised weals on his smooth back.

'I, too,' I agreed.

'I made three errors,' he admitted. 'But he hit me too hard.'

'I made none and he still hit me,' I replied. 'Doubtless the monster Apophis will eat his heart in the end but this does not comfort me, brother.'

'Hotep, can we run away?'

I swung him around so that we were facing one another, floating easily in the water, legs entwined. Re who is the sun was westering, but there was abundant light, spilling over the temple, making the stones glow like gold. Kheperren's brow was wrinkled with thought. He had black hair and the smooth olive skin of the countryman, whereas I was pale, almost ivory, and my hair was tinted with the Theban copper. It was unfair that I, whose father was only a scribe because he had been a common soldier in the army, was as fair as one of the Royal House, and my heart's brother was as dark as a peasant, though he was descended from the high priests of Amen-Re. I liked our contrast as we lay together, his thighs twined with mine.

'We can't run,' I told him. 'Remember when Yuya tried that.' They caught him, beat him, and made him sit for a week with his legs tied together.'

'I can't bear it,' Kheperren wailed, burying his face in my neck. 'If it wasn't for thy love, brother, I would die.'

His mouth was hot against my skin; our breath mingled. Floating, we drifted into a bank of papyrus, and the reeds closed about us. We had often lain here, where no man could see us, clutching each other for comfort.

'We are in a herdsman's hut on the banks of the river,' he breathed. It was our favourite of all the stories we told each other.

'We have stabled our cattle for the night,' I returned, sliding both hands down his body. I found the phallus, hard in my palm as I had always found it, in the dark of the dormitory or the cool of the morning.

'We have left our dog Wolf on guard,' He returned the caress.

'And we are shutting our door for the night, against the demons of the darkness, against the Goddesses of the Twelve Hours,' he continued, his breath catching as my hands, wise in the ways of his body, brought his climax near.

'And sealing our door with the sacred seal of the Brothers,' I whispered, and then could not speak further as he closed my mouth with a kiss.

Careful not to be heard—though such love was not forbidden, it would give our Masters leverage to play one of us against the other—we spilled our seed into the reeds, shivering and kissing. There was no one in the world whom I loved as much as my brother Kheperren.

And as we came up the bank together, still breathless with release, we found a priest waiting for us. We quickly schooled our features into the blank which gives nothing away, but it was not necessary. He smiled at us.

He was not beautiful, being a little fat. The rolls of his belly spoke of good living and his jaw was deformed, but his smile was enchanting and a little wistful, the smile of a man who has shared such delights and possesses them no longer.

'I came to seek a scribe, and it seems that I have found two,' he said politely. I was about to reply when Kheperren grabbed me and dragged me down to my knees and then pushed me onto my face on the paved shore of the sacred lake.

'What are you doing?' I protested as I yielded to his hand.

'Lord of the Two Lands, forgive our insolence,' he begged, and I realised that I had just been spoken to by the Pharaoh's son Akhnamen, Amenhotep IV, co-regent with our own Pharaoh and his only son since Thutmose the Prince died.

And I had almost spoken to a Pharaoh while standing on my feet and looking into his face, for which I could rightly be put to a very nasty death.

'Forgive us, Ruler of Rulers,' I agreed hastily, and put my lips to the curved toe of a gem-encrusted sandal.

A number of people laughed. Out of the corner of my eye—I stayed exactly where I was, face down on the bank in an attitude of complete prostration—I saw the hems of delicate garments and small feet in papyrus sandals.

'Come, let them arise,' said a gentle voice. I dared a quick glance upward and saw the neat dark wig and painted eyes of a very beautiful older woman. Her hennaed hand almost touched my brother's head. Patterns were drawn up to her wrists, which were heavy with chains in the form of lotus flowers and buds. The scent of jasmine enveloped us as the others came from concealment under the outer pillars of the temple of Amen-Re.

'Are they not comely?' asked the Lord of the Two Lands idly.

'Comely indeed, but what does His Majesty want with them?' asked the honey-voiced Queen. She must be the famous Tiye, the red-headed woman, Akhnamen's mother.

'I have need of a personal scribe,' said the King. 'What say you, Lady of the Two Lands, shall I have this or this?' He touched first my head and then my dear friend's.

'Lord of Upper and Lower Egypt, Lord of the River, take both, since they are brothers,' suggested another voice. The speaker sounded male and a little curt. I believe that it was the Master of the Scribes. I didn't know that they knew about us.

'No. One alone, who will love me, is what I want,' said the King. My heart gave a startled jolt, as though a hand had seized it. I slid my hand across and grasped that of my heart's brother, horrified that we were to part.

'This one,' said the light, careful voice of the King, and laid the flail of Kingship gently across my shoulders. I shuddered at the touch.

Thus I was given my freedom, though it was bitter at the time with the parting from the only one I loved. Thus I became personal scribe to the Pharaoh's son Akhnamen, Amenhotep IV, who is called Live the Horus, Mighty Bull, Lofty of Plumes: Favourite of the Two Goddesses: Great in Kingship in Karnak:

Golden Horus: Weaver of Diadems in the Southern Heliopolis: King of Upper and Lower Egypt: High Priest of Re Harakhte Rejoicing-in-the-Horizon, Heat which is Amen, Neferkheprure-Wanre, which means in the common tongue Beautiful One of Re, Unique One of Re.

Chapter Two

Mutnodjme

It is a serious business, marrying a Pharaoh.

This is because he is also a God, the avatar of Amen-Re, Lord of All. He takes many women as concubines and secondary wives, but there is only one Great Royal Wife, and it is through her that the crown is gained. Therefore he is usually required to marry his sister.

The case of Akhnamen was unusual. Everything about my sister's husband was unusual and I found myself wishing, sometimes, that Prince Thutmose, his elder brother, had not died after being bitten by a snake. The physicians and the priests had laboured over him as he shivered and screamed, but their spells had not found favour with the Gods and Thutmose, the eldest son and his father's delight, had departed to the Field of Offerings, the pleasant land where the ka of the person goes after death.

It is well known that a person has five elements: the ka, or double; the khou, or soul, the little flame which burns over the ka; and the ba, or the body-spirit. Then there are the Name and the Shadow, but only priests really understand these mysteries.

I have at last been allowed to stop tormenting flowers and I am sitting at my sister's feet, already dressed in my own best garments, listening to Tey's instructions as the bath-women massage Nefertiti with scented oil. My mother's voice is sharp and precise. She says exactly what she means, and she knows everything.

'This is a great honour, daughter, and it has been bestowed on you because Tiye the Queen may she live is your father's sister. You are required to serve the Pharaoh, please him, and bear him a son.'

'Mother,' Nefertiti murmurs, 'that may not be possible'.

'You have heard the rumours, then?' asked Tey. She is sitting in a leather saddleback chair and she is picking the gold leaf off one of the lion's head finials. I can see her nervous fingers, dark and skilled, smeared with golden dust.

'They say that he is impotent,' Nefertiti did not sound perturbed, but then she never did. Her nature was as sweet and still as cream.

'You must do your best,' said Tey. Then she sat up straight and clapped her hands, gesturing to the door. The servants left without comment—Tey would never keep a servant who did not obey her instantly—and the door closed.

'You know the situation, daughter,' said my mother. 'Amenhotep the Third may he live and his son, are co-regents. The next King was to have been Prince Thutmose but he is gone. The King strives to teach the Lord Akhnamen wisdom such as he himself richly owns, but the Heir was idle and mystical when he was just a prince. Now he wishes to do nothing but consider the deep matters of the Gods which would be better left to priests, whose business they are.

'And the King Amenhotep is aging—health and strength be unto him—so your Lord may soon be Lord of all Egypt, may that day be long delayed! Before this happens, a son is needed.'

'Why didn't my Lord Akhnamen marry his sister the Princess Sitamen?' I asked from the floor. Tey jumped, saw that it was only me, and answered briskly.

'Because his father had already married her. There is no Royal Heiress for the Heir to marry, so he has done this house great honour in choosing Nefertiti. Your questions will not spoil, Mutnodjme, if you keep them in your mouth until later!'

'Do not scold her, Mother,' my beautiful sister drew me closer to her scented breast. 'It was a good question. And the problem remains, Mother Tey. I do not need rumours, I can see for myself that there is something amiss with the Heir; though he is gentle, they say. If no seed springs from him in my womb, what shall we do?'

'We will think of something,' said Tey. 'I will be near, daughter, we will talk again. Let me look at you.'

Nefertiti stood up and Tey herself draped the gown over her; the finest pleated gauze-thin linen, through which her delicate pale limbs moved, as visible as a woman swimming in milk. The fashion for short, neat wigs, the sort that they called Nubian, suited my sister's pure line of jaw and nose. The jewels of the Pharaoh were laid on her shoulders and arms, and I thought that they weighed her down. My sister was more beautiful in her bare skin as Khnum the Potter made her on his wheel, than any lady dressed in the most precious garments, the richest topaz, turquoise and gold.

Tey my mother adjusted the counterweight which held the great pectoral in balance across the slender shoulders and flicked an errant strand of hair into place.

'You are beautiful,' decided Great Royal Nurse Tey, and led Nefertiti to the door. She moved as she always did, with elegance and economy, like a dancer in the temple of Hathor, the Goddess of Love and Beauty, and the attendants, waiting outside until we should please to emerge, leapt to their feet. There were a hundred women in fine gauze and all of their jewellery. The scents of jasmine and myrrh were so strong as to be almost a stench. In homage to her beauty, the naked musicians carried Hathor's sistra before my sister on the way to her marriage with the Pharaoh Akhnamen may he live. We entered the corridor to the music of harps and drums and little bells.

That was the first time I saw him whose wisdom is famous throughout the whole world. Barbarian Kings sing his praises, and his own scribes and priests bow down to his sagacity: Pharaoh Amenhotep, Lord of the Upper and Lower Crowns.

He was old and fat and I was very disappointed.

We came in to the great hall of the Kings, our music about us, to stand before the two thrones. They were on a high dais with eleven steps. The thrones were of black wood, inlaid with lions and lotuses, and the king's enemies were on his footstool; defeated Nubians and Asiatics and Hittites. The carved figure of Amenhotep may he live was holding three of them at once by the hair.

Our sandals made a rustling on the inlaid marble floor, as though the papyrus remembered its reedy home. I was right behind my sister Nefertiti, a little stunned by the drumming and the music and half suffocated by perfumes.

Nefertiti was led toward the thrones by Father Ay, soon to be Divine Father. I had not seen him often during my life. He was wearing so many jewels that he glittered in the dawn light; a stocky man with dark skin, like mine and my mother's. He was scowling, as he usually was. He had shown no interest in me.

The women said that he had been very much in love with his concubine, who bore him one dazzling daughter before she died, and he visited my mother only occasionally. First wife has the position, concubine has the attention; that is what the women said. Perhaps that also was a maxim of Amenhotep may he live! for he had almost a hundred wives; though they said that he doted most on the red-headed woman, Tiye the Queen, who had been his first wife and still lay with him almost every night.

Nefertiti was approaching the throne. She sank down, graceful as a bird, while the music died away and there was silence. It extended for so long that I grew bored. We could not move until one of the Kings was pleased to speak to us.

I tried lining up my new sandals on the golden lotuses on the floor. They fitted perfectly, which pleased me. I peered around my mother, trying not to breathe heavily and risk stirring her delicate gauze draperies. If she felt me moving, she would glare me back into decorous behaviour.

The Lords were looking not at my sister but each other. One was Akhnamen may he live; a young man, heavily decorated and painted, wearing a long wig and the crown of the Upper and Lower Lands. The cobra which was wrapped around the crowns, the uraeus, was of bright cloisonné and so real that I thought I could hear it hiss. The younger King was thick of body, with a strange face; high cheekbones, slanting eyes, a long jaw and soft red lips.

The other King was fat and old. This was the Lord Amenhotep of legendary wisdom. His belly overflowed his beautiful embroidered cloth, and his solid chest bore many jewels; he had thick wrists and stubby fingers overloaded with rings. I was not pleased with him at all until I lifted my gaze to his face and he caught my eyes.

Brown eyes, most deep and considering brown eyes, terribly clever but terribly forgiving. He knew, I felt, as the Divine mouth lifted a little at one corner in a conspiratorial grin, exactly how boring it was to be an overdressed nine-year-old girl, forced to stand in a palace procession and not be able to see anything. He knew why I was peeping around my mother to see what happened to my sister. He even knew, I was sure, how very much I loved her. I smiled back at him with all my heart. Then he shifted his gaze so that my mother would not catch me looking at the Lord of the Two Lands, and returned his attention to his son.

I could not hear what they were saying. My mother was so tense that I felt her quiver like a leashed hunting dog. Was this all for nothing? Were we to take my sister home again? I hoped desperately that this would happen. But finally the strange young man stirred, stood up, and came down the eleven steps to take my sister's hands and raise her to her feet.

Then the music broke out again, loud and exultant, drums and women's voices. Nefertiti mounted the steps. Akhnamen may he live presented her to his father Amenhotep, who kissed her on each cheek. Taking one hand each, they presented her to the gathering and we all cheered.

The gates had been opened. Outside were the people of Thebes, all craning to catch a glimpse of the most beautiful woman in the world. When they saw her a gasp and a murmur ran through the mob. Then they began to yell 'Nefertiti Divine Spouse who lives! Health! Strength! Life to the great Royal Wife!'

As the Kings and my sister walked along the colonnade which led to the temple of Amen-Re where she was to be crowned Queen, flowers rained down from people who lined the walls, so that the golden stone was carpeted with perfumed petals, and the voices followed us, 'Blessings on the Great Royal Wife, Nefertiti daughter of Divine Father Ay, blessings on Divine Nurse Tey, life to Akhnamen, may he live!'

We left more and more people behind as we moved into the precincts of the temple.

The central mystery, of course, is only for the King and the High Priest of Amen. No one but priests see the God, when they tend him every day. The women stopped as though at an invisible barrier but the Kings walked on, Nefertiti between them, and I followed because no one stopped me, at the heels of Tey my mother and Ay my father.

Inside the temple, in the hypostyle hall like a huge forest of carved petrified trees, four thrones were set up beside a statue of Amen-Re as the Hawk Re Harakti. There were priests waiting. One held a crown. I saw that the Lord Amenhotep was talking to my sister, smiling at her, and she was smiling in return, shy in such state and such company. Then he bade her kneel, and the priest, a tall man with a priest's shaven skull, raised the crown and lowered it onto my sister's head.

It was heavy. I saw her shoulder and neck muscles tense to take the weight. With both hands in those of the Lord Amen-hotep, she rose again, and was led to sit down on the throne between the King Amenhotep and her new husband, who had hardly looked at her. I was indignant. Didn't he understand that he had been given the most beautiful of all women as his own?

The air was heavy with the frankincense which came from far-away Punt. It smoked in little dishes on the floor. I felt sick.

Before I could disgrace myself by really being sick in the temple, for which I would probably have been condemned to have my heart eaten after death, I was distracted by the arrival of the Queen, who walked alone up the steps and sat down beside her lord, Amenhotep.

Queen Tiye was plump and smooth, draped in cloth of astounding quality. She wore the Crown of the Upper and Lower Lands, and her skin was as white as milk and her face rounded and smooth. I knew that her hair was red, thought to be unlucky, the colour of Set the Adversary and of Desaret, the Red Waste outside Khemet the Black Land. I knew that there had been trouble with the priests when the Lord Amenhotep had married the foreign woman, although he was Pharaoh and could presumably marry as he pleased, and there were no royal children left from his father's reign. But I also knew that she had borne sons and daughters to the King and he doted on her. I saw the great crown tilt as Queen Tiye smiled at Nefertiti, and my sister sighed with relief.

Then the priests censed everyone, declared a blessing in language so hieratic that I could not understand it, and we were released to go back to the palace at Thebes and feast.

It was a good feast, and I was sick, after all.

Ptah-hotep

When Pharaoh declares his wish, it is as good as done; and so it was with me. I slept one more night with the trainee scribes in the dormitory. My destiny had been declared. I would now not be a priest. I had no great leaning towards such a life, anyway. I had just wanted to be a skilful scribe, if I had to be a scribe, not a priest.

But I was distracted with grief at leaving my heart's brother. The Master of Scribes, for some reason, relaxed his usual rule and allowed us to sleep my last night together. In fact the Master seemed strangely sorry for me, considering the fact that everyone else was congratulating me on my amazingly good fortune. He sent me bread and roasted goose and fruit from his own table, and the servant who brought it had been ordered to stay and serve Kheperren and myself as though we were grown and masters in our own house.

We sat in my little room, one on either side of a borrowed table, dressed in our best clothes, and the servant poured wine for us whenever our cups were empty. And because I was a boy and my heart had already been broken when Pharaoh touched my shoulders with the flail, I began to enjoy myself. The food was good, and we ate heartily and drank deep, and drunkenly embraced. Then we slept in each other's arms all night, and I woke to the dawn twittering of the swallows who nest in the temple of Amen-Re and saw my brother, my spouse, asleep with his head pillowed on his arm. By the cool light he was to me entirely beautiful and unexpressively dear. The light embraced the curve of his olive cheek and the fringe of his sooty eyelashes. Kheperren's other hand had been curled on my chest as I slept beside him.

I stood silently in the doorway, my bundle of possessions in my hand—a few spare cloths, a childhood amulet given to me by my father, the usual belongings. My palette and the gear of my trade had already gone to the palace. I did not want to wake Kheperren. I feared I would not survive a farewell.

So I dipped my finger in lamp-black and wrote 'I will always love you' on the wall near his face, where he would see it when his eyes opened, and went away.

I washed in the sacred lake, put on my best cloth, painted my eyes with kohl to protect them from the glare, and went with the servant who had come from the Lord of the Upper and Lower Lands to take me to the palace.

And despite my best resolutions, I wept all the way.

I was met by a Chamberlain, who exclaimed, 'So young! Amen-Re have compassion on us, boy, you cannot appear before Pharaoh like that. Come in here.' He ushered me into an anteroom where a young woman was bandaging a slave's foot. She dismissed the slave with a pat on the toe and an injunction to rest for at least a week, and then turned her attention to me; as the Master of Slaves scolded her patient for being stupid enough to put his foot under a falling bench. 'And you the King's favourite cup bearer, what am I going to tell him?'

'This is the King Akhnamen's new scribe,' said the Chamberlain, a fussy man of middle age wearing too much jewellery and paint. 'Do what you can, Meryt.'

'Sit down,' said the young woman. 'What's your name, Scribe? I'm Meryt the Nubian. Where does it hurt?'

'Only my heart,' I said as I sat down on the stone bench. She took my hand and her warm fingers found my pulse.

'The voice of your heart says that you are healthy,' she said gravely. Her skin was soot-black and her eyes twinkled. 'But drink this while I clean your face and re-apply your kohl.'

I drank obediently as she washed my face with precise strokes of a wad of damp linen and re-drew my eyes. She passed a red-ochre brush gently across my cheeks to restore the bloom of health. The drink was a warm compound of wine, honey and herbs, and it went down smoothly, not offending my already over-worked insides.

'You have left someone you love to come to Pharaoh's service,' she remarked. 'That is hard. But you will flourish in the regard of the Pharaoh, be happy, and come to your lover again.'

'How do you know?' I asked.

'I am a Nubian and we have some skill in foretelling though I am no oracle. But I know,' she said firmly.

For some reason I was greatly cheered.

'There are many people in the palace today, is it always like this?' I asked, as she straightened my earrings and flicked dust off my wig.

'It's the coronation of the great Royal Wife Nefertiti,' she replied, laughing. 'Where have you been?'

'His Majesty took me yesterday from the School of Scribes to be his personal scribe,' I told her. I felt her draw back in shock, and then she came and knelt before me, her forehead on my sandal.

'I did not know, Lord, pardon!' she whispered.

'Meryt, get up,' I tugged at her shoulder. 'Why are you bowing to me?'

'You are the Royal Scribe,' she said, looking up from her crouch. 'You rank higher than almost anyone in the kingdom, except those of royal blood or the priests of Amen-Re.'

'In that case I order you to stand up,' I was astounded and I needed more information. 'This can't be,' I said.

'Lord, if that is your position, then that is your rank.'

'I don't believe it,' I protested.

'If you will take some advice,' ventured Meryt in a whisper, 'beware the envy of others. Have your food tasted and search your rooms for serpents and your bed for scorpions. I am the lowliest of Pharaoh's slaves, but I know this much; there will be much murmuring at this appointment. No one will say anything to you, Lord, but they will be very angry. The person who was expecting to be royal scribe was the old man the Lord Nebamenet. He has expanded his household on the understanding that he would be awarded the post.'

'If this is true, Meryt, will you come to me and keep the serpents away?' I asked entirely on impulse. She looked away.

'Master, I am unworthy,' she murmured conventionally, which meant 'yes'.

Thus I acquired my first slave, for it was true—I had been elevated to one of the highest posts in the Kingdom, and with much more justice than Meryt I felt like saying, 'Lord, I am unworthy'.

The chamberlain took me into the first hall, where the common people come to speak to officials and those badly treated can appeal to Pharaoh their father. It was decorated with stiff lotuses and stiff papyrus heads, the symbols of Upper and Lower Egypt. A slave was sweeping the stone floor, another was sprinkling jasmine-water, and clearly something was about to happen. The soldiers at the gate had lined up in a long double row, light gleaming off their heavy belts and helmets. The wind carried to me the jingling of their accoutrements. The Chamberlain, muttering something about inconvenience, took me through the Audience Chamber and into the palace behind, and we stood at a window looking down into the hall.

'The Great Royal Wife Nefertiti was crowned not an hour ago,' he said under his breath. 'Both Kings may they live! will be here soon. They will show the new Queen to the people, then come along this corridor into the feasting hall. There the Lord Akhnamen has ordered that you should meet him. Now I really should...'

'Wait, Lord,' I grasped him by the arm. 'The slave Meryt said that I had been given one of the highest offices in the kingdom. She was, of course, wrong?'

'Nubians, they talk too much. Yes boy, I mean, my Lord, you are ranked higher than almost any, and I hope you live your first decan, for I do not know what will save you unless the Gods do.'

This was alarming and I forgot my grief for a little. Still holding him, I demanded 'Explain!'

'I don't know how to explain it,' he wailed, the paint on his cheeks cracking a little with the stress of unaccustomed facial expression. 'Did he know you before, Lord Ptah-hotep, know you...when he was a boy?'

'No, of course not. Yesterday I was swimming in the sacred lake and he just came and took me. I have never seen him before,' I replied.

'Whimsical, whimsical, that's the Divine Akhnamen. I wish that his brother had lived. But at least he has married; a wife will settle him down.' He spoke to himself, then remembered me.

'Now, don't be afraid, boy, my Lord. He won't hurt you, he's the gentlest creature alive, may Amen-Re shine sense upon him! He just doesn't think, you see, he's impulsive. But he keeps his friends, and he needs them. Be a friend to him and no courtier's malice can touch you.'

'Sell me the slave Meryt,' I requested. He patted me on the shoulder.

'Certainly,' he replied. 'Ten ingots of copper and she is yours.'

'Should all this be true, Lord, I will owe you the copper, and you will send her to my quarters as soon as you can. I feel,' I added, as we heard trumpets and the whole honour guard sprang to attention, 'that I will need someone to watch over me.'

I went to the feasting hall as the procession left the Audience Chamber and walked along the corridor painted with a fresco of tribute bearers. I was puzzled and apprehensive but my heart was still too sore to be either really joyful or really afraid.

I heard the swish of the ladies' draperies and their voices, as they were freed from ceremony to speak, pass my window and I slipped out into the passage and came along behind them.

I had never seen such splendour as that feasting hall on my first night in the palace of the Kings. The Kings and their Queens were seated on a raised platform at one end of the hall, with painted frescoes of antelopes behind them and a whole lion hunt on the opposite wall.

The tables were draped with white cloth and laden with all manner of food; bread and roasted fish and dried fish, roasted oxen, goat, roast quail and duck and goose; plums and melons and figs and grapes in black bunches, bursting with juice. There were three sorts of cheese and eleven different cakes, dates, pomegranates, and salads of lettuce and leeks.

I had never seen so much food in my life. In my father's house we were never hungry; we had bread, fish and beans every day and roasted meat occasionally. But this abundance was astonishing and I had to restrain my hand from creeping out and stealing a cinnamon cake. My nostrils twitched with the heavenly scent. Cinnamon and, I thought, honey.

The chamberlain, who may have been feeling guilty about his casual reception of me, took me by the hand and led me through the feast to the Kings.

Everywhere people were tearing apart roasted quail and crunching bones and demanding more wine. Servants flew about the huge room with pots and jugs. Musicians strummed and plucked valiantly, but could hardly be heard above the voices and the demands for more drink, at once!

I was deafened and shaken—it was like being inside a gigantic mouth—by the time I was kneeling at the feet of the young man with the strange misty gaze.

'Ptah-hotep,' he said vaguely. For a delirious moment I thought he might have forgotten me and I would be sent back to my own trade and my Kheperren. Then his eyes sharpened, as if I had come into focus.

'See, my Lady,' he addressed a woman of surpassing beauty, who put down her wine-cup politely and smiled at me. 'This is Ptah-hotep, my scribe.'

The old man sitting next along shot me a look as penetrating as a spear, then smiled and I smiled back. It was impossible not to smile when Amenhotep the King may he live for a hundred years smiled. But the Lord Akhnamen was my master and he was touching my bowed head with his staff.

'Rise, Ptah-hotep, you are Great Royal Scribe,' he said quietly, and the whole hall fell silent. The silence began amongst the great nobles, and spread with surprising speed through the feasting ladies to the door slaves. No one glared, but they all stared, some with curiosity, some with a determination to make sure that I did not keep my position while there was poison in the world. I could read them all. Meryt the Nubian had been right.

I was now required to stand and reply, and I did so. I was, for some reason, no longer afraid.

'Life! Health! Strength to the Pharaoh Akhnamen!' I cried, and the whole hall screamed the salutation, mostly with their mouths full.

'Life! Health! Strength!'

I hoped that it would be so for me, too. But I would not have given high odds on my surviving until the next month.

Chapter Three

Mutnodjme

The problem with my mother Tey and myself was that we were too much alike.

She was sharp, intelligent, determined and curious, and so was I, though she called me insolent, too clever for my own good, stubborn and a spy. All her own attributes, and she didn't like them in me.

Therefore she was all for sending me away, to my father Ay's estates near Memphis. I think she was worried about what I might say, given the extremely delicate nature of my sister's marriage. But Nefertiti would not allow this. Tey's opposition faded away. Nefertiti always got what she wanted. She would persist and persist, never forgetting and never losing her temper, and eventually it became easier to allow her whatever she wanted; rather than to continue, churlishly, to oppose her will. My sister was gentle, but she was neither stupid or anyone's dupe.

And she was determined to love her husband.

Marriages being dynastic or family matters, it was rare for the parties to have known each other before the woman came to live in her new husband's house. Women had lovers, of course, and men had favourites, and we had no bans on youth enjoying itself.

After marriage, naturally, women and men were expected to be devoted to each other because the family was the unit established by the Gods for the comfort and protection of children and the feeding and clothing of the members. Husbands cared for wives, wives for husbands. Did not Hathor the Goddess of Beauty and Music go every year to Edfu to spend two weeks with her husband Horus in feasting and lovemaking? The world was designed for pleasure, and pleasure extended beyond the death of the body. In the Field of Reeds, the dead feasted every day on the offerings which were made in their tombs.

Despite my mother's misgivings, therefore, I went with my sister Nefertiti when she went to lie for the first time with her husband the Divine Akhnamen.

She dismissed the other women at the door, thinking that her husband might be shy, and took only me with her, to undress her before she lay down in Pharaoh's bed. We entered his apartments to the music of sistra and women's voices, and the most beautiful woman sat down on a saddle-strung chair next to the bed on which the strange young man was lying.

He had retired early from the marriage feast, saying that he felt fevered, and there was an unhealthy slick of sweat on his face and his torso.

By rights, Nefertiti should have been in her own apartments, which were certainly grand enough, and he should have come to her. But it was her nature to understand fear, and she knew that he was afraid.

'Is it you?' he asked, reaching out a languid hand, which she took in both of her own.

'It is I,' she said gently. 'Your wife.'

He twitched a little at that.

'Is it your will that I should stay with you tonight?' she asked, stroking the hand, which was long-fingered and elegant, unlike the rest of him.

'It is,' he whispered.

At her signal, I loosed the heavy pectoral and lifted it off my sister's shoulders. I laid away all her jewellery, the rings and bracelets and the heavy gem-encrusted girdle. I loosed her sandals so that she could step out of them and laved her face and hands with cool water in which jasmine blossoms had been steeped. On impulse, I lifted King Akhnamen's soft hands and sluiced and dried them, and then laid the wet cloth across his brow. His strange almond-shaped eyes considered me with some interest.

'Who are you, dark lady?' he asked, and I stifled a laugh.

'I am Mutnodjme, lord, sister of your wife,' I replied. He twitched again. That word definitely worried him. 'Sister of Nefertiti, Lord. We are here to serve you,' I added.

Naked, I could see that his body was like a child's, not the bold genitalia which I had seen on the men bathing in the river. I glanced at my sister and could see no expression on her face but gentle concern.

I helped her lie down on the bed next to the Pharaoh, adjusted the neck rest so that they lay together like statues, then took myself to the threshold, where I would lie for the rest of the night, as was my duty as attendant on the Great Royal Wife.

The sky was black. Little glints of moonlight sparked off the gold leaf of the great bed, which had leopard's heads at one end and leopard's tails at the other. A fine curtain hung from the uprights to exclude mosquitoes. I could only see them as shadows.

They had not moved to touch each other. Finally, his hand shifted and lay heavily on her thigh, and she bared her body. There was no doubt that she was willing to mate with him. She lay over him, her mouth finding his mouth, rubbing her soft cheek across his face, her hands moving to cup and stroke, seeking a phallus.

Evidently these caresses had no effect, because after perhaps half of an hour I heard her say softly, 'Are you not pleased with your handmaiden, lord?' and I heard the Pharaoh begin to sob and scream.

Words tumbled from him, but I could not understand them. He was speaking in some hieratic dialect, some priestly tongue. Nefertiti turned on one elbow and gathered him into her arms, so that his face rested on her peerless breasts, and she soothed him as she had soothed me when I skinned my knees.

'There, my lord, my love, there,' she said in her honey-voice.

'It is the will of the God,' he said, finally, into her shoulder.

'Which God, my lord?' asked my sister. 'Tell me, and I will have sacrifices made tomorrow, temples built. Which God requires your potency?'

'There is only one God,' he said flatly.

Nefertiti said nothing in reply; for it was absurd, only one God? Everyone knew 'the Ennead'—the Nine of Thebes: Isis, sister-wife of Osiris; Nut the Sky, Geb the Earth, and Shu the Air their father, who comes between the mating of sky and earth and makes Day; Amen-Re who is the Sun; Set the Adversary; Anubis, God of the dead; and Thoth, God of Learning. Then of course comes Horus the Avenger, child of Isis. There are also the Twelve Gods of the Night and the Twelve Gods of the Day, and the countless other little Gods of house and village all up and down the Nile—who is himself a God, Hapi. One God? Which one?

I leaned back against the door, which was uncomfortably studded with copper nails, and listened in scorn.

'Aten,' whispered Akhnamen. 'My father and I believe that there is one God, only one, who rules all the Heavens.'

'But, my Lord,' protested my sister. 'What of Hathor and Horus? What of the others whom our fathers worshipped?'

'They are nothing,' he said fiercely, this King who lay on my sister's breast. 'They are delusions, fantasies of men who did not know the truth. There is only one. Unknowable, invisible, uncreated.'

'Khnum the potter, who made men on his wheel?' hazarded my sister, who had never been very interested in religion.

'No! Your mind is corrupted, like all the others.' He sat up abruptly. 'Go, leave my presence.'

'Lord, do not distress yourself,' said Nefertiti. 'I spoke only from ignorance, and did not the Divine Amenhotep your father say that *Ignorance is the one disease which has an easy cure?*'

He did. I had read that maxim of Amenhotep to my sister only the week before. The agitation of anger had tired the young King, and he sagged down into my sister's arms again.

'Ah, my lady, ' he said softly. 'Thy breast is a pillow for my aching head.'

'That is as it should be, lord,' she said softly, 'Let me sing to you, and then you will sleep.'

He must have nodded, for she began to sing very softly a lullaby sung by all mothers on the banks of the great River, from mud huts to palaces.

'*Sleep little child,*
Thy mother is here.
Sleep is on the water
Sleep is in the reeds.
Birds rest with wings folded
Winds sleep in the sky,
The Gods guard the night
The Gods guard the Nile.
Khons counts the hours
The moon wanes. Sleep,
Mother's breast bears you,
Little child, sleep.'

The Pharaoh sighed and snuggled closer, and soon I too slept. In the morning my sister went to my mother and reported,

'It is as you feared.'

Tey shot me a hard glance and I nodded, not venturing to speak. 'You are sure that no stimulation can rouse him?' asked Tey, and Nefertiti blushed. 'Is it perhaps that he prefers men?'

'No, I do not believe that he is potent at all,' said my sister. 'Then we shall appeal to the Lord Amenhotep, the Divine One,' said Tey, who always made fast decisions.

'Mother, wait,' Nefertiti put her hand on my mother's arm. 'I would not shame him. He is possessed of a God, I am sure. A new God, one God, he says, Ruler of All. He says that this God requires his seed, that He took it all away from him when he was just grown, and he sickened but did not die. He is gentle, Mother Tey, and I love him. I will not leave him.'

Tey considered. She always put her head on one side when she was thinking, like a predatory bird. I could see what she was thinking. We had position—my mother was now Divine Nurse to the Queen of Upper and Lower Egypt. My father would not abandon this, even though he had married his daughter to a eunuch. And when Nefertiti said that she loved him and would not leave him, she meant it. Was not the household of Tey overloaded with people whom Nefertiti loved, who could not be dismissed and who did no work because they were old, crippled or crazed? Nefertiti has as soft a heart as Hathor herself. It was because of the Divine Nefertiti's devotion to the lost and strayed that we had a one-armed doorkeeper, a cook who crooned all day to a strange little conic fetish, and a watchdog with three legs. Tey had frequently remarked that the concubine's daughter could cherish a crocodile in her bosom, or wet-nurse a snake.

And she had clearly taken her husband under her protection, and there was no remedy for it.

'We will speak privately with the Lord Amenhotep,' decided Tey. 'There need be no shame. But it is his posterity you guard, daughter, and he must know of a remedy. He is, after all, renowned for his wisdom.'

Nefertiti assented and went to her own quarters to be bathed and massaged with oil.

Mother Tey gave me a piece of honeyed bread and a draft of beer, sat me down on a cross-legged stool, and cross-examined me about all the events of the night. I answered as fully as I could, every sound and every word. I also described the appearance of the King, suppressing my comparison with the boys swimming in the river, as I did not think that I was supposed to look at them.

'It is as she said,' she muttered. 'Good girl, Mutnodjme. Stay with your sister. I do not think he will harm her. She is gentle and loving. But you, my sharp-witted creature, do not you argue religion with him. Agree, daughter, and if you cannot agree, be silent!'

'But Mother, he says there is only one God!' I objected.

'He is Pharaoh,' snapped Tey. 'He is a God. Presumably Gods know about Gods. Do as I say, Mutnodjme. And don't gossip. News of this impotence must not spread abroad. Do you understand?'

'Yes, Mother,' I understood enough. I knew that if it was known that the Co-Regent King was impotent, it would harm my sister. I loved my sister above anything, and my lips were sealed.

The next night they lay together again. She held him close, his head on her breast, and talked about Aten the Sun Disc until they both fell asleep.

I was asleep long before.

Ptah-hotep

A servant brought me to my chambers in the Palace at Thebes, and left me at the door. No courtesy could be expected, it seemed, from any of the incumbents. I was persona non grata, an upjumped schoolboy, and my most immediate need was a staff of my own, on whom I could rely.

How did one go about appointing people? Did I own anything? I had a succession of opulent rooms, all painted with rural scenes. One room had the whole process of making flax. One wall was covered with duck hunting. Another was patterned with simple lotus and papyrus in the most enchanting blues and greens. My floor was of marble, set with gold flowers. I walked through my audience chamber, my library packed with shelves of records, my own shabby tools laid out on the inlaid table. I came to my own bathroom, my tiled alcove with water jars, my own closet, into my bedroom, where several rooms leading off it were evidently for the accommodation of my wives and children.

It was dark and cold. Someone had lit several lamps, but the rooms felt unoccupied. My own footsteps echoed. I took a woven blanket off the huge bed and something small and dark clacked to the floor, skittering into a corner.

I laid down my lamp, chased, cornered and crushed it.

It was the wrong time of the year for scorpions to invade the houses of men. It was not even spring. Someone must have gone to considerable trouble to find the poisonous insect in winter. I stood contemplating the still writhing carcass for some time.

Then I shook out the blanket, wrapped myself in it, and sat down in the alcove beside the door to think.

My first thought, that I could bring my dear love to the palace, must be dismissed. Kheperren would be an instrument for the palace to use against me, a hostage to my fortune. I did not greatly mind dying. I would join my grandfather in the Field of Reeds. I still missed my grandfather. But Kheperren was young, he had every right to live, and he could not live if he was with me.

I almost wept again at the thought. The idea that as Great Royal Scribe I could be reunited with him had been a warm glow at my heart for the whole strange day and night I had spent in Pharaoh's palace. Indeed, I could not even see him again, or I might bring retribution down on him wherever he was. I must get a message to him before I took up my duties, for after that I would always be noticed and probably followed. Oh my brother, I mourned in the darkness of my elaborate rooms. Oh my heart, I have lost you, I have lost you.

I might have sat there in lonely misery all night if I had not heard footsteps approaching. They were confident and heavy, yet not mailed; not a soldier. I threw open the door, more angry than afraid, about to demand of the visitor whether they had any more scorpions.

'Master,' said Meryt, dropping to one knee. I laid one hand on her curly hair in token of possession. She gave me the invoice for ten copper ingots which made her mine.

I was so glad to see her that I could have embraced her. She was dressed in a patterned cloth, which must have been the parting present of her previous master. On her strong shoulder she bore a large basket, and in her hand she carried a bundle of papyrus rolls. She lowered her burden to the floor and smiled at me.

'I thought that they would not have attended to you, Master,' she said deferentially. 'So I brought some food from the King's kitchen. No hands but the cook's and mine have touched it,' she added, drawing forth some cooked duck, several loaves of bread, some grapes and a cinnamon cake. 'There is also wine,' she added.

'You are kind,' I said gratefully. 'But you are in danger the whole time you are with me, and possibly I should not have done this to you after all, you showed me nothing but good will. Come, Meryt, look here,'

I showed her the remains of the scorpion, and she looked grave.

'It is as I said, Master,' she commented. 'Tomorrow you must find some companions—such as can be trusted. But tonight we can search the bedding and remove any more. I am a slave,' she said to me, her dark face hard to read in the dim light. 'But I will serve you gladly, Master, for they seek your death, and that is not just. This appointment was none of your seeking, Lord Ptah-hotep. They gave me these, Lord, telling of your estates.'

'My estates?'

I unrolled the papyri on the table. I read them. I rubbed my eyes. I read them again. I was indeed rich. I owned the yearly tribute of five villages, eleven vineyards, two hide-dressers and a stone quarry in Syene. My goods were all stored in the palace warehouses. I could have bought the School of Scribes and had goods left over for the Sacred Barge at Karnak. I felt dizzy. Meryt saw this and pushed me gently down onto an ebony chair.

'Sit there, Master, have some wine and some of this good bread, and I'll search the bedroom and make sure it is safe. Tomorrow my lord will be pleased to consider who may deserve the honour of a place in my Lord's household. Tonight my lord needs rest.'

I drank wine red as blood and ate some meat and bread. I heard Meryt shaking out bedclothes, humming to herself and then singing softly. Light bloomed golden as she lit the big alabaster lamp in the shape of an ibis, symbol of Thoth God of Learning, patron of scribes.

'Come, Master, it's all well,' she called, and I took my wine into my bedroom.

'Meryt, eat,' I said belatedly, and she hauled the basket into the room and closed the studded door. It latched with a click and I suddenly felt a good deal more secure. The bed was comfortable and I leaned against the painted wall and began to relax for the first time since I had entered my apartments.

Meryt sat down cross legged on the floor and ate. I liked watching her strong white teeth as she bit and swallowed, saying, 'I never fed this well, Master, since I came to Pharaoh's palace!'

'How did you come here?' I asked. I needed to know all about her, this woman whom I had so casually bought and paid for.

'My father was a chief,' she said matter-of-factly. 'He ambushed and killed a trading mission. Then the soldiers came, killed our young men, captured us and burned our village. I was a child. I have always been hungry since then. Not starving, Master, no slave starves in the palace. But there has always been a corner that could be filled. When I grew tall I showed a talent for healing, and the Chamberlain made me his healer, to attend to the slaves.'

So, taking me to Meryt had been an insult. It had, however, not been recognised at the time, which meant that its aim had been bad. And it had given me Meryt, who liked me. And if my estates sufficed to continue to feed her to satiety, she would probably be faithful. I was pleased with the outcome of my first insult in Pharaoh's service, and sure that it would not be the last.

'And then you bought me from that old man and here I am,' she concluded, breaking the last cinnamon cake and giving half to me. 'And I am yours, Master.'

I bit into the cinnamon cake and returned the grin.

I lay with her in the Great Royal Scribes' bed, and refused her offer of her body. She was a little puzzled, but not offended, and we huddled close and warm until morning.

I woke with an arm over my chest. For a moment I was flooded with affection, believing that I lay with Kheperren, then I heard a woman cough, and realised that it was Meryt my slave and that I had to get up and assemble a household.

I was drinking warmed wine and nibbling a honeycake when I heard someone come in and kneel down. I looked up from the last census, which seemed to have been carried out with commendable efficiency, and saw the one I loved more than any other in the world. He was prostrate, his hand touching my foot, as any scribe should be before the Great Royal Scribe.

'Meryt!' I called. 'Shut the outer door and stand guard!' and as she ran to draw the big portal closed, I seized my dearest companion, dragging him into my arms. He fitted perfectly into my embrace, as he always had.

'Oh my heart,' I said into his hair. He hugged me for a moment, his fingers digging into my shoulder, and then whispered ' "Hotep, why did you not send for me?'

'Because that would have meant your death, and still may if any marked you coming here.'

'I don't think so,' his brow corrugated, as it always did when he was thinking. 'I did not need to ask the way. I have been here before, when I took a message for the Master of Scribes to the old Royal Scribe. No one would have noticed me, particularly. What do you mean, I'm in danger? That means that you are in danger!' He held me closer, his mouth against my jaw. 'Let me stay with you,' he begged.

'No, I can't, don't ask me, brother of my heart. I love you too much to put you in such peril.'

His scent was on my skin, the dear scent of my own brother, and I allowed myself a moment to hold him tight, as though I could imprint his body on my body. Then I drew away from him. I felt strangely weak, as though I was bleeding from some invisible wound. If Kheperren argued with me, if he pleaded, I did not know whether I would be able to resist him. And I must resist.

But he did not speak, at first. He looked closely at me, as though he was memorising my features. He grew more beautiful every moment. His eyes were gentle and his mouth was soft. He kissed me, lips parting, tongues touching. I drank the sweet silkiness of his inner lip. Then he laid one hand very softly on my thigh, and my body reacted at once. He nodded, as though some private theory had been confirmed. Then he sat back on his heels and said diffidently, 'What do you want me to do, brother?'

'Forget me,' I said. He shook his head so that his golden earrings tinkled.

'I cannot do that,' he said. 'What else?'

'Leave the palace without being observed. Never come here again. I am rich now, brother, I can give you an estate in the country, if you wish.'

'I will never go there without you,' he replied. He was not arguing, but he was definite. 'If you are afraid for me, brother, you cannot give me anything without the envious ones knowing. That will attract their attention. Is this not true?'

'Yes,' I agreed, rather taken aback by his calm acceptance of the situation. Yet I was sure that he loved me.

This was confirmed when he took a seal cutting knife from my table and sawed off a lock of his hair. He gave it to me without speaking. I cut off a similar tress and he wound it around his fingers and stowed it in his cloth, against his skin. Such gifts are love gifts, yielding great power to the recipient. Any competent sorcerer could cast a curse on the giver if he had some of his hair.

Kheperren said abruptly, 'They are taking scribes today for the army. I will go with Horemheb, the captain who is required to travel the border. I will write to you. And one day we will lie in our hut in the reeds, with a dog called Wolf on guard. The oracle said so,' he told me.

He leaned forward and kissed me again. Our tears mingled.

'But never ask me to forget you,' he said.

Then he bowed to me. Meryt opened the door, and he was gone.

I stared for a time at the closed door. It had brazen studs in the shape of lotus blossoms. Then I sent Meryt to bring to my presence the Master of the House of Scribes.

I needed advice and a household before I called on the Chief Priest of Amen-Re at Karnak, the most powerful man in the kingdom, apart from the Son of Re.

Chapter Four

Mutnodjme

Tey my mother and Nefertiti the Queen and I went to see the Great Royal Wife Tiye, our relative, and nearest way to the Pharaoh Amenhotep's private ear. We found her bathing. Her hair was loose, uncovered by her usual Nubian wig, and it was indeed red and long enough to reach to her waist. She lay back in a pool of water in which leaves had been strewed, and I smelt a sharp herbal scent; mint, perhaps, and wormwood. Her body was swelled with pregnancy. She was pale, as pale as marble, as pale as milk. I had never seen such skin before. The colour of her hair—Set the murderer's colour—would have caused her early death in some parts of the Kingdom. Even in the enlightened and civilised city, she usually kept her head covered in public. But the hair was not red, I realised, it was like copper wire; a fine, fiery tint, a fox colour. She looked tired and the herbs she was bathing in were selected to refresh an exhausted woman.

But her eyes, when she opened them, were slate-coloured and bright. She saw us come in, motioned us to sit down, and dismissed her attendants, three young women and one old woman who drew away beyond the door-curtain, block printed with indigo lotuses. The maidens seemed reluctant to leave Tiye, eying us suspiciously. The Lady of the Two Lands, the Queen of all Egypt, sat up unaffectedly, flicked her hair over her milk white shoulder, and smiled.

'You have come to tell me about my son,' she said, reaching out both hands so that we could help her out of the pool. I rushed to help. She was not like my beautiful sister, slim and delicate; but was wide hipped and her breasts were big and slightly sagging as she left the buoyancy of the warm water. She wrapped herself in a wide length of linen and motioned us to chairs.

Tey sat down and I sat, as I always did, at her feet. Nefertiti, a little nervous at being in the presence of this powerful woman, examined her sandals and did not venture to speak.

'Hmm.' The Queen exchanged a long look with my mother. 'The lady has lain with my son?'

Tey nodded.

'And it is as I feared?'

'If you feared that he would be impotent, Lady of the Two Lands, then it is so,' said Tey bluntly. Nefertiti blushed purple.

'She is very young; she can not have had many lovers. Can it be that she does not know…' Tiye smiled at Nefertiti, who was still too miserable to return it.

Tey shook her head so decisively that her earrings rang like bells.

'I have examined her account of what happened and my other daughter agrees. Nefertiti is fresh and beautiful and skilled, and entirely willing. She tried in all ways to please the son of the lord may he live but to no avail. She doubts that he is capable of producing an erect phallus, and without that there is no seed, and with no seed….'

Tiye wrapped the rope of her hair meditatively around her hand. 'Does she wish then to return to her mother's house?'

'No, Lady,' Nefertiti came to life and threw herself to her knees at the Queen's feet. Tiye, surprised, embraced her in the curtain of her coppery hair.

'Daughter, can it be that you love this weakling who cannot even lie with you as a man does with a woman?' she asked in an astonished tone.

'Yes, yes,' whispered Nefertiti into the linen towel. 'It is not his fault, it is the will of the Gods, who made him so. He is crippled, but he is so gentle. He did not hurt me, as another man might have done, disgusted by his failure. He did not blame me.'

'What, then, did you do all night?' asked Tiye, a little amused.

'We talked, Lady, and then we slept.'

'What did you talk about? There, daughter, be comforted, I will not tear you from your heart's longing. I wished merely to be sure that you were not discontented. Egypt does not need an unhappy Queen.'

'We talked about the Aten, Lady.'

'The Aten? Ah, religion,' said the Great Royal Wife, her mouth twisting as though she had bitten a persimmon. 'Sometimes one questions the wisdom of attempting to penetrate such mysteries. In any case, I am no guide, daughter. My son is philosophical, even whimsical, and perfectly unreasonable on that subject. I have always found it best not to argue with him.'

'What happens if you do argue with him?' I asked. Three sets of eyes turned on me. My mother's glare was as hot as a silversmith's furnace.

Tiye, however, was looking at me with great interest. She tipped up my chin with a strong forefinger and looked into my face.

'A good question, little daughter, and one that not many would dare to ask, Mutnodjme. I wonder what your father means to make of you, questioner?'

'She will be a wife,' snarled my mother. 'To an old man who will beat her.'

'There are worse fates than to be loved by an old man,' said the Queen gently, who was herself so married, and Tey bit her lip. I had made it possible for her to make a mistake in speaking with the Great Royal Wife, and she was going to beat me until I bled when she got me home, I could tell. But the question had not been answered and I looked at the Queen again. She laughed.

'What does my son do when he is crossed? He argues, and then if he is further opposed, he screams, and if anyone persists with their opposition, he throws himself on the ground. I recall that his nurse would not allow him to play with one of the guard dog's puppies, because she was afraid it would bite him. He shrieked until he turned blue and she was afraid and sent for me. I agreed that the prohibition was wise. My son found that he could not move us, and seemed to surrender. But the next day the puppy was found dead, its head beaten in by a stone. If he could not have it, no one could. It is not wise to persist in opposition to his desires.'

I stared at the Queen while my heart slowly chilled. Into what blood-stained hands had my Father delivered my beautiful and innocent sister?

'If he is…thwarted,' said my mother carefully, 'what remedies do you suggest?'

'Instant compliance,' said the Queen, still with her bitten-persimmon mouth. 'And if he is foaming and screaming, an infusion of valerian and reed-heads will calm him. I never expected to raise him,' she said slowly. 'When he was thirteen he was struck with a fever which raged for three days. He was as hot as a smith's brand and no medicine could quench it. All the physicians said that he would die. But then, quite suddenly, he fell into a sweat and then into a sleep, and when he awoke he was…distant. His ka had travelled, he said, to the Field of Reeds and found it empty but for the god Aten, the sun-disc.

'And then he did not develop like other boys. I thought it was just laziness—he has never liked to run or fight—when he fattened like a heifer, growing breasts and belly. I told myself, he is young and his father is solid and stocky, may he live forever. I thought nothing of it. By the time I knew that it was not so with my son, he was changed into what he is now. You are gentle and beautiful, Nefertiti, and he likes beautiful things. Love him as best you may. I can only hope that this child,' she caressed the mound of her belly, resting heavily on her thighs 'is a boy, for if my son Akhnamen becomes sole ruler, I do not know what will become of the Land of the River.'

She clapped her hands and her four suspicious maidservants came through the curtain. They did not look on us any more kindly, and I wondered if they disliked us on principle, or if they were defending their mistress, whom they evidently loved, from exertion. The old one knelt for her orders.

'The presents for the Great Royal Wife and her mother and sister, Sahte,' said Tiye gently, and the old woman blushed, muttered something, and gestured to the others, who brought a large basket. According to custom this could not be opened until we were back in our own apartments, so we bowed and kissed her sandal and were going away with a lot to think about, when the Queen Tiye said to my mother, 'I will send a scribe to your daughter Mutnodjme, Lady, if it please you. I think that she should be literate.'

'She can write and read as much as any princess,' said Tey, displeased at this slur on our household.

'I think she should be able to do more than that,' said the Queen, and now there was no doubt that it was a command. 'I will send a scribe tomorrow for the lady Mutnodjme, and a companion. She is a stranger here, and I think that she will be a friend to another stranger.'

'I and my family are in the Queen's hand,' replied Tey conventionally.

The plump woman shifted in her chair, cradling her burden. 'Yes, you are,' she agreed. 'So do not beat your little questioner, Great Royal Nurse Tey. It is never wise to beat children for exhibiting intelligence.'

'As the Queen says,' responded my mother through gritted teeth.

I walked behind her out of the Royal Bedchamber, thinking hard. A companion? I had been torn away from my friends when we had moved into the palace, and there were few children of my own age in the marble halls of Amenhotep may he live. And although I could read and write at least as well as my sister, my father had not considered that women needed much education, and had recalled his scribe to his other duties after we had mastered letters and numbers in the ordinary script enough to keep our household accounts, and understand recipes and prayers.

Father's scribe had been the old man Ani, a stern greyish man in a linen cloth with ink stains on his clever fingers. He had kept his eyes averted from us. I expected that a Royal Scribe would be sterner and older, and hoped that he would not hit me and my new companion if we made mistakes, as Ani had.

Running to keep up with my mother as she walked briskly down the corridor of tribute bearers, I did not ask questions. I had escaped one beating by divine favour, and I did not want to press my luck.

And the problem of the impotence of the Son of Egypt had not been addressed. Instant compliance, as recommended by the Queen, would not make an impotent King potent.

It never occurred to me that it was not my problem. I was intent on a solution. I could only think of one, and had already dismissed it as impossible.

When we were back in our own quarters, my mother not only did not beat me, but gave me a quick, fierce hug. My face was pushed into her breast and my cheek dented by her elaborate pectoral. I was eye to eye with a vulture, but Tey hugged me so seldom that I was resolved to enjoy it.

'Little questioner,' she held me out at arm's length and smiled at me. 'Tey's true daughter! Always one to ask the question that is on every tongue and to which no one dares to give voice…I wonder what will become of you?'

'Will you marry me to an old man who will beat me?' I asked slyly, and Tey laughed again and replied, trying to look stern, 'It might at least curb your inquisitiveness. You did well, daughter. For now we know, and otherwise she might not have told us.'

'About Akhnamen may he live,' I said.

'About him, yes. I had not heard about his… temper, 'Nodjme, had you?'

'No, Lady,' I replied honestly. 'They say that he is vague and gentle and lazy, that he sleeps a lot, that he is impulsive and pays no attention to right conduct or precedence. No one said that he is cruel, not where I heard them, or that he has tantrums.'

'Hush! That should not be said, daughter, not outside our home. Neferiti, are you determined to stay with your husband?'

'Yes, Lady,' said my sister.

'Even though he may be dangerous?'

'He will not be dangerous to me,' said Neferiti.

I had heard that tone before. Just so had she spoken before she had knelt down before a mastiff, her beautiful face inches from its teeth, and freed it from the wire snare which was wound around its leg. The dog had been wild with terror and pain, snarling and struggling, but under her hands it had lain quite still, even when she unwound the wire and hurt it afresh. The leg had never recovered, but the mastiff had been devoted to Neferiti ever since, though it bit everyone else.

She was probably right about the devotion of the King. But men, I had heard, were more cruel than beasts, taking pleasure in pain, and who knew what gave a eunuch pleasure? I resolved to ask, and to watch. I would know.

Ptah-hotep

To whom can I speak today?
I am heavy-laden with trouble
I have no friend of my heart.
To whom can I speak today?
Gentleness has withered
And violence rules the world.
To whom can I speak today?
Faces are averted
No man trusts his brother.

'What are you reading, Lord?' asked Meryt.

I let the papyrus roll up. 'It is called The Man Who Was Tired of Life,' I said.

She looked worried. 'You haven't had time to get tired,' she chided. 'And if you despair, your enemies will rejoice, for they would have no need to stain their hands with murder.'

'True. And you would not have my enemies pleased?'

'No, Lord, I would rather watch their hopes wither down to a forgotten grave,' she said, a serious curse. 'The Master of Scribes is here to see you, Master.'

'Send him in, bar the door, and serve wine,' I said hurriedly.

I had lived in the house of Ammemmes, Master of Scribes, for many years, and thought I knew him well; ancient, testy, short-sighted from construing ancient writings. He hobbled into my office now faster than I had ever seen him move and was about to sink to the floor to kiss my sandal when I caught him by the arm and led him to a chair.

Nothing was going to stop him, however, from conducting the proper verbal forms of address to a Great Royal Scribe. He rattled through my titles like a sistra in the hands of a musician from Hathor's temple.

'Humble greetings to the Great Royal Scribe, Whose Hand Moves as the Favourite of Re Akhnamen Lord of the Two Lands Keeper of All Secrets To Whom No Heart Is Hidden Marvellous in Wisdom Whose Heart is the King's Ptah-hotep,' he said, all in one breath. 'How are you, boy? I rejoice to see you still breathing.'

'I almost succumbed to a fatal accident with a scorpion,' I replied. 'My food is now tasted and I am about to appoint a staff of scribes who owe their positions to me.'

He gave me a shrewd look from his reddened eyes.

'Pharaoh's choice, though it seemed random, may have been better than he knew, my pupil. Now, give me some wine, and we will talk. Outside this room, you are the Great Royal Scribe. Inside, you are my pupil, Ptah-hotep, a young man forced into an intolerable situation who has a claim on my advice—if the Great Royal Scribe should desire it.'

'Master, I am...' I was touched almost to tears. He patted my hand briskly. Meryt came with my best vessels and poured wine. She sipped from both cups, swallowed, and nodded. Thereafter Ammemmes tasted it approvingly.

'Zythos Tashery vintage, if I'm not mistaken, from the vine-yards to the south. In the year 12?'

I consulted the terracotta label on the amphora and nodded. He was quite right.

'Keep it for the most honoured of visitors,' he advised. 'You have acquired one slave already, I see.'

'This is Meryt,' I introduced her. She dropped to her knees as was proper, but her eyes were directed at the Master of Scribes, as was not proper. He returned her gaze evenly. They were examining one another, the Nubian woman and the elderly scribe. Meryt had put on the new clothes I had ordered for her. Her printed cloth was knotted beneath her breasts in approved fashion, and her wild hair was plaited under a beaded cap. But she was still Meryt whose ancestors were hunters and warriors, and she was not abashed in the presence of the Master of Scribes. He was as different from the slave as possible; male, scholarly, sharp; but the look which they both directed at me before they considered each other again was identical; a slightly exasperated affection, which I did not deserve. Meryt I had taken from her position and placed in danger of her life. The Master of Scribes would now share her peril.

When Ammemmes spoke it was clear that some sort of agreement had been reached without need of words. He laid one veined hand on Meryt's decorated head in token of approval and asked 'Well, maiden, do you approve of your change in fortunes?'

'Yes, lord,' she said in her strong, liquid voice. 'The Great Royal Scribe honours this humble person with his trust.'

'He must be guarded and protected, Meryt the Nubian, for his foes ring him around like an embattled lion.'

'Lord, they will have my life first,' declared Meryt.

'And mine,' said Ammemmes in his precise scholar's tone.

I did not know what to say. Meryt, making up her mind, kissed Ammemmes' ringed hand, and he patted her cheek. Then she got up and poured more wine.

'Now, Ptah-hotep, what advice do you require?'

I was suddenly flooded by a strong sense of my own bot-tomless ignorance.

'Master, I haven't paid any attention to the situation of the Court. I know nothing. Tell me anything and it will add to my knowledge.'

'Hmm. Well, you have been appointed to a situation far above your merits by the co-regent Akhnamen, whose motives are obscure. He is Heir to Amenhotep the third may he live and that King, though robust, is over fifty and must die. Then the Heir will rule alone, an alarming prospect. You must consolidate your position while Amenhotep may he live forever is alive. As Akhnamen's appointee you cannot directly consult the King, which is a pity, because he is justly famed for his wisdom. The only other Heir is the Lady Sitamen, who is healthy a woman, it is said, but has not borne a child; and the Great Royal Wife is pregnant and due to deliver, if Isis is kind, soon.

'Medical opinion says that the co-regent is not expected to live a long life, but that does not solve our immediate problem. The person who was expecting the appointment may have sent you the scorpion; he must be curbed, you cannot spend all your life watching your back. Even your admirable Nubian must sleep sometimes.

'You sent Kheperren away, boy, that took courage and I am proud of you. That should preserve his life. Now, who should you appoint as your second in command?' He thought about it, drank some more wine, and stared absently at the papyrus heads painted around the cup.

'Who is the least favourite scribe in the palace?' I asked. Ammemmes was silent for a moment, then barked a short laugh.

'Mentu, by the crocodiles of Sobek, Mentu is the perfect choice!' He laughed again. 'Mentu belongs to one of the best families, a relative of the co-regent Akhnamen's new wife Nefertiti; a cousin, I believe, of Divine Father Ay. Mentu trained as a scribe after a fashion. He is boisterous, lazy and incompetent and Akhnamen finds him vastly attractive, being everything that Pharaoh is not. Mentu wishes to do nothing except race chariots and drink in the houses of ill repute by the river. No one can speak against his appointment, because Lord Akhnamen favours him. No one would want him to succeed, because he is immoral and stupid. Excellent. If you cannot have an efficient and devoted second, Ptah-hotep, there is a lot to be said for an idiot who pickled whatever brains he was born with in lowbgeh palm wine years ago.' Ammemmes rubbed his dry palms together with a whispering sound.

'I will appoint him immediately,' I said. I was beginning to feel a little better. I began to think that I might live out the day.

'Now, as to the staff—I think that you may as well have boys. You'll need a sensible man to watch over them, but most of your work could be done by anyone who can add, subtract, and write a fair hand. You don't want to be overawed, Ptah-hotep, in fact you cannot afford to have anyone with a lot more experience than you have yourself. What do you say to Khety? He is a commoner, though he shows no peasant good sense. He is skilled enough, in fact he was due to leave before Opet to go back to his father and become scribe on his estate, and I know that he was unhappy at the prospect. His father is a dreadful bully.'

I remembered Khety, a pleasant boy with an excellent memory. He was always in trouble for day-dreaming, but he told wonderful tales as we lay in the shade at noon. I nodded and called for a writing board. Meryt brought it with a speed which suggested that she had heard every word of my Master's discourse.

'Mentu and Khety,' I wrote on a scrap of pumiced papyrus.

'Hanufer, I know he's not a bright cheerful boy but he's determined and he's thorough.' I nodded and wrote down the name. I did not see much scope for cheer in my present situation. Hanufer's stolid solemnity would suit my office.

'And the supervisor?' I asked.

'Great Royal Scribe, you may command all of my men,' said my Master. 'Who would find favour in your eyes?'

'I need someone who understands politics,' I said, taking a sip of the wine—it was delicious, I noticed. Tashery was an excellent vineyard. And, as I now recalled, it was mine.

'Not Snefru, then, he is interested in nothing except ancient scripts. Let's see, it's Ephipi now, isn't it—that's why it is so foully hot—but in seven days Hathor goes to Horus and we have the festival of Apis. Bakhenmut might be your man and he'll be back from Memphis after the bull-sacrifice. He is a priest of Osiris, not allied to the priesthood of Amen-Re, which might be useful. He's shrewd and no gossip. Also he is married with three children and an ambitious wife.'

'And that is good?'

'An ambitious wife will be pleased by his ascension and she will know that he owes his position to you. That means you will have an advocate in his household.'

'Ah,' I agreed, having not thought about this before.

'Remember the Divine Amenhotep's sayings, my pupil. *The wise man educates the ignorant to wisdom and those who are hated become those who are loved*,' said my Master.

'*He brings to shore him who had no profitable voyage. He who was famine-struck is the possessor of harbours*,' I rejoined. 'What-ever that means.'

'One must always meditate on the sayings,' said Ammemmes, 'then their meaning will become clear.

'Though you will doubtless understand this message which I was bidden to give you by a young scribe who left this morning with the soldier Horemheb. He did not dare write anything, but said that I should bid you to remember a hut in the reeds, and a dog called Wolf.

I blinked back tears, suddenly possessed of memory; Kheperren's hands, his soft breathing, the way his eyelashes lay fanned on his cheek.

The Master of Scribes coughed, sipped more wine, and remarked, 'I reminded this young man of his duty to write to me, his master, of his progress. I recalled to him his apprenticeship in my house, and told him that I expected a report every decan. *Those he loves he favours; he dries their tears*,' he quoted.

'I suggest that you send Hanufer to me at intervals—shall we say, a decan or so?—as he is still my pupil, and he may carry such messages as the Great Royal Scribe sees fit to send to the Master of Scribes. And such as that humble official may be required to send in dutiful reply.'

He did not look at me or smile but I felt that a great weight had been lifted from my heart. I could know of my dearest one, could even communicate with him, without bringing him into any more danger than he would face ranging out along the borders with the guard.

'I will send the boys as soon as I return. Your office will, of course, be responsible for their board, and a suitable payment will be made to the Master of Scribes for the trouble of beating knowledge into a new collection of illiterate dirty boys.'

'For yourself, Master? I have great wealth, it appears.'

'For myself? A grant for the school for the acquisition of old manuscripts that will please Snefru's heart. And you could order the sacred lake cleared of weed.'

'I could do that,' I agreed, wondering how.

'Now, with your leave, I must go. I will instruct your staff suitably, and you will send news to Mentu of the honour of his appointment. Farewell, Ptah-hotep.' He kissed me in familiar fashion, then knelt before I could forestall him and kissed my sandal, whispering something to my ankles. His voice was urgent and soft, so that I had to strain my ears to catch it.

'Ptah-hotep, beware of the High Priest of Amen-Re. He will call for you soon. Tread as carefully with him as if you were walking barefoot through a field of serpents. He's the most powerful man in the kingdom.' My Master then rose, with Meryt's assistance, and left.

I sank down on the floor, cross legged, to write out the appointments for the names he had given me. But before I began, I wrote a draft on my Tashery vineyard for one hundred jars of the best vintage to be sent every year to Ammemmes, Master of Scribes in the Residence of the Pharaoh at Thebes in the 28th year of the reign of Amenhotep III and the first of his co-regent Akhnamen, Lords of the Lands of Upper and Lower Egypt, Shining in Thebes, Enduring in Kingship, Establishers of Laws, Lords of Strength and Mighty of Valour, may they live.

Chapter Five

Mutnodjme

We opened the basket and it was full of treasures. Nefertiti exclaimed as we spread out cloth worth half a Nome—finest gauze, the sort which we call 'woven air,' which takes a skilled spinner and weaver half a season to make and for which barbarian kings pay their weight in silver.

My mother doubled and redoubled a length and found that even folded ten times it would still go through a finger ring. It was beyond price.

Under it were well-made lengths of printed material, a handful of silver bracelets and jewellery made by some Theban craftsman, delicate beaten gold and small bright stones. There were also several heavy arm-rings.

In the midst of this a nurse was announced and came in pushing a reluctant miserable child before her. This, it appeared, was my new companion.

She had hair the same silvery brown as sycamore bark and eyes like good beer. She was dressed in a tunic of strange fashion, covering her shoulders instead of knotting around the waist. Her skin was milk white, like the Great Queen Tiye.

'This is the Lady Merope the Klepht, Princess of Kriti in the Islanded Sea, Royal Wife of Amenhotep may he live. On the orders of Queen Tiye, Favourite of the Two Lands, she is to be the companion of your daughter the lady Mutnodjme,' said the nurse, gesturing to a slave who was carrying a clothes-case and a basket to set them down. The basket yowled and something struggled within it, almost tipping it over.

'Please send my thanks to the Great Royal Lady and convey our understanding of her condescension,' said Tey.

The Lady Merope looked into my face with her strange brown eyes. I put out my hand and she took it. Her palm was damp with sweat. I could see that she was lonely and frightened and her loneliness matched my own. I smiled. So did she.

'Where is Kriti?' I asked. 'And why are you a Royal Wife?'

'I was sent as wife to the Pharaoh to seal a treaty, I mean, to the Lord Amenhotep may he live to ensure peace between Kriti and the Black Land,' she corrected herself hastily.

I was shocked. Egyptian princesses are never sent to another country, for in them resides the succession. Merope was continuing, 'And I will lie with the King when I am old enough, that is after my woman-blood begins. But now all I do is teach a slave how to speak the language of my home and learn Egyptian and wait. The lady the Queen Tiye may she live sent me here because she told me that you were in need of a companion. Is that true?'

'Yes,' I answered, suddenly made aware of how much I needed someone to talk to, preferably someone with something interesting to say in reply. 'And we are to have a scribe to teach us.'

'I have yet to learn to write,' said Merope. 'At home we do not use writing for anything important, only for lists.'

'Lists?'

'Of tribute to the temple and palace,' she explained. I knew about this.

'We do that here, as well, but there are many other things written down, the wisdom of our ancestors. "If you do not write it down, the words of wise ones will be lost." I quoted Ani, my father's scribe.

'We do not need to write it down. We remember. Bards can recount the story of a man dead a hundred years,' returned Merope with spirit.

'Here we know what words were said a thousand years ago,' I boasted. Tey my mother broke up the promising argument.

'Lady Merope, choose a gift to celebrate your arrival,' she said, gesturing at the array of treasure on the floor.

Merope smiled shyly, lifted aside the cloths, and pounced on the jewellery. She laid it out gently: pectoral and counterweight, elaborate earrings and chiming bracelets such as temple-dancers wear, and solid gold arm-rings.

'I like these,' she said, and my mother gave her an armband of thick gold, inlaid with little ibises for Thoth.

'Thoth is the protector of scribes, little daughter, and that should be worn while you are being instructed. I am glad that you are not greedy of gain, daughter Merope. Now my daughter will show you where to sleep and we will all lie down. And be quiet. The wind has given me a headache.'

Nefertiti had gone to lie down with her husband, my mother had lain down on her saddle-strung bed in the coolest corner, and I took Merope and the vociferous basket into the next room, where there were no windows and the air came up coldly from the staircase down to the cellars.

'This is Basht,' she said, undoing the basket. A striped cat shot out swearing, landed in a remote corner, glared wildly around to make sure that there was no threat in her immediate surroundings, then sat down to make an elaborate toilet, licking every ruffled hair into place deliberately and slowly. She was anxious to make perfectly sure that we didn't think that we had disturbed her at all by stuffing her into a nasty smelly basket and dragging her halfway across the palace without her leave.

'She is very beautiful,' I commented. Our own animals had been left at our house, and the palace cats had not seemed interested in our apartments.

'She is a gift from the King may he live. She sleeps on my mat, when she feels like it.'

'You have seen the King?' I asked.

'Yes, they brought me to him when I came, and he patted my cheek and told me to try to learn Egyptian, and gave me

Basht to be company for me. He is a nice man and I will not mind in the least when I can lie with him, even if he is old. He has kind eyes.'

'I know,' I agreed, remembering that shaft of understanding and fellow-feeling he had sent me at the coronation.

Basht finished her wash, stood up, yawned, and walked over to Merope, indicating that it was time for a rest. Merope had a sleeping mat of clean reeds, and we unrolled it and lay down, still too new in our acquaintance to sleep.

'Are you a wife of the Pharaoh, too?' asked Merope, settling her neck on a headrest and pulling out an errant strand of hair as it caught and pulled.

'No, I am just a daughter of Divine Father Aye and the Great Royal Nurse Tey. My half-sister is Nefertiti the Divine Spouse of Akhnamen may he live.'

'Oh,' she murmured. 'Not King Amenhotep, then.'

'No.' There was something pointed about the way she made no further comment, but it was too soon to talk about that dangerous subject. I did not know if I could trust her yet, this barbarian princess. What was always a safe subject?

'Tell me of the island of Kriti,' I urged.

'It's a fertile and green place, an island ruled by Minos the King, a nation of sea farers. Our ships go all over the Islanded Sea, as far as the river Oceanos extends, half across the world.'

'Is it a peaceful place?' I had heard that barbarians spent all their time fighting.

'Certainly,' she seemed offended. 'I don't know why Egyptians always think that their ways are superior to all others!'

'Divine Amenhotep says: *Go around the world, speak to all peoples, and you will not find one who will change his country's customs for another's.* And he is right. I beg your pardon, sister, but don't be so touchy. I wish only to know.'

'I'm sorry, I've been so lonely and everyone thinks I'm a savage. But that is what the men of my island would say about Egypt, I expect. Is it always this hot here?'

'No, this is Ephipi, the hottest month. That's when the lion-wind blows, the poison-breath of the Eastern Snake. Soon it will be Mesoré, and the grapes will ripen and we will have the harvest festivals.'

'I don't understand your year,' she said plaintively. 'At home we had four seasons, but here there are only three.'

'That is because we are the gift of the river. The Nile is our mother. We have three seasons of four months each, made of three decans of ten days,' I instructed my foreign sister.

'Shemu, which is harvest, that's now; Akhet, which is flood; and Peret, which is sprouting, the time of plants. Every time has its festival and every day its god, and over all of them is Amen-Re, Lord of Lords.'

'It is well known that Gaia Mistress of Animals is the head of the gods!' objected the foreign princess.

'Not in Egypt. But we will ask the scribe about gods; Mother says that they are not fit subjects for humans.'

'I know.'

She might have been about to say something more, but Basht walked off her chest and onto mine, dipping her head to sniff delicately at my neck and settling down with her pin tipped feet folded under her richly-patterned body.

'We were meant to be friends,' concluded Merope. 'Basht is never wrong about people.'

'Of course not. She's the avatar of Basht the Lady, Goddess of love and motherhood.'

'She couldn't be just a cat, then?' asked Merope slyly.

'No more than a crocodile is not the avatar of Sobek or a hippopotamus of Set the Destroyer.'

'But the crocodile will still bite and the hippopotamus break boats,' she argued. 'Acting like animals, not gods.'

'It's a mystery,' I replied, thinking about it for the first time and taking refuge in the scribe Ani's invariable response to such questions.

'Egypt is a strange place,' concluded my new sister, and we drowsed into sleep.

For the first time I had met someone who asked more questions than I did, and I thought the Queen Tiye wise to put us together. It might even preserve my own mother's temper.

◇◇◇

The Kriti princess was equally pleased, it seemed, with me as a companion. Though she refused to abandon her tunic, which covered her chest, for a proper knotted cloth, and would not have her head shaved to a sidelock, as we did for cleanliness and convenience, she adapted to life in her new country well. She had learned the language very quickly, though some words still eluded her, and some of the grammatical constructions which I had learned before I knew that I was learning them gave her trouble. She could not differentiate between the three levels of formal address, so spoke to all persons as though they were Pharaoh or a High Priest, which gave her a reputation for humility. And she asked me why my mother had commended her for lack of greed when she had asked for a solid gold bracelet.

'Because you did not ask for silver, the most precious metal in the Black Land,' I explained.

'In Kriti the most precious metal is gold,' she protested.

'Here gold is as sand,' I replied, beginning to laugh. After a moment she joined in. 'Whole shiploads of it come from Nubia in Upper Egypt every day. Whereas silver has to come from barbarian lands and is traded for three times its weight in gold.'

'Come, then you shall learn some Kritian, if I must learn Egyptian,' she said.

'Why should I do that?' I teased.

'Because it would be sweet to speak again in my own tongue, and I shall never see my home again,' she responded, and burst into tears.

I was shocked at my insensitivity. I would never be sent away from my country, never have to learn difficult words in another tongue to speak to my captors. I tried to imagine how much she must miss the green island and the sound of her own language, and thought how I would miss the land of the Nile, the speech of the women, the scent of dung fires which kept off mosquitoes, the taste of plum and melon. I imagined it so well that I made myself cry and hugged her close and she wept into my neck, strong sobs which hurt her slim body. When the tears had died down a little, we kissed, I mopped her face with a linen cloth and we began to learn Kritian as I re-drew the kohl around her strange brown eyes.

'Adelphemou,' she taught me as my first words, which means, my sister.

Ptah-hotep

The summons from the High Priest of Amen-Re came for dinner the next day, when I had settled my scribes into my office and instructed them in their duties. It was basic record keeping, really, as the master had said. Not difficult, but requiring steady attention and some skill. Few actual orders issued from the office of the Great Royal Scribe, but he acted as auditor for the whole of the nation, expected to uncover fraud and misreporting, to protect the common people from over-zealous officials and extortion, and to oversee the administration of the kingdom.

He was—*I was*—also responsible for receiving the Nomarch's accounts, the Chief Watcher's report on the state of lawlessness in Egypt, and for recording the Lord Akhnamen's thoughts and orders.

That seemed to be enough for one very youthful scribe whose previous heaviest responsibility had been as overseer of a class of ten boys.

And Pharaoh still had not sent for me. I wondered if he had forgotten me, and if I should ask for an audience with him. Perhaps he was leaving me for a decan to find out if I could avoid assassination for ten days.

That might prove to be harder than I thought.

Meryt had come to me at dawn, brow wrinkled.

'Lord, someone tried to get into my chamber last night.'

'There could be many reasons for that,' I said sleepily. With her beautiful smile and her rounded body, many men would have found Meryt attractive. She shook her head and her earrings chimed.

'Nothing as innocent as that,' she protested. 'Besides, no one would dare. I belong to you, Master. I don't like this. I heard someone try the door; saw the handle move. Lord, I want to spend some of your gold and make you a gift.'

Her face was solemn, and I shook myself into real wakefulness.

'You may spend my gold. I will accept your gift,' I said, matching her seriousness.

'Thank you. I will be gone perhaps an hour, Master. Wait for me, fasting, if you will.'

'Very well,' I agreed. Fasting was no great pain to me. I doused a pang of some unexpected emotion—was it disappointment as to the nature of her gift? Since I had refused her offer of her body, she had not attempted any intimacy. Meryt bowed and left, closing my door behind her.

She had returned within her time, towing a heavy chain behind her. It appeared to be suspended in the air and I was surprised at the size of the hound to which it was attached. He was huge.

'This is Anubis,' Meryt informed me. 'A Nubian hound for a Nubian slave, and he has cost you an ingot of gold, Master.'

Anubis sat down, all paws together, and regarded me with an intelligence which was vaguely disturbing from a canine. He was part-jackal, perhaps, a black, high shouldered dog with a pointed muzzle, long legs and a long whip-like tail. I had seen such hounds racing alongside chariots.

'He's a hunting dog, a war-dog,' I said. 'Meryt, what have you spent my gold ingot on? He surely will not be comfortable in a palace.'

'His kind comes from the Mountains of the Moon; my home now lost forever. Such hounds belong to kings; and his father belonged to my father, captured as loot when my village was raided. He is a Nubian, as I am, and we are faithful to death.'

Meryt stood with her dark hand on the hound's black head. Both pairs of eyes were regarding me almost dispassionately, but with such steadfastness that my own eyes burned and I had to look away. What had I done to deserve such loyalty? I was only a scribe, son of a scribe, no great warrior or captain.

Meryt continued, 'Once he knows that you are his Lord, he will allow no thief or murderer close. He will not bay and arouse the palace, but come and wake you. And at a pinch, Master, he will defend you with his life. That's why I wanted you to fast. He needs to identify your scent, not mixed with onions or wine.'

She led the hound forward and pushed his muzzle into the gap between my arm and my side. I felt the cold nose tickle, and the dog took two deep snuffling breaths, recording my scent. Then he pulled away from Meryt's grasp and lay down, putting his head between my two hands. In that position he was helpless and at my mercy. It was an act of formal obeisance as graceful as any courtier, as graceful as the other Nubian in my service.

'Anubis, I accept your fealty,' I said gravely, deeply touched. Meryt nodded and went to fetch our breakfast. Anubis accepted the two scribes, sniffing them as they came in, carrying bundles of possessions and their working tools.

'Lord, it's a wolf!' exclaimed Khety.

'It's a dog,' Hanufer reproved him. This was typical of their relationship. Hanufer had no imagination at all. Khety had too much. Together, I hoped, my office would be balanced.

We laid out the work for the day and the two scribes sat down to become familiar with the extent of the Great Royal Scribe's responsibility. It did not look so unmanageable with someone else to read the endless reports and tell me what was happening. We were in the middle of the Hare Nome's report on the repairs to the canals when there was a disturbance in the outer office and I went out.

'Call him off!' gasped a tall young man wearing an expensive, food-spotted cloth and a wig which had evidently not been cleaned since last night's feast. The perfume cone which had dripped scented oil was matted into it and he stank of wine. Anubis had backed him against the wall and the oil from his headdress was marking my lotus frieze.

'Anubis, release him and come here,' I said quietly, wondering if the hound would obey me.

Meryt had spoken truly, as was her habit. Anubis left the cowering young man and came to me, sitting down composedly at my side.

'Who are you?'

'I'm Mentu; you called for me,' blurred the man, straightening the wig and wiping more oil over my delicately painted wall.

'Come away from there,' I ordered. 'Anubis will not hurt you, unless I so order him. Meryt, some wine, if you please. Sit down,' I told my second.

'What a remarkable hound,' said Mentu, sitting down as ordered and discarding the wig. He dropped it to the floor where it lay like a dead rabbit. 'Where did you get him, Lord?'

'He comes from Nubia,' I evaded the question, because I did not know from whom Meryt had bought him. 'From the Mountains of the Moon. Mentu, I am minded to appoint you as my Second Scribe. Will you accept the appointment?'

Now that I was close to him, I could see that he was not so young. Hard drinking and some hard exercise—chariot racing, perhaps?—had put harsh lines into his face and crow's feet around his eyes. Though presenting a picture of dissipation, he was examining me with eyes which were quite bright and present.

'It would please my father, and he holds the key to the treasure-chest,' said Mentu consideringly. 'What would you wish me to do?'

'You can do as you like,' I said. 'You can attend here and help in the management of the kingdom, or you can race horses and drink every night.'

'I see,' Mentu accepted a cup of Tashery vintage—the amphora was already open—and sipped. His eyebrows rose.

'I see your plan,' he commented. 'I would be the last person anyone would want as Great Royal Scribe.' This was a rather alarming insight, but I said nothing. 'In fact, the scheme may work to both of our advantages, Lord Ptah-hotep. I wish to feast and enjoy myself, you wish to run the kingdom. Or maybe it is true that you were just selected at random out of the school of scribes solely to annoy the old man Nebemanet, who made his disapproval of the Divine Akhnamen's religious views so distressingly plain to Pharaoh's Royal Father?'

'I was selected by Pharaoh may he live out of the school of scribes,' I agreed. 'Why, I still do not know and I have not seen Divine Akhnamen since.'

'He will call for you,' said Mentu, sipping more of my wine. 'Do not, if you will accept my advice, argue matters of gods with him. They say that he is perilous if crossed, and as he elevated you out of the school, he can cast you down again, and all those who hold with you.

'Do I wish to involve myself in office, when I could thus be ruined if you make a false step; or if Divine Akhnamen takes against you? A pretty problem. I believe that the answer lies in the bottom of another cup of wine.'

Meryt poured more wine for him. He looked at her.

'A Nubian hound, a Nubian slave they are powerful arguments for your influence, Lord. Neither give their allegiance lightly. You, woman,' he addressed Meryt roughly.

She knelt. A slave is required to kneel if she is spoken to by the nobility. Her face was perfectly blank, like a carving in ebony.

I struggled with rising anger.

'Lord, what do you require?'

'Are you owned by this young man?' he pointed at me. Meryt nodded.

'Has he your loyalty?'

'He has,' said Meryt. Mentu considered her, then reached out and playfully tugged a tress of beaded, plaited hair.

'You're a good girl,' he commented, and gestured to her to rise. She did so with perfect, athletic ease. 'I might be of use to you, Lord, though not as a scribe. I know the palace, Lord Ptah-hotep. I accept your appointment. I will serve you faithfully. Now, what do you want to know?'

'Tell me about the Master of Scribes,' I said, as a test of his accuracy.

'A good man, if dry as the papyrus he studies. From an old family. Reliable, loyal, all those cold virtues.' So far I agreed with my new second in command.

'The Nomarch of the Nome of the Hare?' I asked at a venture, having just read his report.

'Drinks too much and quarrels incessantly with the Nomarch of Heliopolis. They share family connections—his First Wife is the Heliopolitan's sister. Spends too much of his inheritance on boats and huge feasts.'

'Is he cheating on his taxation?' I hazarded, not knowing how far Mentu would be willing to go in informing on his friends.

'Probably. Look for inconsistencies in the returns on fish; it's been a wonderful season for fish. And turtles.'

'How about Heliopolis, then?'

'Fat and lazy, do anything to avoid trouble. Wouldn't run the risk of cheating, because it would mean that he had to make an effort. Has a longstanding argument with the Temple of Osiris on the bank opposite the city. Study the temple's share closely; he'll shave their ingots if he can.'

'And Thebes?'

'Ah, that is my cousin.'

Without being asked, Meryt filled the cup of this loquacious informant. I found myself beginning to like Mentu, though he was everything I disapproved of in a man.

'Your cousin?'

'Indeed. Now he will pay more than he is required to pay to the Temple of Hathor, because he and the temple priestesses have an understanding. Whenever he feels the need of comfort, he calls for them and they attend his palace and relieve his… monotony,' Mentu laughed and I joined in.

'They are very skilled, the ladies of the Lady of Love and Beauty. The feast of Horus and Hathor is famed all over the known world. Achaeans and Trojans and Klepht travel many leagues to lie down in their smooth arms and taste their divine kisses. May I hope that my Lord will come with me to Edfu when the season comes?'

This was a loaded question, and I contented myself with a nod. I had never lain with a woman and did not know if I desired to taste such well-travelled flesh.

'Apart from his fascination with the priestesses?'

'Thebes is rich in his own right, no commoner's son.'

I allowed the silence to grow long after the initial discomfort. Mentu shifted on his chair. Finally he said, 'No insult was meant, Lord. But if he is rich in his own right, he is less likely to peculate. Except for his expenses in love, you can trust the Theban Nomarch.'

I recalled my invitation to the temple at Karnak. 'The High Priest of Amen-Re?' I asked.

'Death in a white robe,' said Mentu promptly.

Chapter Six

Mutnodjme

Merope and I had slept, though we were not aware of having slipped into a doze until we were woken abruptly by a flurry of movement in the outer chamber, and voices crying, 'The Queen is in labour, send for the great Royal Nurse Tey, the Queen's midwife!' I heard my mother grunt as she rose from her saddle-strung bed.

'Quick,' I whispered to my new sister. 'Put on your sandals and we can follow in the confusion.'

'Why should we?'

'Because it's childbirth, and I've not been allowed to see it.'

'Nor me,' she agreed, tying strings rapidly.

We slipped into the outer chamber, where my mother was stripping off her robe and stepping into a decorated tub. Slaves sluiced her down with cool water and scrubbed her with handfuls of oatmeal mixed with laundryman's lye and then rinsed her. She then tied a clean cloth about her waist, another around her head, and raised her voice.

'I am coming!' she cried. 'Be silent, women. The Great Queen Tiye has already borne children. She knows what is happening. But she will not be assisted by a clamour like a marketplace on the day before a feast! The birthroom has been prepared; has anyone thought to carry the Queen thither?'

She stilled the babble of replies with a gesture.

'Good. We will go there now, and she who makes an outcry which upsets the Great Royal Lady will be beaten until she bleeds.'

This threat calmed the crowd nicely and Tey walked composedly out of our apartments and into the corridor. Merope and I followed.

The mammisi was prepared. It had bare walls, a bare floor, and a pallet made of clean linen on the floor. The birth chair had been scrubbed and repainted. Not for the Lady of the Two Lands the peasant delivery, squatting on bricks. The chair was bottomless and at an easy height for the attendant to catch the baby as it was delivered.

So far, so good. The Queen was standing with two women massaging her back. Her hair was dark red with sweat and she looked old. She greeted my mother with a smile which was a sketch of the one I had seen before.

'Lady,' she said.

'Where does it catch you?' asked Tey.

'My back, it always hurts my back,' replied the Queen, and Tey directed the women to massage lower down, in the flat space just above the buttocks. The Queen seemed to feel some relief. She was offered an infusion and drank it.

'Now what?' whispered Merope.

'We wait,' I replied.

Nothing happened all afternoon. The sun sank towards night and still nothing happened. I was carrying a scroll, one of the few which I owned myself. Ani had copied it for me. It was the tale of Ptah and the Destruction of Mankind. Merope and I sat down against the wall, out of everyone's way, and peered through the legs of the attendant women. Nothing still seemed to be happening, and we were getting bored, so I opened the scroll and began to read, telling Merope of the sins of humans which made Ptah the creator disgusted with his creation:

Humans blasphemed against the god, saying, 'His bones are like silver, his limbs are like gold, his hair is like lapis, in truth he is old and weak.' Then Ptah called to him the gods who were with him in the primeval ocean and took counsel with them. . .

'Who were the gods from the primeval ocean?' asked my sister.

'Shu who is air, Tefnut who is water, Nut who is sky, they were the first ones, in this story,' I replied.

The Queen groaned, and we strove to see, but a rush of attendants blocked our view. I consulted my text again:

The gods came and bowed before the majesty of Ptah who made the firstborn gods out of words, out of his lips and teeth, Lord of Speaking Creatures, Maker of Humans. They said before him, 'Speak to us, for we are listening.'

A woman stubbed her toe on us as she hurried to the door for more cloths and another infusion of the birth herbs, and did not even stop to notice who was sitting in that corner. I continued the tale:

Ptah said to his gods, 'Tell me of humanity, what shall I do to these blasphemous ones? I have given them the world, and they say that I am old.'

The gods took counsel, and they replied to Ptah Creator, 'Lord, you must slay them, so that they shall know fear of the gods.'

'Who shall I send to slaughter men and women?' asked Ptah.

The Spreader of Terror rose, lioness-headed Sekmet who is out of Hathor the Goddess, and said, 'It shall be I.'

And Ptah agreed that it should be so.

'Who is telling a tale?' asked the labouring Queen. 'Bring them here.'

We were discovered, hauled out of our corner, and shoved into the middle of the room where we stood, heads hanging, before Tey's wrath. The Queen was sitting on the birth chair and laid a sweating hand on my mother's shoulder.

'Let her read on,' she ordered. 'Sit down, little scribe, and continue. I need something to distract my mind.'

'Lady, this is not a good story for one in your situation,' warned Tey, but the Queen merely said 'Read on.'

'Do as you are bid,' snapped Tey.

Greatly wondering I sat down, Merope at my side, and continued with the story of the destruction of the world.

Sekmet Destroyer went forth, and great was the slaughter amongst men and women. She struck fear into their hearts; and Ra said to Ptah, 'Behold them fleeing into the mountains in terror, and there terror waits for them.'

I stopped as the Queen groaned again. My mother wiped the Lady's forehead with a wet cloth and instructed me 'I don't know what you are doing here against my express orders, Mutnodjme, but now you will learn the way of birth, so pay attention. The pains come at intervals, getting closer and closer until they are almost simultaneous and then the child is born if the gods are kind. While the pain is upon her, she will not hear. When it has passed, she will listen again. This story may not last long enough; do you know any more?'

'Yes, Lady.'

'Good. Go on.'

The Queen was attending again, and I resumed the tale:

Great was the slaughter, great the mourning. Corpses littered the mountains and the living could not bury the dead, because there were too many.

Fearing that they would all be destroyed, Re said to Sekmet, 'Return, return in peace, Sekmet, you have slain enough.'

She replied, 'You gave me life and this power to kill. I am not glutted, I will not return but slay and slay until no one lives on the earth.'

I risked a look at the Queen. Her thighs were tensed, tendons shaking under immense strain. Her female parts were wet with escaping fluid. I felt elated, frightened and compelled. I could not look away from this body in such agony.

Tey slapped me over the ear and recalled me to myself. I began reading again:

Then Re spoke to the priestesses of the Lady, saying, 'Do thus and you shall be saved. As women pound barley for beer, they shall crush mandrakes from Elephantine in great number, and they shall make beer which is as red as blood and fill seven thousand vessels.'

And such of the women who lived pounded mandrakes instead of barley, and made seven thousand jars of beer as red as blood.

It was not a groan this time. It was closer to a scream. I waited out the contraction and continued:

Therefore came the Majesty of the South and the North, Re who is Amen and the Sun, Glorious in Might, sailing up the Nile in the barge which is called Glory of Amen-Re and he came to the fields of Suten-henen where the goddess waded in blood.

Another pain, another cry. A priestess from the temple of Isis laid an ankh, symbol of life, on the Queen's stomach, swollen so tight that I thought that the skin might split. Tey did not have to scowl at me, however, I resumed as soon as I could.

Then came the four, the good gods, and Tefnut filled this field with rain. Then the women poured out the seven thousand jars of beer made with mandrakes of Elephantine, and the water became as blood.

Sekmet the Spreader of Terror snuffed the air and smelt blood, and she dipped her muzzle and drank. And merry was her heart as she drank the blood, and she became drunk on this water, and fell asleep and knew not slaughter any more.

There was a shift in the room. Some spirit had come in. Tey was biting her lip, which she only did when she was seriously worried. I saw blood begin to drip from the Queen's genitals onto the floor. Bright red, drop by drop, it splashed on the clean marble and pooled. Tey cast a red cloth under the chair so that the Queen should not see the blood and be afraid, and urged, 'Lady, think, speak, listen,' and snarled sideways at me 'Talk, daughter! It's what you're good at!'

I stood up and spoke louder. Merope was huddled at my feet, overawed. I wished fiercely that I hadn't come, but it was too late to repent and time cannot be poured back once the jar of life has been broached.

'Come, come, oh most beautiful,' called Horus the Eye to the sleeping Sekmet as she lay in the field of blood. 'Come with me, most excellent lady, be my own love, for my heart is moved for you.'

And he was to her eyes as the fairest and most delightful of men, and as she woke she loved him. She took his hand and he led her north to a lake called Bubastis, where he said to her, 'Let us swim, dear one, and be clean.'

And she went in to the water, and came forth a beautiful woman and a cat, and Horus said to her, 'We shall call this your benign avatar Basht, elegant and fair; and you, Lady, shall always have my heart.'

And they lay on the banks of the lake called Bubastis and had great joy. He imbued her with the perfumes of his body, and she was gladdened by his touch.

I glanced at Tey and she motioned me to go on.

And ever since the cat Basht has been worshipped at Bubastis, city of cats, and ever since the priestesses of Sekmet have made barley beer with mandrakes at the Festival of the Deliverance, and thus shall it always be.

The Queen gave a great, forceful shriek, half of agony and half of effort. Her legs flexed, her hands closed on the arms of the chair with force enough to crush the wood. The cry came again, and the child was born into my mother Tey's hands in a slippery flash followed by a fountain of blood.

I heard my sister Merope retch, but I was not sick. I was fascinated. As Tey cleared its mouth, the baby began to gasp and then to cry. Tey held it carefully close.

'Rejoice, Great Queen,' she said to the woman, as the attendants swathed her loins in red cloth, bound tight to stop the bleeding. 'You have given your Lord another son.'

'Smenkhare,' whispered Tiye. Then she collapsed, and we were thrown out.

Ptah-hotep

I occupied the remainder of the day by instructing my new scribes, ordering more wine for Mentu's visits, and inspecting the chest full of beautiful cloths. As a Great Royal Scribe, I could wear what I chose and I did not like much decoration. It smacked of ostentation. I was therefore considering the difference between creamy linen with a thin gold border and a starkly white one when Meryt announced, 'Someone's coming—someone with a lot of attendants—sit in your chair, Master, take your writing board, tell your scribes to instruct you in something; it's the King Akhnamen may he live!'

I did as she bade me, throwing myself into my chair and grabbing a plaster board. Hanufer stood beside me and read the complaint from the temple of Osiris that the Nomarch of Heliopolis was reducing his offerings—just as Mentu had said.

It was a long wait, and I had time to give him orders to send an investigator to the Nomarch and suggest that he hand over the ingot-shavings to the temple or suffer an afterlife spent inside the Great Snake, Apep. What sort of idiot risks his Eternity for a minor quarrel?

Khety, on my other side, had time to begin a summary of the preparations for the feast of Hathor-at-Dendera—she goes to Horus-of-Edfu at the end of Ephipi and there are always problems with public order—when the King finally arrived, flanked by two soldiers.

He stood in the doorway as we registered his presence and threw ourselves to the floor. I crawled forward to kiss his sandal and he signalled to me to rise by brushing his fly-whisk across my shoulder.

'You have only a small staff,' he commented, flicking the whisk at Khety and Hanufer. Meryt stayed where she was until one of the soldiers, shoving her with his foot, said, 'Fetch wine' and she rose and slid away.

'Lord of the Two Lands, more are expected, but not many more.'

'And you have appointed Mentu as your second. Do you believe that he will be of assistance?'

'Lord, I believe that he may be of great assistance.'

I did not specify as to how he might assist me, and it was always difficult to discern how much the Lord Akhnamen understood. I had dared to raise my eyes to his face. He was smooth and well tended, this younger son of the King. His eyes were strange, unfocussed, a dreamer's eyes, a visionary's. I never knew how to read them. Was he pleased with his selection from the School of Scribes? Was he about to order me back to obscurity? Hope rose in my breast. I could go then and find the Captain Horemheb and rejoin my own dear friend Kheperren.

'What have you found out? You gave your scribe an order. What was it?' he asked Hanufer directly.

Hanufer was not over-awed. He stood up straight, smoothed down his cloth, took his ostracon and repeated my order, word for word including the comment about the afterlife, as emotionlessly as though he was reading a laundry list. I held my breath. The King laughed and sat down in my chair.

'I think I may have chosen well,' he commented, accepting a cup of wine from Mery's hand, after the soldier had tasted it and nodded to her to continue. 'You have everything you need?'

No one has offered you affront?'

I shook my head.

'And you have a guardian,' he commented, glancing at Anubis who was sitting as still as a stone hound by the door.

'Yes, Lord, I have.'

'That should preserve you from any annoyance,' he murmured ambiguously. 'I understand that you have been summoned to dine with the Chief Priest at Karnak tonight.'

'I have, Lord. Is it your will that I should attend?'

'Mmn...' he was thinking. 'Who is your god, boy?'

'Amen-Re,' I replied, surprised. Everyone's god was Amen-Re, the Sun.

'You come from the Nome of the Black Bull, do you not? Have you a special devotion to Apis or Osiris?'

'No more than usual, Lord of the Two Thrones.'

'Be careful,' he advised me. 'Yes, you must attend, of course; even I must attend on him if the High Priest summons me. But he will suspect you, Ptah-hotep, because you are young and because I selected you instead of an old man with whom that same High Priest had an understanding.

'My father the Divine Amenhotep says that the priests of Amen-Re are becoming too bold, too powerful and too rich. I am minded to mend this situation, but not yet. I am thinking of a new city.'

'A new city, Lord?' I was following his train of thought as well as I could, but logic was not helping. I decided to just follow this fascinating breeze wherever it went.

'I will speak of it again. I have been given permission by my father to move from Thebes to a new place, clean, unstained by other worship. On the left bank of the river, at Amarna,' he said, waiting for my shocked reaction.

The left bank was reserved for Houses of Eternity, the cities of the dead, but I made no comment. If Pharaoh wanted to build a city in a tomb, who was I to argue? I nodded. The King rose. 'Attend on me early in the morning tomorrow,' he ordered. We all flung ourselves to the floor again, and he was gone.

Anubis, by the door, gave a faint growl and a long considering sniff. The King had, indeed, smelt powerfully of spikenard, and perhaps that offended my hound's sensitive nose.

We had barely recovered from the royal visit when another Divine Personage deigned to enter and we were back on the floor again. Fortunately Meryt had ordered it swept and sprinkled or I might have betrayed my dignity with a sneeze.

'Rise, rise,' said a slightly impatient female voice, and I came up nose-to-hem with the Chantress of the Temple of Neith, the Princess Sitamen, only daughter of Amenhotep and also his wife.

'You are Ptah-hotep,' she observed, motioning to Meryt to bring her a chair. 'Go on with your work, honoured scribes, I do not wish to interrupt you more than I must.'

Hanufer and Khety collected their wits, closed their mouths, which had gaped, and withdrew to the inner room. I was alone with one of the most powerful women in the Kingdom, and one of the most beautiful.

The Princess Sitamen was slim and strong, with wide shoulders and long legs. It was said that she did not wish to wed at all, and had accepted a marriage with her father with relief, as she could not thereafter be pressured to accept another mate. She loved to run, ride, dance and swim, lived with her maidens in seclusion, and was seldom seen at palace functions or feasts. Her charities were legendary. She had endowed a school of priestesses for the temple of the Divine Huntress Neith, sister of Isis, out of her own fortune, telling her ladies, 'Melt down a few thousand bracelets, I do not wish to wear anything more decorative than my skin.' Or so it was said. She certainly wore nothing more than a scant cloth, no jewellery except her badges of rank, and plain sandals such as common people wear.

And her own skin was very decorative. She glowed with health, though she was bronzed with weather, unlike the pale ladies of the palace.

'I am here on my mother's errand,' she began briskly, 'Her labour began an hour ago, but she does not forget promises. I need a scribe for the Royal Daughter Mutnodjme and a little Great Royal Wife called Merope, a barbarian princess. My mother suggests a young man, because they are both inquisitive and mischievous maidens, and would disconcert anyone older. Unless you can think of an older man who has a flexible mind?'

'I have never met one,' I confessed. 'I am honoured by the Great Royal Lady's trust. I will find her a suitable scribe. I will appoint someone, or I will come myself.'

'Good.' She had discharged her errand but she did not seem to be thinking of leaving. Her maidens had arranged themselves around her on the floor and Meryt had already sent a slave to fetch more wine and cold water. In future we would have to keep a greater store of provisions in the office. There was room enough in the empty rooms at the back.

'I saw that my brother was with you,' she commented.

'Yes, lady, he has just left.'

'Many will wonder at your appointment, Ptah-hotep.'

'Lady, they will. I am very young and I have no experience of this work, but I will learn. I will justify the trust which Pharaoh Akhnamen may he live has shown in me.'

'My father,' began the Princess, then abandoned the train of thought. 'No, of course, you cannot approach my father. But should you be able—indirectly, of course—to talk to him, his words are to be cherished. The Divine Amenhotep's reputation for wisdom is not exaggerated.'

'Certainly not,' Lady of the Two Lands. Every wise man quotes his words.'

'Thank you,' she accepted a cup of watered wine from Meryt. Hanufer and Khety, abandoning any pretence of work, had joined the maidens and were handing round wine-vessels. The Lady Sitamen did not seem to object to their presence, so I did not frown them back to their places.

'The Lady Sitamen seeks a scribe to teach two young Royal Daughters,' I said to them. 'She needs an inquiring mind this on the orders of Queen Tiye, may she live. Have you any suggestions?'

'From the School, Lord Ptah-hotep?' asked Hanufer, who liked to have the rules explained before he started.

'There, or anywhere,' I replied.

I occupied my eyes with gazing at the Princess' maidens. They were very like her. They were scantily clad in undecorated cloth, they looked coloured by the sun if not precisely weathered, and they looked muscular and competent. One was wearing an archer's bracer and several carried knives. I would not have liked to approach the Princess Sitamen Great Royal Wife of Amenhotep may he live with mayhem in mind. The attendants of the lady looked capable of mincing any attacker long before he got within striking range. And they looked, to my mind, as if they might enjoy it.

However, Anubis, a war-dog, had sunk down onto his belly and seemed pleased by their company. Evidently they had no unpleasant fate in mind for me.

'Hotep, what about Khons?' asked Khety, who still had not become used to our elevation in status. I stared haughtily at him, until he registered the glare and amended his mode of address.

'I mean, my lord Ptah-hotep, Great Royal Scribe may you live, would you consider Khons for the honour?'

It was a good idea. Khons was young, he was bored, and his back bore the marks of the master's displeasure at his endless questioning. He was supposed to go into the Priesthood of Amen-Re but they had rejected him, and he was presently considering the fact that the only temple that wished to have him was the home of the unfashionable Khnum the Potter at Hermopolis—a soggy and uncomfortable place where half the population died young of marsh-borne diseases. His only other option was to return to his village and be a marker-scribe; an honourable occupation, but possibly even more tedious than the temple of Khnum. And he was a commoner's son, as I was myself, and it pleased me to think of him instructing the Princesses.

'Will he do?' asked the Lady, arching an eyebrow.

'He will, with your royal approval,' I replied.

'Then you may forgive your scribe for forgetting your honorifics, as he is very young and he is sorry,' she said; and Khery grinned with relief. Had I wished, I could have had him beaten with rods for such insolence.

'Write an order for the Master of Scribes,' I directed. 'Send him Ptah-hotep's compliments and beg him to donate another student to the palace. Tell Khons to report to me and I will conduct him to the Royal Ladies Mutnodjme and Merope.'

'Very good,' the Princess still did not move and I wondered what else she wanted. She came to some sort of decision and gestured her attendants away.

'Young men, show my young women the decorative features of your office,' she ordered, and Khery and Hanufer rose obediently to exhibit my painted walls and my precious statue of Thoth made of the hardest grey granite.

The Princess waited until they had gone out of easy earshot and said quietly, 'My brother took you from one you loved, Ptah-hotep, to make you Great Royal Scribe.'

Was this a trap? Did she want to find a lever, and therefore needed to confirm my love for Kheperren? He was safely away with the army. The princess did not try to hurry me. She listened to Hanufer explaining at length the symbolism of Thoth being both the Ibis and the Ape, and waited.

'Yes, there was one I loved.'

'You sent him away?'

'Lady,' I agreed.

'That was wise, for you are surrounded by enemies. My brother's action has plunged you into a pit of snakes. But I know how it is to be threatened by the nature of one's love, Ptah-hotep, more than my brother or my father ever knew. That is why my father married me, to preserve my life and the way I live it. But you will *have* to marry.'

'Lady, in time.' I was not sure of this Divine Princess, or her purposes.

She sighed in exasperation. 'You have no reason to trust me, Ptah-hotep, but you may. So I will say this, if you are assailed, if your only love is in danger, send or come to me. I have a palace of my own where no enemy enters—or if they do, they do not remain. By gift of my wise father, may he live forever, I have position and power and I will protect you. In one respect, Great Royal Scribe, we are as sister and brother.'

I knew what she meant. She was right. She was also putting herself in peril to so speak to me, and was being astoundingly generous.

I slipped from my kneeling stance into a full 'kiss-earth' and laid my forehead on her workaday sandal. 'I am the Divine Lady's slave,' I said with a heart full of gratitude 'And lie at the Divine Lady's feet.'

Chapter Seven

Mutnodjme

The scribe came that evening, before Tey had finished her remarks on how appalling our presence in the mammisi had been. Indeed, I feared that she would never get to the end of them, and I was to be scolded down to my grave.

'The only reasons that I am not at this moment beating you until you scream,' she added 'is that you came with your stories at the right moment, to distract the Queen. She had been labouring for hours before she called for me, and she was at the end of her strength. So, it has ended well. And what did you think of the great female mystery, daughter?' she demanded, more mildly.

'Strange and terrible,' I said. 'Were all of us thus born?'

'All except Amenhotep our Lord may he live,' said a voice from the door.

'Even he, may he live forever, and divine conception aside, was born of a woman,' snapped Tey. 'Who are you?'

'I am Ptah-hotep, the Great Royal Scribe,' said the young man mildly. 'I was asked by the Princess Sitamen to bring a scribe for your daughters, Lady. Here he is. His name is Khons, and he asks more questions than anyone could answer.'

'He should be heart-friend to these two, then,' snarled Tey. 'This is Great Royal Wife Merope, a barbarian princess, and this is my daughter the Lady Mutnodjme, sister to the Divine Spouse Nefertiti. Have you eaten, young man?'

This was a polite enquiry made of all visitors, but it was not delivered in a polite tone. Even Khons raised an eyebrow and looked at the Great Royal Scribe who, I could not help but note, seemed awfully young to be so eminent.

He was good looking. He had very long hair, braided into a plait by someone with a great deal of skill. She had threaded in blue beads and small mirrors that winked and flashed as he moved. He wore no jewellery but his scribal ring, big enough to stiffen a hand to the knuckle. His cloth was perfectly plain. He had the pale skin, high cheekbones and elongated eyes of the Theban bloodline, and those black eyes were wary, giving nothing away. His voice was low, clear and firm and his mode of address very formal.

'Great Royal Nurse Tey, Gracious Lady, I am sure that you will wish to be exceedingly hospitable to the Teacher Khons, because I will be obliged to report to the Princess on his progress and I would be very loathe to have to say anything to your discredit. I am bidden to dine with the High Priest of Amen-Re so I cannot stay long, but I would enjoy a cup of beer and a little conversation with your daughter Lady Mutnodjme and Great Royal Wife Merope.'

Merope, who had been hanging back, came forward and offered him her hand to kiss. He sank to one knee and did so with due solemnity. My mother flicked a hand at the slaves, and chairs were brought. We all sat down.

Great Royal Nurse Tey was examining the scribe closely and suddenly decided to like him, which was how Tey was. If she loved you, she loved you no matter how she might later scream or slap. If she hated you, she hated fiercely and could not be diverted. It was a pity that she had never loved me and I did not know how to change her mind.

'I greet the Great Royal Scribe,' she said formally. 'I beg that he should forgive my hasty words. I have just come from the childbirth of the Queen Tiye may she live and I am fatigued.'

'May we hope that the Great Lady was safely delivered?' Scribe Ptah-hotep matched her in courtesy.

'Indeed, of a son. She has called him Smenkhare. As you are dining with the High Priest, please inform him of this event. Do me the honour of tasting this brew,' she said, as the slaves brought a jar of the very light ale which we drank on very hot days.

Ptah-hotep handed his cup to a slave who stood by the door. A Nubian woman with beaded hair sipped and nodded and returned it to him.

'Your precautions are wise, Lord, if you will forgive me saying so.'

'I forgive you, certainly,' said the young man. Honours were, I decided, about even. Tey was interested in the Scribe but could not, in politeness, ask any more questions.

Teacher Khons was older than the Scribe Ptah-hotep. He was thickset and looked strong, and I wondered at the mess that someone had made of his back. He had been beaten many times. I wondered who had beaten him and why. He had a shaved head and golden rings in his ears and a fine, wide, dazzling grin which showed teeth like seeds. He grinned at us and we smiled back, a little nervously. I wondered if his teeth could bite as well as smile.

'Let us see if we will suit,' he said to me. 'Greetings, Lady Mutnodjme, Lady Merope. What would you ask of your teacher?'

'Tell us about the divine birth,' I said. Birth was on my mind and I had privately resolved to see it again.

Teacher Khons spoke promptly:

The Divine Amenhotep's mother lay down in her bed one night, and behold! her husband came to her, and lay down with her, and did such things as were pleasing to her.

And she said, 'You have pleased me and lain inside me, and I felt your seed spring in me. I am scented with your essence; my soul took flight; I love you.'

But he did not speak in reply but left her and was gone.

That night she conceived the Lord Amenhotep; and yet her husband had slept the night alone.

'How?' I demanded. 'How can she have conceived if her husband slept alone? You just said he lay with her.'

'It was Re the Sun, even Amen-Re himself, who lay with the great Royal Wife,' explained Teacher Khons.

We thought about it.

'Amen-Re in the shape of her husband?' I puzzled it out. 'He came to her in her husband's form?'

'She was a virtuous woman who took no lovers,' explained Khons. 'Therefore he had to come in her husband's shape, or she would have rejected him, even the god, even the Sun himself.'

'But…' I began. The Scribe Ptah-hotep lifted a hand.

'I must leave you, I regret. Teach them well, Khons, I leave it in your hands. You will lodge here, and the Great Royal Wife Tiye is responsible for your expenses. Farewell, ladies.' He stood up. The Nubian woman opened the door for him.

'Come again,' urged Tey, making one of her infrequent bows. The young man returned the bow and his mirrors glittered.

'Lady,' he acknowledged, and left.

'Tell us another,' urged Merope.

Tey flapped a hand at me. 'In a moment. Teacher Khons, you may lodge here, and the young ladies will show you where you can lay your mat. It is very kind of the Queen to send you, and I appreciate it. If you can answer some of the ladies' questions, you will be performing a valuable service.

'Tell me,' she said, escorting him to the small chamber next to ours and instructing a woman to lay out his mat and refold his bundle of creased garments, 'What do you know of the scribe Ptah-hotep? He has impressed me very favourably.'

'Lady, he took me out of the school of scribes and rescued me from a marshy fate. He was the best scribe at the school, which is why the Master offered him to Pharaoh Akhnamen may he live! Otherwise, I did not know him well,' said Khons, watching a slave lay out his frayed and damaged wardrobe with evident embarrassment.

'We will ask the Queen for some new cloths,' said Tey, slightly amused. 'Where do you come from, Teacher?'

'From the North, Lady, the Nome of Set. My father trades in pots in the market,' he added, fiercely rather than humbly.

'Mine trained racehorses,' returned Tey. 'It is difficult, is it not? To live in a palace that knows no lack, with people who have never walked on hard earth or lived on fish and beans? But we manage, Teacher.

'Now, even though it is still so hot—will the Southern Snake never stop blowing?—I must be away to visit my Lady the Queen, and you can tell stories to these voracious maidens. Ask the slaves for whatever you want,' said Tey, and went.

I heard the outer door slap closed. Then I drew a deep breath, echoed by my new sister, and we both sat down on Teacher Khons' sleeping mat.

'Tell us another,' we said, almost in unison.

'First you will tell me,' he said in a guarded fashion, 'Is the lady your mother always like that?'

'How?' I asked.

'So short, so brisk, so … decided.'

'Yes,' we both agreed.

'Ah. Then we had better make some progress in learning or I'll be off to Khnum at Hermopolis faster than a vulture flies. Tell me what you already know, Lady Mutnodjme.'

'I can read and write cursive and understand most of the hieroglyphs. I can tell stories. Do you know a lot of stories?'

'Hundreds.' He turned to Merope. 'And you, Lady?'

'I never learned to write,' said Merope. 'But I can tell stories, too.'

'And you can speak Kritian,' he added. 'An accomplishment that many of us would envy. Very well. While you are learning cursive, my Lady will learn hieroglyphics. And we will tell lots of stories. Will that please my ladies?'

'Yes. Who beat you?'

'My Master at the school of scribes.'

'Why?' I traced the scars where thin canes or whips had cut his smooth flesh.

'For asking too many questions. For arguing.' He smelt pleasantly of frankincense, now that I was close to him. Merope also edged nearer, and Teacher Khons began to look nervous.

'Sit further away,' he ordered. 'It is too hot to be close in this wind.'

'Where does the wind come from?' I asked, as I moved to another mat.

'It is the breath of Apep, the great Southern Snake, foe of Re the Sun since the beginning of time. At Ephipi, and into Mesoré, the power of Re is diverted to the other side of the world, and Apep roars, desiring to take the Black Land again into his maw and slake his thirst by drinking the Nile dry.'

'Could he do that?'

'Once he did just that,' said Khons. He slid down until he was leaning on one elbow, chin in hand, examining us with his black eyes.

'When?'

'Shall I tell you the tale?'

'Tell us about Apep and Re,' we chorused. Merope and I lay down also on reed mats, and Basht came padding in and settled down with her chin on Merope's chest. It seemed that the striped cat liked stories, too.

'Apep is a gigantic serpent,' he began.

'How gigantic is he?' I asked.

'He is two hour's walk from end to end, and in the middle as wide as the Nile at flood,' replied Khons. We gasped and he continued the tale:

You know that the Lord Amen-Re sails his sun-boat under the world into the Tuat every night? Every hour of darkness he must fight off some attacker or fiend, for the otherword is not as here, my students, it is dark and the water is troubled. Fiends stalk the darkness, and the evening carries more dangers than just robbers and thieves.

As the sun boat navigates the Tuat river in black darkness, Apep comes swimming. Each undulation of his body is as high as the sky, and five armies could march under him abreast. Slithering he comes, for he is cold. Faintly he shines, for he is slimy.

In the night frightened wayfarers see the gleam of his teeth under the cold stars, and dig holes in the sand to hide from the cold stare of his eyes. For he is the great devil, the everlasting Foe of all that is warm, and breathes, and lives.

'What about fish?' I asked. 'They do not breathe and are cold. Do they belong to Apep?'

This would have been the point where any other storyteller would have snapped at me for interrupting, but Teacher Khons took it in his stride.

'Fish breathe, Lady, they just breathe water, not air. And they are warmer than the water in which they swim, and they can be eaten by humans, so they are not of Apep. But the green viper and the horned viper are his own children, and live to slay anyone who touches them.

Now this Apep attacks the boat on which the Sun who is Re rides through the Tuat, and the kind gods fight him; even She who is Beauty and Music, even the gentle Hathor.

Apep roars, and the stink of his breath burns the sail of the Sun Boat; he dives, and the river banks are flooded and washed by his bow-wave. And the gods kill and dismember him, he who is Destruction, and cast him into the river.

But every day, while the Sun Re is in the sky, Apep reforms and draws his bones and his flesh together, and every night he attacks again.

Some men say that one night, if belief fails, then he will win; and that will be the end of light, and warmth, and the world.

We shivered pleasurably. 'You have the spell which they recite every day in every temple of Amen-Re in the Black Land,' said Teacher Khons. 'The priests say it as they destroy a wax image, melting it and spitting on it and crushing it underfoot. We will listen while you read it, Lady Mutnodjme.'

I took the scroll, scanned the cursive script and began to read:

Apep is fallen into the flame; a knife is stabbed into his head: his name lives no more. I drive darts into him, I sever his neck, cutting into his flesh with this knife. He is given over to the fire which has mastery over him.

Horus mighty of strength has decreed that he should come to the front of the boat of Re: his fetter of steel ties him and binds him so that he cannot move. He is chained, bound, fettered, and his strength ebbs so that I may separate the flesh from the bones, cut off his feet and his arms and hands; cut out his tongue and break his teeth, one by one, from his mouth: block up his ears and put out his eyes. I tear out his heart from its throne: I make him not to exist. May his name be forgotten and his heirs and his relatives and his offspring, may his seed never be established: may his soul, body, spirit, shade and words of power and his bones and his skin be as nothing.

I looked at Teacher Khons. 'Why, then, is the serpent still alive?' I asked.

'Because spells cannot mend everything,' said Teacher Khons, turning a gold ring in his ear. 'Because gods are a way of looking at the world. Because there must be a balance, and while there is good there must be Amen-Re, and while there is evil there must be Apep.'

That sounded reasonable. I began to think that having a teacher was going to be very interesting.

Ptah-hotep

The temple of Amen-Re at Karnak is colossal.

Because I was uncertain if I would return—some people never do return from the temple—I made sure that Khons was settled with the alarming Great Royal Nurse Tey and her two charges. I gave a very unwilling Meryt enough gold to get back to Nubia and a scroll which freed her from slavery. I left Khety and Hanufer with the task of understanding a particularly convoluted tax appeal from the Nome of Set and I farewelled Anubis, who was the only one who didn't contend with me. I would take no one with me into danger, though I had to have a furious argument with all of them before they agreed to let me go alone.

Meryt plaited my hair with beads, but otherwise I was undecorated, except for the Great Scribe's ring-seal, which weighed down my hand. I had a right to wear that. Otherwise I was a mere appointee of a Younger Royal Son and did not consider it proper to make a display of my wealth, so recently gained and so easily lost. I was more afraid than I have ever been as I walked unescorted out of the palace of the King and into the avenue of ram's-head sphinxes which led to the complex and castle of the most important temple of the Black Land's most important god.

To walk from the palace of the King to the Temple of Amen-Re takes but an hour; and to walk the extent of the Temple of Amen-Re just along the river bank takes four hours. Every Pharaoh since the earliest has added his image and a few temples to the Theban temple, and some have added whole palace sized buildings. The central mystery, of course, is not open to anyone but the King and the High Priest, but the common people can see inside the great pylons or gates when the festival comes, and Amen-Re is carried along the avenue of sphinxes to his wife Mut, to stay for a decan in her arms.

The Heb-Sed festival too centres on this temple. It is celebrated when a Pharaoh has reigned for thirty years, and the Lord Amenhotep may he live looked strong enough to survive another two years and celebrate it. I prayed for the King's health and my own as I walked along the sanded path, carefully cleared of stones every morning by slaves of the temple. No leaf or bird was suffered to land on that path. Men spent their whole lives warding them off, which struck me as a sad way to spend a life.

The temple is built of sandstone which catches and reflects the rays of its lord. Golden at noon, the stones were red as ochre as I approached them. The serpent wind had died away, the endless maddening scratching sound of blown sand had ceased, and I was wet with sweat and fear. No one spoke to me as I passed several cheerful parties of young men, redolent of wine and pleasure. One woman called to me from the houses of wine by the waterside, but I ignored her. I was praying to Osiris that I might find favour in his eyes because I might be joining him soon, to Neith the Hunter and Isis the Mistress of Magic who protect such creatures as the Princess Sitamen and I, and to such of my ancestors who could spare their attention from feasting in the Field of Offerings.

'Help me, all gods and venerable ancestors, help me to survive this interview and this night,' I prayed, but received no answer.

Amen-Re the Sun was descending into the underworld as I came to the pylons, turned aside and said to the soldier guarding the priest's door, 'I am Ptah-hotep. The High Priest and Servant of Amen-Re the Sun, Bringer of Blessings, has summoned me. I am here.'

He admitted me instantly into a courtyard. My feet crunched over carefully arranged patterns in unseen mosaic as I was conducted by the soldier who did not speak through a colonnade and into a wide hall. The pillars were shaped like stems, the capitals like lotus flowers. It was of inhuman size, vast and shadowed, with only a few torches for light. An elderly priest, head shaved, eyes down, beckoned me to follow him into another hall, and handed me over to a younger man, who took a torch from a slave and led me up a flight of stairs.

None of them had spoken. This treatment was evidently designed to rattle me, and I was determined that it should not do so. I had not asked or schemed or even desired to be Great Royal Scribe, but I was, and I had a feeling that if I had been the old man Nebamenet I would not have been walking through the halls attended by priests who seemed to have been struck dumb by my eminence. When the young man picked up his pace, wishing perhaps to have me arrive at my destination out of breath, I kept to my usual walking speed until he noticed and came back for me. Then I saw some expression on his expressionless face; it was not a smile but a softening of his rigidly schooled features. I did not speak to him, because I would have been at a disadvantage if I spoke and he did not reply. I had played this game at the school of scribes, and I had always won.

We came to a painted door, and the priest called 'Ptah-hotep,' and a slave opened.

I stepped inside. The room was bright with torchlight which revealed painted walls, a marble floor inlaid with golden sun discs, a ceiling made of golden rosettes placed so thickly that they looked like spiderweb over a lapis lazuli sky, and a throne.

It was made of wood overlaid with gold. The high back was of electrum, an alloy of silver and gold, the cushions were covered with golden tapestry and the footrest was of solid silver. It would have bought a small town.

Since I was not required to bow to an empty throne, I stood where I was and considered the situation. The slave who had admitted me had gone. I knew what I was expected to do: get angry, or fidget, or wander around and finger the ornaments, or fret, or tremble.

I did none of these. I sank down into the scribe's cross legged position, folded my hands in my lap, and sank into thought.

The high priest was assuming a lot about the nature of my appointment if he dared treat me so discourteously. He was also making certain assumptions about me which I could not like. He was expecting to evoke an emotional reaction, well, I was certainly an emotional being, but all my love was given to one human, and he was with the army.

I knew how powerful the high priest was; did he know how powerful I was, with my patron the king behind me? Was it wise, in short, to slight me without doing some research to find out how I was likely to react? The Pharaoh Akhnamen could have ordered—though such a thing was unthinkable—that the worship of Amen-Re be abandoned and no taxes be paid to the priests, and where would that leave the high priest? A discredited old man forced to beg his way along the roads.

That thought pleased me and I may have smiled a little.

I sat still for about half an hour by the sand-clock on the table when I heard a scraping sound and an unexpected door opened in the painted wall. I had had time to memorise the decorations, and this wall was unusual; it was painted all over with doors of all sizes and shapes, half-open like the false door in a tomb which allows the ka to enter. One of these doors was now opening, and an old man came through, attended by two entirely naked, very beautiful women, who assisted him to climb the step and sit down on the throne.

I had enquired as to the correct greeting of Great Royal Scribe to High Priest. I rose and waited for him to acknowledge me.

He raised his eyes and gave a slight nod.

'Ptah-hotep,' he said, a mild discourtesy.

'Servant of Amen-Re,' I bowed to the correct depth and no lower.

'My name is Userkhepesh,' he said. He was required to tell me his name by protocol agreed between the palace and the temple.

I was tired, hot and weary of these manoeuvrings.

'My title is Great Royal Scribe,' I pointed out, as the thing which he clearly did not know about me.

There was a moment when we stared straight into each other's eyes. He was very old. His shaven head was as white as chalk, his limbs trembled with age, and his robes hung on his rack of a body like nets on a fisherman's wire traps. But his eyes were deep and full of will and strength. Neither of us looked away for an uncounted time. I do not know what he saw in my eyes. But he finally broke the contact with a grunt, waved at the women to begin laying out a feast, and did not speak until I had a cup of wine and they had helped him descend to sit on a low chair at a well-filled table.

Even in the driest month the temple of Amen-Re, it appeared, had melons, golden fruit from the jungles of Upper Egypt. A naked woman leaned over me and put a piece of fruit into my mouth. I smiled at her, but she did not respond.

'So you are the Pharaoh's lover,' the old man broke the silence. I said, 'Lord, I am the Pharaoh's choice,' and ate some more melon.

'How old are you?' he asked, and I told him my age. He thought for awhile, seeming not to notice the curved belly or breast before his face, or the melon juice mopped from his chin by his attentive slave. 'Your father?' he asked.

I was sure that he knew all about me, so I answered 'He is a scribe in the city of Apis in the Nome of the Black Bull, Lord.'

'I know.' He tasted a roasted pheasant, then indicated to the slave that she should serve me some of the scented flesh.

We ate in silence for awhile. I sensed his puzzlement. I was not reacting as a boy-lover should react, or an over-awed child, or a scheming creature who has kissed Pharaoh's feet for his favour. I like silence, and I let it continue. I had not been well fed lately and this meal was a feast of all that was tasty and light, perfect for a hot evening.

'The pheasant is delicious,' I commented, a social statement required of a guest. 'You are a generous host, Userkhepesh, Servant of Re.'

'I am delighted that my poor fare should please you,' he said absently, again the correct reply.

I ate some good black grapes, spitting the seeds politely into my hand, and he watched me as if I was a newly-created beast and he was Khnum the Potter, wondering what to name me.

'Are these from the Tashery vineyard, Lord?' another social comment. 'My second in command says that they are the best grapes in the Black Land.'

'Mentu? He would know about wine, though nothing else. You know that. You appointed him.' The High Priest leaned forward. 'So far you have not put a foot wrong, Lord Ptah-hotep. You were not awed or improperly curious. You know the value of silence. You do not fear me.'

'Lord, I fear you, and your office, your god, and your power,' I responded honestly. 'But since this meeting is a test, set by my wise elder to find out my worth, I would dishonour my office if I did not at least pass it.'

He laughed, a dry laugh which had little merriment in it.

'What did happen at the lake?' he asked. 'How did Pharaoh choose you?'

'I was bathing, and I was called out of the water. Pharaoh laid his flail on me; possibly my master recommended me. That was the first time I ever saw the Lord of the Double Crown.' I took some more of a curious, luscious mixture of beans in oil.

'Whimsical. That is the Lord of the Two Lands, Akhnamen. I could wish that his brother Thutmose had not died. However, Amen disposes of men as he wishes.'

There was another silence, then I remembered that I had a message for him.

'Lord, I am bidden with a message from the Great Royal Nurse Tey. The Queen Tiye was delivered this afternoon of a son called Smenkhare.'

'Good.' I had no doubt that he knew this already. 'No, don't take any of the fish, Lord. It would not agree with you.' His old fingers were laid on my wrist. Despite the heat, his skin was cold. A slave woman took the dish away.

'As a priest, you, of course, my Lord, do not eat fish,' I said slowly, thinking it out. 'Fish are the phallus of Osiris, and may not be eaten by priests. But I, as Great Royal Scribe, have no such taboo. And the fish would not have agreed with me, High Priest?'

'No,' he said, showing no sign of any other emotion. 'It is over-rich for a young man such as yourself, a young man of sense and courage, who is likely to prove adequate for his high office.'

'If he lives that long,' I replied.

He patted my hand. 'If Amen-Re is kind,' he agreed, 'Do you play Passing-Through-The-Underworld, the game also called senet?'

'Yes, Lord.'

'I thought that you might. Another time, Ptah-hotep, Great Royal Scribe, will you come and dine with me, and perhaps play the game of the dancers?'

'It would be an honour, Userkhepesh, Servant of Re, High Priest of Amen-Re at Karnak.'

He smiled, this time, and I returned the smile.

I had left for the temple of Amen-Re in trembling and in silence. I returned, by order of the High Priest, in a litter, escorted by priests, announced by a trumpeter.

I was so relieved that I slept most of the way back.

Chapter Eight

Mutnodjme

Tey my mother reported the Queen recovering, the child suckling his wet nurse, and herself pleased with our silence and attention to our teacher. Because of a lack of brothers—my only brother was grown and married—and my father's frequent absences on matters of estate management, we had been a female household, and the presence of Teacher Khons put us on our best behaviour. Tey was less likely to shriek, I was less likely to ask so many questions because Khons was there to answer them, or—his especial strength—ask me another, even curlier, which would keep me silent and thinking for hours.

We adjusted to the presence of the teacher very well. He slept on his reed mat in the smallest sleeping-chamber, never went out to get drunk, (except on the festivals, and he was a very considerate and quiet drunk) and told us stories every day. Merope my sister learned cursive, I mastered the priests pictured letters, Khons learned Kritian, and peace reigned in the household of the great Royal Nurse and Divine Father Ay. Even he noticed the change in the atmosphere and approved of the deferential young man whom the Queen had sent. He also approved of the fact that his expenses were paid by the Great Royal Wife. My father was a very rich man, and stayed so because he regarded every bead, every thread, every scraping of copper as a close personal friend.

Tey my mother regarded me with more tolerance because Teacher Khons told her that I was clever. He delighted in arguing with me and, though, so far, he had always won, he told my mother that I had an original mind which would take me far, especially if I was to study in the temple of Isis among the priestesses of the Lady of Magic and Learning. Since Tey had often despaired of finding me a husband so wealthy that Divine Father Ay would not have to pay a dowry, this presented her with a possible solution to the problem posed by Mutnodjme.

Thus I was allowed to come along with her and Nefertiti as the hot wind died down and we moved into the month of Mesorʐ̌, seasons of harvests. We were going to renew our interrupted consultation with Queen Tiye about the impotence of the King Akhnamen may he live. The situation had not improved, and my sister was worried. She had tried getting the royal lord drunk. She had tried all manner of baths and unguents, and also the attentions of pretty dancers of both sexes. But the King Akhnamen, when merry, fell into a laughing fit and then into a heavy sleep from which it proved impossible to rouse him. When bathed he drifted into a trance. When massaged he sighed and dozed; when caressed by the dancers he had giggled as if they were tickling him and fallen asleep. He was pleasant and loving, but utterly impervious to all sexual advances.

'Nothing,' sighed Nefertiti in reply to my mother's questions. She herself was nervous, prone to start at sudden noises and to fall into periods of despondency. Mother Tey, after Nefertiti had gone back to her loveless bed the previous evening, had snapped at Father Ay, 'That maiden needs a man, and if something is not done, she will find one, or one will find her.'

'Impossible, she is Great Royal Spouse and a virtuous girl,' my father had puffed, then added, 'Do you really think so?'

'*Love will have love, heart will have heart, mouth will find mouth,*' quoted Tey 'As Divine Amenhotep says. I will go to the queen again tomorrow, husband. She said that she might have a solution. I hope that she has.'

'If the lord Akhnamen may he live, dies without an heir my endowment of royal estates will blow away with the wind,' snarled my father. 'The red-headed woman is astoundingly fertile and so is King Amenhotep may he live forever. She has already borne him two sons, and though Thutmose died early it was by accident. The young Smenkhare is thriving. She may yet bear more children. Go, wife, and ask Queen Tiye. We must have an heir, and she must contrive it.'

'I will go tomorrow,' said Tey, and I stopped listening.

So we walked along the corridor to the queen's apartments. As usual, they were crowded with petitioners, slaves, maids and the Great Royal Heir's household. The baby was crying and someone was commanding, 'Put him to nurse, he never cries unless he's hungry'.

As we came in the Great Queen was saying to a pair of farmers lying at her feet, 'Yes, yes, I see the justice of your claim and I have given you a note to the Great Royal Scribe, the Lord Ptah-hotep, who will listen to you; go now. A slave will guide you. Sahte, I am going to lie down until the noon meal. Bring some wine for the Great Royal Wife and the Great Royal Nurse and the Lady Mutnodjme.'

Sahte, the thin-faced sour maid who had been the Great Royal Lady's own nurse, sniffed and announced, 'My Mistress is retiring for a rest. Make way,' and she led us to the Queen's Room of Silence, where no raised voice could be heard from outside. The door, unusually, was of thick wood and had a bolt on the inside. After Sahte had brought the wine, the Queen shut the door and latched it and sank down into a chair with a sigh.

'Greetings, ladies, have you eaten?' asked the Queen conventionally and wearily. We assured her that we had and poured her some heavily watered wine. Tey rose and laid a professional hand on the ivory forehead and chided, 'The Great Royal Wife needs to rest more and talk less.'

'True, but the Great Royal Wife has petitions to hear and household matters to arrange, and that cannot be done by resting,' agreed the queen. She looked tired. The coppery hair was loose and fell in waves down her back. I noticed that a streak of white had formed at each temple. She was wearing a cloth with fine blue patterns along its edge but little jewellery. We waited until she had recovered a little and sipped from her cup, and even then we did not have to introduce the subject. She knew what we had come to discuss.

'He's impotent, isn't he, Nefertiti? You've tried everything. Including a troupe of very well skilled dancers. And nothing has worked.'

Nefertiti nodded. Her hands were clenched in her lap.

'And this is not what you expected when you agreed to be Great Royal Wife, is it?' asked the Queen kindly. 'You are a young woman and unmated, and your body is restless.'

'Yes, lady,' said my sister. She was so beautiful that she hurt my eyes, but there was an edge to her beauty now, a fine grey shadow like a spiderweb over her comeliness.

'The heirs of the Pharaoh have to be heirs of a Pharaoh's body, but not necessarily...' began the Queen.

I caught her drift at the same time as Tey did. Her eyes lit. 'The Pharaoh Akhnamen,' Tey finished the sentence.

I did not speak, but I was horrified. To give my sister to that old man! A nice old man, admittedly, a kind and very wise old man, but old.

'Will you accept this?' asked the Queen. 'It is entirely your choice, Nefertiti. This will be the only way you can conceive a Great Royal Heir.'

Nefertiti was thinking. She was never good at quick decisions. Given a chance to consider for long enough, she usually made a wise reply, but she hated being pressured. And now she was on the edge of panic.

Tey said 'Come, daughter, this is a way out of all our difficulties. The Lord Amenhotep is fertile, as he has amply proved, and he is gentle and wise. Make up your mind, Nefertiti!'

But Tiye, whose slate coloured eyes saw very clearly, took Nefertiti's slim hand in her own strong ones and told her, 'You need time to think, lady. Go to your own apartments and consider what you wish to do, all on your own.'

Tey shot the Queen a glare which expressed how much she wanted to take Nefertiti home and rage at her until she agreed. Queen Tiye returned the look with one which said that she knew exactly what Tey wanted to do and was determined that she would not do it; and which, by one arched eyebrow, posed the question which could be summarised as, 'Who is Queen?' Tey looked away first. I was delighted and strove to keep my face straight.

'No one will disturb you, but before night falls you will send your sister, the little scribe, and she shall bring your answer to me. I will not have you take my lord unwillingly; or with half a mind yea and half nay. He does not deserve that. To conceive you must enjoy him—ask any physician. To do that, you must want him. He gets no enjoyment from rape. Have I not lain with him all these years, and never left his arms without regret? Unbolt the door, Lady Mutnodjme, and call Sahte to me.'

I did as I was bid and Sahte's disapproving face appeared at the door.

'This young woman will come with a message for me tonight,' said the Great Queen. 'I wish to hear it, wherever I am and whatever I am doing. Do you understand, Sahte?'

Sahte sniffed, but nodded. This order was essential, because she was frequently known to banish all visitors from her Royal Mistress' door and often kept messages until the time of arising the next day if they arrived after the Queen had retired. I was delighted at being referred to as a young woman. I was, of course, now ten, and my woman-blood was expected next year, after which I would be fully female.

'When I receive it, I may want to speak to my son. Make sure that you know where he is tonight. Now, Sahte, we will allow the lady Nefertiti to leave, and perhaps the Great Royal Nurse will assist me in some of my household problems?'

Nefertiti left without a backward glance at my mother, and Tey subdued her rage. The Queen was keeping us with her so that King Akhnamen's wife had time to get to her own apartments and lock herself in. So I was more surprised when I saw the beautiful Great Royal Wife Tiye and my mother exchange a grin.

'Oh, very well, Lady, I will not rail at her. But the Divine Father is worried by this lack of an heir, and this seems like an excellent solution if the silly girl will but see it.'

'She is very young, and I will not have my husband imposed on a shocked and frightened maiden; it would hurt his feelings as well as hers. Nefertiti the beautiful must make up her own mind,' said Tiye.

'Now, what shall I do with this baker? I am sure a lot of flour is going astray. Look at the accounts! He must think we are stupid, or cannot read plain figures. He has drawn twenty sacks from the grain-store, and made of it only a hundred loaves of bread.'

'Fine or coarse?' asked Tey, after a marked delay. Peace had been declared. I exhaled the breath I had been holding. Although she was midwife to the Queen and had her confidence, there was something about the affable, smiling Queen Tiye which made me sure that Royal Midwife or not, Great Royal Nurse or not Great Royal Nurse, Tey and all of us would be out of the palace before nightfall if we dared to seriously cross her. And Tey in a temper was not discriminating in her choice of target.

After Tey had scribbled some figures on an ostracon, it became clear that even if the baker was wasting a large amount of grain in attempting to make the finest flour, he was stealing about five sacks for every twenty he drew. Finest flour is sifted three times and there is a certain amount of wastage, which, as Tey pointed out, is not actual waste, because the coarse flour makes bread for the mill-workers or the baker's household and the husks fatten his pigs.

The palace, of course, never ate of the flesh of swine. Teacher Khons had informed me that this was because the pig was an avatar of Set the destroyer, and certainly wild boar were terrible creatures who ate babies and wrecked whole vineyards.

But since people in some places on the Nile ate crocodile, which according to place was either the God Sobek or an avatar of Set, and which also ate people, this did not strike me as a good explanation. And in any case, the commoners all kept pigs, which were slaughtered every year for the feast of the Victory-of-Horus-Over-Set and roasted, after which sausages and smoked meats were made from the remains and many a poor household fed for the summer on this cursed beast.

Khons had agreed that this was not logical but stated that Egypt had so many interesting local customs that visitors never made sense of them and that, anyway, if I wanted to taste swine he would take me and Merope to the Victory-of-Horus feast in the village of Thebes and we could eat it there. He emphasised that all meat from pigs must be cooked thoroughly, and that it was unsafe to eat it raw.

Merope and I had had no difficulty in promising faithfully not to make a meal of raw swine.

I realised that I was considering the swine problem because I did not want to think about the soft flesh of my sweet sister pressed and impregnated by that old man. It seemed wrong, cruel. Youth goes to youth, that was the way it had always been. I was very angry with my mother and father for marrying the one beautiful daughter to an impotent fanatic, and lost my train of thought.

'What shall we do with this thieving baker?' asked the Queen. Tey gave her invariable answer to all problems involving humans.

'Flog him,' she said, shutting her mouth with a snap.

Ptah-hotep

Things went more easily for me and my office once the approbation of the high priest was known—and it was known with amazing speed. Palaces have very efficient gossip-networks and the gifts-of-welcome, which had been conspicuously absent, began to pour in.

I had to purchase two more slaves to open and catalogue them and hire another scribe to send thank-you notes. On Meryt's advice, I bought Nubians, and that caused some murmuring. People said that I had a taste for black flesh, or that I was secretly part-Nubian. This might have been true. My father was always cagey about who my mother's family had been and where he had acquired her. But what I needed was a household which would get along with Meryt, my chief slave and housekeeper, and she naturally preferred her fellow countrymen. Hani, Tani and Teti were pleasant people, cheerful enough, though showing marks of cruel usage, and seemed to be happy with their change of occupation. It never once occurred to me, as someone suggested, that the Nubians might mutiny and massacre me during the night. The people who were trying to kill me had all been pure-bred Egyptians.

I was delighted to find that my principal scribes were attentive and intelligent, and by balancing Khety's account against Hanufer's, I could arrive at a reasonable view of any situation.

My office was complete when the Master of Scribes brought me Bakhenmut, returned from the feast of Apis.

They found me listening to Hanufer's account of the depredations of a landlord, who was demanding higher taxes than the Inspectors had assessed, in return for what he said was a spell for conferring magic fertility on seed, direct from Isis herself. The farmers who had *not* bought it had found their promising fields of barley and spelt-wheat withered overnight. This might, of course, have been supernatural but it seemed suspicious.

'A letter to the Chief Watcher of that village, Hanufer,' I dictated:

> '*To the Chief of the Watchers of the village of the Son of Horus, Greetings. May your eyes never grow dim and your vigilance be maintained. Find out the movements of men around the stricken fields at night, and taste the soil of the fields where the crop has died. If you have reason to think that they may have been spread with salt, arrest the landlord and bring him before the court of the Nomarch.*

'Call also the Principal Priestess from the Temple of Isis and ask her to perform an apology to her goddess, who will have been affronted by this fraud—this to be paid for by the landlord.

'If you find nothing to suggest fraud but instead divine intervention, then divert the debts of the farmers to the Temple of Isis, who presumably had a reason in bespelling some fields and blighting others. Convey this to the priestess also. Know that if you are virtuous and diligent, Pharaoh and the gods are well aware of what you do and you will be rewarded. Report the result to me so that I may instruct the temple to adjust the taxes.

The Lord Ptah-hotep, usual titles.

'How is it that you know of that trick about the salt, my lord Ptah-hotep of the usual titles?' asked my amused Master, alerting me to his presence.

'Master, how good to see you!' I exclaimed, getting up and laying aside a sheaf of reports on the maintenance of dykes and walls. I noticed, as I put them down, that I might have to levy some labour to repair the worst, and that would be costly. Levied labourers eat like donkeys, but not, alas, of the same food.

'Master, a landlord tried something very similar in my own village, though in that case it was sowing weed seeds through the crops.'

'There are advantages in being a commoner, lord,' he commented. 'I have brought your scribe, as we agreed.'

'Welcome.' I took the hand of the short stocky priest with pleasure. He smiled shyly and said, 'I am honoured by the Lord Ptah-hotep's condescension and will strive to repay his trust.'

'I'm sure you will. Now, here are Khety and Hanufer, you will remember them, and here is Meryt, she is my housekeeper and ruler of all matters which do not involve my office.'

Meryt knelt and Bakhenmut patted her shoulder gingerly. Meryt's subservience had a royal arrogance about it now which made nervous people more nervous. She rose and smiled at him and he smiled back in relief.

'Lord Bakhenmut, will you take up your apartments today?' she asked practically.

'Yes, yes, my wife is moving our household there now, very beautiful rooms. She is pleased,' he told her, beaming. 'She is a woman of refinement, you know, my Henutmire, and of noble lineage, and she is delighted at our elevation.'

'But you will have a room here for late work, lord, and if you will come with me now I will show you,' said Meryt.

Did I notice a shade of more relief on the devoted husband-of-Henutmire's face? It was gone too quickly for me to be sure. I left Meryt to settle the new overseer of scribes into his room and took my Master into the inner office, to which only my household had access. One of the Nubian twins poured wine.

'Tashery?' asked the Master of Scribes, smiling at me.

'Did you get them?' I asked.

'Certainly, Ptah-hotep, and they were a generous present. My ancient colleague Snefru is beside himself with joy at the cartload of old manuscripts you sent and he has plans for the purchase of so many more that he may have to be dug out of the pile. That was kind, lord. And I hear that you acquitted yourself so well with the High Priest that he declared you to be almost adequate and invited you to play senet with him.'

'You are well informed, Master of Scribes,' I smiled. It was very pleasant to revert to being a student again.

'Many have had to alter their view of you, Chief Royal Scribe,' he returned. 'But I knew, of course, all along. Can you tell me of the interview, lord, before I perish of curiosity?'

I recounted the whole evening, including my silent, lonely walk along the avenue of sphinxes.

'He would have liked that,' chuckled Amménemes. 'No attempt to bolster your position with soldiers or guards, just the solitary young man and the terribly dangerous old man. A duel of more than wits, and you have impressed him. Very well done.'

'Now, Ptah-hotep, you seem to have ordered your work in the approved way—as I would have done myself. There is only one thing which I would venture to suggest and before I do that I think I will have some more wine.'

I gestured to the Nubian. He filled the master's cup, and then left at my signal.

'The Princess Sitamen visited you, did she not?'

'Yes, she did.'

'That has caused gossip. It would not be wise to have too close a friendship with that Great Royal Wife. You know how palaces are.'

'I am beginning to learn,' I said stiffly.

'One you know of is well and has sent word; I bring this,' he handed me a letter which I slipped into my cloth. 'To preserve him, Ptah-hotep, it would be a good idea for you to marry. The followers of supplanted Nebamenet are restrained, but not muzzled. They speak against you and who knows what will incline the Pharaoh's heart one way or another? Take a wife, my pupil.'

'I do not want a wife,' I said. 'I do not want to take on the responsibility of a household and children when my own position lies on the edge of a knife. I will not take anyone into peril with me.'

'That is the only impediment?' his eyes were as sharp as pins.

'No, I do not know if I desire women, and I would not like to make anyone miserable. Then the word would go out to all the gossips, Master of Scribes. A mysterious young man who may or may not love women is one thing; an impotent husband is a laughing stock.'

'You have a point,' he said. 'And I would not presume to instruct you in your private life, my lord. But I do think,' he added, getting to his feet and ordering his cloth, 'that you should try and find out. Secretly, of course. With a trusted lover.'

I nodded, and the Nubian saw him out.

Meryt came in to announce that Bakhenmut was pleased with his accommodation and had already taken some of the tax-returns off the pile to be read.

I surveyed her. She was elegant and well-made, this woman whom I owned; for she had resisted being freed, saying that a freed slave had no place in my service, and that she would keep the paper for some later date, when fate might make it useful.

Her hair today was loose and floating, confined only by a length of gold ribbon. Her body was full, her breasts round, her limbs well-shaped. Did I desire her? Could I make love with her?

'Meryt, sit down. I have something to say and I want you to listen.'

She sat down promptly at my feet and I slid down to join her, so that I could see her face.

'Lord?' she asked politely.

'Meryt, I value your service and I could wish for no better housekeeper and companion.'

'Thank you,' she said, puzzled.

'The Master of Scribes has told me that I must marry, but…'

'But your heart belongs to another,' she finished the sentence. 'Yes. But there is another problem. I do not know women, and I do not know…'

'I will lie with you tonight,' she said, reading my heart as she often did. I seldom had to spell things out to Meryt. 'Then you shall know. Is that all, Master?' Her voice sounded careless, as if it was a minor matter in a busy household.

'Yes,' I answered.

She relented and stroked my cheek, a caress which felt as intimate as a kiss. 'It will be all right, Master,' she said, and was gone.

◇◇◇

She came to me after the household was bedded down for the night. Hanufer and Khety in their room, my new scribe with his family, Anubis on guard, the three Nubians in an untidy heap on their mats before the door.

There was a breathing silence, and Meryt came in naked on the wind of it.

'Look at me,' she whispered, and I saw by lamplight the rich curves of her shoulder and hip, the rounded belly, the full breasts. She came closer and I smelt a strong female scent, oil of Hathor from the temple. It mingled with the scent of her skin and made me giddy.

She knelt beside me and guided my hands to her nipples, to the wet cleft between her thighs. I had never touched a woman, and slid one finger inside, feeling her slippery flesh with curiosity but, as yet, no desire.

Then she bent her head and kissed my mouth, and she tasted of honey. Her lips parted and I felt her tickle my inner lip with her tongue. Still, though I felt interested and a little breathless, I was unaroused.

'Isis lay with Osiris after he was murdered,' she whispered, and her hands caressed my body, sliding down over my chest to my belly and then to my phallus, which at last began to rise.

'I will show you how she conceived Horus the Revenger,' Meryt said softly. 'I will show you how she received his seed inside her.'

I moved under her hand, and she pushed me down firmly. For a startled moment, I felt her mouth encompass my phallus, a sudden indescribable wetness, and then she was astride me, her knees on either side of my hips, and my phallus was inside her, in the soft liquid heat of her vessel, and it felt wonderful. I lay still, transfixed, and she rode me like a warrior rides a horse, rising and falling, and the stimulation passed towards unbearable until it flowered in a gush, a stream of semen, a sensation so strong that it hurt deep in my loins, and she exclaimed with pleasure.

She would not let me withdraw, but rolled so that we lay side by side, and strong muscles held my softening phallus inside the Nubian woman until it hardened again and we moved now with some confidence, and at the second climax I heard myself cry aloud.

Chapter Nine

Mutnodjme

Nefertiti thought for a long time, and she did not tell me what she thought. But she had cast aside her cloth when she came into her own rooms, and as she lay naked across her bed on the reed mat I saw one hand stray to her nipple and roll it gently, a self-caress full of sorrow. She had never been a 'woman of a hundred lovers' even when she had played with our cousin, her first lover, in the stooks of cut hay. She had told me that he had pleased her and that she loved him, but Divine Father Ay had plans for Nefertiti—'the beautiful one who is come'—most saleable of daughters. Our cousin was sent away to the army and later we heard that he had been killed in a border skirmish somewhere south in Kush.

I wondered suddenly about Horemheb, the captain, who had known his way to her bathing pool and bed-chamber when I had fallen into the Nile and nearly been eaten. Had he lain down in her arms as well? But Horemheb was also away on the borders, and in any case he was young and strong. He was not an old man.

Nefertiti sighed. She rubbed her temples as though her head hurt. Then she moved to the window, where she could catch the last glimpse of Amen-Re sinking over the edge of the world to traverse the Tuat, the twelve hours of night and the battle with the monster Apep of Teacher Khons' story.

'Lord Amen, you who know the hearts of all creatures, tell me what to do!' she exclaimed. 'I must conceive, my womb is hollow, it aches for a child. To do so I must lie with another man.'

'He's a god,' I said, and she started at the unexpected voice, though she knew that I was there. 'The Pharaoh is the avatar of the Lord Amen-Re; Teacher Khons said so. You aren't lying with a man, but with a God.'

I realised, too late, that I had succeeded in arguing my sister into doing what I least wanted her to do, and bit my lip. For Nefertiti was smiling at me. She took me into her scented embrace and kissed me, and then turned me around by the shoulders.

'Most intelligent little scribe! Go tell the Queen Tiye that I will do as she advises, as long as my lord knows and approves.'

I went, but I still didn't like it.

I don't know what the Great Royal Wife Tiye said to her Royal Son that evening, but she did speak to him; I saw him come and go from her apartments. I watched as the Queen's maids cleared the corridor with a great tumult, screaming that there was a snake and that no one should come near until the snake-catcher could remove it.

Then I saw the King's door open, and the old man came out into the empty hallway. He moved easily, though it was clear from the drooping of belly over his cloth and the laxity of the flesh at his throat and armpit, not to mention the white hair, that he was very old. His face was all lines, around his mouth, across his brow. He was scented with the rarest of oils and his hands, as he reached down to pat my shoulder, were long fingered and very clean with close cut nails. He wore only one ring, his coronation ring of the beetle Khephri who is Amen-Re at noon. I knew that he had been a soldier in his youth. There was a lateral scar across his chest where a spear had slashed him in the battle in Nubia. A battle which had decided him against any more wars, or so they said. So he must have once been young and strong and brave, like Horemheb.

He saw me and smiled, his understanding, intelligent smile. 'Well, little maiden, we meet again.'

This was true and I saw no need to comment, but he held out his hand and I took it, kneeling as I was required to do when addressed by a god.

He lifted me to my feet and said, 'Tell me, Mutnodjme, is this with your will?'

His dark eyes were very kind but exceptionally sharp and I could not lie to him.

'No, Lord,' I wriggled with embarrassment.

'Is it with the lady's will?'

'Yes, Lord,' I replied. His face, which had been troubled, cleared.

'Then show the way,' he said, and I led him to my sister's door. She opened it and he went in. I went too, as was required, and was immediately ordered by my sister to stand outside the door and keep watch in case anyone defied the Queen's diversionary viper and came this way. Affronted, I did so, and only heard a little of what went on inside.

I heard her say to him, 'Lord, has my husband agreed?' and heard the soft voice of the King say, 'Lady, he has,' and then I heard the creak of the bed-strings as Nefertiti lay down. I could picture her, spreadeagled for a sacrifice; but there was no other sound but conversation too quiet for my ears for a long time; no other creaks.

Unbelieving, I heard Nefertiti laugh, a light laugh as though there was no great responsibility on her. Then I heard wine being poured. There was an interval, and then I heard her giggle, a giggle which broke into a soft gasp. Still the tell-tale strings made no noise. What was she doing? Was the old King impotent as well as the young?

Then the gasp broke into a strange cry. It was repeated on a rising note, like a bird's voice. At last I heard the bed respond to another body being added to it. The bird-voice went on until it broke and silence fell. Then more speech, more conversation, more wine. I began to think I was going to sit outside my sister's door all night, and wondered how long the snake-panic would keep everyone away.

At last I heard a man groan, over the rising notes.

A span of time later, the door opened, and the king came out, smiled at me, and walked away. I went into the room.

There was a scent of the herb unefer—the holy plant, which exudes a pearly sap which women call 'seed-of-Horus'—in the air; and such a strong atmosphere of mating that I paused at the portal, overawed. Finally I shook myself roughly, had I not a right to be there?—and walked in. Nefertiti was lying asleep on her bed. I threw a light cloth over her. The cool air of the night was stirring her hair across her face, and she sneezed and almost woke, then rolled on her back, her thighs open. She was slick with perspiration and utterly relaxed, and she was smiling.

I began to think that I had underestimated both the king and the love of men, and lay down on my mat to think about it. I had not got very far before I too fell asleep.

She made no verbal report to my mother the next day, but smiled at her like Hathor herself; and Tey said, almost gently, 'I wish you joy, daughter.'

Tey ordered Khons, Mutnodjme and Merope to join the Great Royal Wife as she accompanied her Divine Spouse, Akhnamen, to the office of the Great Royal Scribe to inspect the plans for a new city. I was delighted. I had liked the young man who had brought us our teacher. Khons, too was pleased.

'The Lord Akhnamen is building a great city at Amarna, on the other bank of the river,' he informed us. 'Now, my pupils, do not disgrace me before my master. Keep the questions until later and I will answer them as well as I can. Do you hear me, Lady Mutnodjme?'

'Yes, teacher,' I agreed. I had discovered that Khons would give me a better answer in private than I could hope for in public and I had never shocked him with any comment or request. In any case I was still thinking about what I had heard in the apartments of the Queen Nefertiti the night before.

She had seemed so different this morning, so relaxed, so beautiful; as if the old man had given her a great gift, had loosened some tight thread within her weave which had been distorting the whole human garment. There was something in this matter of human love that I did not understand, but I was determined to find it out. Mother Tey, when asked, had told me flatly that I would not know what it meant until I too lay with a man, and that was at least a year or two away, if ever, and then only if I was exceptionally lucky.

We were passing through the hall of the tribute bearers when Merope cried 'Kriti! There are the men and women of my island!' and we halted to survey the copper-skinned warriors, bearing cow-hide shaped ingots of copper on their muscular shoulders. Around their loins was a fringed garment; otherwise they were bare and very beautiful, with long elaborately curled ebony ringlets.

'Indeed, Lady Merope, they are the men of your island,' agreed Khons. 'But we cannot linger, we will come and look at them again,' and he took the hand of the now-disconsolate Great Royal Wife and led her on after the guards and maidens who were escorting the King and Queen.

Merope was struggling to hold back tears. To distract her, I began to whisper to her; I thought it might comfort her to hear of the excellent results obtained by my sister and the pleasure she could expect from the love of the king, even though he was old. I kept my voice low and mentioned no names, because one never knows who is listening in a palace. Merope listened and forgot to cry.

Khons, who also may have caught what I was saying, looked away and did not comment.

Nefertiti and the King were close together. His arm was around her waist and he was smiling at her as though he thoroughly approved of her lying down with his father. This was strange, but presumably it had been explained to him by the alarming red-headed woman his mother, and he had accepted it.

I could not, in fact, imagine someone not accepting anything explained to them by Queen Tiye, who would have kept explaining until there was no alternative but to agree. Not that she would have overborne his will if he had been strongly opposed, but he had not been. I reasoned that he was not sexed, so why should he bother that his father was, and why should he grudge his spouse, whom he certainly seemed to love, such pleasure as the Divine Amenhotep could provide?

And there was no doubt that he had provided it. The arrangement was that Nefertiti should lie with the King every second night for a month. She told me that she was longing for the next time.

It was a puzzle.

Ptah-hotep

I woke the next morning with Meryt asleep beside me. Her coarse black hair strayed across my face and made me sneeze, and I awoke with such a feeling of pleasurable languor that I embraced her again for the pure luxury of touching a warm breathing living creature.

She murmured, and her half-asleep hand slid down my body, found and clasped the phallus, which was erect as it usually was at that hour. She made a complicated movement which entwined our legs and I was inside that female vessel, so soft and wet and strong. Four or five strokes, not more, and I was seeding her again. She was a little disappointed, I think, but she merely held me close and said nothing.

'Well, Master, what of the love of women?' she asked, disengaging our bodies and kneeling up to find her cloth, kissing my mouth in passing.

'It is very fine,' I said truthfully. I did not love Meryt as I loved my heart's friend Kheperren, who reported that he was well, enjoying great favour from the captain Horemheb, and missing me beyond endurance. I did not yearn towards her as I yearned towards Kheperren. But I was delighted to find that I was potent with women and she pleased me in a purely animal way. I wondered how her other masters had used her. I asked.

'Most do not desire black flesh, so I was not raped. When the house-steward bought me I was warranted virgin, though I was not. My people have a great feast at which all virgin girls are required to lie down with the King. Since that was my father I lay under my uncle, who was heavy. He did not hurt me but he did not please me, either. If you wish, Master, I will teach you the art of pleasing women. Then, if you marry, your wife will be happy.'

'What we have done is not pleasing to you?' I asked, getting off my bed.

'Not precisely, Master, though it was not unpleasant. Some men have the skill of making a woman scream with joy; they are the ones surrounded by adoring maidens begging for their attentions.'

'Like the Lord Amenhotep may he live?' I sluiced my body down with cool water and dried my male parts with a linen towel. My phallus was a little reddened, but not sore.

'Yes, he is the master of love-making, it is well-known,' agreed Meryt. 'I will show you the caresses women use amongst themselves to give each other pleasure, after they have done their duty by harsh, unfeeling men. Then your wife will adore you and never murmur against you.'

'I would like to please you,' I said, overcome with a rush of pure gratitude to this generous Nubian, who had awarded me her loyalty as well as her body.

'Then you shall,' she said, giving me a quick kiss. 'Now, I must order your household, for the Royal Architect is coming, even Imhotep himself, to show the King Akhnamen may he live the plans of a new city he is intending to build. I have drawn more wine from the kitchen, and we should serve them some food. Hani and Tani can attend. Is that according to your will, Master?'

'It is,' I replied, and she went away.

My clerks were grinning at me. Did everyone know what I had been doing? I adopted my most serious manner and they grinned even more. Khety whispered to me, 'Well done, lord!' and I was within a finger-span of clipping his ears, as my own master might have done to an impertinent student.

However, it did mean that the palace gossips would have a new morsel on which to mumble their jaws. Man-loving Ptah-hotep has lain with his Nubian—well, well. I could easily bear the imputation that I cared only for black women. That would only mean that I was a commoner and had commoner's tastes. And I am a commoner, and I do have common tastes. My most dangerous secret would be safe; but there must be something for such persons to know about the great, and I was happy if they knew that.

Imhotep had already arrived. He was a thin fussy youth with grand ideas, especially about his own station. He had slapped Hani, the clumsier of the twins, for approaching too close in serving him wine; and Hani, shocked, had spilled a full cup into the imperious architect's lap. Meryt was mopping him, but the cloth would have to be pounded in lye before it could be worn again. Hani was crying, Tani was comforting Hani, and their brother Teti was glaring and picking up the shattered remains of one of my best wine-cups. I reminded myself that I outranked all of them.

'Hani, stop crying; it was an honest accident; I'm not angry. Go and help Meryt set out the feast. Tani, get some more wine. Teti, finish cleaning the floor and accompany Hani.

'My lord Imhotep, do not be distressed. My slaves are not used to being struck, I would be obliged if you do not do so again. Come into my quarters and I will be honoured to give you my finest cloth to replace the one you are wearing.'

Imhotep, knowing that he was in the wrong—one is not supposed to strike slaves, it reveals one as a man with no self-control—came with me and selected a cloth I had inherited along with my office. It was almost solid with gold embroidery and he was welcome to it. He stripped off the wine-stained one and dropped it on the floor.

'I should not have slapped your Nubian, lord, forgive my hastiness. But the King Akhnamen may he live is going to look at my plans and by Thoth who is our protector, I'm so scared,' he said frankly. I looked on him with immediate approval.

'I know how you feel,' I told him. 'But we shall make a good production of this. Meryt has the feast ready. The wine is the best. Tani and Hani shall serve it, and they will catch the King's attention, being identical twins.'

'Yes, where did you get them?' he asked as we left my sleeping chamber.

'From the temple of Khnum, which is selling some of its surplus prisoners. They are relatives of Meryt, my housekeeper.'

'And as long as you sleep with their sister, they will be loyal,' he commented. 'A wise precaution, my lord.'

'Now, what plans have you and how can we display them to their best advantage?' I asked, passing over the comment about Meryt. That aspect of our relationship had not occurred to me.

'I have drawn a big map, perhaps that should go on the wall,' he said, fussing again.

It took a long discussion before we decided that Tani and Hani should hold up the large drawing, providing an amusing reflective effect; while Teti served the wine; and Khey, Hanufer and Bakhenmut answered any questions about the office which it might please the Lord of the Two Thrones to ask. Meryt would meanwhile take charge of Khons, the barbarian princess and the Lady Mutnodjme and answer their questions, preferably out of earshot.

Then they came, the King and Queen may they live, and their attendants. When the Great Royal Wife Nefertiti came in, accompanied by the inquisitive Lady Mutnodjme and the Kritian princess, I knew instantly that the expression on her face matched my own. The Queen had lain in love as I had myself. Her body, as mine, was feeling loose, comforted, warm. She glanced at me briefly, and whatever she saw in my countenance made her shy, because she lowered fringed eyelids and looked away.

This caused me a moment of intense puzzlement. Had some God endowed the Lord Akhnamen with potency?' It was well known that he was unmanned by disease.

I had to store my astonishment for later consideration, as my royal guests were tasting the tidbits prepared for their delectation, and Imhotep was beginning to explain to the King Akhnamen all about the new city of the sun at Amarna.

'In the centre of the city will be the palace and temple, as you have ordered, Great Lord,' began Imhotep, his voice shaking with nerves. The strange profile inclined. The King was interested. I looked at the drawing, flanked by two solemn Nubian faces. The palace and the temple were one; strange, but not impossible. The buildings were laid out in a huge court, the palace on three sides and the temple on the other.

'And here, Lord of the Two Lands, is the Window of Appearances that you ordered. It commands the whole square. From it all people will be able to see you and your Queen Nefertiti may she live. If this is what you require?' asked Imhotep.

I could understand his uncertainty. This was a very odd request. Women in the Black Land were free and visible, of course. Only barbarians who are ashamed of their own brutality and have peculiar ideas about how the world works, hide their women away in stifling tents in the desert lest other men should see and covet them. Indeed in this same dynasty a queen had made herself into a king, the Divine Lady Hatshepsut, who had declared herself Pharaoh and reigned alone for thirty years.

And in every market the sellers were women, the traders and some of the makers, though weaving was still largely a male task and field workers tended to be men, because they were stronger (and according to my mother, closer to the mentality of the ox or horse). The washers of clothes were all men, as the lye they used in removing such stains as the wine soaked into Imhotep's cloth, was very strong and was thought to affect the fertility of women.

But Great Royal Wives conferred the kingship on their husbands, and took no official role in running the country. What they did unofficially, of course, was not known. Certainly their favour was strongly solicited for mercy or justice.

Great Royal Wife Tiye had sent me a couple of oppressed farmers recently, and on their testimony I had ordered an investigation of the administration of a mismanaged village which might well have escaped notice otherwise. And if the headman of that particular village had done half of what was alleged, he would shortly be examining an executioner's knife at uncomfortably close quarters.

I had missed some of Imhotep's speech while lost in thought, though from the smothered yawns from the king's attendants it had not been gripping. Imhotep was listing the labour he would need to survey the site, and the wording on the boundary stones. No one lived in the area, it was desolate Desaret, red waste, so there were no disputed farmer's claims to adjudicate. I did wonder where the Royal Lord Akhnamen was going to get his water for the lakes of lotuses which Imhotep had designed. I was answered in the next sentence.

'And I estimate that it will take three seasons to build the canal,' said the architect, and sat down.

Tani, who had forgiven the insult to his brother, gave Imhotep a cup of the strong beer which he preferred, and he gulped it down and held out the cup for more.

'Good,' said the king. 'Good. The breadth of your imagination pleases me, Imhotep. Consult with the land registry and with my scribe, here, and draw the labour you need. No slaves; this city will be built by freeborn men.'

'Lord, they are expensive,' protested Imhotep. 'Indentured labour can only be used during Shemu, the harvest season, when no one works in the fields; and then only really for the months of Pakhons, Paoni and the first decan of Ephipi, after which it becomes too hot. And they demand not only the best food—which is in any case wise, as a healthy workforce is more productive—but priests, physicians and an army of cooks and overseers.'

'Nevertheless, that is my desire,' said the King softly. Imhotep took one look at the determined royal countenance and threw himself to the floor, kissing the king's jewel-encrusted sandals.

'Lord of the Two Thrones, Master, I will do all that you wish,' he said, and the king left a measurable pause before he lowered his flail and let it slide across Imhotep's back.

'Ptah-hotep,' he said to me, ignoring the man lying at his feet. 'You are happy?'

'Great Royal Lord, I am,' I replied.

'Come to me tomorrow, early in the morning,' he said. His voice was always soft. Nefertiti, the Great Royal Wife, was sitting close beside him. His arm was around her waist and his soft fingers were stroking her bare side, just as though they were lovers. She blushed and nestled closer to him, her slim arms around the bulk of the king. It was most odd, but rather charming.

'Lord, I will come,' I agreed, though I had no need to reply. He knew that no one in the palace would oppose any order he cared to make.

'I am thinking of a hymn, which I will write,' he said. His elongated eyes glowed with fervour.

'Lord?'

'A hymn to the Aten,' he told me, and with no further word, he rose and left.

Meryt came to me after seeing Imhotep to the door with all his plans and papers.

'The little princess Mutnodjme has grown,' she said. 'She did not ask anything which might be considered impertinent, except about men and women, and I told her what I could. What are you worried about, Master? I think the twig-broom my lord Imhotep's speech went well and they have eaten a lot of the food.'

Apart from knowing that Imhotep had now been named and would be forever after known in my household as Twig Broom, which suited him perfectly, I was troubled because the king had named a god I had never heard of; and I thought I knew all of them.

'Khety,' I said, 'Have some of this honeyed quail, it's delicious, and then look up the lists of gods, and find me what it says about the Aten.'

Chapter Ten

Mutnodjme

The conversation with the Nubian woman in the Great Royal Scribe's service had been brief but so packed with information that I went straight to my mat and lay down to think, astonishing my sister Merope, my mother and my teacher.

But I did not have time to really consider the implications of what I had heard, because the Priestess of Isis was announced and both Merope and I were banished to be thoroughly washed and perfumed and to have our hair combed and arrayed fittingly.

For the Chief Priestess of Isis is the mistress of magic, of learning and of spells; and was it not Isis who by her sorcery collected up the pieces of her murdered husband, put them back together, all except for his phallus which the fish had eaten, and then magically compensated for that loss, and mated with him to conceive and birth Horus the Avenger? That class of power differed from that of the Pharaoh, but was not to be slighted.

We were ushered back into the big room with the beautiful frieze of flowers—cornflower, lotus, sunflower and all the riverine grasses—a little breathless but terribly clean, and knelt to the tall slim woman in the green robes.

Isis' Lady was old. I knew that the proper title was 'Singer for Isis' but she sounded too old to sing. Her feet were hard and calloused like a dancer's; and her robes smelt of moon-leaf and unefer, magical herbs.

Tey my mother introduced us, and as is proper, we did not move until the old hand had moved to touch first Merope, then me, on the bare shoulder.

'Mutnodjme,' she said consideringly, dismissing Merope with a delicate wave. 'You are learned, I am told.'

'Lady, I have a little learning,' I agreed. I knew how much I did not know.

'And would you have more?'

'Lady, if I am allowed to ask questions.'

Khons grinned, and Tey scowled.

'Mutnodjme, my life has been entirely spent asking questions. Whether you will receive answers, well, there is a question.'

I was looking into her face. She had the papery skin of the aged, deeply lined, and her voice was high and trembled a little. Her dark eyes were unreadable, but might have contained a glint of humour. I gambled on this and replied honestly.

'Lady, as long as there are questions there will be answers, or there is no sense in asking them.'

'And you are sensible?' At least she was continuing the conversation.

'Sometimes, Lady of the Lady Isis.'

She gave a short laugh; almost a grunt. 'Sing,' she said. I rose to my feet. I had always liked to sing and Nefertiti liked to listen to me, though I gave Tey a headache. I sang one of the spells which people used to charm snakes.

A face has seen a face
A face is against a face
The mottled knife
Both black and green
Goes forth against
What is seen
Back with thee, hidden one!
Hide thyself, venomous!

Back with thee, hidden one!
Hide thyself, toothless!
In Nemi's name, the son of Nemit,
Thou shalt do no hurt.

I finished with an elaborate twirl on the last three notes and sat down. The old woman did not comment on my voice but asked, 'You banish the serpent in the name of Nemi. Who is Nemi?'

'Lady, the woman who taught it to me did not know. Teacher Khons thinks he might be a servant of the Nine of Thebes; my sister Merope says that the name is not Kritian and she does not know; and the Nubian woman who cleans the floor says that it is not Nubian. Therefore I would derive the title from our word for wanderer; so it would mean, Wanderer son of Wanderess, which is a good description of a snake. So I think that's what it means, and it's a way of naming the snake. So maybe the song should say 'I name thee Nemi, son of Nemit' which would scan, too.'

'And the value of knowing a name?'

'If you know someone's name...' I groped for words. 'You know them, Lady, and can hurt them. All the spells depend on knowing a hidden name.'

There was a pause in which I wondered if I had said something terribly wrong. Then she nodded.

'My name,' said the old woman, getting to her feet with my mother's assistance, 'is Duammerset, Priestess of Isis, and you may come to me for more learning, little daughter, if you will.' She made a complicated gesture of blessing and was gone, escorted by three attendants in the same green robes.

They were the most beautiful of greens, deep and rich, the colour of malachite, and I wondered what dye they used.

I was surprised by my mother hugging me and Khons offering me a honeycake.

'That is a very alarming lady, my daughter, and you spoke up well, and sang well. I am pleased with you,' declared Tey, 'And so will your father be. That settles your future, daughter. If you wish to marry from the temple, then Isis is your dowry.'

Khons was so delighted at how well I had acquitted myself that he offered to take us for a walk to the walls, and Tey was so pleased with me that she allowed this.

The town of Thebes baked under the sun of the month of Mesoré. We could practically hear the old mud houses in the village creaking as they dried. The village was large, and on one side of the river the temple of Amen-Re stretched out of sight, pile on pile of glowing golden buildings. A few fishing boats slid across the river, the reed ones which the fisherman use only in this season when the river is almost stagnant. No one was stirring in the small houses where linen bleached on the roofs of the laundrymen and new spun threads hung limply at the dyer's. All sensible people were asleep in the dark, waiting for a change of weather. No work was done in the fields in this season. There is no sense in ploughing dust. I remembered Merope saying that in her island the fields were watered from the air, by rain, but here the Goddess Tefnut contented herself with the Nile. I had only seen rain perhaps ten times in my life.

There was not a breath of air, which was an advantage. The poison-breath wind had gone and soon we would be feasting and rejoicing in the five intercalary days on which the common people got married, and then the rise of the river again at New Year, when there was another feast, Opet. Merope leaned on the marble wall and exclaimed, pulling back as the hot stone scorched her tender arms.

'I don't like Egypt,' she said, 'you were my only friend and now you're going away.'

'Not for years,' said Teacher Khons consolingly. 'She cannot enter the temple until her moon-blood comes, and even then the priestesses may send her home if she is not mature enough. Isis deals with the great mysteries, birth and death, and they cannot be contemplated by anyone who is still a child. We will go on as we have been doing, Princess, and learn as much as we can. And anyway, you must go and be a Great Royal Wife in truth when the time comes for you.'

'That's true, Teacher,' Merope appeared to be comforted.

'What is this Lady Isis, anyway?'

'Come and sit down under the awning, pupils, and I will try and tell you, but first I will call for some small-ale and some fruit and Mutnodjme will tell us what she knows about the Lady Isis.'

'She is the Lady of a Thousand Names,' I said as I sat down next to Merope in the thick shade. 'Lady of Bread, Lady of the Wheat Field, Star of Mariners, gentle and learned. When Set the Destroyer murdered her husband she sought for him and saved him and rules the Land of Sekhet-hetepet, the Field of Offerings, with him. Her child is Horus and her sisters are the Ladies of Motherhood, Hunting and Protection: Tawert, Neith and Nepthys.'

'A very good start,' encouraged Teacher Khons. 'Do you know the tale of the theft of the Name?'

'No, tell us,' we said, our invariable answer.

'First, tell me why Great Royal Nurse Tey said that Isis would give you your dowry,' asked Merope.

'Because a woman learned in the mysteries of Isis needs no dowry,' I answered. 'Women of that temple can deliver babies, tend the sick, make spells, draw down Khons by the hair,' I added, referring to the God of the Moon and Time and grinning at Khons the teacher, who slipped off his Nubian wig and revealed an entirely bare scalp.

'You might have trouble pulling this Khons down by the hair,' he chuckled.

'She is a wise woman, a skilled woman, and worth a great dowry. That is, if she lasts for the whole time. Priestesses are required to stay in the temple until they are eighteen, and I may not live that long, of course.'

'If the gods are kind, you may survive and become a good magician. Do not take to sorcery, Mutnodjme, I beg,' said Teacher Khons, replacing his wig.

'Because I mightn't be good at it?' I asked.

'Because you might be altogether too good at it,' he responded.

Then we settled down with a cup of small-ale each, Khons produced the papyrus, and we read it by turns. Merope, who still had trouble with Egyptian, began:

Behold the Goddess Isis lived in a woman's body skilled-with-words. Her heart turned away from millions of humans and turned to millions of gods. How could she become esteemed on earth, how could she make herself Lady of Knowledge by means of the knowledge of the Great Name?

'This is too difficult, Teacher,' Merope begged. 'Can I give it to my sister? In any case, she reads better.'

'Very well,' said Khons, giving me the roll. I took up the tale:

Behold Re came each day in the sacred ship, lord of the double crown. Divine Re had become old. He dribbled at the mouth. Now this Lady Isis took his spittle and earth and moulded it into a serpent in her hand, even a serpent with fangs sharp as arrows, and she placed it on the path before the Lord Amen-Re's foot.

When the Most High walked on his way, the serpent drove its fangs into his ankle, and the life began to depart from the Eternal's body, and the creature of Isis began to destroy the Lord of the Sun.

Then that mighty god opened his mouth and cried aloud.

The gods said, 'What is the matter?'

And the Lord Amen-Re found that he could not speak, for the poison was running in all his limbs as the Nile conquers the lands through which it flows.

Then the great god steadied his heart and spoke, and said, 'I have been stung by some deadly thing of which I have no knowledge, which was not made by me and is not of me. Never have I felt such pain. Can it be fire? Can it be water? My heart is burning, my limbs are shivering, let there come to me all those who know words of power and banish this agony from me.'

And all the gods lamented, for they knew no remedy.

I could see it all, the little serpent the colour of earth, the bite and the great god's cry of pain. The part of the story which I liked most came next, and Khons took the scroll from me to read at an even pace, for when I was excited I always read too fast. I listened with bated breath as I always did to Isis' clever manoeuvre.

Then came Isis with her words of power and in her mouth was the breath that is life. She said 'What is this, Lord? Has some created thing dared to bite you? I shall overcome it.'

And the Divine One said, 'I walked the road of this country my own Khemet to look on my own works and a serpent bit me. Can this be fire? Can this be water? I am hotter than any fire. My limbs tremble, I sweat, my eyes fail. I cannot see.'

Isis said, 'Divine One, tell me your name, and I shall cure you.'

And Amen-Re said, 'I am maker of mountains, I am creator of all, I am maker of waters. I have created love. I am he the gods know not; I am one who is hidden. I am he who commands and the Nile flows forth to water the land. I am the creator of hours, time, festivals and years. I am Khephri at dawn and Harakhte at noon and Temu in the evening.'

And those names were named but the poison still tormented him.

So Isis said to him, 'Declare your real name, your hidden name, and you will be healed.'

And the poison burned in Amen-Re like a smith's fire, and he said, 'I will allow Isis to search my heart, and my name shall go from my body into her body, from my heart into her heart, and she shall know my name.'

Then Isis the Great Lady of Magic kissed his mouth and the Name flowed into her, and she said, 'Flow, poison, I make you to fall upon the ground, for you are conquered, in the name of the Great God which he has told me. Re shall live and the poison shall die, for if the poison lives then Re shall die.'

These were the words which Isis spoke, the Queen of Magic, and she had knowledge of Amen-Re's name.'

'But what good did it do her?' I objected.

'She knows still the secret name,' said Khons. 'And secrets known to only one other make the other very powerful. The Lord Amen-Re endowed her son Horus with his two eyes, the sun and the moon, and they helped Horus in his battle with Set the Destroyer. And the Lord Amen-Re healed Isis when that same son injured her, because she let Set loose from his chains.'

'Why did she do that?'

'Because he was her brother,' said Khons.

It was very hot, and we lay down in the shade to sleep. How could the Lady Isis be the sister of Set the destroyer? It was very confusing.

Ptah-hotep

I went to the King very early the next morning, as he had ordered, and sat down at his feet with my whitened board to listen as he was shaved and tended.

'My father may he live first quarrelled with the High Priest of Amen-Re when he was minded to take the Lady Tiye as his Great Royal Wife. She was a commoner, no Princess, but there was no Great Royal Heiress for him to marry and he was sure that Tiye, my mother, would be a good queen and she was his choice.

'That High Priest remonstrated with Amenhotep, who was a boy, thinking that he could overbear him and alter his mind, but my father was not convinced or afraid. He had already fought one battle then, and said that there should be no more wars in Egypt.'

The barber, who was trying to shave the king, stood patiently with his bronze razor in his hand waiting for a break in the conversation. I tried to provide one.

'Lord, as it says on the scarab: *I married the Great Royal Wife Tiye and made for her a lake called Lake Tiye on which I sail my barge Gleam of the Aten,*' I said, watching as one side of the royal face was oiled and scraped. He had hardly any beard but shaving is good for the skin.

'And further, my lord, I have read the account of the Battle of Kush, where it says: *One came to the Lord, saying, "The foe, Kush the wretched, has planned war in his heart. The King went forth. Kush knew not this lion which was before him."*'

The King murmured along with me, as though he too knew this inscription by heart. I only knew it because I had been forced to copy it perfectly seven times in dictation or suffer the consequences. I recited:

Kush came, their hearts eager to fight, and many fell. The might of the King took them in an hour; making a great slaughter of them, their king and their cattle. They planted the harvest, but the King reaped it, mighty bull, strong in heart; great things were in their hearts, but this fierce-eyed lion slew them by the command of Amen, it was he who led them in victory.

I added the words of the viceroy, and my Lord Akhnamen knew them also.

The king's son, vigilant for his lord, favourite of the good god, the king's scribe Mermose said, 'Praise to thee, good god! Great is thy might against him that affronts thee; thou hast caused the rebellions to say, "The fire we have kindled rages against us." Thou hast slain his enemies and they are under his feet.'

'Amen again,' muttered the king.

I observed that the barber had now shaved both sides of his face and was sliding the razor under his chin, so I kept talking.

'They say that the construction of the lake only took fifteen days, remarkable speed,' I observed. 'It is a fair place and I hope to see it when the family moves back to Djarukha after the New Year. I believe that the palace is beautiful beyond belief.'

The royal throat was shaved and the King was now free to answer. 'It is beautiful, but not as beautiful as my new city of Amarna will be, once the canals are built and there is water. You saw the plans, Ptah-hotep, are they not splendid?'

'Absolutely breathtaking,' I agreed, for they were, although I didn't think that there was enough gold in the world to build them; or enough labour.

'Do you know your titles, Ptah-hotep?'

'Yes, Lord.'

'Then, Keeper of All Secrets to Whom No Heart is Hidden Whose Heart is the King's, listen.'

'Lord, I listen.'

As he talked, he allowed his hand to lie on my shoulder, and it was probably only my imagination which made it seem very heavy. Servants came and replenished his cup and mine, made him stand to replace his cloth, and painted his eyes with kohl, and he did not seem to notice them. The Keeper of All Secrets was going to share his knowledge with at least eight people, I estimated.

'In the beginning was nothing,' he said, and I seized my stylus. 'Void. The primeval chaos before Nun the primeval ocean, before the gods, all these later pretenders in which an ignorant people believe. My father is renowned for his wisdom, is he not? And he believes in the Aten, the spirit before the beginning which made all things, the visible god who manifests himself every day to all humans, the sun-disc is his symbol, but it is not he. He is himself and no other and cannot be known.

'Lord, I hear you,' I said. So far it seemed a harmless mysticism.

'My father believes in the beginning, in Aten the voice in chaos which said to the world, 'Be!' and it was. All men shall believe it,' he said.

I began to feel uneasy. 'Lord, does not your father may he live renowned for his wisdom, also say, *Enquire not into another man's gods?*'

'He said that, but he is an old man, and does not have the heart for the great work which is before us. All men shall speak to god, not through the medium of priests and their prattle and their useless rituals, but to the Aten himself by the sun-disc which gives life to all of the Black Land. I shall simplify,' said Akhna-men the Pharaoh, making a broad gesture with his soft hands.

For a moment, I caught his enthusiasm. Without priests or sorcery or words, without the trade in sacrifice and charms and spells, a man could speak directly to the source of all goodness, to the breath of creation. He saw my understanding in my face.

'Away with the mumbling old men of Re and the toothless old women of Isis. Away with faithless promises of an afterlife! There is no afterlife but to be reborn as another human, as a beast, as a tree.

'I would like to be a tree, planted in a garden, fruitful and full of life, fed by the water and breathing gentle vapours like prayers to my maker, even to Aten the symbol of the Creator. What would you like to be, Ptah-hotep?'

'Lord...' I hadn't considered it before, but I could think of nothing else. 'Lord, I would be a dog, who could guard the farmer's crop against thieves and his household against robbers, and I would sleep every night on his doorstep.'

He seemed pleased with this idea—they had told me that he valued loyalty—and stroked my cheek.

'You have not even begun to sprout a beard,' he mused.

'No, Lord, and I may not; my father has no beard.'

'Nor mine,' he said. 'My father is still too wary of the priests of Amen-Re to take such action as should be taken against them, and I am not yet strong enough. But when Aten transforms my father and I rule alone, then they will be chastened for having the effrontery to admonish my father about my mother, and for promulgating false gods to the people.'

I was about to say, 'Lord, false or not, the people need their gods,' when I caught his eye and decided to be silent. It was, in any case, unlikely that I could argue my obsessed Master out of his cherished beliefs.

'Why do men need gods?' he asked, having picked up my thought, which he was reputed to often do.

'Because their lives are hard,' I replied. 'They work all day for bread, and though they are seldom hungry in this rich land they have not enough of what they like to eat. They may have married the wrong woman, they may have no children or no sons and too many daughters, they may have lost their only love, they may be in mourning for wife or parent, and they weep, saying, "How can I endure this?" And they are comforted when they consider that after death they will live pleasurable lives in the Field of Offerings, drinking beer which will never sour and eating bread which will never rot.'

'Dreams,' scoffed my lord Akhnamen.

'Or they can attribute their own failure to the ill-humour of a god, as when the Nile flood is too low and the fields parch into dust, spoiling the young seedlings; or too high, and the people watch their houses melt in the water and take to the boats, weeping, screaming insults at Hapi.

'If the canals are ill maintained or the ducks stray or the fish desert the nets they can always blame the god rather than themselves or their own carelessness. And when pure misfortune strikes, it is always better to have something to curse by,' I added.

I waited for a moment, hoping for an interruption, but he was thinking.

'I know nothing of the life of the common people,' he said at last. 'You were a commoner, were you not, Great Royal Scribe? Tell me of your life.'

'Lord, it is not interesting, I was the son of a scribe.' I suddenly remembered that I had not written to my father to tell him of my elevation, sending some large present so that he would not call me undutiful. I wondered what he would like. A vineyard?

'Tell me of a commoner's life,' he said.

'Lord, let me recite to you from the *Satire of Trades*,' I offered, not capable of so much description without some time to prepare.

'Recite,' said Akhnamen; so I began:

Consider the field worker—cruel is his fate! His skin is like leather, and he tends his crop in tears. He eats bread by the side of the meadow and is burned by the sun…

'He is honoured,' said my lord, 'for the sun is the emanation of the Aten.'

I didn't know what to say.

Chapter Eleven

Mutnodjme

My sister mated with the King every second night for a month, and she conceived.

We tested her urine by watering barley seedlings with it. For if a woman has new life growing within her, shall not every emanation of her body be imbued with life? Tey watched over those seedlings as though she was Isis herself, and I wondered that any of them ventured to grow, so fiercely did she glare at them, daring them to tell her that her daughter was not carrying a child. But by the beginning of the new year, it was clear that one group was growing much faster than the other, and by that time my sister was beginning to swell at the waist.

Her husband was delighted. He would sit with her by the hour, his fingers stroking the curve under which the child lay, naming her Phoenix, self-created, impregnated by the god, Mother of Miracles. He ordered artisans to paint her rooms with the story of the Benben bird, which flew through the sky in a burst of cosmic flame and laid a black stone egg which one day would hatch to produce another firebird. Nefertiti was so delighted that she glowed. She adopted the stance of the pregnant woman long before her burden became heavy, the hand to the small of the back, the slowed movements; she who had been so lithe and quick.

Meanwhile it was Opet, the festival of the New Year and the day when Amen-Re came to his wife Mut and stayed with her a decan. I knew that the Sacred Barge had been refurbished and repainted, that the priests of the god and the goddess were fasting in preparation for the Mystery Play, where the Chief Priest and the Chief Priestess would enact the roles of the gods and ensure that the Nile rose to flood the thirsty land.

The royal family would attend, of course. Nefertiti insisted that she was well, had never been so happy, and would not be denied; and her husband the Lord Akhnamen may he live did not protest, saying that the Phoenix knew what was fitting for her avatar.

I asked Teacher Khons about the Phoenix, and he had no more to tell me than the story I already knew, which seemed curiously pointless, though circular. He did add that the Bennu or Benben bird had been worshipped a long time ago by the ones who built the pyramids, those Houses of Eternity which dotted Desaret, huge, strange, and of mysterious purpose. The capstone of each pyramid, he said, was carved with the Phoenix. This did not make my sister's husband's remarks any clearer.

Nor did his endless insistence on the primacy of the Aten, an immortal, unknowable creator whose visible symbol was the disc of the sun.

In the Black Land we knew of the sun, of course, it shone every day, it was the god Amen-Re who appeared in many forms, but sunlight itself was dangerous. The rays of Re could wound and blister, and only field workers and the common people went out into it, and no one could look at Him. But I saw my lord Akhnamen staring into the sun at noon as though the heat and brightness would not blind his eyes, and wondered how long he could do that without sacrificing his sight to his Aten.

In any case it seemed to have nothing to do with the festival of the New Year, and I was going out with my sister Merope and Teacher Khons to enjoy it.

We began our walk before dawn. We could have travelled in a carriage, and Mother Tey had urged my sister to do so, but she said that the motion of the horses made her sick and left her bruised and she was perfectly capable of a gentle pace for a few shoeni along the well made temple road between the rows of ram-headed sphinxes.

I love processions. Ahead were the trumpeters, the drummers, the players upon both the short and the long pipe, and the women shaking sistra—which made a sound like a rattle. Everyone was wearing their best clothes to honour the god; everyone was hungry after the strict fast of the Epact Day of Set, on which no work is done and no food consumed. The early morning was cool, with some condensation still on the trees, and the river was already beginning to rise.

I could smell green things and growing waters, when the gusts of perfume from the nearest people cleared. We smelt lovely. From the lotus and galbanum of my sister and King Akhnamen may he live to the robust male scents of labdanum and cassia and the aromatic Nubian oils from the Chief Royal Scribe who walked next to the King. My lord Ptah-hotep smelt of clove and cinnamon and I walked closer to him and drew in several deep breaths.

They said that he had a fascination for black women, that he was conducting orgies with his Nubians and that he was a commoner, but I did not mind. It was none of my business; though I did wonder what it would be like to lie down with identical twins. He was attended by two gigantic slaves with red feathers in their hair and I could not tell the difference between them. They looked like a mirror images, but clearer than any polished bronze one could show. They were preserving their countenances very well amongst the noise and music, which must have been very strange to them, coming from a people without such spectacles.

Ptah-hotep noticed me and smiled. He was a sedate young man, I thought, unlike his boisterous second in command Mentu, who was already drunk and singing along with the Hymn to Amen-Re, out of tune and out of time. There was something wrong with seeing Mentu on foot. He belonged in a chariot. We had often watched him racing through the narrow streets to gain the desert, where he competed against the finest charioteers in the army. And won, or so they said. His father and my father were friends, and Mentu's father had always despaired of his drunken careless son finding any office. When Mentu had been named Second Scribe his father had given a party at which everyone had been merry for three days.

Ptah-hotep glanced at Mentu, smiled, and said, 'It's the festival, Lady, everyone should rejoice.'

'I do,' I replied, a little in awe of this powerful person but enjoying his attention. The palace said that he was arrogant and proud and spoke to no one. But he seemed grave to me, even sad. The Nubian woman had arrayed him gloriously, in a red cloak embroidered with the icon of Thoth the Ape as befitted a scribe. Around him were his household; three slaves, three scribes, and Mentu, who was attended by a servant to carry his wine jug.

The household of the eldest scribe Bakhenmut included an over-decorated woman with the stretched neck and popping eyes of a camel, her two sons, and a gaggle of maidservants who might have been chosen for their ugliness. This usually meant that the Master of the House had a roving eye and his wife was worried that he might take a concubine, but the scribe who seemed to belong to her looked unasserive and crushed and was attending meekly to whatever it was the camel-lady was hissing into his ear.

Then we heard trumpets. Ptah-hotep grabbed my hand as the crowd surged forward and pulled me into the lee of his tall Nubians. The mob broke on their satiny backs and strong legs like water on a rock, and flowed around them. Pharaoh Akhnamen's soldiers closed around him and fended off the people. The Sacred Barge was coming.

In a roar of voices, a flourish of trumpets, a mutter of drums, the god came. The Sacred Barge of Amen-Re was carried by forty priests. It was a real boat, capable of voyaging on water, and it must have been heavy but they bore it up on their shoulders; and the people seethed noisily around it, striving to touch it and be assured of good luck in the coming year. Even so—over the screams and the cries of *Amen-Re!* and the curses of those who were trampled underfoot, over the chanted litany *The God comes, he comes, even the Lord Amen-Re who is master of all*—I heard the Pharaoh Akhnamen say, 'Superstition!' Then the crowd swept me away and I thought I was lost until Ptah-hotep noticed, retrieved me, and pulled me closer to one of the twins.

'Stay close to Hani, little daughter,' he ordered; and I did, for a change, as I was bid, for I was afraid of the press of people. In their desire to get closer to the god, they were impeding the procession, and they were being shoved aside by the priests and falling. As each one fell, they tripped a few others who fell in their turn and there were cries of distress from under the heap of people. I saw a child fall under her mother, a man collapse over them. My vision was filled with snarling mouths and blurring fabrics and arms and legs and the sudden stink of fear.

The Chief Priest, a very old man who was being carried in a litter before his god, flicked his sceptre of office and the bearers picked up their pace.

I put my back to the Nubian Hani's legs—my head was about level with his belt—and he smiled down at me, a huge watermelon grin which showed all his white teeth. He was oiled with the same scents as the Great Royal Scribe. He was fending off the crowd without any difficulty, standing steadfast like a colossus, and I suddenly felt safe. The procession was now moving on, the Sacred Barge was past, and the pile of people disentangled themselves with much personal abuse and settling of crumpled garments and straightening of holiday garlands.

I admired Hani's strength. His legs were like columns and his body was thick and solid, like ebony. Muscles moved under his oiled skin as he breathed. I dared to look around him at the retreating procession and he said, 'Come up, maiden,' and lifted me without any apparent effort and set me on his shoulders.

I looked through the nodding red plumes on his braided head and saw the whole procession stretched out like a brightly coloured river. At the head, the Chief Priest and the Sacred Barge, then the Pharaoh's family, then the press of the households of all the people employed at the palace. My fear had gone and I felt immensely proud to live in the Black Land where such spectacles could be seen. Not even in the Island of Kriti, where the Bull-King lived, could there have been such a magnificent sight.

'Hani, Tani, Teti, all my staff, we follow,' ordered Ptah-hotep, but I had seen someone I knew and grabbed Hani's hair to make him stop. Between two ram's head sphinxes stood a man I had not seen for years. He was a tall man with a blue bead on each lock of long hair. 'Horemheb!' I screamed, and because my voice was high, it carried over the multitude of voices and he heard me and wove a path through the people to me.

'Such a mount, little Princess,' he grinned, reaching up to me to take my hand and kiss it. 'Such a horse only a princess could ride.'

'His name is Hani and he just rescued me,' I told him. 'This is the lord Ptah-hotep, Great Royal Scribe may he live. This is Captain Horemheb, my lord,' I said formally, because even if I was sitting on a Nubian giant's shoulders, I was still aware of protocol and I wanted to show Horemheb how much I had learned since he rescued me from the Nile. He seemed impressed.

'My lord,' he bowed to Ptah-hotep, 'I have returned to deliver a report to Pharaoh Amenhotep may he live of events on his border. Might I ask you a favour? Offer my scribe some assistance in writing his report. Here he is,' he reached into a group of soldiers and extracted a young man, somewhat dusty and crumpled by his passage through the mob of worshippers. 'His name is Kheperren, and he has been valiant and faithful. I want to ensure that he does not censor his own part in a recent victory over the vile Kush.'

'Captain, I will do as you request,' said Ptah-hotep with surprising formality. He took the young man by the hand, as token of agreement with the captain. But from my vantage point on the Nubian's shoulders, I saw his eyes widen as though he had been given a sudden shock.

The crowd shoved us and we shifted, throwing the scribe almost into Ptah-hotep's arms and pushing even the massive Hani into close proximity with Horemheb. They were almost of a height. Horemheb grinned at Hani, and his equally huge twin Tani, and punched him lightly in the chest. 'You are slave to the lord Ptah-hotep? Have you never thought of joining me as a soldier, little one?'

I thought that this was an insult, but Hani laughed.

'We had enough fighting in Desaret against the Tribes,' he replied. 'Our sister is concubine to the lord Ptah-hotep, and we stay with her.'

'Then you must be from the Village-between-two-trees, ' said Horemheb. 'Yes, that would be enough fighting for any stomach. We will be in the palace for the festival. Come along to the field if you fancy a little exercise. Mentu of your office will be there, I have no doubt. He has a new chariot team; matched greys, faster than the sun, he says.'

I could not see Hani's face, but Tani his twin was regarding Horemheb with approval. 'We will come, lord, if our lord allows,' he said.

'What did he mean about where you came from?' I asked.

'In the Village-between-two-trees, men are loyal to their sisters,' said Hani. 'The brothers accompany the sister to her new husband, and stay with her. If Tani, Teti and I marry, our wives will stay with Meryt our sister, and we will be a new tribe, with Meryt's name.'

'A very good custom,' I declared. Hani patted my knee. 'Are you not loyal to your own sister, little Princess? I have seen the way you care for her.'

'She is the most beautiful woman in the world,' I said, and he grunted an agreement. 'But,' I added, 'what about the Desaret tribes? I have never heard of them. Who are they?'

Tani replied, 'They are the Sharu, the Wanderers, little Princess, and civil folk enough except when they are possessed by a call. Then they sweep across the sands, screaming that their god requires them to take land or prisoners—foolish, who can take land? Land stays in one place, or it would not be land. But every now and again, they come, and then they fight like lions; even as the lion of the peak, who is called Sekmet by the Egyptians. They even have beards and hair like a lion's mane.'

'They are carved on the footstool of the King who stands at the pylon of that temple,' added Teti, who had been listening with interest.

'Oh, yes, I have seen them,' I said, remembering. 'Beards and long hair caught at the nape of the neck.'

'Indeed,' said Teti. 'They have visionaries, and these prophets lash them into wars. One day they will attack Egypt in force, and then they will be a real menace, for they do not know when they are beaten and fight until they are all dead, for the sake of their god. My father used to say that the worst thing that could happen to a people was a new god...'

Hani reached out a huge hand laden with gold rings and clamped it over his brother's mouth.

They all looked at me, and I had a sudden flash of power, and a stronger flash of shame. Was I to inform on these kindly men who had spoken freely in answer to a question?

'What did you say?' I asked Teti. 'I didn't hear, the trumpets are so loud.'

Ptah-hotep

I had him again, I touched his hand, I embraced his body. And by the grace of Captain Horemheb, I had a reason to take him home with me.

I don't think that anyone in that mob of drunken, dancing, reeling worshippers could possibly have been as happy as the Chief Royal Scribe, Ptah-hotep.

We saw the god into his resting place, the temple of his wife the Divine Consort Mut. We saw the Chief Priest Userkhepesh walk into the welcoming arms of the priestess of Mut, who embraced him, kissed his mouth and led him inside. The door of the temple was shut on the bride and bridegroom and the people spread out into groups with their temple-provided beer, bread and roasted goat to sit down and feast.

I distracted myself for a while by wondering how that austere and aged man liked being kissed in plain sight of a multitude, who cried out advice as to what he should do with the Goddess Mut, how many times her should do it and in which positions. I found the idea amusing, and when I met Kheperren's gaze he laughed, for he had been thinking just the same.

Hani was bearing the princess Mutnodjme with no apparent exertion, Tani and Teti were standing close to him, and Horemheb and his soldiers had gone off to the barracks for the returned soldier's wash, massage and feast, all provided by the Pharaoh may he live. There was nothing for us to do but to return the little Princess and go back to the palace. The scribes, of course, could stay for the feast if they wished, in the huge tent and awning set up for the palace outside the temple.

Both Amenhotep and his royal son were in the temple, watching the mating of the gods, which had to be perfect or the Nile would not rise. This was the most important festival in the calendar, and any deviation from normal practice would have caused disaster. In view of his age and general fragility, I hoped that the Chief Priest of Amen-Re had been well nourished and rested in the days before this feast, and that the priestess was skilled and both were fitting vessels for the gods, or the omens might be truly ominous.

Kheperren was thinking the same. I could tell from his side-long look. His eyes still crinkled when he smiled. He did not touch me but I was stingingly aware of his presence, his breath, the rise and fall of his chest, his scent so achingly familiar and sweet.

Of all the people around us, the only one who showed any sign of being aware of what was between Kheperren and me was the little princess, sitting easily on Hani's shoulders as though she had been riding Nubians all her life. She was looking at us, a wrinkle forming along her brow. The Lady Mutnodjme was destined to be a priestess of Isis, and such women are very observant. I moved a little distance from my dearest friend and then bit my lip, for that had given me away more surely than any stillness might have. But the Princess was watching the pylon and had seen the great gate open.

'Amen-Re the Mighty!' roared the crowd with their mouths full, for the presence of both Pharaohs meant that the mating had been accomplished and more free beer was about to be distributed. The Chief Priest had acquitted his task once again, and we could go back to the office.

'Would it cause comment, Lord Ptah-hotep may you live,' asked Kheperren, using the most formal of modes of address, 'if I accompanied the Great Royal Scribe to his apartments and delivered my report for his most honourable attention now? I have newly returned from the borders and I am fatigued and wish to rest.'

'It would please the Captain Horemheb to have his report earlier rather than later,' I replied gravely. 'Therefore we will return there now. A scribe who has been wounded in the service of the Lord of the Two Thrones deserves all consideration.

'Hani, Tani, find the lady Mutnodjme's teacher Khons and give her into his care, then join the feast. Meryt and Teti will come with me and join you later. Khety, Hanufer, you will wish to attend the merrymaking. Bakhenmut, I am sure that the Lady of your House will appreciate the seat of honour which has been prepared for her in the Pharaoh Akhnamen's tent. I am awarding you my two most trusted slaves to be her escort.'

Bakhenmut gave me a grateful smile and even the unbeautiful wife unbent sufficiently to smile on me. Hani and Tani exchanged rueful glances, anticipating an afternoon of being ordered around by Bakhenmut's wife but consoled by the amount of food they would manage to consume in the process. Everyone else seemed content. The lady Mutnodjme leaned down from Hani's shoulder and gave me her hand and I kissed it. She squeezed my fingers a little and let go, and the household made their way through the picnicking families towards the awning under the pylon where both Kings were feasting.

Meryt and Teti escorted Kheperren and me to my office, picking up various tidbits from trays and tables on the way, which Meryt loaded into her ever-present basket. When she had come to me, she had carried a brightly coloured basket in Nubian weave, and it never left her. She said that women of her tribe were responsible for feeding the people, and picked up anything edible which they saw, and the habit had not left her.

She set out some food on a cloth on the desk, patted my cheek, and drew Teti with her to the outer office. She and Teti and Anubis sat there, cracking bones and breaking bread, while I took Kheperren into the inner rooms, shut the door and secured it.

'Oh, my brother,' whispered Kheperren.

I wanted to look at him, to touch him, to make love to him, all at once. Our mouths met and I was lost. My bones melted; I burned. We fled into my bed-chamber and threw ourselves down on my bed, and embraced so closely that there was no room between us, the wet skin of his belly against my belly, our hands sliding across flesh which was oiled and sweating.

We locked thighs and thrust, once, twice, and then we dissolved into an orgasm so strong that the day became night before my eyes and I thought that I had died.

I had not died, for when I awoke I saw not the face of the First Doorkeeper demanding to be named Understander of Hearts or he would not let me pass into the afterlife, but the curly hair and the dark eyes, burned now even darker by the fierce Eye of Re.

'You look older,' he commented, kissing my neck. 'Severe. Quite the Great Royal Scribe, my dearest brother.'

'So do you, quite the soldier; and oh, my heart, my love, you have been wounded!' I stroked a gentle finger down a transverse cut, barely healed, which seamed one arm almost to the elbow.

'It's nothing, it doesn't even hurt any more. A Kush warrior hacked at me and nearly missed, only not nearly enough. It was in Horemheb's Battle of the Mountain. He saved my life. He saved all our lives. How have you been faring, brother? Did you receive my letter? I sent it to the Master of Scribes and he said he was able to get it to you without endangering our secret.'

'He did, and I rejoiced to hear that you were alive and missing me, because I was alive and missing you. Oh, Kheperren, I missed you so much!'

'Show me how much you missed me,' he said, guiding my hand to his phallus. I kissed down his body, slowly, relishing the taste of his skin, engrossed in his perfumes. He gasped, his hands on my head. 'I love you,' he crooned while he could still speak, 'Oh my love, my heart, my desire, my brother.'

Like Ptah Creator-god who swallowed his own semen to bring forth the world, I brought him slowly to a climax which shook us both to the bones.

We woke and it was dark. In sleeping, he had curved around me and hugged me to his breast, and I have never woken feeling so sated, so loved, so pleased. I tasted the divine herb unefer in my mouth, and kissed him to share it.

'I suppose we should get up,' I said, stretching lazily.

'I'm hungry,' he commented. 'In fact, I'm starving. Will the Great Royal Scribe allow a portion of bread to a humble army scribe before he delivers his report?'

'Only if the humble army scribe accepts a wash in the purest water, a sumptuous meal and swears that he will love me forever,' I bargained.

'I will love you forever,' he said seriously, holding my right hand as one does when swearing an oath to another. 'By all the gods both seen and unseen, I swear.'

'So swear I, Ptah-hotep, Great Royal Scribe,' I said. 'Come and wash, for we smell like a couple of rutting goats.'

He sniffed and agreed.

Later, we sat down in the inner office and began on Meryt's collection of comestibles which she had gathered for us. There was a leg of roasted duck each, some dried grapes and dried melon, several loaves of different breads and we washed it down with good wine.

'I observe that you have not taken to soldier's fare,' I said. 'Or would coarse barley bread and beer suit you better?'

'No, coarse barley bread and beer would not suit me better. Hand over some more grapes. Oh, the sweetness. I used to lie awake at night and cry; firstly for you and secondly for dried grapes. Let me tell you, brother, there is nothing sweet about being a soldier and no one would ever do it if it were not for Egypt's need and the calibre of such captains as Horemheb.

'It's hot and unprotected and dangerous and unbelievably uncomfortable. The common soldiers grumble all the time about the food and the officers grizzle for their wives. No one is happy. But Horemheb can command men and they know that they are his care and that he loves them.'

'How much did you love Horemheb?' I demanded, instantly and to my astonishment, jealous.

'How much do you love your Nubian?' he responded sharply.

'We take our loves where we find them, Ptah-hotep.'

'I am ashamed,' I told him. 'But I am also answered.'

'So am I,' he said.

There was silence for a moment, and then we leaned forward and kissed, a deep kiss flavoured with raisins. We concluded an agreement in silence; that we would lie with whoever we liked, for ease or pleasure, but I would be his only love, and he would be mine.

'We came down into a defile and we were attacked,' he went on, as though the exchange had not happened. But his free hand was in mine as though he never meant to let go. 'Kush attacked. There were more of them than us, and they had the advantage of surprise. We were guarding the only road through Desaret into Egypt for a hundred shoeni either way, and we could not let them pass.'

'What happened?' I caught my breath.

'Kush did not know that Horemheb always expects surprises. He had half of his force dismounted from their chariots—their complaints must have reached the gods, you would think that charioteers have no feet—and clambering along the ridge of the mountains on either side. The ridges were thickly wooded, so

Kush didn't see them until they were on them and shoving them down the cliffs into the waiting grasp of the mounted men.'

'And who was leading the scouts on either ridge?' I asked.

'No one of consequence,' he squirmed.

'You, and which other?' I demanded sternly.

'Yes, it was I,' Kheperren nodded. 'And his name was Tuy; he was killed. My people come from the mountains they call the Edge of the World, and I was the only person present who knew anything about climbing. That's why I volunteered; though the charioteers didn't like it. They told Horemheb that they would not take orders from a scribe.

'He told them that my orders were his orders, and if they got someone killed because they were being snobbish about rank, then he would personally flay them alive and leave their skins drying over a memorial stone that said, *Here lies a moron right-fully executed by his captain. His name is forgotten.*

'Did he mean it?'

'With Horemheb it is always safer to believe that he does mean it. Can I have some more wine?'

I filled his cup and my own. I was getting used to the sound of his voice again. He had a sweet voice, my Kheperren, very pleasant to the ear.

'So we poured down the cliffs after the Kush, and they were caught between a hammer and an anvil, and they were all killed. You know how we used to read accounts of battles, "Hotep, where each move is described and the storyteller knows what is happening all over the field? It's not like that. You can see maybe an arm's length around you and it's all dust and yelling and weapons appearing out of nowhere.

'The only thing to do is try to stay alive and the only way to do that is to kill the man who is trying to kill you and I am no good at it, no good at all. The man who gave me this, he was young, strong, I looked into his fierce eyes and knew that he was a man like me. When he raised his weapon he saw the same and missed my heart, perhaps on purpose. Then he struck at Horemheb and I deflected the blow on my shield. I didn't see what happened to him but he must have been killed, they were all killed, all of them. We despoiled the bodies and buried them all in a great pit in the sand, killing the wounded with a blow to the back of the neck. I made a note of them and their numbers. There were eighty-three corpses; only nine of us were killed.' His eyes were filling with tears. They ran down his face and dripped into the wine, and I took away the cup and gathered him into my arms.

'I'm not brave as the captain says,' he said desolately. 'I didn't run away because there was nowhere to run. I fought because I was attacked.'

'There, my brother,' I held him close. 'You need not go back, I can keep you here. No scandal can touch us while Meryt lies with me.'

'No,' he said, lifting his wet face to mine. 'If I stay I will have to marry. I cannot marry. I tried to lie with a woman in a border wine-shop and I could not. I only desire men. I must go back with Horemheb, my brother. But it is you I love, and one day...'

'One day,' I replied as steadily as I could, for what he said was both true and painful. 'We will draw the latch on our hut in the reeds, leave the dog Wolf on guard, and sleep together all night in peace.'

I could not see that it would ever be so, but it comforted him, and presently we went to bed and slept and made love and slept again.

Chapter Twelve

We sat at our teacher's feet and construed the *Satire of Trades*, written years ago by Dua-Khety for the instruction of his son.

'This was quoted to me so often by my father when I was a child that I loathed it, but it is nevertheless good literature,' said Teacher Khons, giving Merope the scroll. She began to read:

It is miserable for the carpenter when he planes the beams of a roof. It is the roof of a room measuring ten by six cubits.

'What's a cubit?' she asked.

'The length of my forearm,' said Khons. 'A digit is the width of my finger. There are six digits in a palm, and there are six palms in a cubit. *The measure of the world is the measure of a human,*' he added, quoting another wise scribe.

Merope continued:

He spends a month in laying the beams and spreading the roofing material. All his work is done, but his wife and children are hungry while he is away.

The bricklayer is in pain. He works outside in the wind with no garment but a cord for his back and a string for his buttocks. He is so exhausted by his labour that he can hardly see, and he eats with his filthy hands.

But I have seen the bricklayers, Teacher. They seem happy enough, even if they are naked. They sing. And at night they get drunk and sing more. Just under our window, where they are building the new rooms,' commented Merope, puzzled.

'That is true, my pupil, but this is a satire. It exaggerates for the purpose of making a point.'

'The point being that Dua-Khety wants to make his son decide that a scribe's life is the best?' I reasoned. Teacher Khons nodded.

'But he's lying,' I said. 'I mean, exaggerating. That is not the way to make a proper argument. *The Maxims of Ptah-hotep* which you made us read last decan say:

Truth is great and its effectiveness endures forever; it has not been confounded since the time of Osiris.

Khons sighed. 'A little colouring is necessary even for truth,' he told me. 'Do you not remember the *Tale of Truth and Falsehood?*'

'No,' we said, hoping to escape more of the *Satire of Trades*. Khons obliged:

Truth came home one day, naked and wounded, having been beaten and cursed by the people who did not wish to hear, while his brother Falsehood went dressed in the brightest garments and feasted with every household.

'What shall I do?' cried Truth to the gods. 'No man wishes to hear me and all beat me and throw things at me; look, I am covered with dung.'

'You are naked,' said the goddess Maat, sympathetically. 'No naked one can command respect. Therefore take these robes and you will walk without fear and all men will sit at your feet to hear your stories.' And she dressed Truth in Fable's garments, and he was welcome at every house.

'What's a fable?' asked Merope, who also did not like the Satire of Trades. Khons smiled and began:

The lion summoned all beasts to come to his court.

All animals attended, except for the desert fox, the clever, sand-coloured slinker who steals rather than fights. The lion waited, and still the fox did not come to offer obeisance.

At last the lion left his cave and came to the fox saying 'Why have you not come to offer your obeisance to me?'

The Fox replied, 'I judged that it would not have been good for my health. I have seen many tracks going into your cave, Lord, but none coming out.'

'And that is a fable about...what?' I asked.
'The nature of government,' replied Khons shortly. 'The Satire of Trades, Princess Merope, if you please.'

The message-carrier leaves on his journey after giving his property to his children, as he does not know if he will return. He is always afraid of lions and ambushes. He only relaxes his vigilance when he returns to Egypt, and by then his house is only a tent. He does not come home to a feast.

Why not?' asked Merope. 'Even if he did give his property to his children, wouldn't they be pleased to see him again?'

'Perhaps we should read something else,' said our Teacher. 'The satire might be too sophisticated an art-form for you literal young women.'

'Good speech is as rare as malachite, yet can be heard in the conversation of slave women at the millstone,' I quoted from the Maxims of Ptah-hotep, and Khons laughed.

'On second thought, we will write,' he ordered, and we took our writing boards and opened the pot of ink. I found my favourite stylus in the bunch and Merope sanded away her previous essay with pumice.

'What shall we write about?'

'The festival of the new year,' said Khons. 'Did you have a good feast, little Princesses?'

'Wonderful,' declared Merope. 'I love roasted duck and I had a whole one to myself. But I didn't get to see it as well as my sister, because she had enough wisdom to be swept away by the crowd and lifted up by the Nubian of the Great Royal Scribe Ptah-hotep may he live. Why are we having lessons, anyway, teacher? It's only the third day of the holiday, which is twelve days long. Amen-Re lies in the arms of his wife Mut. No one else is working. The commoners are all sleeping to store up energy for tonight's feasts. Why are you working?'

'As a favour to your mother, to keep you occupied while she arranges the move to the palace on the lake. You will have visitors today, my pupils, and she wants to keep you occupied. But we can tell stories if you would like.'

'Take us for a walk?' we coaxed.

'Where would you like to go?'

'Down into the village,' suggested my sister.

'Out onto the water,' I asked. I had never got over my fascination with the river, even though it had tried to eat me.

'Sorry,' said Khons. 'Neither. The village is full of drunken people and the river is rising fast. You remember what happened to you on the day that the river was rising, Mutnodjme.'

'Then to a temple,' we said.

'Which one?' asked Khons warily.

'Basht,' said Merope. Basht the cat came to her name and walked delicately over the tiled floor and onto Merope's lap.

'That is in the village, and we cannot go to the village.'

'Story, then,' I said, for we were clearly not going to join the interesting crowds and noises which we could hear outside the walls. At least we were not going back to the *Satire of Trades*. Khons nodded and began:

Isis and Osiris were brother and sister and loved each other with a love greater than death.

Isis was the most wise of all the daughters of Geb and Nut, and she said to Osiris, 'Be my lover; oh most beautiful of all men, and I will lie in your arms and I will never leave you.'

And Osiris beheld her and replied, 'Most lovely of all women, I will lie with you, and love you, and I will never leave you.'

But Set their brother was jealous and said, 'Why did she not choose me? I am as strong as Osiris, and I am good at lovemaking, yet she has chosen my brother and not me.'

Therefore he decided to kill Osiris, hoping that Isis would love him after her husband was dead. So he had a sarcophagus made, exact to the measurements of his brother, taken from the print he had left sleeping in the sand, and he challenged the gods, that whoever fitted into the valuable goldwork should have it for his own.

Osiris climbed in, and lo! Set clapped the lid down, and welded it shut. He flung Osiris into the Nile, and so he perished miserably, suffocating in the dark.

And Set said to Isis, smiling, 'You shall be my wife.'

'Wicked!' cried my sister Merope. 'What happened? Did Isis take Set as her husband?'

'Of course not,' I argued. 'Isis is the lady of wisdom, she wouldn't do something so stupid.'

Khons raised a finger for silence, and I subsided.

Not only did Set fail with Isis, who scorned him saying he was a scorpion among brothers, but his own wife Nepthys, disgusted by this murder, left him also, taking with her their son Anubis.

Isis and her sisters lamented for Osiris, then turned themselves into birds; and Isis and Nepthys and the Divine

Huntress Neith flew low over the Nile, seeking the coffin, crying to lost Osiris, 'Come to thy house!'

And many people saw the birds and wondered, for they called with human voices to the dead man, 'Come to thy lover!'

But they could not find him, until a bird told them that the tamarisk tree had found the coffin and grown lovingly around it to preserve it from destruction, and that the tree had been cut down and made into the pillar of a King's house. That tree has ever since been sacred to Osiris.

Isis came in the form of a woman to the King's house and offered to suckle his child if she could ask for anything in his house. The baby was sickly and not likely to live, and they had no other children. So she nursed the child, dipping him each day into the fire to make him immortal, and at night changing herself into a swallow which mourned around the pillar, crying for lost Osiris.

Thus it went, until one night the Queen found the woman putting her child on the fire, and cried out, so that the child lost his chance of immortality, and the nurse was transformed into a mourning swallow.

The swallow then spoke with human voice, saying, 'Take your child, he is strong though now he will not live forever, and give me the pillar of your house.'

And greatly wondering they obeyed, and the pillar was replaced and a woodman split it open with his axe to reveal the marvellous sarcophagus inside.

Then Isis was a woman again, and opened the coffin and wept over the dead Osiris inside, and all who heard her weeping were afraid, for it contained all the sorrow in the world. Then she took the coffin with her and rowed it down the Nile and placed it in a thicket while she slept. But while she slept Set came, and found the body; and, in his malice and misery, hacked it into pieces and flung the pieces into the air; and they scattered all over Egypt.

Then Isis called her sisters and Anubis the black dog, son of Set, who came to her and mourned with her afresh.

Then they collected the pieces, crying, 'Come, holy one, be one, be alive, for Isis has thine hand and Nepthys thine arm.' But they did not find the phallus, for the fish of the river had eaten it.

Then Isis assembled her husband and made her magic, drawing down time and the moon, even Khons himself as her ally. And making a phallus out of the mud of the river, she descended onto the phallus as a woman, her thighs wrapping his hips, and he entered into her and seeded her body with the divine child, even Horus the Revenger, born to contend with his uncle Set.

'But what happened to Osiris?' I asked. 'He did not come alive in the world again, did he?'

'He rules the otherworld, my pupil,' Teacher Khons said.

He reigns over the Field of Reeds, a pleasant place of feasting and little waterways, of lotus and canals, where no sunlight blisters or cold bites; where no sandfly stings or crocodile threatens. No hot winds blow there, where the happy dead live in their houses, attended by their shabti, the answerers who are buried with them.

There each family has its own fig tree and grape vine, and all live in peace with one another. And in the centre of this pleasant place is the House of Osiris, where Kings and Queens dwell and feast and laugh forever.

'It is not so in the Island,' said Merope.

'Tell us,' I said, leaning on Khons, who nodded at Merope.

'There all dead persons explain their lives to Gaia, Mistress of Animals, and Dionysus the dancer, her consort. There they say: *I have been just, I have not hurt or killed, I have loved and been loved, there are those who will mourn my death.*

'And Gaia welcomes them into her kingdom, to dance with the Dancer and sleep in the green grass, on the mountains where the goats crop, in the Island Underworld where Gaia sits on her flowered throne,' Merope said.

'Here, too, one must confess before Osiris,' returned the teacher. 'The dead one must say: *I have done no murder. I have not oppressed the widow and orphan. I have fed the hungry and given water to the thirsty; and to those who could not cross the river I have given boats.*

'The more power the person had on earth, the more chance they had to do the wrong thing and the more likely they are to see their heart sinking in the balances against the feather of Maat. For the herdsman has little chance to commit sins; he is too poor for gluttony and too ugly for lechery and has too little power to oppress the poor. But the great man has a correspondingly greater scope, and therefore can more easily fall into sin.'

'What happens to those whose heart is heavy in the balance?' asked Merope.

'The heart is eaten by the monster Aphopis, half crocodile and half dog, and they are forgotten,' replied Khons.

'Even if they are embalmed in the proper way and all the spells said and offerings made?'

'Even so,' said Khons seriously. 'Unless the dead person is good, they will not survive to live in Osiris' kingdom. In the *Tale of Se-Osiris the Magician*, it is told that the good poor man goes on rejoicing to feast with Horus, and the rich greedy and corrupt man lies down at the first keeper's door, and the socket for the door-pivot is his eye.'

We thought about this. It was a sobering image. For if the more powerful had more scope to commit sins, what could we make of the changes being wrought by the most powerful of all, who had just announced that he was changing his name and would henceforth be known as Akhnaten; and that in his new city there would be no feast of Amen-Re at the New Year?

Ptah-hotep

Many people came to visit us over the next two days. The report was written, with Kheperren's reluctance to declare his own bravery overcome, mostly by main force—by which I mean that Hanufer sat on him while Bakhenmut made a fair copy of the report and gave it to Khety to copy five times, and I sealed it. It was then an official document and it would have been treason to meddle with it or erase so much as a line. This was explained to Kheperren with due solemnity and he agreed to allow the report to go to Horemheb and the King without emendation.

The holidays were always marked with a round of visiting and a lot of eating and drinking, and Kheperren and I wandered from gathering to gathering, arriving when we wished and departing when we felt like it. I had never drunk so much in my life, but consoled my conscience with the notion that soon I would be back at work; and then my mind shied away from the thought that Kheperren must leave me again at the end of the twelve days. He must go with the captains and depart into the waste, and risk his life every day, a life so precious to me that I did not know if I could live without him.

However, we were enjoying our leisure. The palace was loud with the noise of parties, the stink of lamps and the cloud of perfumes; wine, roasting, melting fat as the scent-cones dripped oil down the faces and wigs of the guests. We were lurching down a corridor, arms around each other, in the middle of the second night, and Kheperren was saying how difficult navigation was in the half dark when we almost fell into the arms of Horemheb and an old man.

We dropped as soon as we saw who it was with the brave captain, and kissed his sandal toes. I tried to force my wine-soaked wits to remember the proper forms of address but I was hauled up by the shoulder before I could get through half of the titles of Amenhotep the King, may he live forever.

He was regarding us with very shrewd dark brown eyes. I leaned on Kheperren and he leaned on me and together we remained more or less upright. Horemheb said, lips twitching, 'Here is the Great Royal Scribe of your Royal Son, Master, and my brave army scribe.'

'Come with us,' said the King, and we followed him into a little antechamber, past two ranks of soldiers. There a woman sat nursing a child. It was Great Royal Wife Queen Tiye, the red-headed woman, and she smiled indulgently upon us and called for wine mixed with water and plain bread with sesame seed, reputed to be good for hangovers. We sagged down onto a precious carpet before the King's feet and Horemheb took a chair.

'I am always pleased to talk with chance-met companions,' said the King slowly, making sure that his words penetrated even the most wine-sodden skull. 'It would not be proper for me to interfere in my son's household, of course, but I admit I was curious about this young scribe, especially since the Great Royal Lady tells me that he deals most impartially with the matters she sends.'

I had investigated the farmer's complaints, discounted ten percent for exaggeration and found a case to answer. The Headman was now awaiting trial for oppression and theft, though what would probably seal his fate was defrauding the King's taxes. The new Headman would be required to watch his predecessor's execution, which should ensure exemplary rule in that village for a generation or so. Since then the Queen had seen fit to send me three or four other matters, which I was considering.

Not that I was capable of considering all that much at the moment. Kheperren, always a happy drunk, was showing a tendency to giggle, and I felt as though every thought had to be dredged up as from a deep well. When the wine-and-water came, I took some deep draughts and ate some bitter herbs, which the slave had also brought. They were the dark green nettle which we call gallus, a strong restorative. I felt slightly sick, but clearer in the head. The King looked approvingly on me and smiled.

I could not see any of my lord Akhnamen, now Akhnaten, in the king. He had none of the dreamy aura which surrounded the Royal Son. He was immensely alive and alert, though old, and if his gaze had been sharper when he was younger then he would have been able to stare holes in a stone door.

I realised that I had been fetched, accidentally on purpose, to a serious meeting which palace procedure would have totally forbidden, and sat up straighter. My dearest friend appeared to be sobering, also. No one ever said that Kheperren was unobservant.

'General Horemheb,' said the King, 'what shall we say to this Great Royal Scribe and this decorated soldier?'

'We shall say that they hold the fate of the Black Land in their hands, and explain the situation without frightening them too badly,' replied Horemheb, flicking a blue-beaded tress back over his shoulder.

'You trust them, despite their youth?'

'I trust them because of their youth,' he replied. 'And because although he has no taste for war, Kheperren saved my life. He did not flinch and he did not run, and that is much for an untried and scholarly young man. And I trust them because they are brothers.'

'Very well,' said the King Amenhotep may he live.

'General,' said Kheperren, wavering down to kiss Horemheb's foot, 'congratulations on your elevation.'

'Scribe,' said the general, 'I thank you. I have here your mark of valour, which you will wear in memory of the Battle of the Mountains.'

He took Kheperren's hand and slipped a heavy gold arm-ring onto his wrist. It was figured with silver bees.

I knew that Kheperren was about to protest and I wanted to hear what the King had to say, so I pulled him back onto our carpet and said, 'Congratulations, soldier! My lords, we are at your disposal. What did you wish to say to us?' I was worried as to how long my sobriety would last and I did not wish to disgrace my office by falling asleep.

'Egypt,' said the King, a little amused by my presumption, 'is at its fullest extent. We control more land than we ever have, and we control it mostly by diplomacy. The army, of course, is important,' he deferred to the general in a way which was most pleasing to watch, 'but mostly we have maintained this empire by diplomacy. My entire foreign office spends all its days in writing letters to the surrounding kings and princelings and in patching up alliances and in fostering quarrels between our enemies.' The old man got up and began to pace the room, occasionally pausing to stroke the cheek of the sleeping child or take a strand of the Queen's coppery hair between his fingers.

'Consider,' he continued, 'on both sides of the Nile there is Desaret, a bleak waste, where nomads roam. They are not immensely important on their own, being quarrelsome and uncertain of purpose. If they can ever ally one with the other, settle their differences and invade in force that will be a different matter, and I have agents amongst the tribes to warn the throne of the emergence of a new god, which is the only thing which could make them dangerous. Beyond them on one side there are the kingdoms of Mitanni, Babylonia and Khatte, who are bitter enemies of each other and must be kept so. For if they combine, then Egypt will fall before their combined might, and we will be subjugated just as we were under the Hyksos.'

'How can they be kept at variance?' I asked.

'By a sedulous fostering of quarrels, my scribe, by a careful application of flattery and gifts, by marriages and alliances. On the Great Green Sea our messengers sail to Achaea and to Kriti; there is a Princess Merope of that Island amongst the Great Royal Wives, here to bind her father Minos to our treaty. We sail to Ugarit, to Tyre, to Byblos unmolested. Our boundaries stretch across most of the Known World, but take heed of this: no army in the world could protect them if they were assailed at more than one point. However big the army, however well led—and General Horemheb, I mean no insult—they could not get to a troubled spot in time if an invasion in force was attempted. Only diplomacy can keep Egypt, and that is why you are here, young and honourable men, I fear..."

He was standing by his wife and she reached up and took his hand, drawing it to her breast. For a moment, I saw fear in the heart of the Lord Amenhotep.

'My son is building a new city, and you will go there with him when it is finished, Ptah-hotep,' said the King, 'I doubt the King Akhnamen—Akhnaten now, of course—will bother with a foreign office, so I am asking you to do me this favour. Take with you several scribes from my service who speak the foreign tongues and write the barbaric cuneiform. Receive the ambassadors politely, send out such presents as will please them, and try—for me, for Egypt—to balance the allies and suppress the enemies. You can maintain a link with the army by your letters to your heart's brother Kheperren who will stay with the General Horemheb, who will keep him safe for love of me.'

'Lord of the Two Crowns, I will try to do as you wish,' I began. 'But I do not know what the Lord Akhnaten intends for me, and at any moment I may lose his favour. Already I am worried by this man Huy, whom he took from the cattle-market.'

'Ah, yes,' said the King, sitting down heavily, so that the straps of his chair squeaked. 'Huy. He has named him Chamberlain?'

'Yes, Lord. Huy is insolent to his superiors and cruel to his inferiors and he has great ascendancy over the Great Royal Son. I know that he is disliked by everyone; but the same could be said of me,' I added, conscious that I was telling tales.

'No, the same is not said of you,' said the King. 'Ever since you came back alive from your interview with the Chief Priest of Amen-Re, you have been respected.

'It is my fault, you know; all of this,' he added.

We stared at him.

'I began to attack on the power of the Priests of Amen-Re. It seemed to me that they had grown too great. A kingdom must have balance, young men; it must lie between contending powers on a fine point, like a pair of scales. I saw the Amen-Re temple taking over more and more administration until my father was almost helpless to act at all; for they ran the kingdom, and he was merely a figurehead. That was not my idea of royalty, though it would have been better if I had not meddled.

'I thought the Aten a charming philosophy, rooted in ancient belief, that I could use to remind the Amen-Re priests that they were not as important as they thought. I managed to retrieve a number of operations from them. Now I believe that I was wrong.'

He began to pace again, an old man under a great burden.

'Lord, you were not to know that your son would be sick…' began the Queen, saying something which I would not have dared to voice.

'But such things happen,' said the King. 'There will in the nature of history be weak kings and mad kings, and the kingdom must be able to cope if the head of state is an infant or incapacitated. I took all the reins into my own hands in my arrogance, and now it may be that the next driver is going to steer the chariot off a cliff, to the ruin of all.'

'It shall be prevented, if our lives can do so,' said Horemheb, and we agreed aloud.

'I may not be able to speak to you again,' said King Amenhotep may he live, laying his hand on my head then on my brother's.

'Particularly beware of Mittani. Tushratta is a devious, greedy and unprincipled king who will tear up any treaty if it suits him. His main enemy is Khatti; luckily they love gold. Send them cartloads of statues. Do what you can to mitigate the effects of my son's fanaticism. Report to General Horemheb. The gods bless you and keep you, my sons.'

As we were leaving, carefully reproducing our previous stance though we had never felt less drunk, we heard him whisper, 'And may the gods save Egypt.'

The last I saw of the Pharaoh the Lord Amenhotep may he live long, he had slumped down next to his wife, burying his face in her neck, and she was stroking his white hair.

Book Two

Aten in Splendour

Chapter Thirteen

Mutnodjme

The temple sent me to the funeral rites of King Amenhotep, now Osiris-Amenhotep, and, standing at the wall of the palace, I had never seen such widespread mourning.

Ten years had passed quickly for me, because I was always learning, I knew, now, almost all that the priestesses could teach me, and I delved into their stored scrolls and construed puzzling inscriptions in temples which were so ancient that only the old man Snefru the Scribe in the temple of Amen-Re could read them. I sought always for more knowledge.

I had not seen the king since he had fallen ill, though the physicians had sent to the temple of Isis for more and more of the narcotic black resin we extracted from the white poppy seed-capsule. They spoke of his death as a gentle one, and I hoped that it had been so, for he had given my sister Nefertiti six fine daughters; though after the birth of the third I had not seen her either. My Lord Akhnaten had taken her away to his new city at Amarna, and Nefertiti had never been good at writing letters, though she sometimes sent me presents.

I wore the green robes of the Lady Isis now, and I was of a great age; eighteen, nearly nineteen. There were villages in the marshes where that was the usual age for a woman to die, worn out with the dangers of childbearing and disease.

I lived in the cool stone palace built for the Mistress of Magic, high above the sandflies and the mosquitoes, and illness was rare in the temple. I had not borne, because few men pleased me, and what seed I had allowed into my body had not taken root. The temple wished to keep me and I had no wish to leave. I could have gone to Amarna and lived with my sister and my mother; but Tey and I had never been friends and my mother had grown very proud, so that she looked down on a mere priestess. I could not have my own establishment because I was unmarried and I had no wish to marry.

I had heard very strange rumours about what was happening in the new City of the Sun and I worried about my sister, though she always said that she was happy.

I stood in my malachite-dyed robes, my head crowned with the Isis symbol, the jewellery of my rank weighing down my shoulders and arms, while the keening grew from the river banks. The barge was coming with the King Akhnaten and his family, and I could hear the weeping as the priests came forth to line the road to the Temple of Osiris.

The King Osiris-Amenhotep had lain in dry natron for forty days. His body was dried and pickled like a salt fish. His entrails had been preserved and put into jars beside him. It hurt me that such a wise man should be so mutilated; and it struck me for the first time, to wonder how anyone could know that the dead, so treated, came alive in the Field of Reeds.

Then my heart forbade further inquiry. Our ancestors as far back as we could reckon them knew that this was the case. My own Lady Isis had made it so. It was true.

And I had a part to play in this funeral, as representative of my own Goddess, and I must not fail.

The walls were warm under my hand, almost as warm as flesh. The season was Shemu and the month was Pakhons, month of Finding Osiris, and unseasonably warm. The common people said that since the Divine Akhnaten worshipped the sun, He had come closer to us.

The old women in the temple said that such fluctuations had occurred twice in their memories, and that more grain should be stored against bad seasons. They had reported this to the King Amenhotep, now the Osiris-Amenhotep, and he had increased the storage rates so that the bins were full.

Now all his wisdom was lost to us. His translation to the Field of Reeds took with it the last of my childhood.

I could see all the way down the river, from the new temple of the Aten at Karnak, golden in the early sunlight, to the white and yellow ochre cliffs on the other side, which marked the landing place of the Houses of Eternity, where only Kings are buried. We would take Osiris-Amenhotep to his tomb which had been prepared for a long time; he had ruled for thirty-seven years.

Now his son Akhnaten had named his brother Smenkhare as his co-regent. This was thought wise. Smenkhare was eleven and had shown no signs of the illness which deformed his brother. The red-headed woman Tiye the Queen had lately borne a child, the last of the children of Osiris-Amenhotep. She had called him Tutankhaten.

A thought occurred to me. By this transfiguration I would also lose my sister Merope, the Kritian Princess, who had gone into the Palace of Women when she had first bled in purification. She had not conceived. We had been such close companions for such a long time that I would find life difficult without her. But now she would belong, as would all the royal wives and concubines, to Akhnaten.

And that meant that Merope, too, would move to Amarna. My future was looking more and more lonely.

Beneath me the people wept, tore their hair, threw ashes into the air in token of mourning. I had stood contemplating too long. I hurried down the marble stairs to the street and ran, robes bundled up in one hand, along the alley and into the small square before the Osiris temple where the women's gate stood open. There my sister Merope straightened my headdress and smoothed down my gown, without a word, and led me into the House of Life, where the embalmed body of Osiris-Amenhotep lay.

They had painted him and given him glass eyes, and stuffed the loose skin of his face with mud, so that he resembled a corn doll, such as children make of cornstalks with a plaster face. There was no trace of the man he had been, the sweet lover, the wise speaker. Two priests of Osiris were standing beside a heap of torn cloth, waiting for us to begin so that they could enfold Osiris-Amenhotep in his last garments. I took the hand of my sister Merope who was linked to Queen Tiye and Princess Sitamen, whose grip was as strong as a man's. We were there to represent Isis and Nepthys, Selkis and Neith, protecting the dead king's body while it was still vulnerable from the attack of fiends, the children of Set the destroyer. We stood in a circle around the body, singing our lamentation.

The bandages were carefully wrapped around our transmuted Pharaoh, the heart scarab in place, the amulets scattered across his body, the phallus bandaged into erection, the fingers wrapped separately. All the time the priests chanted the protective spells and the scent rose, resin and aromatics, frankincense and sandalwood oil with an underlying stench of putrefaction dreadful to smell and cruel to consider.

'Do not be afraid, my Lord,' whispered the Queen Tiye. Her long hair was tangled and muddy, her breasts were bare, her face disfigured with long parallel scratches which she had made in her grief. 'Anubis will make you beautiful, Osiris will take you to his bosom, oh, my heart's darling'.

We walked around under the palm boughs of the embalmer's makeshift hut—this structure would be burned the second the Osiris-Amenhotep was removed, and there was no point in burning a good building—singing the lament of Isis and Nepthys:

Hail thou Lord of Otherworld, Bull of those that live there,
thou image of Re, most beautiful babe! Thou driver-away
of evil, thou maker of gentle fortune, come to us, thy sister
and thy wife, even to Isis and Nepthys.'

Merope and I moved to the head of the Osiris-Amenhotep as the priest chanted:

Homage to the divine father Osiris! We embalm all thy members, for thou wilt not perish and come to an end as beasts do: thy breath is strengthened, O Osiris, the winds blow into thee. Thou are established, thou art strong, thou wilt live. The worms shall not devour thy body, thou wilt not fall into rottenness, thou wilt never see corruption when thy soul has gone out of thee.

The priest was a fat spotty youth with a nasal voice, most unfitted for his post, though I presumed that he was ritually clean, not having had intercourse with a woman, eaten meat or consumed wine for forty days. That should have improved his complexion.

When the soul hath departed, a man seeth corruption; the bones of his body crumble and stink, the members decay one after another into a helpless mass which falls away to foetid liquid, thus he becomes a brother to the worm and is made into worms and an end is made of him as for all things that perish.

I wondered how Tiye could bear this dreadful litany; Tiye who had loved the Osiris-Amenhotep for so many years. Her skin was grey, and she had bitten into her bottom lip, trying not to scream, though we would be required to scream soon and that might give her some relief.

Merope's hand was in my left and Sitamen had my right and she was grinding my bones in her grasp, for she also had greatly loved her father.

It was hot in the House of Life under the palm branches, and I felt sweat run down my breasts and into my eyes. The ritual was horrible, forcing the reality of death into our mouths, the words falling like ash on our heads. All must die, even the wise and generous.

Homage to thee Divine Father Osiris who lives!

Thou didst not decay, no worms made food of thee, thou didst not rot, thou didst not putrefy. Osiris-Amenhotep shall not rot, shall not decay, shall not putrefy. He shall not see corruption. He shall live, he shall live, he shall live! He shall flourish, he shall flourish, he shall flourish! He shall wake in peace, he shall be whole; he shall not lose form or savour of life. He will be stabilised and established; he will never be destroyed on this earth.

The amulets with their attendant spells were placed, even the garland of cornflowers and lotus was laid around the head of the mummiform coffin, which was of gold. This was then laid within a bigger sarcophagus, and then a larger, so that Osiris-Amenhotep was shut away from us within three shells of precious metal.

As Isis, it was my turn to speak. I said:

I am come to be a protector unto thee. I waft unto thee breath for thy nostrils and the north wind which comest from the god Tem into thy nose. I have made whole thy throat, I make thee live like a god. Thine enemies are crushed under thy feet. I have made thy word true before Maat, and thou art mighty among gods.

As Nepthys, my sister Merope said:

I am around thee to protect thee, my brother Osiris, my strength is near thee, thou art raised up. The gods have heard thy call and have made thy words to be truth. Ptah hath overthrown thy foes, and I will be with thee forever.

As Neith, Siramen said in a loud voice:

I have come quickly, behold, I have driven back the footsteps of the hidden enemy, I have illuminated thy face, Osiris-Amenhotep. Brother, I watch to protect thee, I stand with my bow and my arrows to repel the demons which assail thee.

As Selkis, Queen Tiye delivered her speech in a low, tight monotone:

I protect thee with the flame of my life, Oh Osiris-Amenhotep. I have gathered thy limbs and collected thy bones. I have brought thy heart and placed it on the throne within thy body. I will make thy house to flourish after thee, oh thou who livest forever.

Then the litter bearers came to lift the sarcophagus and carry it to the boat which would cross the river with our lord, and as expected we shrieked and wailed our lament, tearing our faces with our nails and fending off the bearers who would take him away.

'Come to thy house!' screamed Tiye, embracing the coffin. 'Oh my father and brother, oh, my dearest love, return to thy sister who loves thee!

'Father and brother and lover, return,' shrieked Merope, who clawed after the coffin as it was lifted. 'Return, my lord, return!'

'Great lord, sweet lord, come back to thy sister; he whose mouth was of honey, whose body was my delight,' Tiye begged, and was pulled respectfully back by Sitamen, who had not spoken.

I took Merope in my arms. She was shaking with expended emotion. Tears ran down her face and down mine, and Queen Tiye collapsed into her daughter's strong arms. Even Neith-devoted Sitamen was weeping, even that muscular warrior maiden whose hair was too short to dry her mother's tears.

Ptah-hotep

I was back in Thebes and he was dead, the wise old man. I was to accompany my lord Akhnaten to the funeral, and he was very reluctant to go.

'I do not believe in these gods, these fraudulent gods of the otherworld and the Tuat,' he protested when messengers brought the news that the Pharaoh Amenhotep had gone to Osiris. 'Tell me, Ptah-hotep, why should I go to this funeral?'

'Because although you are wise, Lord, the people are not, and they believe. They would think badly of you if you did not,' I had replied.

But when we had arrived at the palace of Thebes my lord went first to visit his remarkable temple of the Aten, which had taken a year's sandstone and untold amounts of labour to build. It occupied the ground between Karnak temple and Thebes village, a sandstone city in itself. I was met at the gate of the palace by Sahte, Queen Tiye's nurse, who demanded to know where the Lord Akhnaten was. I pointed and she spat on the ground.

'Come and speak to my mistress,' she urged. 'She has always respected your learning, Ptah-hotep. Merope the Kritian is with her and we are waiting for Sitamen, but she is mourning and cannot be comforted.'

'That is to be expected in the loss of so great and wise and gentle a husband,' I responded, allowing her to drag me by the arm up two flights of steps and onto the first balcony.

'Yes, yes, of course,' snapped Sahte crossly, 'But she will not rouse. There are many things she needs to do, and she just stares at the wall, or at that new temple of the Aten, and then she sighs, and then she stares again. I'm worried about her. She's got courage, my lady. I don't know. What is the world coming to? New gods and new temples and not enough to eat in the villages, that's what. In here,' she shoved me through a door curtain.

The room seemed empty. Then I made out the figure of a woman sitting on the floor; her hair hanging around her bare shoulders. My sandals whispered across ash on the floor. I knelt down next to the Queen Tiye and took her hand and kissed it. It was quite limp and curled empty on her lap when I released it.

'Lady, I am here on your orders,' I reminded her gently. She reacted slowly, but she reacted.

'I gave no orders,' she said. Her throat was torn with weeping and the voice creaked unwillingly from her strained throat.

'But you would have,' I continued, 'if you had not been crushed under a burden of despair. Where is the Great Royal Wife Merope?'

'I sent her away with unkind words,' confessed the Queen. 'I wish for no comforts.'

'Lady, you grieve,' I said, sitting down on the floor beside her. 'But consider. He died easily, without pain. He loved you all his life and you loved him. You were his heart, Lady, such pain never vanishes. But you will have some comforts. They are time and distance, and the memory which is cherished.'

'You are a ruthless young man,' said Queen Tiye after a pause in which she debated whether to order my instant execution.

'Lady, I am here because my lord Akhnaten is coming, and I wish to warn you that...' I paused to choose my words.

'Well then, warn me,' she said sharply.

'He is a devotee of the new god Aten, Lady, and I fear that... the funeral, you see, involves mentioning the gods of the underworld, and...'

'He would deprive his father of the afterlife because of his thrice-blasted and damned new god?'

I would have felt better if her voice had been raised, but it was perfectly level.

'He doesn't believe that there is an afterlife, Lady,' I began, but she closed her ash-stained hand on my arm—that arm was going to be bruised—and said, 'I hear him coming, go through that curtain and wait. Sahte will show you the way out. Thank you, Great Royal Scribe, I will never forget this.'

To my astonishment she pulled me close and kissed my mouth. She tasted of starvation and salt. I heard footsteps outside—it the guard who never left the King Akhnaten—and I scrambled through the curtain just in time. Sahte was beside me, a twisted shadow. She took my hand and kissed it but did not speak.

I heard the Pharaoh say to his mother, 'Lady, I have priests who will bury my father, in the new religion of the Aten, despising all fraudulent gods.'

And I heard her reply; though I did not know the voice, it was so cold and flat, like the voice of the dead. I shivered.

Queen Tiye said, 'If your father, my dearest love, my husband Osiris-Amenhotep is not laid to his rest in the House of Eternity as his father and his father before him, I will curse you.'

I heard Akhnaten step back, papyrus soles rustling in ash. He got as far as a shocked, 'Mother!' before the cold voice continued as if he had not spoken.

'If one of your priests of Aten touches the Osiris-Amenhotep and defiles his ritual, I will curse you both waking and sleeping, I will blight your ways, your board and your bed, slay your wife and your daughters though they are also my daughters, and death will be about you and follow you.'

She was actually beginning on the most potent curse of all, the curse of Set, which is complete destruction to the body, the spirit, the shadow, the fire and the soul, the posterity and the name. Akhnaten gasped again, 'Mother!' and she paused long enough for him to speak.

'Lady, I will do as you wish,' he whispered.

'Do so,' said the icy voice. 'You may go and learn your part as Sem-priest at the Opening of the Mouth. One word wrong, my son, and my curse is on you. Purify yourself,' she said.

There was an interval. A woman came and stood beside me. The Princess Sitamen, warrior-woman of Neith, had been listening intently to all that went on. She stood as still as a shadow, reminding me of a soldier on guard. She put a hand on my shoulder as soldiers do and I reflected the gesture.

'Scribe,' she acknowledged.

'Lady,' I replied.

We heard the outer curtain swish shut after the Pharaoh and his guard.

'Your lord has gone, best follow him and make sure that he has the text of the *Recension*,' she said. 'Fare well, most honoured comrade.'

She punched me lightly and Sahte led me out and along some corridors and showed me into the courtyard in time to catch my Lord Akhnaten and his escort.

'Ptah-hotep,' he said. 'I have decided that it is proper that my father should be escorted to eternity by the old ritual. He believed in it when he was alive. Have you a copy of the ritual?'

'Lord, I will obtain one immediately,' I said, and left him to find my master Ammemmes in the School of Scribes.

The temple of Amen-Re was empty. Wind carrying dust blew through the massive pillars. After wandering for a while I caught a straying boy and asked him to lead me to the master of the school of scribes, and he took me through a series of winding paths between walls to a small building within the main temple.

Then he ran away before I could reward him.

I paused on the threshold, as was polite, and clapped my hands for permission to enter, and someone let out a held breath. As my eyes grew used to the light, I saw that it was Ammemmes himself, who had been about to bludgeon my brains out with the large club he was lowering.

'Ptah-hotep, you should have warned me. I was about to kill you.'

'So I noticed, can I ask why?'

'We are moving the last of the scrolls today and I promised Snefru before he died that no harm would come to them. A promise to the dead must be honoured.'

A pair of boys were completing the wrapping of a huge bundle of papyrus. They had vanished when I had appeared and now returned to their work. I searched through it swiftly and removed a copy of the *Theban Recension*, then bade them continue.

'The worship of the Aten has taken all our funds,' said the Master. He looked well, though much relieved at not having to murder to carry out his promise. 'The estates of the temple have been given away; this was your Lord Akhnaten's order, we received it three decans ago. So we have gathered all our learning and we are leaving,' he added.

'How did Snefru die?' I asked, watching the boys stagger outside with the bundle. I did not wish to know where they were going to hide it.

'They came to the temple and told us that, on the orders of the Pharaoh Akhnaten, the temple was closed and all of the written material which named the god Amen-Re was to be burned,' said the Master sadly. 'Snefru cried out and clutched his chest and died of shock. As he was dying he made me promise to store his cherished scrolls, and I have done so. And we will bury him properly when his time is completed even if I have to do the whole ceremony myself in the dark.'

'Master, who will train scribes for the service of the people and the god?' I asked, horrified. I had not seen this order. It must have gone through Pannefer the Master of the Household or Chamberlain Huy.

'Aten, I suppose,' the Master shrugged. 'I'm going back to my own village, Ptah-hotep, to wait out the storm.'

'Take these,' I loaded onto his thin arm all my bracelets and put round his neck my pectoral of electrum, a very valuable thing which ought to feed him for the foreseeable future. He smiled at me and kissed me. His eyes were very weary and his hair was quite white under the Nubian wig.

'Thy brother Kheperren?'

'Still with the General Horemheb, and alive,' I replied. 'I am glad to have found you, Master, and he will be glad to have news of you. But all things pass, Master,' I said. 'The Osiris-Amenhotep is to be buried in the old way.'

'Return the copy of the *Recension* when the funeral is over,' said Ammemmes. 'Send it to me near Sais, at the village of the Crossed Arrows. And survive, dearest son; survive. But do not do evil in the name of any god. The only one who accepts evil deeds is the demon Set—oh, no, I am mistaken. Set does not exist any more.'

'But evil does,' I responded, and left the temple.

Thus I stood with the King Akhnaten at the door of the tomb in the Valley of the Kings and prompted him as he recited the litany of offerings to Osiris-Amenhotep. A priest at his right side offered the things as he named them, and passed them to another who piled them in the tomb.

Outside the funeral procession waited, thousands of mourners weeping and crying. There were no colours, no dyed fabrics or rich jewellery. Every person wore a white cloth now stained with mud and ash. Their hair was loose and tangled, as was mine and the King's. Four sacrificial oxen lowed their displeasure, children cried and the chorus never ceased of women calling for the Osiris-Amenhotep to return. They wailed:

Come to thy house, thy lovers, thy sisters.

Overhead, no good birds flew, but the birds of ill-omen, the vulture and the crow. The vulture was the Goddess Renenet once, before Aten had come upon us. Now she was just a carrion-eating bird. On consideration, I liked the goddess better. Akhnaten had almost conquered his loathing for the ceremony, overruled by his fear of his mother. He recited:

This libation is for thee, I have brought thee before the eye of Horus, that thy heart may be refreshed thereby. I have brought it unto thee so that no thirst may torment thee.

Queen Tiye was at the door of the tomb, linked with her daughters and the Priestess of Isis Mutnodjme; and Queen Tiye never took her eyes off her son for the whole long, long recital. Her obedient son, Akhnaten, who implored:

Open thy mouth, Osiris-Amenhotep. I cleanse thee, I cleanse thee, the fluid of life shall not be destroyed in thee.

He presented milk in a clay vessel.

Here is the nipple of the breast of thy sister Isis; milk of thy mother has found thy mouth.

The other Sem-priest, an ugly youth, took the vessel and put it on the sarcophagus; and my lord Akhnaten, presenting two iron instruments to the south and the north, continued:

Osiris-Amenhotep, the two gods have opened thy mouth.

He was doing quite well. I remembered what my master Annmemmes had said about fear being a bad teacher, but clearly it had done wonders for my lord's powers of concentration.

Day hath made an offering for thee in the sky, and the south and the north have caused an offering to have been made. Night hath made an offering to thee, and south and north have caused an offering to be made. An offering hath been made to thee, thou seest the offering, thou hear'st it. The King giveth an offering to the ka of Osiris-Amenhotep.

He repeated this four times. He then began the long—and mostly jumbled and nonsensical—ritual involving cheeses, cakes, beer and perfumes, which seem to some scholars to relate to plays on words whose original meanings are forgotten.

My mind wandered. I had already mourned for the death of the wise old king, and for the future I felt nothing but unease. I did not like the way the rule of my lord Akhnaten was going. His edicts, for a start, had caused the death of an innocent old man, harmless and learned Snefru, who loved his scrolls and hoarded writings as much as any father loved his children. I was keeping my place in the *Recension* with one finger, and was amazed to find that my tears were blotting the ink. I hastily wiped my face. It was probably not for Osiris-Amenhotep that I was weeping.

Chapter Fourteen

Mutnodjme

We wept ourselves out. The Queen was led wailing from the door of the tomb and the priests sealed it with the great clay seals of the City of the Houses of Eternity, and we left Osiris-Amenhotep to the silence and his interviews with the various doorkeepers in the Tuat.

'He was a good man and a good king and he will dwell with Osiris forever,' said the Princess Sitamen to her mother, 'Will you come, Mother, and live with me? Thebes is being deserted by the royal court and there are beggars in the streets. Now that the temple has been closed there will be no one to care for the poor. The priests of Amen-Re are dispersed.'

'You are my daughter and I love you, but I will go where I might still be of some use,' said Tiye the Queen, so softly that the tall princess had to bend to hear her.

'So far the temples of Isis have not been attacked, daughter,' the Queen said to me. 'But I do not know how long their immunity may last. Sitamen will go back to her estates, which are hers in her own right and cannot be removed. She may visit us, perhaps, if you will come with me and my widow-daughter Merope? We leave in twenty days.'

'Where are you going?' I asked, though I knew the answer.

'To the City of the Sun,' said the Queen with great determination. 'To save what can be saved.'

So it was settled. I officiated at the secret funeral of the old man Snefru, cried for him and saw his tomb sealed. The new edict was making the city nervous. It was rumoured that all worship was to be forbidden except that of the Aten; and people were burying even their little household gods, the pottery statues of the fanged dwarf Bes who assists in childbirth, and the little images of Amen-Re as a ram or Osiris as a bull.

At the end of twenty days I gathered my texts and my robes, packed up in oilcloth and buried what I could not carry with me, and left the temple where I had been happy for many years. The Singer of Isis, Lady of her own kingdom, escorted me to the great door.

'Be of good cheer about us, daughter, we have places to go and things to do, and we are not without resource,' she said.

Duammerset had died a year before, and this Lady of Isis was young. Her name was Peri, and she had a sweetness of character. A childhood accident had burned one side of her face, and her parents had abandoned her on the temple steps, hoping Isis might heal her. Isis had not removed the scar, but she had accepted Peri as her most intelligent and devoted priestess, a natural successor to the old woman. Some even whispered that she was Duammerset come again; that her spirit had passed from one body to the other. Certainly she had a lot of the old woman's mannerisms, including a low, soft voice full of authority.

'But what will you do if your worship is forbidden?' I asked.

She smiled—it was certainly Duammerset's smile, a cool, calculating turn of the mouth. 'Better that you should not know. Now, do not forget what you have learned of us, daughter Mutnodjme. Even if humans forget Isis, she will not forget us. Farewell,' she said, and kissed me, and I went with my bundle down the steps of the temple and into the street.

I had abandoned my robes, and felt naked. I was wearing just what every woman in Thebes was wearing, a white cloth and a delicate square of fabric covering my breasts, and I bore my bundle on my shoulder as women do. But voices fell as I walked into a market, and I heard hisses behind me, saying, 'The woman of Isis, there is no Isis, there is no god!' and I had to exercise considerable self control not to run. I reminded myself that I was still a priestess of a very strong-minded deity who did not care whether people believed in her or not, and picked up my pace unobtrusively.

There were soldiers at the palace gates. There had never been soldiers there before. They were well armed with spear, sword and shield, and they wore the Pharaoh's red plumes, his personal guard. They crossed spears before me and opposed my entry.

'I am Mutnodjme, sister to the Great Royal Spouse Nefertiti, let me through,' I said into their unmoving faces. They looked like statues, not men, and they did not react. I was wondering what to do—kick one in the shin, perhaps, to test whether he was stone or flesh?—when I was relieved of the burden of decision.

'Let the lady in,' said a quiet voice, and the statues snapped to attention, unbarring the way.

It was the slim and decorative Great Royal Scribe Ptah-hotep. His hair was still dressed in the Nubian fashion, threaded with gold and mirrors. He was older. There were crow's feet at the corners of his eyes and a permanent double line between his brows; evidence of bad temper, perhaps, or overstrained sight. He did not seem to be bad tempered. Instead he seemed gentle and rather sad, as he had always seemed. But he was taken aback at the sight of me.

'Lady Mutnodjme,' he began, bending lower than a Great Royal Scribe need bow. 'It has been ten years since I last saw you, and time has been very kind to you.'

'You saw me at the funeral of Osiris-Amenhotep, though you did not look at me,' I replied. 'I was Isis.'

'Lady, that name is not to be said aloud,' he took my hand and led me to the palace, where more soldiers waited at the inner door.

'Why do we need a guard?' I asked, and then fell silent, responding to the hushing gesture which he made, very quickly, with one hand.

I did not speak again until he had taken me through the palace to the apartments of the Widow-Queen Tiye. She was not there but a number of harried looking slaves were rolling tapestries, packing wine vessels into baskets and folding cloths.

'You may pay your respects later,' said Ptah-hotep. 'Will you come to my humble quarters and drink a cup of wine with me?'

'Certainly,' I replied. His eyes were begging me to agree, though I could not see him being overcome with either love or lust. 'That would be very welcome.'

We were clearly conversing for the benefit of listeners and I found a safe topic.

'Tell me the health of my sister and her children,' I asked.

Ptah-hotep replied, 'There are now six daughters of the Lord Akhnaten may he live! They are called Mekhetaten, she is the eldest daughter, then Meritaten, Ankhesenpaaten, Nefernefer-aten-tashery—little Nefertiti. Then there is Neferneferure, and the baby is Septenre. She is sickly and your sister is very worried about her. My lord intends to take the little princess Mekhetaten to be Great Royal Wife as soon as she is old enough—she is only ten, but a beautiful little maiden.'

I wondered privately who was going to take over the task of providing children for the eunuch King, but if Isis was not an acceptable subject of conversation then the king's impotence certainly would not be.

Ptah-hotep continued to tell me stories of the beauties and charming ways of the children of my sister until we reached a fine door. This had no soldiers, but when Ptah-hotep pushed it open disclosed two very large Nubians and a huge dog standing solidly in the way.

Anubis walked over to me, inhaled my scent and lost interest. I was not an enemy. Tani and Hani grinned and said, 'Here is the little princess who rides Nubians,' and I was touched and sat down as my eyes filled with tears. Meryt the Nubian with the rounded contours of the well-fed and well-treated brought me a cup of wine. Three scribes looked up and then looked down again. Ptah-hotep led me into the inner apartment and closed the door and we heard the creak as one of the twins leaned his back against it in a casual fashion.

'We meet again,' said Ptah-hotep, sitting down in a throne-like chair and bidding me take the other.

'So we do, and we are all bound for the same place.'

'You accompany the Queen to Amarna? I hoped it might be so, lady.'

'Why did you hope so?' I asked suspiciously.

'Why, so that I might profit by your conversation, though not too often or too secretly. The palace is full of eyes and none of them are the Eyes of Horus.'

'Or the ears of Khnum?' I matched his reference with another.

'No,' he agreed.

'The School of Scribes is closed, the master is banished and you, my lord, are deep in whatever plots the King is concocting,' I said angrily, for I had lost a friend in the scribe Snefru and the cult of the Aten looked likely to eat all Egypt.

'Not deep enough, it seems, for I knew of no order to close the School of Scribes. If I had not gone there purely by chance, the master would have gone and I would not even have said farewell to him or given him any gold for his sustenance.'

'Snefru is dead,' I told him.

'I know,' he said sadly.

'Well, what are you going to do about all this?' I demanded.

'What can I do? Temper the King Akhnaten as much as I can, put reins on the power and pride of his officials, that is all I can do.'

'There must be more than that,' I said. He stretched out both hands to me and said, 'Tell me what more, and I will do it.'

'I do not know,' I said, and he sighed. 'I do not know, yet,' I added. 'Let me look at the situation and listen and learn. When we reach Amarna, can you get me quarters separate from my mother and my sister?'

'Only if you marry someone,' he said. 'But I had thought of another solution.'

'The Great Royal Wife Merope will have her own establishment; I will stay with her,' I said.

'And you will speak with me again?' he asked, not wanting to pressure me but greatly desiring my company. It had been a long time since I had been wooed, and it felt very pleasant.

'Indeed I will,' I said, and drank some more wine. His eyes were beautiful, brown and deep, like the eyes of my sister Merope whom I loved.

'How is your household, Lord?' I asked, belatedly.

'My wife died two years ago,' he said. 'We had no children. Since then I have taken no other woman; my Lord Akhnaten approves of my piety in the Aten, which is immortal and unknowable.'

'I never met your wife,' I said.

'She was a daughter of a connection of Divine Father Ay. A pleasant girl, not very interested in great matters, and Meryt liked her.'

I hoped that if I ever married, my husband would have a more impressive epitaph for me. I remembered something and delved into the band I wore around my waist to find it. I had to grope for the package, because it had worked its way around behind my hip, and the Great Royal Scribe showed no embarrassment and no curiosity as to why I was disrobing in his presence.

'You are very beautiful,' he commented dispassionately.

'Thank you, but I am not trying to display my erotic charms, but to find ah, there is the letter.'

I found the elusive packet and began to replace my garments, when suddenly he seized me and pressed me close. His mouth was on mine. It was so unexpected that I did not resist. His fingers pinched my nipple. Unexpectedly, I found that my body, which had been so unenthusiastic with other lovers, was reacting with zeal and I kissed him back in earnest. His back was muscular under my caressing hands. We shed the remnants of clothing and slid together to the floor… where my swimming eyes beheld a pair of jewelled sandals, and I looked up along the length of thin shanks, fat thighs, swollen belly to the amused face of the Pharaoh Akhnaten may he live and I felt myself blush purple.

Ptah-hotep released me and we prostrated ourselves in a 'kiss earth' which allowed me to hide my burning face.

'Lady Mutnodjme, Ptah-hotep,' said the King in an indulgent tone. 'I was told that you were secret together and came to find out what you were talking about—and I see that my informants were mistaken about the subject of conversation.'

I was quite naked but Priestesses of Isis have never been disconcerted by nakedness. Was not our lady Isis naked? At his signal I stood up and looked the King in the face. My garments were in a crumpled mess on the floor and under them was the packet which I had been carrying.

'Lord Akhnaten, Favourite of Aten, Only One of the Great God, Master of the Two Thrones, Mutnodjme, the humble and unworthy sister of the Great Royal Wife gives respectful greetings to the Most High Pharaoh, and hopes for his favourable attention,' I said in the most formal mode of address.

'Lady Mutnodjme, sister of Nefertiti Neferuaten Great Royal Wife and Priestess of the Phoenix is high in the regard of the Lord of the Two Lands and he welcomes her to his palace,' replied the Pharaoh, his strange eyes warm with some emotion.

'And he rejoices that she is loved by the Great Royal Scribe Ptah-hotep; the Pharaoh has been concerned for his scribe's grief since his wife died, and delights in the delight of his faithful servant.'

At the term 'faithful servant,' the Pharaoh cast a sharp look at the thin man standing behind him. He wore an overdecorated bag-wig and far too much perfume. He seemed consumed with chagrin, biting his pale lips and twisting his ringed hands together.

'So, Pannefer, you were wrong,' said the Pharaoh. 'This is innocent and charming. Neither party is married and I expect that they will reach some arrangement. Nefertiti will rejoice that her sister has come to her, and that love has brought the adherent of a false cult to reason. Ptah-hotep, do you love the lady Mutnodjme?'

'Lord, thou knowst the secrets of all hearts,' replied the Great Royal Scribe. He also was naked, and he was very well-made. Living mostly with women I had not tired of the sight of male flesh, and he was finely and sparely handsome.

'Lady, do you love the lord Ptah-hotep?'

'As you see, Lord,' I said, matching my lord Ptah-hotep for obscurity.

'Then I give you each other,' said Akhnaten, joined our hands, and left, taking Master of the House Pannefer and the soldiers with him.

As soon as the entourage had gone, Ptah-hotep hugged me to his breast and said, 'Oh, most quick-witted of women!' and I began to laugh and couldn't stop until the slave Meryt, ruler of the household, bought me a cup of undiluted wine.

'Master, he just walked straight in, and I didn't even have time to warn you,' she said in an undertone to Ptah-hotep.

'It's all right, Meryt, not your fault. Pannefer is clearly watching me even closer than I thought. Now, some more wine for the lady and you can leave us.'

Then they all went away again, and I said to Ptah-hotep, 'Perhaps we should lie down, in case we are still being watched, and then you can explain.'

He led me by the hand to his bed in the inner apartment. A woman had arranged the room, it was clear. There were lamps in the form of lotus flowers and a statue of an ibis. The walls were painted with scenes of fishing and fowling and were old fashioned but charming.

We lay down together on the big bed and I pillowed my head on his bare smooth chest. I have never felt comfortable lying with a man—except this one. I fitted into his embrace; there was none of the preliminary shoving as one worked out what to do with arm and elbow and knee. He seemed to feel the same sense of rightness, for he stroked my cheek gently with his free hand.

'Lady, I have importuned you, put you into a false position, and by nightfall it will be all over the palace. Everyone will know that you are my lover. I apologise as profoundly as I can,' he began hesitantly.

'Lord, I have no particular objection to being known as your lover, I need an excuse to see you and be private with you, and you need not apologise,' I replied.

He smelt lovely, of cinnamon oil, his own skin and the scribes' scents of papyrus, sand and ink. 'In fact the apology is due to you, because I have clearly endangered you by bringing a letter from Ammemmes into this exceptionally spy-ridden palace. I thought the Temple of Isis was gossipy,' I said heatedly. 'How long has the palace been like this?'

'Ah, lady, a long time,' he sighed. He sounded so weary that I moved, taking his head onto my breast, and he snuggled down into my embrace as though he had been lying with me for years.

'It was kept in check while Osiris-Amenhotep was alive, that wise old man. He spoke to his son, saying that he was surrounding himself with sycophants and that he needed at least one counsellor who would tell him the truth, but my lord just looked at his father with those vague eyes. You see, he is convinced that there is no god but Aten, and when that was his own religion and no pain to any other, it was no trouble. But now he is so petted and encouraged by Pannefer and Huy and the others that he is intending to impose this Aten on all of Egypt. There is no god but the One, he says. There shall be no god but the One.'

'So he has closed the temples of Amen-Re,' I said. 'And the others, as well? Are all the gods to be abandoned? What, then, will happen to the people?'

'I do not know,' he sighed. I stroked his shoulder and cheek and he nestled closer to me, twining his legs with mine.

We did not speak for a while, and I wondered if he had fallen asleep. His skin was in contact with my skin the length of my body, and his free hand cupped my breast. I was so aroused that I would have opened to him if he had made any advance at all, but he did not and I reflected that it was not fitting that I should turn a political ruse to my own pleasure.

'It was the fate of Khons which settled my mind,' he said unexpectedly, so that I jumped. I had not seen Teacher Khons since I had gone to the temple of Isis and he had been appointed tutor to the royal children. The last I had heard of him he was attached to my sister's household as teacher to her daughters.

'What happened to Teacher Khons?' I asked in a whisper.

'You remember Khons, the questioner? The Lord Akhnaten came in one morning when he was instructing the little princesses in the names of the states of Egypt—each Nome had its god, and he was saying something like, 'Nome of Hermopolis, symbol the frog, god Khnum the potter,'—you probably learned the lists the same way, lady.'

'Yes, I did.' I could hear Khons' deep voice saying them and Merope and I repeating the list. I had a sudden flash of lying on the cool floor on a reed mat with my sister beside me, Basht the striped-one sitting with her front paws on Merope's prepubescent breast, and the prospect of honey-cake if we recited the Nomes without fault.

'The King said, "There is no god but the Aten" and Khons argued with him. No, he didn't even argue, poor Khons; he just said "In the old days, Lord, each Nome had its god and it is still easier to remember them thus." And the King flew into a rage, screamed that Khons was perverting the minds of the divine princesses. Instead of pacifying him, Khons continued. He told the King that Egypt's history was made under the old gods, and they were worthy to be studied regardless of the advent of the Aten. So the King gave an order and the guard—you notice that he always has a guard?—speared Khons as he sat on the floor with the children; and he died.

'I was summoned by the King to see what fate came to a scribe who questioned the primacy of the Aten. Khons was dead by then, lying on the tiles with a spear through his neck and blood spilled around him; and in the middle one terrified little girl and a scatter of building blocks and toys. You know how the mind fixes on one small thing which exemplifies the scene forever after. To me, the picture of Khons' death is a pull-along painted clay horse in a pool of bright red blood.'

'By all the gods, 'Hotep, is he mad?' I asked, horrified by the picture I too could see now of Khons lying dead on the tiled floor, blood pooling around the little princess and her toys.

'Oh yes,' he whispered into my shoulder. 'He is quite mad.'

Ptah-hotep

Lady Mutnodjme was a surprise. I had not seen her for years. When she had left for the temple of Isis, she had been a small dark child with bright eyes, her breasts not yet budded, weeping a little at the loss of her sister Merope—though the Great Royal Wife visited the temple at least every week, or so Pannefer told the King. But as her sorrow at leaving her home I sensed in her measureless appetite for learning, matching even my old friend Snefru.

And when I saw her again at the palace gates, contemplating the guard—and I am sure that I got to her just in time to prevent an incident, for she never lacked courage—she was still small, no taller than Kheperren, but a woman in truth, tending to plumpness (which is very unfashionable but very attractive) and clever-handed, deft, and still with that quickness of thought which had made her remarkable as a child. She had brought me Kheperren's last message, sent through Ammemmes, and she had melted into my embrace when I kissed her, sighting the Pharaoh's soldier's boots under the door and knowing that we had to conceal the reason for our meeting.

She had handled the interview with the lord Akhnaten with promptitude and confidence, and I was very impressed with her.

My wife Hathor, called Hunero, had been a pleasant maiden, only interested in the doings of the other women in the office, Khety's wife and Hanufer's concubine. She had occupied her days in a companionable feud with Bakhenmut's wife Henutmire. They each required more and more jewels of their respective husbands, and I reached an agreement with Bakhenmut that I should provide new trinkets for both, so that he was not driven to peculation or theft to supply Henutmire's greed. Hunero had been fourteen when I married her out of her father's house, and she had seemed happy with me. All my love was still given to my dearest Kheperren, who managed a visit to the capital at least once a year. But Hunero seemed content with what I could give her and the skills which Meryt had taught me had pleased her body. She had conceived twice, both children being miscarried before they were well-formed, and then the fever which had ravaged the City of the Sun had taken her away.

Now the rooms where she had lived seemed empty and cold, and I had closed off that part of my apartments.

But the woman who lay down with me and listened without exclamation to the death of Khons, she was a different matter from the meek little mouse who had been sold to me by a connection of Divine Father Ay's whether she would or no. Once Priestess of the dissolved cult of the so-called goddess Isis, the Lady Mutnodjme was strong willed and strong minded and meat for no man's bargain. Her arms were strong and her breast very soft and I rested my aching head in her embrace without fear. It was only when I woke from a light doze, which I had not meant to take, and found that she was still there, holding me gently without any sign of impatience, that I realised how badly I had missed a friend and how beautiful she was.

I had been afraid—not terrified, but afraid, watching every expression on every face, tasting every drop and nibbling every crumb and especially examining every word for heresy before I allowed it to leave my lips, for so long now that I only realised the extent of the strain when it relaxed.

The Lady left me with an ostentatious kiss in front of the whole staff, promising to come again, and I gave orders that she should always be admitted whenever she wanted.

Khety, very happy in his wife and four sons, smiled at me. Hanufer, as stolidly pleased with his three children as he had been with his faithful and unimaginative wife, nodded. Bakhenmut, cursed with Henutmire's greed and shrill nagging, raised an eyebrow as if asking me was I sure that I wanted to do this again, having escaped unscathed last time? Meryt and the Nubians grinned. Meryt had liked Mutnodjme since childhood, and Hani still talked about being ridden, for this had given the three men an acquaintance with General Horemheb, now famous for his courage and strategic skill. They always went out to meet the General when he returned to report to the palace, and joined in the athletic contests—and the feasts—which the soldiers conducted. Mentu, who was visiting us because he had broken an arm in a chariot accident, clapped me on the back.

'Well-chosen,' Mentu said. 'A close relative of the Divine Royal Spouse and therefore unassailable; another guard for your back, my dear Ptah-hotep.'

'Also, she is very beautiful,' I reminded him. He grinned.

'There is that, also. Though you should come and see my new dancers. Blonde, I swear, not bleached, and they dance with bells on their feet.'

'Perhaps later. Khety, we are supposed to get copies of all the orders issued from the Master of the Household's office. Do we have the order which closed the school of scribes?'

'No, Lord,' Khety searched through a huge pile of documents. 'The tax returns have come in from all of the Nomes, there is a difficulty with some walls and bridges which need to be repaired, a woman gave birth to a goat in one village…no, nothing from the Master of the Household's office at all.'

'Mentu, take my compliments to my lord Pannefer and inform him that you are there with Hani and Tani. They are to carry back all the copies of the orders which he has issued and forgotten to send to me—doubtless through pressure of business. Can you do it without getting anyone executed?'

'Certainly,' Mentu assured me. Sending Mentu was, of course, an insult to the commoner which Pannefer had been. Mentu, however dissolute, had been schooled from babyhood in the subtle nuances of rank, which Pannefer did not understand at all. I was just as common as he—my father had been a village scribe and so had his—but I had applied myself to learn how my new society worked. By his false accusation of me, Pannefer had massively lost face with the Lord Akhnaten may he live and would have to comply with my request. Mentu would make sure, without words, that Pannefer knew that I knew this.

Thus I played the game of tit for tat, while the teachers from the temple were driven away and the Father of the Two Lands thought only of his god.

Chapter Fifteen

Mutnodjme

The first thing my sister said, as I walked into the royal apartments past the ubiquitous guards, was 'Oh, Mutnodjme, my heart is glad for you! Ptah-hotep will make you a fine husband!'

'I am still thinking about it,' I replied. Even after years in the temple of Isis I was not used to the speed at which gossip travelled. 'How do you fare, my dearest sister?'

She had aged. She was breath-catchingly beautiful still, perhaps more so, since with age had come dignity and queenly self-possession. Her long neck was unmarked, her profile perfect, and her breasts despite six children still as firm as a maiden's.

She lifted the last child from her knee and said to it, 'See, little princess, here is your aunt!' and I had to kneel and coo over the baby Septenre. I have never liked babies—which is strange, because I have seldom been bitten by any animal and I even handled snakes in one ordeal with the Lady whom I must no longer name—but human young look unformed, furless and puddingy. The baby gaped at me with a toothless grin which was almost charming, and then was obligingly sick, so that her mother gave her to her nurse and slaves mopped the Queen and replaced her cloth.

I wanted my sister to herself.

'I am coming with you to Amarna,' I told Nefertiti.

'Of course, my lord has closed the temple,' said my sister tactlessly.

'No, I am in...' I was about to say 'love' but my sense of truth revolted; and so I said, 'two minds about the Great Royal Scribe. Also my friend Merope is going as part of the establishment of Lord Akhnaten may he live.'

'Oh, yes, the wives of the Osiris-Amenhotep; no, I mean the dead King,' she corrected herself. 'Things are so much simpler now that there is only one god,' she said, accepting a cup of light beer from a slave. 'Except that I sometimes forget.'

'Nefertiti, sister, has your lord told you of the changes which are taking place in the Black Land?' I asked, knowing that every word was going to be reported to one spy or another and choosing my speech with extreme care. Nefertiti put down the cup and took both my hands.

'Yes, it's a miracle,' she said solemnly. 'It's a revelation. My lord has seen the land all under one god, one worship, one truth. He is the high priest of the Aten, may it be forever adored.'

'And you?'

'I am the High Priestess of the Phoenix, the Star-bird, the Fire-wing.'

Her face shone. She was so transfigured by her devotion to this cult that I knew that I would waste my breath attempting to convert her to anything approaching sense.

'You shall come with me,' she whispered, conferring a great favour. 'You shall see the temple of the firebird, the columns of marble, the carvings in stone, the paintings in fresh colours. We leave for Amarna tomorrow. You will stay with me? I shall order a room prepared.'

'No, sister, I thank you, but I have already agreed to lodge with the Widow-Queen Merope.'

'And that is near the apartments of the Great Royal Scribe,' she patted my cheek with her elegant fingers. 'Sly sister, wanting to be near your lover! Tell me, is he as skilled as the lady Hunero used to say? Does he make you faint with delight?'

'He is all they say,' I said warily. This was an aspect of Ptah-hotep which I had not considered. 'What of you, sister? Your children, are they healthy?'

'They are. My lord Akhnaten may he live has taken them for a walk to the Window of Appearances in the Temple of the Aten, or I would introduce you now. But there will be time. Travel with me tomorrow, sister, bring the lady Merope with you. I have not seen you for years. You have grown beautiful,' she said, untruthfully.

'And Divine Nurse Tey, my mother, she lives?' I asked.

'She is well and awaits us in the City of the Sun. I must go to my lord now, sister, the sun is setting and we have evening offerings. And here is Sahte, come looking for you, I'll guarantee. The slave will take your bundle to the Widow-Queen's quarters and I will see you tomorrow.'

Thus dismissed, I accompanied Sahte to the rooms of Queen Tiye, where I also found my sister Merope. They both smiled at me and congratulated me on my choice of lover, Tiye adding something extremely rustic on the subject of phalluses and the goddess Isis.

'Lady, live forever, and if you wish to continue to live, you must not mention the name of any other god but the Aten,' I said, sitting down and hauling Merope into a close embrace. I had missed her and she always felt good in my arms.

'Ah,' said the Queen Tiye. She wrapped a tress of greying red hair around her plump hand and asked 'My Royal Son's religion has a firm grip on him?'

'And on his officials. Pannefer the Master of the Household and Huy the Chamberlain are both fervent believers in the Aten, or at least in their own power and position.'

'Such is always the case in weak rulers,' said Tiye, far too clearly for my newly-discovered sense of peril.

'And the walls have eyes and ears,' I added.

'Doubtless,' agreed the old queen, not moderating her tone in the slightest.

'If it would please you, I would like to lodge with you when we reach Amarna, and the Widow-Queen Merope and I are ordered to join my sister tomorrow in the royal barge,' I told her.

'That is acceptable,' said the lady Tiye. She was still mourning. Pain was on her countenance like a tight grey veil. Merope helped me to my feet and led me into the outer chamber, where more slaves were binding the last bundles of belongings.

'Are we not taking the lamp?' I asked. It was a fine alabaster one, carved in the shape of Sekmet, the lion-headed woman.

'No objects with other gods on them may be taken into the City of the Sun, we have received orders,' Merope said quietly. 'Apparently we will have much more splendid rooms in the new palace. Come, sister, let us eat and then let us sleep, for I am very weary and confused.'

I listened as she ordered a servant to fetch us a light supper, ate most of it for I was hungry, and we lay down together. I dreamed—strangely, not of fear or danger—of Isis descending on the phallus of Osiris, and woke shivering and wet with desire. I slaked it in the arms and breasts and sweet mouth of my sister Merope, but it was Ptah-hotep who had awakened it.

◇ ◇ ◇

It is sweet to sail on the bosom of the Nile and watch the cultivation slip past, hear the voices of the boatmen and the bleating of goats on shore. Priestesses of the unnamed lady travel sparely and eat lightly, and the last time I had taken to the water I had been on the way to attend a fever in a distant village and had travelled in a fishing boat made of reeds, which had leaked and wallowed and threatened every moment to throw us to the crocodiles.

I was now seated in the boat *Aten Gleams* with my sister Merope. Little Ankhesenpaaten was lounging on my lap. With the usual perversity of children, she had divined how I felt about small humans and had decided that I was the one she would favour with her royal attention today. She was solid and heavy and would not sit still, so my thighs were being gradually flattened. I could feel every knothole in the wooden bench I was sitting on.

'I like you,' announced the small princess, unexpectedly. She was entirely naked except for the strings of beads and her earrings, which were evidently a source of great pride to her.

'Thank you, Great Royal Lady,' I replied cautiously.

'You're comfortable,' she explained, digging her elbows into my side as she wreathed her arms around my neck.

'I am honoured,' I said, lifting her a little to free my breast from her knee.

'My father is the Royal One of Amarna, Akhnaten may he live,' said the little princess. 'And if you aren't nice to me, he'll order his soldiers to spear you.'

'I see,' I replied evenly, concealing my shock at such a cool pronouncement.

'Like he did to Teacher Khons. He was making me learn a long list. I didn't like him and the Pharaoh may he live killed him for me.'

'Ah,' I choked down rage, which boiled up in my throat as bile. My dear Khons, he of the ready grin, dead on a mad King's whim and here was this barbarous child threatening me with the same fate. There was a lot of water very near; I had already seen several crocodiles, and one swift movement would drop this royal monster into a fanged maw which would end her presumption in one bite, snap, wrench and swallow.

Ankhesenpaaten might not have been civilised, but she was perceptive enough when it came to her own safety. She climbed promptly off my lap and went to her mother, not saying a word more, and I stared out over the water while Merope my sister whispered, 'Consider how it must have been for her, her tutor slaughtered! She had to invent something to explain it. Do not blame her, sister, she is only a child.'

This was true but not helpful. If I could not blame the little princess I could certainly blame the Royal One. And I did—vengefully and darkly—watching the fronded vegetation, the Nile blue and Nile white waves, the palm trees and the farmers, and a naked boy washing a horse in the river, all with a gaze Merope that said was ferocious enough to wither barley.

'We must present a pleasant appearance,' she whispered to me, burying her face in my neck. 'They will suspect you of belonging to the goddess we cannot name; and they suspect me of being associated with the old king—as I was, and I miss him so much! And our lady the Widow-Queen is not, I fear, going to temper her opinions, and that may get us all killed as dead as poor Khons.'

'All right, Merope; yes, you are correct,' I said softly into her nut-brown hair. 'We should talk to my sister. How long has she been a fanatic?'

'Oh, years,' said Merope. 'I've got used to it, you know, it's only now that you are back that it seems strange. Ask her to tell you about the children, it's all she's interested in; that and the cult of the Phoenix, of course. And you'll be taken all around the temple.'

'What about my father, Ay?'

'Ah,' Merope's expression said it all. Clearly Ay was as mean as ever and must, I assumed, be the richest man in Egypt by now. 'He is High Priest of the cult of Aten in Amarna,' Merope told me.

'Is she,' I commented as tonelessly as I could. I had not seen Divine Father Ay for seven years, and on the whole, they had been happy. On the last occasion, he had given me a long, cold, appraising look, growled, 'Too old for marriage now' with a certain complacency, and had gone away to spend more time with his treasure. I could not think of anyone less-fitted for a religious office than my father. I diverted my thoughts by imagining short fat Father Ay in a priest's leopard skin—the tail would certainly drag on the ground, and perhaps he would trip on it.

'He has expressed his joy to the lord Akhnaten at seeing you, his daughter, again,' said Nefertiti, who had been listening.

'My father said that?' I was instantly suspicious. The only reason that Father Ay could have for wanting to see me again was that he had some gold-producing scheme and he intended to use me in some way. I was never, unlike some maidens, under any false impression that my father cared for me.

'Yes, I told him that if I could persuade you to come with me, sister, I could induct you into the worship of the Phoenix.'

'For which privilege he is paid some fee?' I hazarded. I was on safe ground, for Nefertiti may she live was nodding.

'Certainly; for you are dedicated to the temple, and your father must be paid the equivalent of a dowry.'

'I see,' I relaxed. In the confusion of a new worship, at the head of a new cult, living in a new city, it was comforting that at least Father Ay had not changed. 'Tell me about this dedica-tion, lady and sister.'

'Not here,' said Nefertiti, shocked. 'It is a mystery.'

In the temple of Isis, whence my thought instantly flashed, I recalled Duammerset, the Lady's Singer, instructing a group of young women: *If anyone tells you that they cannot explain their actions because it is a mystery, then you know you are in the pres-ence of woolly thinking.*

I had a feeling that belief in the Amarna cults might require enough woolly thinking to denude whole flocks of sheep.

But I remembered Khons, and kept my tongue safely between my teeth.

Ptah-hotep

We shipped all our furniture and I sailed with the King Akhnaten and his officials, leaving my four Nubians to care for my goods and my scribes. Bakhenmut's family were loaded last because his lady was prone to sea-sickness, and then she complained bit-terly that she must ride in the same barge as Meryt and her clan; between them and their wives, my slaves had seven children, and they were admittedly noisy and prone to romp. Bakhnemut's children immediately joined the Nubians in a spitting contest, to their mother's loudly-expressed disgust.

'My lord Ptah-hotep may you live,' Huy greeted me with his oily smile. 'I trust that your burgeoning Nubian family is comfortable?' This was a hit at my well-known addiction to black women and suggested that all of the Nubian children were actually mine.

'Indeed, I thank the Great Royal Chamberlain for his condescension. His own household is suitably bestowed on soft cushions?' This was a moderately nasty response, because although Huy had three wives and several concubines, he had no children, and general gossip suggested that this was because of his insistence on anal intercourse.

'Indeed,' he replied. Honours, it seemed, were about even.

'My lord Akhnaten Lord of the Horizon may he live looks well?'

'As the Divine One of Amarna always does,' I agreed.

In fact, the King looked flabby, sunburned and sick. Travel by water did not agree with the Lord Akhnaten may he live and his indulgence in the sacramental wine of the Aten, drunk always at midday, had not improved his digestion. Two servants stood by the Divine One of Aten to make sure he did not fall as he waved to the assembled people on the bank at Thebes. They then seated him in his throne under the embroidered canopy. I noticed a discreet pot, beside one royal foot, in case the royal stomach should prove to be overtaxed by the motion of the water.

But the river was running gently. At this season it should have been strong. Inundation this year had been low, the inner canals had not filled and fully a quarter of the cultivation could only be watered by the use of a shaduf, a sling arrangement with a leather bag on the end, used to raise water up and over a bank. The whole population would need to be employed in keeping the crops wet or the yield for the tax inspectors would be low. And who then would pay for my lord's new city?

I saw the lady Mutnodjme in the Queen may she live's barge, *Aten Gleams*. She was glaring at the river bank as though wishing to put a curse on the whole stretch of the Nile, and I did not want to attract her attention. I did not think that she would be able to play at being lovers while she was in such a mood, and I wondered what she had been told. I had never had any difficulty understanding my wife or Meryt, but the lady Mutnodjme was a puzzle which might easily prove engrossing.

'So, my lord, do you marry?' asked Chamberlain Huy, following my glance.

'The lady has not answered me yet,' I replied honestly.

'Surely you do not need her answer. Send a load of treasure to her father and you will have her,' said Huy, who was very jealous of Divine Father Ay. I shared his opinion that Ay was a timeserving unreliable miser who would sell his own grandmother for crocodile meat to the temple of Sobek (if he still existed) but I saw no reason to tell Huy that. The less that any of them knew about me, the better, and the more I could keep them guessing about each other the less they would enquire into my real secrets.

'I will have her own will in this, not her father's,' I said, again with honesty. I thought that I had felt a fervent response in the lady Mutnodjme but I did not know and I have never forced anyone. Huy grunted. Meryt said that Huy chose very young maidens, insisted on virginity, a strange taste, and liked hurting them, requiring their blood. I felt a great distaste for his company. He knew this instinctively; he who had earned a living previously selling asses in the market-place had an intuitive understanding of the buyer. He hated me for it. But there was nothing that he could do but say to Pannefer, 'Look! We are rounding the island. Soon we shall see the City of the Sun in all its glory.'

The city was, in fact, a long day's sail away but it meant that Huy was bestowing his conversational gifts on someone else and I had leisure to eat some bread sprinkled with sesame-seed and think of the last time I had seen Kheperren.

He had come to me in extreme secrecy in Thebes, and although he was older, weatherbeaten, and had a new scar, I thought him surpassingly beautiful above all the sons of men. The point of a spear had torn his forehead and scalp, so that his dark brown hair was white along the length of it. I accused him of dyeing it.

'No need, soon the rest of the hair will match,' he had said, laughing, but there were new lines around his eyes and he was worried. We had made love but he had been distracted.

'Tell me,' I had begged, and in the darkness, guarded by all of my slaves, he had told me that the borders were unstable and that little raids were crossing all the time. So far they had been small and easily beaten off. Tests, General Horemheb thought, to try Egypt's state of readiness. Shasu had come from the desert to steal goats and horses. Warriors of Kush had sacked and burned a little village in Nubia, and Horemheb had followed and captured them, executed the chief and enslaved his people. Khatim, secret and clever, had crossed into Mittani their neighbour and looted a temple, escaping into Egyptian territory, for which they were punished by the local commander and returned to their king in chains.

But this is all in preparation for a major incursion, Horemheb says,' had whispered Kheperren into the darkness.

'Then it will be beaten off as we beat them before,' I said, not understanding.

'No, 'Hotep, it won't; don't you know? The Pharaoh Akhnaten may he live is calling his soldiers into Amarna. There will be no one to guard the borders,' said my dearest friend.

'But that's… Why is he doing that? What great task has he for the army?' I wondered. Kheperren shook his head. I felt him move against my chest.

'I know not, and my general is worried. Perhaps you can find out more.'

'I'll try, I promised the wise old man as much; and I have been reading the foreign correspondence. So far it's mainly begging letters, and I have been sending treasure as requested; the lord Akhnaten is very generous with his treasure. King Tushratta of Mittani has a permanent feud with the king of Khatti, and this is being fostered with presents. If ever Mittani and Khatti settle their differences, we will be in serious trouble. But the King prefers not to bother with letters. He's having a sed festival, you know.'

'A sed festival? To celebrate thirty years' reign? He hasn't reigned long enough for a sed festival, and where are the priests to run it, if he has closed the temple of Amen-Re?' objected

Kheperren, and I put a hand over his mouth before he could name any more forbidden gods.

'A sed festival,' I said firmly. 'He says that he wants to re-establish his reign over all Egypt under the auspices of the Sole and Only Aten. It will be conducted like the other except with the Aten; and the Phoenix, of course, for the Benben bird is the Queen's avatar.'

Kheperren was silent for awhile, and then he kissed me instead of speaking. It was warm and close in my bed and we were agreeably occupied for some time. It was only after we had consummated our love and were lying back, cooled by sweat, that he spoke again.

'Explain this Benben bird cult to me. Where did it come from, and if the King says that there are no gods but the Aten and is willing to kill to prove it, how could there be another object of worship?'

'That I do not know and cannot explain. The worship of the Benben bird is very ancient, in the old temple at Karnak there was a pillar where it was to roost when it returned. It only comes back every one thousand six hundred years or so. When my lord built the Aten temple at Karnak, he ordered a hall of the Phoenix and it is decorated with portraits of the Queen Nefertiti may she live making offerings to the Phoenix. Now in the City of the Sun too there is a temple, a very large one; it occupies the whole of one side of the palace complex. As to what goes on there, Kheperren, I do not know.'

He laid his head down on my shoulder as though he was very tired and said, 'These are strange times, Ptah-hotep, my heart, my brother, but I know one thing; I know that I love you and you love me,' and he fell asleep.

I stayed awake, staring into the darkness. If my lord pulled all his soldiers out of border country, what would stop an invasion from west or east or south? At the beginning of the present 18th Dynasty, Egypt had groaned under the heel of the Hyksos, who had come in chariots and swept an army before them. What was to prevent Mittani or Khatti—who were constantly testing each other because they could only expand into each other's territory when Egypt was strong—from detecting that the guard was elsewhere and crossing the desert in force?

I could see nothing that would stop them but the legend of Egypt's strength. I would continue to send presents, continue to correspond as though I was in a position of power, and see how long I could keep the boundaries intact.

How long, I wondered, with Kheperren snoring gently beside me, could one—one man—keep a kingdom by bluff?

I was recalled to myself by a passing boatman, who hauled on his rudder to pass close by, calling to us to beware of hippopotamus ahead. The sail-boat was past before the King's guard could punish the fisherman for describing the animals as 'creatures of Set' and I envied the man. He could speak his mind, did not have to continually guard his tongue, and his boat was as fast on the water as a running horse on land. It carried him swiftly to safety beyond bowshot. In any case the King Akhnaten was too ill to bother, which was a mercy.

'See your servant Ptah-hotep, my lord!' cried Huy to the King, 'He dreams of sweet delights with the lady Mutnodjme!' And as I was, indeed, dreaming of sweet delights, I smiled in assent. I was glad that I had not known Huy when he sold beasts. He would have sold me a broken-winded hobble-legged old child of an ass, and I would have had to buy it, because he would have known instantly, from my expression, what I was thinking.

'I have made a dedication stone for the sandstone quarry, Lord Akhnaten,' Huy's attention was diverted from me as soon as I had acknowledged his acuity. I am thinking of putting this inscription on it:

Living son of the sun disc Aten father of all Akhnaten said to me his most humble servant, let there be stone for the new city, the city of the sun. I, Huy, made it to be so in the name of the beautiful child of the sun-disc, one without peer, who formed and fostered me! The lord knows which servants are not diligent; such give themselves over to the power of the King may he live, for the taxes of other gods are measured in handfuls, and those of the Aten in cartloads!'

'Huy,' said the King slowly, 'you have said there are other gods.'

Huy paled. 'There is the worship of the divine Phoenix, my lord!' he protested.

Pannefer, who had been subdued, brightened immediately. 'But her worship is also rich beyond price,' he put in.

The king nodded. The guard leapt to their feet. I was about to interpose a word—after all, if one has two enemies, it is better to have them in plain view and at each other's throats; and it would not have suited me to have either Huy or Pannefer on their own as King's sole counsellor—when the King Akhnaten said, 'But it is time for evening worship. I like your inscription, Huy, just omit the heretical reference.'

'*Hail to thee, most beautiful, sole child of the living god,*' I began loudly, the first line of the Hymn to the Aten which the King had written so many years ago, dictating it to the boy from the school of scribes who had been me.

Huy, reprieved and shaking, continued:

Thou shinest upon us all, father of creation,
self-created, self-sustaining, light of the world.

Pannefer took up the hymn, in his high dissonant twang:

Thou art indeed comely, great, radiant and high over every land.
Thy rays embrace the land for thou art Aten
and subdueth them for thy beloved son Akhnaten.
Thou art remote though thy rays are on earth.
Thou art in the sight of all, but thy ways are unknown.

Then I sang:

The Two Lands are thy festival.
They awake and stand upon their feet for thou hast raised

them up.

They wash their limbs, they put on raiment, they raise
their arms in adoration at thy appearance.
The entire earth performs its labours. All cattle are at peace
in thy pastures. The trees and the grass grow green. The
birds fly from their nests, their wings raised in praise of thy
spirit. The animals dance on their hoofs; all winged created
things live because thou hast risen for them.

This had always been my favourite part of the hymn. I recalled
how enchanted I had been when I first took it down in my fast
cursive, how the poem had grown on the whitened board under
the spell of the soft voice of the King.

'*How wonderful are thy works!*' declared the King, forgetting
his water-sickness, as he spoke his own words:

How mighty and how manifest to thy children!
They are hidden from the sight of men, Lord of the Sky,
Sole God, like unto there is no other!
Unique One of the World, how sweet are thy ways!
Thou didst fashion the world according to thy desire when
thy wast alone—all men, cattle great and small, all that
are upon the earth that run upon feet or rise up on high on
wings.
And the lands of Syria and Kush and Egypt—thou
appointest every man to his place and satisfieth his needs.
Each man receives sustenance and his days are numbered.
Their tongues are diverse in speech and their qualities
likewise, and their colour is different because thou hast
distinguished the nations.

My lord Akhnaten stood up and raised his arms as he declared
the final blessing:

O Divine Lord of all,
All men toil for thee,

The Lord of every land, the Aten disc of the day-time,
Great in majesty!'

And it occurred to me for the first time—considering how often I had repeated the hymn the realisation was late in coming—that unlike the previous hymn to Amen-Re, the Aten as a god had done nothing but create and provide. There was nothing in the hymn about compassion, or mercy, or justice, or kindness, or love.

And there were precious few of those qualities in the King, or in his Egypt.

Chapter Sixteen

Mutnodjme

I had never seen such a beautiful palace. Ankhesenpaaten, who for some reason had decided to like me—and there was nothing I could do about this—took my hand and led me through all of the rooms of her mother's palace, and it was remarkable.

Because the artisans were forbidden the use of the old outlines of gods—no falcon-headed Horus or cat-headed Basht—they had to invent entirely new ways of depicting the world. The child told me that thousands of men had worked for months on the walls, and it showed.

Everywhere was light and colour and beauty. One whole room, for instance, was decorated with grapevines so real that one looked to pluck a handful of fruit. I stopped abruptly on what seemed to be the brink of a fish-filled pool, and Ankhesenpaaten laughed; the first natural sound I had heard out of that unnatural child. The pool was not real; it was a tesserae mosaic of fish and weed, so realistic that I had thought at first glance that I was about to step into water.

There were depictions of the royal family too; endless scenes of my Lord Akhnaten playing with his children, being anointed by his wife, offering piles of food to his sun god, and one delightful frieze of naked children playing games. The colours were bright, reds and browns and gold and blue.

We were alone in the centre of a room decorated all over with cornflowers and lotus, when the strange child suddenly said, 'I was afraid,' and I knelt down so that I could see into her face. She was thin limbed and big-bellied, like most children of that age, and instead of her usual bold stare she was eluding my gaze and biting her nails.

I decided that this was probably not a ruse of some sort and asked softly, 'When were you afraid?'

'When the soldier speared the teacher. There was blood. I was afraid.'

'Yes, I'm sure that you were,' I agreed, wondering what I could say that would not be reported back to every spy in the palace, or quoted where it would do most harm by the child herself.

Her little monkeyish face screwed up into a grimace, she whispered, 'Will they kill me, too?'

'No,' I said firmly, clutching her as she threw herself into my arms. 'No, Ankhesenpaaten, they won't kill you. Your Divine Father loves you, you know he loves you.' And I was perfectly sure of this.

'Then why...' I could not tell her the real reason—that her father was completely mad—so I temporised.

'People sometimes do things which we cannot understand,' I said. 'But you are safe, little royal daughter, of that I am certain.'

'That's all right, then,' she concluded, wriggled to get down, and continued to show me through the palace.

I began to wonder about my sister Nefertiti's care for her children. Mother Tey would not have liked answering a question about such a happening, but she would have answered. This child's fears had gone unassuaged and she was obviously choosing her confidant, and her moment, carefully, with a tact not to be expected in one so young. I resolved to look into the state of the others. And what was Tey my mother doing about it?

As it happened, nothing. Tey my mother summoned me later that day to a room decorated with a harvest; the most beautiful, delicate, full-coloured painting I had ever seen. Tey, however, was just as ever, though older and thinner, a spare dark crone in the atmosphere of exotic richness which enfolded the palace of the City of the Sun.

'Well, daughter,' she offered her hand for me to kiss, and I sank to my knees to comply.

'Well, Divine Nurse Tey?' I asked in return. Her black eyes dissected me, flaying me skin from bones. I held her gaze for some time, until she looked away.

'You are older, daughter, you are getting fat, which will not do; and you are just as inquisitive and selfish as ever,' she commented.

'True, mother, I have not changed, though I have learned a great deal,' I replied, trying not to lose my temper.

'False learning in service of a false god,' she sneered.

'But learning none the less,' I returned.

'Why have you come to Amarna?' she demanded, and I told her that I had come with Widow-Queen Merope when my temple was closed. She leaned forward and grasped my upper arm in hard fingers.

'Listen to me, daughter, you have come and I cannot send you away, because there is nowhere to send you now that the false worship you followed has been exposed. But if you have come to break apart your sister's peace, to annoy her or interfere with her management, or come between her and her husband, I will send you to work as a prostitute in the worst tavern on the waterfront, do you hear?'

'I hear,' I said equably. She could certainly send me there, but nothing could make me stay there.

'Nefertiti is happy, she is content, she has position, she is a priestess of her own cult, and I will not have you meddling, daughter!'

'Mother,' I agreed, knowing that the title would annoy her. Having made her point, she decided to push matters further, to demonstrate her control over me. Tey never wanted partners or even co-conspirators. She would never think of trying to persuade me to be nice to my sister and to acquiesce in her husband's insanity. Tey only ever wanted slaves.

'And I forbid you to marry Great Royal Scribe Ptah-hotep may he live.'

'Oh?' I asked. The temple's training in self control was beginning to slip. I would have to leave soon, or I would lose my temper. 'Why is that, Mother?'

'He is far above you, disgraced daughter of an outmoded religion.'

What to do? If I argued with her I would have to stay in the same room as this tyrannical woman, and I was anxious to leave and breathe free air again. But I would more willingly spend a hundred years in the belly of the serpent Apep than obey Tey's whim. However, she had given me an escape route. I was not being forbidden to see Ptah-hotep, just to marry him. I threw myself on my face, so that she could not see my lack of tears, and began to sob, clutching at the hem of her garment.

'Mother, please do not deny me this marriage—it is my last chance!' I wailed, which was true. I felt her satisfaction, heard it in her voice.

'I forbid it,' she purred, and weeping, I concurred.

'I will not marry the Great Royal Scribe,' I whispered, and she laid her hand on my head and called me her good daughter.

Then she dismissed me. I went out with my stole over my dry face, and reflected that luxury and position had not improved the character of my mother.

It had also not done wonders for mine. I had just lied to my mother; or rather evaded the truth to deceive her. I would have to confess that at the end of my life. Assuming that Osiris and Isis still judged the dead and weighed their hearts against the feather of Maat.

I walked through the painted palace to the apartments of the Widow-Queens Tiye and Merope, and arrived in time for the noon meal.

'The arrangements for the sed-festival are far advanced,' commented Tiye. 'I would have forbidden them if I had known. A sed festival—for a king who has reigned for such a short time? Ridiculous! But now it is too late.

'Have some of this pheasant, child, it is delicious. My son has excellent cooks, it is plain. Do you know how much bread and beer the palace is providing for the residents of Amarna? Thousands of loaves, oceans of beer. My own lord Amenhotep-Osiris, may his soul be joyful forever in the Field of Reeds, gave lavish feasts and no one left without being fed properly, but this is beyond belief. He distributes this much food every decan, for the festival of the Aten on the tenth day. How can Egypt afford it?'

'And the river is low,' I agreed, taking some of the perfectly cooked flesh. It was very tasty and I took some more.

'How was the lady your mother?' asked Merope.

'Much as ever, and she has forbidden me to marry the Great Royal Scribe.'

'Why?' asked Merope.

'She is demonstrating her power over me.'

'I see. Would you like me to speak to my son about this marriage?' asked Tiye the Queen, eying me keenly.

'No, Lady, I have agreed. I am too old to marry, anyway, I am almost nineteen. But she did not forbid me to see him,' I added, and Merope chuckled.

'We played that trick on her when we were children,' she said. 'She still hasn't learned it!'

'No, Tey has always been straightforward. Unpleasant, but straightforward,' said Tiye. 'She was a good midwife, but she no longer attends births. In fact, I believe that she does nothing but intrigue for more land and more power for the Divine Father Ay, who has, in my view, enough gold and power already. Tey was a better woman when she had tasks to perform. What is that noise?'

'People are gathering in the square,' said Merope, looking out of the window.

The windows of the palace of Amarna had deep embrasures. I could lean my elbows on the sill. I did so, next to Merope's uncovered head.

The sun was bright even though it was only Khoiak, the season of the birth of Osiris, once the festival of the breaching of the sluices into the inland plain. The next month, Tybi, would bring the sed festival, and the time which had been the mystic marriage of Isis and Osiris. Khoiak was not usually terribly warm but midday in any season was hot in the full glare of the sun.

'What are they all doing out in the open without any canopy?' asked Merope. 'Midday is the time to avoid the gaze of Amen-Re, I mean the Aten. They'll be burned.'

'So they will,' I agreed. The crowd outside began to chant, all at once, the Hymn to the Aten, a poem which I had seen many years ago as a child. The scribe Ptah-hotep had shown it to me. Akhnaten may he live had written it. At intervals the crowd, courtiers and bricklayers alike, raised their arms to the disc of the sun. I could see them squinting and blinking as sweat ran into their eyes.

'There are the Pharaoh and the Queen, at that window over there,' Merope pointed. Safely out of the full glare of the sun, Akhnaten raised his hands in homage to the sun-disc, and Nefertiti my sister held out handfuls of arm rings and necklets which glittered so brightly that I could not look at them.

The service concluded. There was my father Ay, dressed as I had imagined in the leopard skin of a full priest, and as he held out his hands Nefertiti dropped a golden necklace into his grasp. His fingers snapped shut, as they always did on gold, and the crowd scrambled for the golden beads and bracelets which were sown broadcast through the mob by the King. 'Hail, lord of brightness!' they cried, tripping over one another and elbowing their way to the front. 'Hail, most favoured child of the Aten!'

'What a spectacle,' said Tiye, who had joined us. Her voice was indulgent. 'He always wanted to be worshipped,' she added.

'And this is probably the only way that it could be managed.'

'We should have been told about this,' I was worried. 'Is someone trying to make us commit blasphemy?'

'No, no women can worship the sun in its full splendour,' said Merope. 'Or so Huy the Chamberlain told me. He said that it would defile the Aten's worship if we were to go out into the courtyard. We are allowed to watch from the windows, provided we are pure at heart and have not had intercourse with a man the preceding night.'

'That must sort the sheep from the goats,' said Tiye, chuckling. 'But luckily we are all ritually pure,' she said, and then she clutched her forehead as if her head hurt.

'What is it, lady?' Merope embraced her.

'The only man I have ever wanted to sleep with is dead,' snapped the Widow-Queen. 'I have no other sorrow, but that is enough.'

We had no more to say, and ate the rest of our meal in silence. Then Sahte sent in a group of musicians, who began to play such sad melodies on pipe and drum that they comforted Tiye, or roused her, and she bade them play music to which one could dance.

And Merope and I danced, to and fro in the painted rooms, on the floor tiled with pictures of baboons, to a tune which had once been called, *Hathor takes pleasure of Horus*.

Ptah-hotep

I was allowed to join the worship of the Aten at noon, which argued that the King was pleased with me. It was very hot in the square, and I am fair though I am a child of the common people. I knew that I would be coloured if not blistered when the season advanced and the Pharaoh held his outdoor worship at noon, and wondered if his preference for pale ladies had led to the prohibition on women attending the service.

I had no need of gold bracelets, so I did not strive to get close to the King as he threw his usual larges to the crowd.

I was worried about a letter from Tushratta, King of the Mitani.

Khery, who spoke various languages easily, had become my foreign advisor. He was given the letters and messages as they arrived, and I was responsible for bringing such matters as the

King needed to know to the royal attention. So far, acceptances for the sed festival had come from most of the surrounding kings, including the three most important: Niqm-adda the Third of Ugarit; Tushratta of Mittani; and Suppiluliumas, the new and rather touchy king of Khatti. The kings, naturally, would not travel themselves—it was never safe for kings of the barbarous nations to travel far from their capital lest they be overthrown in their absence—but each would send a son or other person, on which a kingship had been conferred for the purpose of the event. This was common practice and in view of the King's poor manners—he had yawned at the recital of a messenger from vassal Rib-Adda, who was reporting that the city of Sumur was assailed—it was fortunate. I felt for Rib-Adda and I could not see any chance of relief for him, though I would try once again at the next audience for foreign visitors.

King Tushratta, however, was powerful. The Mittani occupied a lot of the border and were a proud people with profoundly foreign ways. I had talked to Menna and Harmose, the old scribes whom I had brought with me to Amarna, and they had told me that Tushratta had actually asked Amenhotep-Osiris for an Egyptian princess as a concubine.

No Egyptian princess could ever be given to a foreign king, for in them resided the kingship. No Egyptian princess had ever been given to a foreign king. But apparently it had taken two stiff letters and a severe visit from a messenger to explain this to the barbarian. He was still writing, but now he was demanding gold; which was easier because Amarna had a lot of gold.

'Tushratta,' murmured Khety beside me as we walked away into the grateful coolness of the palace.

'I know,' I groaned. 'But what can I do? If Pharaoh won't listen, he won't listen and I can't make him!' I was beginning to feel dizzy, as though the sun had struck me.

'Perhaps we could just read the letter to Akhnaten may he live,' said Khety.

'He wants unworked gold,' I said. 'That would be possible, though he wants lots and lots of it—the exact term is 'gold in very great quantities'—and we can manage that too, but what shall we tell Tushratta about Keliya?'

'He is still in fetters,' said Khety.

'I know,' I replied. 'He greeted the King in the old manner, and when reproved he argued. I managed to save him from instant death, by getting in between him and the soldiers; but the fact remains that Keliya—Tushratta's principal envoy and royal son of his body, and heir of the King of Mittani—is in durance in Egypt. What will happen when his father finds out I do not know, and I cannot think of a solution,' I replied.

Khety put an arm around my waist as I felt myself sag.

'You are faint,' he said, heaving my weight up into his arms. I do not remember him carrying me to my apartments, but I do recall requesting very urgently that he send not for the palace physician but for the lady Mutnodjme.

Time passed. I swam up into consciousness to the sound of a sweet voice—Meryt, singing to the small drum; and a sweet smell—not the thick rich fragrances of the palace but a bracing scent from the river.

'Galbanum, prince of herbs,' commented a cool female voice a second before I identified it. 'Lie still, my lord, you are fatigued. Your slaves keep the door.'

'Who veiled the window?' I asked, for this was forbidden, as was anything which cut off the sun god from his people.

'I did, and if asked I will say that the strength of the Disc in his glory is too great for mortal men; and that you, his loyal servant, are prostrated in prayer before the majesty of the Aten,' she replied.

I lay down again under her firm hand; for that was, indeed, an acceptable answer and I wondered why I had not thought of it before. I saw Meryt pat the lady Mutnodjme in a familiar fashion, as though they were sisters, and Teti's son brought me a draught of cool herb-flavoured water from a pottery vessel.

'What happened? I was suddenly without strength, as though all the marrow was gone from my bones,' I said.

'The heat of the sun, lord Ptah-hotep. Also you are worried, overworked and underslept. I have permission from the Widow-Queen Tiye Mistress of Egypt to stay with you tonight. She believes that this will preserve your repose. Presently we will have a little supper, and then you will sleep again. Meanwhile little Hani will bathe your forehead and Meryt will sing to you; and I will report on your condition to the Lord Chamberlain Huy, hoping that he has not left an indelibly-greasy stain in your office by his contaminating presence.'

I relaxed into Meryt's voice and the attention of Hani's little son, who was very gentle, and wondered why I had not appreciated the lady Mutnodjme when she was a child. Her very presence in my apartments was making me feel stronger. The temple of the unnameable lady had sharpened her tongue and her wits; and the customs of the City of the Sun, seen through her dispassionate eyes, seemed even more ridiculous than I had imagined them.

I heard her voice, reporting my overwhelming devotion to the Chamberlain, heard his feet retreat and the outer door close. Then she returned and asked, 'Which particular problem were you considering when you collapsed, my lord? We had better solve it, then you will sleep better.'

'Ask Khety,' I instructed. 'Bring him in here and he will tell you about the King of Mittani's son.'

She did as I bade her, and Khety recited the whole problem and read her the passage in which King Tushratta asked:

Why have you delayed my messenger?
Where is my son and the light of my eyes, Keliya?
Why has he not written to me, and is he well?
I do not understand why you do not tell me what I want to know.

'And we can't really tell him what he wants to know, can we?' I asked.

'He's imprisoned, you say, not dead?'

'Not dead,' agreed Khety. 'I go down to the cells and bring him food and assure him that he is not forgotten.'

'All things can be cured except death'; that is what my Mistress Duammerset used to say,' Mutnodjme was thinking aloud.

'There is no sentence, no execution order?'

'No, he's been put there and there he stays until the Lord Akhnaten may he live releases him.'

'It is no use asking my sister Nefertiti may she live for she is completely immersed in her husband's religion and would never go against his wishes. I will be back in an hour,' she said, putting back her long black ringlets and straightening her cloth.

'What are you intending to do?'

'I'll tell you if it works. Meanwhile, my dear Ptah-hotep, drink the infusion I left you and sleep. I will be back, if it works or not,' she assured me, and was gone in a scent of galbanum. She walked like a countrywoman, a solid, firm, decisive stride, with a swing of the buttocks.

Khery and I looked at each other. He shrugged. I drank the infusion.

Barely an hour later—daylight hours are longer, of course, in Peret—she was back. I was sitting up by then, remarkably lazy and sleepy, and I could tell from her triumphant smile that she had achieved her aim. Behind her came a slim young man with the white bands on his ankles which indicate that copper fetters have just been struck off. He was naked and newly cleansed and Meryt sat him down and supplied him with a cup of beer, pieces of bread and meat and a clean loincloth.

'Here is Keliya, Prince of Mittani,' Mutnodjme introduced him. 'He wished to write to his father to complain about his treatment, but I have explained matters to him so that now he wishes to take up his residence, awarded to him by the King Akhnaten may he live. The Great Royal Scribe is requested to report to his father that he is well and happy and will attend the sed festival in Tushratta's place.'

The bewildered young prince stretched out a hand to Khery, called him brother, and wept a few tears before addressing himself to the beer and the food. Keliya seemed otherwise well, had not been beaten and, apart from being hungry, was undamaged.

Hanufer wrote the letter for him, and he sealed it with his seal ring. Then the lady Mutnodjme opened the outer door to reveal a litter decorated with feathers, ten servants who cried out with joy on seeing him, and four strong bearers. The litter was loaded with gold, jewellery, and a pile of folded cloths to replace the Prince's lost wardrobe.

Prince Keliya left, kissing Khety in the Mittani way and bending right down to kiss the bare foot of the lady Mutnodjme. If she had engineered his release, she deserved it. It was more than Khety or I had managed.

'There, my lord, that is one worry the less,' she said briskly as the entourage left. I waited until they were definitely gone and we were alone in the bed-chamber before I demanded,

'How did you do it?'

She eased me back into her lap—she had offered her thighs as a pillow for my head—and replied softly, 'It was the Widow-Queen Tiye. She told her son that his action had been justified but now he must restore the prince to his position in time for the sed festival; and he obeyed her instantly, like a calf obeys a cow. I thought that it might be so,' she said.

'Now, my lord, you must sleep,' she ordered, and who was I to disobey this masterful woman?

I closed my eyes and slept.

Chapter Seventeen

Mutnodjme

Time passed. I knew that Widow-Queen Tiye may she live was willing to help in mitigating the effects of her son's fanaticism after the release of the Prince of Mitanni. The King did not visit his mother often, for fear of what she might say.

Every tenth day treasure was distributed to the inhabitants of Amarna, every day the sun-disc was worshipped according to the King's ritual, and the Nile did not flood, and the land grew drier, as though ousted Amen-Re was angry with us on behalf of Hapi, God of the Nile.

At the beginning of Tybi, Merope and I were inducted into the mysteries of the Phoenix.

Nefertiti came for us before dawn, a time when sensible people are still asleep. She led us in darkness to a door in the Queen's Palace which gave onto a set of steps and we groped our way down, for apparently no light must penetrate the place of the Phoenix before Aten's own rays.

In that case it might have been wiser to leave the initiation until after dawn, I thought, but I said nothing. Meekness was my name and butter would not have melted in my mouth.

Merope was walking behind me, holding on to my shoulder, for she was as blind as a bat in the dark. I reached up and took her hand and she impudently brushed my nipple in passing, trying to make me laugh. I did not laugh, but pinched her earlobe hard to warn her that this initiation was to be taken very seriously, with the solemnity that my sister Nefertiti was exhibiting as we walked along a complicated corridor in the darkness.

Some little light leaked down through joins from the soldier's torches above, and I could in any case feel that there were many doorways on either side. The openings breathed vacancy and cooler air. Nefertiti was confident and led the way, her hand in mine, and Merope and I followed after, oppressed by darkness and no longer in the mood for tricks.

We came into a small round chamber where I struck my shins on a large pot of water and bit back a curse.

'You must strip and wash,' said Nefertiti. 'Did either of you lie with a man last night?'

'No,' said Merope. I nodded, realised I could not be seen, and said, 'I did not lie with a man last night.' Of course, I had lain with my sister Merope, but that probably did not count.

We were required to strip naked and bathe very thoroughly with laundryman's oatmeal and lye. This stung the skin but certainly rendered it clean. Our clothes were left behind, our jewellery and all our goods.

Nefertiti did not know, and I did not tell her, that the insignia of the Goddess Isis was tattooed on my scalp. It had been done when I came to the temple, when my head was shaved of the lock of childhood, and the hair had long since grown. I had a distinct feeling that being permanently marked with something which effectively meant, 'This woman belongs to Isis' might not be the advantage it was meant to be, and in fact might mitigate against my survival.

Breathing an inaudible prayer to my Lady Isis to assure her that I had not forgotten her worship, I followed the naked Merope out of the chamber into what seemed to be a large underground room and thence into a tunnel.

We emerged into the open. I heard water running. A channel of some sort was near. Nefertiti led me and we walked into water. It was only shin deep but it was a surprise. Merope clutched my hand as if she were frightened. I smelt spices and dust. Then I heard voices—women's voices—chanting in harmony:

Hail, bird of fire.
Hail, fire-feathered, emerald-eyed,
Hail thou who nesteth in spices!

I was through the channel and hauled my sister Merope up behind me. There was a grey predawn light in the sky and we could now see, though at that hour all faces are ghastly and haggard and all colours are absent.

We were in a courtyard, roofed over except for the open space at the end where there was a Benben pillar, a stele with a rounded top; the perch for the Phoenix when she flew into Egypt. This was open to the sky. Each doorway had a channel in front of it so that no one could enter without walking through what was presumably sacred or blessed water. Thus purified, one could approach the worship of the Phoenix.

We were naked, more naked than I can recall being, for I had no jewellery, no sandals, and I felt as though a protective layer of skin had been removed by the lye. Merope crossed one arm on her breasts and shivered, though it was not cold. I held her other hand in mine as Nefertiti brought us forward to face a choir of women, all robed in red and gold robes of great richness and weight.

I could discern the red and gold; the sun was rising. Nefertiti shivered with pleasure as the chorus sang:

Hail, most excellent lady,
Avatar of the fire-wing,
Lady of splendour!

And Nefertiti cried:

This is the worship of the Phoenix,
She who bears her own self inside her,
She who is unique,

For there is only one Phoenix, ever, Self-created, self-generating, lady of fire!

The women, raising their arms, cried:

She comes, she comes
Behold the Phoenix!

Merope and I cried out in amazement. I saw the Firebird, a huge creature, bigger than every bird that flew. In the new sunlight she shone like metal. I could not look at her. And still the women chanted:

She is coloured like the pomegranate,
like the wild poppy;
her wings are gold,
and the rainbow has coloured her head.

My eyes filled, I blinked and looked again, and then I realised that I was seeing an image made of gold with red and copper feathers and coloured glass melted into every scale of her legs. Her eyes were emeralds. She was a masterpiece.

And as the women cried out:

She who is last and first, she who is unique, worship her!

Merope and I dropped to our knees and then kissed earth in front of the Phoenix, while the women did the same. Some of them were crying, some moaning. I had been staggered by the apparition, which was made the more startling by the long journey in the dark.

Nefertiti raised her arms, her robes falling back to reveal that she was draped in red and gold feathers, and the women cried:

Hail most excellent lady,
Keeper of the Firebird,
Prophet of the Phoenix.

The Pharaoh Akhnaten was not the only one who wanted to be worshipped, it seemed. Merope and I screamed along with the rest as they repeated this three times.

Nefertiti said:

She comes from Africa bearing spices for her nest.
She flies into the Black Land escorted by all of the birds of
the air,
For she is their monarch and they delight to serve her.

'They delight to serve her,' repeated the women.
And Nefertiti continued:

Soaring she settles into the perch we have prepared for her,
And there she sings her last song,
Marvellously sweet to hear.

'Marvellously sweet,' murmured the women.

There she gathers cinnamon and balsam and cassia;
She makes her cradle and her sepulchre of frankincense and
spikenard.

'Frankincense and spikenard,' said the chorus.

Here she lays an egg which is her,
A ball of myrrh and seed which will hatch her again,
And then she cups her wings and summons fire.

'Summons fire,' breathed the women, echoing Nefertiti.

And the fire of Aten her lord licks up into her limbs,
And she burns

'She burns,' murmured the chorus.

Hail to the Phoenix!
For though she is burned to ashes,
Yet she leaves her own self to hatch again from the ball of
precious spices,
And she is herself never dying and never dead,
For in her own death she finds life.

'Hail!' cried the chorus.
And Nefertiti, her creamy voice rich with triumph, called:

Thus we shall rise.

'We shall rise...'

We shall rise like the Phoenix.

'We shall rise...'

We shall rise over death, which has no power,
For we are as the Phoenix.
Hail!'

'Hail!' cried the women as they leapt to their feet.

Pipes and drums began from a group of musicians in the centre of the courtyard. I noticed as I was swept into a step-dance that they were men and that they were blind, and I was consumed not with religious ecstasy but pity as I danced, Merope holding one hand and a court lady the other.

And as we danced we chanted the Phoenix litany, and I apologised to my lady Isis for taking part in this paltry ceremony.

Isis demanded that I starve three days before she accepted me, in order that I should understand hunger. Isis required that I should not taste water a day and a night, so that I would understand thirst. To Isis I swore to alleviate pain and misery, to feed the hungry and nurture the fatherless.

The Phoenix only wanted me to strip naked and dance.

But I could do that, and I did. We went round and down in a chain, split into pairs, and then into the round again. The pace was fast and the drums throbbed like heartbeats in fever, and as the sun rose higher we were wet with sweat. Hands slipped out of my slippery grasp. I was out of breath but I could not break the chain, and I reminded myself that I was a priestess of a much sterner lady than this bird, and kept moving.

Fortunately my sister the Queen, who has never had a lot of stamina, left the dance and brought us with her. The priestesses continued, round and round the Benben pillar, and I flopped down on the tiled floor as the drums throbbed and the pipes trilled, making bird calls for the silent image.

When the courtyard was fully lit, Nefertiti raised her arms again and silence fell.

'Listen,' she said, and no one breathed.

'One day,' she told the worshippers, 'You will hear the rustle of feathers, and the song of all the birds in Egypt escorting her to this place. Listen every day,' said Nefertiti, looking so beautiful that I could hardly bear to see her. The lines of her throat and breasts were perfect in the bright light, and she shone ivory, carmine and gold. She was alight with joy, with triumph, as enchanting as a goddess, and the worshippers fell to the ground, screaming and weeping and kissing her feet.

Had this been what my sister had always wanted?

We were escorted back to the palace blindfold through the passages under the ground, and I had no real idea of where the courtyard of the Phoenix lay.

Before we came into the palace again, Queen Nefertiti said, 'If you have any questions, sisters, ask them now, for you may not speak of the mystery of the Firebird outside this place.'

'Lady, what of the musicians? I thought all men were banned from this mystery.' I was curious about the musicians; the mystery itself seemed self-evident.

'They are not men,' said Nefertiti in her gentle voice. 'Their goddess castrates them. She is called Astarte; they are priests of Attis. So they are no longer men, and being blind cannot see the Phoenix, so they are allowed.'

'Who carries out such a terrible deed?' I asked, a little taken aback.

'They themselves, with a curved knife. But we blinded them, of course. Have you any other questions?'

'No, lady,' I said. 'We blinded them? Who was we? Mutilation was sometimes imposed by the law, when a judge ordered that a traitor or a murderer should be deprived of nose or ears and banished to the desert as an alternative to execution. It was not something which anyone could just do so that a Phoenix could have male musicians at her ceremony.

Nefertiti was waiting. Something more was obviously needed, and Merope, my clever Kritian sister, supplied it.

'We are overcome by the honour you have shown us,' she said, and knelt for the Queen's blessing, closely followed by me. After all, *knees are made to bend*, as Lady Duammerset had said. I resolved then to survive if I could, but to do as much as I could to ensure that no more excesses were ordered in the name of the Firebird, even if it meant becoming head of the cult myself. I was beginning to lose my taste for the beauty and airy lightness of the palace.

The rescue of the Mittani prince had been easy because I had Queen-Widow Tiye's trust. How long could the Lady live, so grief-stricken for the old man Amenhotep-Osiris? And when she was gone, would there be any check on the King Akhnaten and his Lady Nefertiti at all?

The eldest remaining son of the Queen was with her when Merope and I returned in mid morning, having bathed again and been oiled and massaged to soften skin which had been dried out by the lye. Another sorrow was on Tiye may she live, and I didn't know how much more she could stand. Her youngest daughter, Bekhetaten, her last gift from Amenhotep-Osiris, had died in the arms of her nurse on the way to Amarna. Many children were dying. There was a plague of summer fever amongst the babies. It began with a high temperature, an unwillingness to feed, then the child developed diarrhoea which could not be stemmed, and so died of weakness. Setepenre the youngest Amarna baby was also ill, and I did not think she would survive.

'My husband the King is dead, and his children are dying with him,' mourned Tiye, dry-eyed. 'Perhaps it is better so. Soon I will join him.'

'Mother, live,' begged Smenkhare. He was a beautiful boy. His mother had given him fineness of bone and her coppery hair, and he was straight and slim.

His tutor reported him intelligent and studious, though that meant nothing. After the murder of Teacher Khons, no tutor was likely to overtax a royal child.

Smenkhare had also inherited, it seemed, his father's shrewdness, because he was using on his despairing mother one of the few arguments that might persuade her to stay on an earth which had become void for her.

'Who will advise my Royal Father when he is confused, if you leave us?' he demanded, moving away from her embrace. 'What will become of the Black Land without you? Do not the foreign kings write to you, Lady, as Mistress of Egypt? What will Egypt do without its Mistress?'

Tiye said nothing, but I saw her drag in a deep breath.

Prince Smenkhare may he live forever saw that he was having an effect and added, 'My father was a wise man and a faithful man, he will build a house for you in the afterlife with the Aten, lady. He will not forget you, how could he? He waits for you. But there are those here who love you almost as much. There is my little brother Tutankhaten, he is only two years old, he needs you, Mother, and I need you. You cannot leave us yet!'

He allowed the Queen to lay her head on his smooth shoulder and stroked her cheek, adding with just a trace of mischief, 'And you have to come to my coronation,' and Tiye laughed. It wasn't a very good laugh, being bitter and brief, but it was a laugh.

'Very well, sweet son,' she agreed. 'I will stay awhile yet,' and Smenkhare kissed her.

Ptah-hotep

I woke, hearing voices at the door, very late on the night which was once the feast of Isis and Osiris, and a sleepy Meryt admitted a lamp-bearing woman into my chamber and shut the door after her with a slam. Meryt hates to be woken from her first sleep. My sandclock showed the time to be almost midnight. I heard the guard changing outside.

'All well?' asked the relieving guard.

'All well,' answered the soldier, and I heard him march away.

No wind was blowing. It was so still that I heard Meryt grunt as she lay down beside Teti in the outer chamber where she insisted on sleeping so that I could not be surprised. Meryt had appetites and her brother Teti supplied them. I wondered that the Nubians had similar customs to our own Royal House until I found that Teti was not the son of Meryt's father or Meryt's mother, but what in Egypt we would call a cousin. I had lain alone more nights than I could count, hearing them making love, which emphasised my loneliness.

Now I was not alone. I knew of only one woman whom Meryt would have allowed into my bedchamber without introduction.

'Lady Mutnodjme,' I said, struggling up onto one elbow and tipping over my neck-rest. 'This is an unexpected honour.'

'I mean you no harm,' she said, crossing the room with her peasant's stride. She set down the lamp. It was a small saucer-shaped oil lamp in the shape of an opium-poppy. It gave very little light, just a small bead of pale flame. In the half-darkness I saw that the lady Mutnodjme was quite naked.

She was rounded and full, with heavy breasts, wide hips and strong thighs. Her ringletted ebony hair fell almost to her waist and she shook it back impatiently. At the junction of thighs and belly was a perfect triangle of pale flesh and a cleft which was the entrance to the female mystery.

'What do you want of me, lady?' I asked. She came closer and sat down familiarly on the edge of my bed.

'I want you to listen to the mysteries of the Firebird,' she said, and I listened to her voice as she whispered to me of blinded musicians and a sister possessed of a strange worship. I wondered why she had come to tell me such things in the middle of the night and caught myself in a yawn. I knew now what no man knew, but it was not a useful secret. Misuses of the law had become commonplace. I said so.

'Lady, the King orders whole provinces flogged if they do not pay his bounty,' I said, my mouth almost touching her ear.

'He ordered the Nomarch of the Nome of the Black Bull to have his ears cropped for not providing labour, even though it is the wrong season.'

'He sent the Nomarch of Set to the quarries and he sends men who are not slaves to work in the mines. And they die, but he does not care, for they provide him with eye-stones for his statues and gold for his bounties.'

'That is true,' she sighed, and for some reason we lay down together, her thigh touching my thigh, her hand clasping mine on her rounded belly.

'There is no justice in the Black Land, and no peace, and no safety for any man, for at any moment the Pharaoh Akhnaten may order his home, his sons and his cattle seized to pay a tax which he has just imposed for the construction of Amarna and the glory of the Aten,' I said, a litany of misery which I had never voiced before.

'It is true,' she responded, very sadly.

'The Nile does not rise and the farmers will hunger this year,' I said into the dark, rush-scented hair. Her mouth was very close to my mouth as she breathed, 'This is true.'

'And the old gods are angry, for their altars are empty and their worship abandoned; their priests wander the roads and their fires are cold,' I added.

And then the lady Mutnodjme said, almost inaudibly, 'But tonight is the marriage of Isis and Osiris.'

Then I knew why she had come to me.

The marriage of Isis and Osiris is—was—celebrated with a feast, after which a priest and priestess re-enact the mystic marriage in the light of the star Sothis, which is Isis and Orionis which is Osiris. This is done when the lights of both stars are in the sky, as they were tonight, before midnight when the stars move in the great wheel which takes them, during daylight, below the earth to the Tuat.

After the marriage of the gods is consummated, all people lie down with their lovers and dedicate their love to the festival, and that which is done this night is pleasing to the god and the goddess.

I allowed my mouth to meet her mouth. Meryt had taught me about women. I breathed in the scent of her skin and her hair, sour, not sweet, a biting sourness like persimmon or the golden apples of Nubia. Her mouth tasted of wine and honey and herbs, and she held out her arms to me.

I felt her hands slide surely across my chest and down to find the phallus, but she did not immediately clasp it, but with her nails and a touch as weightless as a butterfly alighting on a petal she stroked and teased my loins, until I was shivering. I reflected her caress, finding the cleft and touching it as gently as I could, a repeated tapping until I felt her thighs loosen and open, parting easily to allow me to find the pearl which is the centre of all female mysteries.

I felt my skin flush with heat. Beside me, my lover burned. I slid down beside her, finding first the nipple as hard as a metal bead in my mouth, then as her thighs wrapped my shoulders I found myself lapping at the waters of the womb which gave all men life.

Something took me then. Something flowed into my receptive body, some great force which had roamed the night, seeking an outlet. My hands were magnetised like the wise iron and everywhere I touched gave pleasure. Three times I felt the womb convulse under my tongue, heard a moan of delight, not from my lady Mutnodjme but from woman herself, all women, and I was making love to her as all men.

She reclaimed my mouth, sweet with her waters, drawing me into her embrace, her breasts soft under my weight and on that kiss I entered her with a shock like being struck by lightning. We were fused together. Thus must metal feel in the welding. I cried out; so did she. We moved slowly to begin with in a sacramental dance of female and male, of Isis reclaiming her dead husband, of life making love to life.

I abandoned thought; I was no longer Ptah-hotep. She was no longer the dark woman Mutnodjme who came to me in the night whom I had known as a little maiden. We had no history but the god's, no story but the legend. The phallus that moved in and out of the sheath in slow strokes that made the woman cry out like a bird was not mine; the sheath was not hers.

We were one entity; one perfect union of god and goddess, earth and sky, fire and water. We were elemental, strong, unimaginably pure. I saw her face in starlight and she was transfigured, the goddess Isis under my hand, enfolding me, embracing me, so beautiful that my eyes dazzled.

There seemed to be no time. I was in her body, feeling the phallus inside me, the soft flesh close tightly about it, and every movement brought me such delight that my bones were filled with honey. She was me, feeling the penetration of the woman, the skin of my belly on her belly; the union of opposites which were the same.

We reached a climax. Lights exploded in front of my eyes. The rush of fire along my bones was close to pain, beyond pain. Still part of her, I felt her convulse as the womb grasped and sucked at the fluid of generation as though the womb was mine. We bled inside each other, shared veins and heart beating wildly, breath panting. We were one in the triumph of the consummation of the mystic marriage of Isis and Osiris.

I lay beside her, my phallus still inside her, her arms locked around my neck, my mouth on her mouth. We were soaking wet, shuddering with release, dazed.

'Don't let go of me,' I whispered, for I felt unreal.

'Hold me close, for I am afraid,' she replied. We did not move for some time until our bones began to complain. Then we separated, reluctantly, and lay side by side, still touching.

'My lady,' I said uncertainly, for I did not know how to address the avatar of Isis.

'My lord,' she whispered. There was a quaver in her voice.

'I was inside you, I *was* you, did you feel...,' I began. And she answered me, 'I felt you. I was a man and a woman, I was the lady and the lord; such a thing has never happened to me before, I am very frightened and I love you.'

'I am also afraid,' I said very softly. 'I am awed before the power of the gods and I love you.'

We slept the rest of the night without dreams. When I awoke she was lying with her head on my breast. She opened her eyes when she felt me looking at her. We were sensitive to each other. I had only heard of this happening in the case of twins. The night had twinned us.

'You pleased me,' she said, sounding bewildered, tracing patterns on my chest with the very tips of her fingers.

'You pleased me,' I told her, caressing her rounded shoulders and strong thighs.

'It is a strange matter. My lord I do not know what to say to you…' she began. I didn't know either. I solved the problem by kissing her and putting back the black hair.

'You are my lady, and I am your lord,' I said, and that seemed to satisfy her, for she called to Meryt for bread and wine.

Thus the lady Mutnodjme became my lover indeed, just as palace gossip said she had always been, and I never argued with palace gossip.

But the night remained unaccountable. Something had come to us, even to Ptah-hotep the scribe and Mutnodjme the priestess, who had lain down together on a sacred night in an Egypt which had abandoned its ancestral gods.

Chapter Eighteen

Mutnodjme

That strange possession, that pouring into the human vessel of the spirit of the gods, had never happened to me before, though I recognised it from the description of a priestess of Isis who had lain down with Osiris-priest one night of Tybi and had risen forever changed.

It was so strong that it felt as though Ptah-hotep had been branded on my body. For days after that Isis and Osiris mating I could feel the phallus inside me, the hip bones butting the inside of my thighs, the sense that I was inside him and he was inside me. After much thought I concluded that it had been the gods, seeking a place where they could meet and mate, and my lover Ptah-hotep and I had been willing receptacles for their divine lust. I was honoured, though bruised.

The day of the sed festival dawned fresh and clear. I clothed myself in a long robe, hoping to escape the notice of the others, though I was wasting my effort. They all knew. Widow-Queen Tiye told me solemnly not to watch the worship of Aten from the window this morning, as it was patent that I was not ritually clean. I was not. But I felt exalted, raised high, pure. I wondered if my lord felt the same.

I could see him, standing by the King Akhnaten, outwardly collected and calm as he always was; inwardly worried about the festival, the organisation, the weather—would a sandstorm blow today of all days when everyone was required to be outside?

I came away from the window as ordered, but not before I knew that I had just seen into another human's heart. I knew what Ptah-hotep was thinking. Not exactly as to this matter and that, but what he was worrying about.

This was new, and I did not know what to make of it.

Merope relayed the sight to me as I sat on the floor, nursing the mortally sick child of my sister Nefertiti, the little Princess Setepenre. As my dear Kritian talked, life gently left the little body and it slowly cooled. I had seen many babies die—some fathers do not even see a child under two years old, because in a bad season more than half of them will perish—but her little body was so light and her life had been so brief that I wept quietly as Merope told me of the festival.

'The king is out in the courtyard, wearing a loincloth. Now he is surrendering his crown to your father, who is dressed in his leopard's skin. He looks indescribable. He can hardly move under the weight of his decorations. Now the king is running, it's a pity you can't see this,' she broke off to laugh. 'He's come to the eastern corner and bowed to it and is being splashed with water. Now he is running to the west, and there is a priest with a torch for fire. Now to the north, for earth; and now the south, for air; but he's slowing down—will he make it? Yes, he's back before Father Ay. Now there's a ritual combat. He has to kill a bull. They're leading it in now.'

'Give me the child,' said Queen Tiye, and took the lax body out of my arms. 'I will dispose of her fittingly. I do not fear the touch of the dead.'

She took the baby from me and cradled it in her arms, moulding the little limbs into their final position and wrapping the body in a long, heavily embroidered cloth. She gave the parcel to Sahte, who nodded and slipped away. Royal children under five are not embalmed, but buried fittingly in the nearest royal tomb. Setepenre would join her father indeed, although Sahte would have to send her back to the Valley of the Kings for that purpose.

I wondered who in this City of the New Sun was willing to carry out the duties of Osiris Priest. Sahte, however, knew everyone. I was sure that the small dead creature would be in a suitable tomb by nightfall tomorrow. It is not proper to mourn over the death of a baby, for it happens so often that if full rites were observed no family would ever be out of mourning.

'The mother will have to know of this, but not yet,' said Widow-Queen Tiye to me in an undertone. 'Princess the lady Setpenre has gone to her father Amenhotep-Osiris in the Field of Reeds, and he will care for her. Better so, perhaps, than the fate which might meet her in the Black Land. Now, what is happening outside the window? Has my son killed his bull?'

'No, he's chasing it around the courtyard. Now the priests are holding it still. The blade comes down, so!' commented Merope. 'A bad blow, but Divine Father Ay has completed it and now the bull is dead. What happens next, Lady?'

'There will be an offering of roasted flesh to the god and then a great feast,' said Tiye. 'Come down from the window, daughter. We should sit down on the floor. The little princess is dead.'

'Oh, 'Nodjme, you should have called me!' said Merope. 'Poor little princess. The season has been cruel. And I fear that Neferneferure is ailing, as well. She will not suckle. The nurse was here this morning, asking if we had any healing infusions for the baby. I told her to ask the palace physician.'

'That idiot will infallibly murder the baby,' said Widow-Queen Tiye. 'Why did you not supply her with some poppy?'

'Because the King Akhnaten has forbidden any woman to practice medicine, and I do not want to be deprived of nose and ears and sent into exile,' said Merope frankly. 'I would not mind if they were going to send me home to the Island in the Great Green Sea, but lately they have been sending prisoners into the Red Waste, and nothing lives there for long except snakes and scorpions.'

'No women can practise medicine? What nonsense!' said Tiye wearily.

'The Lord King says that only outmoded and forbidden cults teach herbs and spells, so that they must not be used.'

'Gods of all Egypt, that my early sins should be punished by such a son!' Tiye got up with some difficulty and straightened her back. 'Send the poppy to the nurse, Merope, in my name.'

'Lady,' I said, touching her arm. 'He might kill you if you disobey his orders.'

'Then let him kill me, for if they are foolish orders I will disobey them. But he would never dare,' said Tiye without heat.

I hoped that she was right.

Meanwhile, I was glowing, in love with a man for the first time in my life. I would see him at the great sed festival feast. Ptah-hotep, Great Royal Scribe. My lover. The thought was new and intoxicating.

We spent the rest of the day in bathing and combing our hair and anointing ourselves with our favourite perfumes. I always liked the river-scents. Labdanum, a tree-resin, and galbanum, an oil derived from the scented rushes which fringed the river wherever papyrus would not grow.

A scribe from the office of the Great Royal Scribe was admitted, however, a little after noon, and he gave into my hands a small flask made of alabaster, made in the shape of a nesting bird. In it was oil of cinnamon and cassia, a precious gift from my lord Ptah-hotep. Combined with my usual scents, it was a new compound, erotic and cool, hot and considered. Very like, I thought, our relationship, which had been formed in conspiracy and was now heavily-charged with emotion. The others exclaimed at the delightful smell.

'There is more in you than meets the eyes, Mistress of Isis,' said Widow-Queen Tiye, inspecting me with her slate-coloured gaze. I flicked a glance at the scribe, but he preserved a blank countenance as though he had not heard the King's mother using the name of a forbidden god. I bade him thank my lord Ptah-hotep for his present, and he left with one of my finger-rings wrapped in a veil as a return gift.

'If I didn't know better I would swear that the perfume was a morning-gift,' said Tiye may she live forever. 'But such is only for the first time, not for lovers of such long standing as you and the Great Royal Scribe. Fortunate Mutnodjme, to have such a grateful lover!'

Widow-Queen Tiye's guesses were always close to the mark and I turned away to sniff at my wrist, where the new blend was ripening into a truly devastating scent.

'Was it good?' asked Merope wistfully. I was unwilling to talk about the mating, it had been so strange, but I owed her something. Merope would not lie with a man again. Theoretically she now belonged to the heir of her husband, which was King Akhnaten. She knew as well as I did that her body would not be demanded by that King.

'Tell me about making love to Amenhotep-Osiris,' I said, and she drifted away into erotic reminiscence of the old man, his soft mouth, his gentle ways, his sure fingers which found the way to every centre of response. The account sounded remarkably like my experience of Ptah-hotep, and I said so.

I would never reveal, because no one would ever believe me, the sudden intimacy with his mind as well as his body, the sense of fusion of opposites into one being. Even sitting with Merope in the Widow-Queen's apartments and combing the long hair of Tiye may she live I could feel Ptah-hotep's concern for many matters; feel also his memory of me, which was precious to him, as he was precious to me. I had no words to describe this experience. They all belonged to mysteries, where there was a fusion of worshipper and worshipped, and it had not been like that. We were equals, primeval, one flesh.

'He was sweet, so skilled that he melted my stiff sinews and made me cry out,' I said, and Merope sighed. 'I loved the fragrance of his skin, and here he has given me his own scent. His chest was a pillow for my head and his mouth delighted me. And if I add a little oil of unefer, you shall perceive him as we lay together.'

I dropped a little oil of unefer on my wrist and the perfume became unbearably erotic. I stank of mating. The mingling of scents came to Merope and she closed her eyes and blushed red.

'We are glad that you have found a lover, Mutnodjme,' the Widow-Queen told me. 'But leave us to mourn, dear daughter, for I cannot bear to smell that scent anymore.'

'I will wither,' wept Merope. 'I will dry up. My flesh will contract on my bones like a corpse laid in the sun. My dearest love is dead, is dead, and no man shall desire me again!'

'I will grow old,' said the Widow-Queen in response. 'My hair will become grey and then white and lines will etch themselves on my face. My heart is with my love, my dearest love, who was taken from me, who waits for me, but I will come to him an old woman, and no man will lie with me again.'

I took myself and my scent of mating out of the room, and their litany went on, and I hope that they comforted each other. I had no comfort for them and no comfort to carry, for I was going to tell my sister that her youngest child was dead.

Fortunately I found Tey in the corridor of glossy marble, lined with fresh pictures of bearers of tribute to the Aten. I caught at her arm as she hurried past me and knelt on the cool stone, a picture of submission.

'Great Royal Nurse, please wait. Your humble daughter has that to carry which is heavy news for her sister, and wishes to consult with you about when to deliver herself of it.'

'Setepenre is dead?' snapped Tey, looking down into my face. I nodded.

'Your behaviour is most becoming, daughter. I will tell the Great Royal Spouse. Make sure that no one else knows of this who might tell it carelessly. She will be sorry, but it can't be helped. The body is disposed of suitably?'

'By the Widow-Queen Tiye and my sister Merope, Lady,'

'Good. Daughter, have you lain with the Great Royal Scribe?' She knew this as well as I did.

'Yes, lady, but I have obeyed your orders. I will not marry him.'

'It is as you like,' she said carelessly. 'Your dowry will be paid to him by the temple of the Phoenix, so it does not concern your Divine Father Ay.'

It was typical of my mother that she forbade me to do something one day and then acted as if it was of no importance the next. Being Tey's daughter had kept me on my toes for years, never certain from whence the next blow would come. The noise of the sed festival, which was attended with a lot of people blowing horns, came to us dully through the stone walls. A squad of soldiers passed, on the run, spears lowered. Still Tey kept me on my knees. Fortunately the service of Isis had given me strong limbs. I did not move and she relented. If I had been palace trained I would have been in agony; and I allowed a wince to appear on my face. It would never do to let Tey know how little she was inconveniencing me.

'Very well, daughter,' she touched my bowed head and went on. I let her get a good way along the passage before I climbed to my feet, rubbed my flattened kneecaps, and walked away.

I could not see Nefertiti in case she asked me about the baby, I did not have any tasks, and the royal women were mourning their loss. There was no room of books in the palace of the Aten, as the texts were still being written. I could not while away the time until the feast by consulting some old writings, because Amarna had no history. I still smelt divine and I wondered whether my lord was feeling as kindly towards me as I was to him. In fact, I knew that he was, so I went to find him.

Ptah-hotep

I was in love as I had not been since I had first lain with my Kheperren, and I was more than a little confused. What had I to do with a woman, when I had given my heart to a man? What especially had I to do with loving a woman, when Kheperren lived and still loved me?

I banished all my servants and sat in my room, where her scent still lingered, and thought, closing my eyes. Somehow I was aware of her. I felt a sudden stab of sorrow—what had happened? It was not my sorrow, it was hers, it was flavoured with her emotions. What could I do to comfort her?

I sent Hanufer's scribe to my lady with a present of perfumes, and felt her pleasure as she blended them and remembered me.

This was altogether strange and I did not know what to make of it. However, there it was and there is no use in continually re-testing something which is true, as my Master of Scribes used to say.

And after long reflection, I realised that I could love Kheperren, that I did love him as well as ever. He still had my heart, but so did my lady Mutnodjme. Unusual, perhaps, but my entire life had been marked by odd events. My mother had told me when I was still a naked child that a star had fallen when she gave birth to me, and that she knew I was destined for great things.

My parents were still proud of me. When the King allowed, I would go home to the Nome of the Black Bull and they would hold a welcoming feast, very rustic and delightful, and all the men of the village would congratulate my father on his son. I decided that, when I could, I would take the lady Mutnodjme home to meet my parents and drink the wine of their vineyard, lying under the sycamores by the fish-pool, one of my favourite places in the world. I could imagine her there without any sense of strain, the strong woman with the peasant walk, swapping recipes with my mother and discussing the ancient texts with my father until they proclaimed, 'She is a jewel who holds our son's heart!'

My mind was made up. I did love the lady Mutnodjme, I did love Kheperren, and I could do both at once.

Having reached this decision, I got up, washed and dressed in an entirely new cloth and a good selection of jewellery, the lady Mutnodjme's unobtrusive ring on my finger, and went to the sed festival to see the king rededicate his kingdom to the Aten.

The king did not cut a very good figure at the festival, though we all cheered dutifully as, at the fourth attempt, he finally managed to slay his bull. I suspected that Divine Father Ay actually delivered the killing blow but I was not watching carefully. The bull, in the end, died, and the flesh was butchered by the King's Aten priests and roasted in the fire which was kindled by a burning glass, a sacred fire lit by the sun itself.

The courtyard began to be redolent less of expensive oils and more of cooking and the commoners of Amarna beyond the walls smelt this and cried out blessings on the King Akhnaten.

'Joy to the blissful child of the Aten!' they screamed. 'Hail the most favoured child of the Great God!'

Fill-belly-love, nurses call it. As soon as I decently could, I left the ceremony, while the foreign dignitaries were still falling at the feet of the re-crowned king and delivering themselves of laudatory messages. I was pleased that Keliya, the son and heir of King Tushratta of Mittani was there, looking well-fed and shining with oil. I waited to make sure that he gave voice to no complaint about his outrageous treatment—he didn't; and left the ceremony to return to my office, where the new diplomatic correspondence had come in. The tablets were piled in a basket, and no one could read them but Khety and the two old scribes I had brought from Karnak. Khety and his family would be at the festival, but I might be able to find either Harmose or Menna. They were old and had limited taste for new gods or festivals.

I found them both in close conference with my lady Mutnodjme. Now I had supplied these old men with lodgings and food and greeted them with honour and they had repaid me with respect and the exercise of their learning, translating difficult words in all possible ways and doing their utmost to make the writer's meaning clear. They had been diligent and polite, but I had received no sign of friendship from them and had decided that their learning had dried out their hearts and that they did not particularly care for humans.

And here they were, lounging—Harmose, lounging!—and drinking beer and instructing the Lady Mutnodjme in basic cuneiform as though she was a favoured child and they were both her doting uncles.

I stood at the door for a while and watched them. Menna, who had never broken into even a brief smile while I had known him, was actually laughing at something my lady had said, and Harmose was a little taken aback and surprised as she commented that the name of the king must mean 'lion' because the same word was used in three Nubian dialects.

'My lady,' I said, and she looked up. Our eyes met and our gaze meshed, like sunlight and lamplight, though I could not have said which was the sun and which the lamp. She did not even have to touch me to know me intimately, but she did.

She took my hand and laid it to her cheek and told the two old men, 'Here is my lord.' She poured me a cup of beer and moved a chair so that I could sit, disarranging my office, and then resumed what was evidently a learned conversation.

Menna and Harmose were so enchanted by my remarkable Mutnodjme that they did not resume their previous gravity.

'I believe that you are correct, Mistress of the House,' said Menna. 'If that form means 'lion' then the determinative is here, 'the lion' meaning the sole and only one, the royal lion. Hmm. Tushratta has written to the Widow-Queen Tiye, master,' he said to me. 'It is a difficult passage with many possible meanings. But this is what Harmose and I think it means—with some help from the Mistress,' he nodded at Mutnodjme.

'So, what says Tushratta?'

'To the Mistress of Egypt, Royal Queen Tiye Whom the Royal Lord Akhnaten Loves, Greeting,' deciphered Menna. 'The situation of the royal lion is grave, for do not his enemies surge against him like the sea? Do not the birds scorn him, screaming insults into the ears of the King? Send therefore some wise counsel to the lion, lest he be overthrown and his kingdom lost.'

'Cryptic,' I said. 'But one grasps the meaning.'

'Does one? What does it mean? Who are these birds?' asked Mutnodjme.

'Khatti's banners are always painted with an eagle,' I told her. 'King Suppiluliumas of Khatti is young and ambitious and the only way he can expand is into Tushratta's territory, because of his neighbours. The Apiru are dangerously unstable, the Babylonians well-organised, the Assyrians very aggressive and the borders of Egypt are guarded. In any case he could only get to the Assyrians through Mitani. Suppiluliumas is taking a huge risk, however, if he is attacking Tushratta. That king has forgotten more about diplomacy, treachery and extortion than Suppiluliumas has ever known, or his father before him. Is there any other way you can read this but for a request for arms?'

'He's asked for "wise counsel", my lord,' Mutnodjme pointed out.

'Look at the sign next to it,' Menna touched the clay tablet with his old, clean hands. 'See that sign? It means counsel, but it has a secondary meaning.'

'What is that?' she asked, leaning close to see and rendering me dizzy with her scent.

'It means "spear",' said Harmose. 'And written like that, it means a hundred spears.'

'I see. Clearly this diplomacy is a study for a hundred lifetimes.'

'Indeed,' Menna smiled at her. 'What shall we do, lord Ptah-hotep may you live?' he asked.

'We must tell the Widow-Queen,' I said. 'We have a treaty with Tushratta and mutual defence was one of the first sentences. We are required to go to his aid if he asks for it.'

'There have been three letters prior to this one,' Menna said uncomfortably. 'The King came in one day when we were working on the translations and took them away with him, saying that his Master of the House would deal with them.'

'Why didn't you tell me?' I demanded, seriously worried. The Aten alone knew what the King might have done with a demand for aid, let alone Huy the unreliable.

'The King said not to bother you with such matters,' Menna was equally uncomfortable. 'So we assumed that it was taken care of. And now here is Tushratta writing to the Queen Tiye may she live so he must have received no answer.'

'Don't make such an assumption again, my scribes, if you love the Black Land. And make sure I know what is going on.'

How can I make political decisions if I am not fully informed?' They seemed suitably abashed and it was not their fault, so I stopped berating them and thought.

'Let the Lady Mutnodjme take the letter to the Widow-Queen,' Menna proposed. 'She is wise and discreet.'

'I will certainly do that gladly, Master Scribe. She needs something to occupy her mind, but what can the Queen do if she wants to send troops to Tushratta? All the soldiers are coming here,' replied Mutnodjme.

She was right. By order of the King Akhnaten may he live as many serving soldiers who could be summoned were converging on Amarna to receive new orders from the King. Only the very farthest borders were left garrisoned, and that only because General Horemheb had insisted and the Widow-Queen had backed his orders with her own. And if Khatti took Mittani, we would have a victorious foe on our border and no army to repel an advance.

'Tushratta must live or die, may his gods protect him,' I said despairingly, 'for there is no help we can send him.'

Chapter Nineteen

Mutnodjme

The sed festival feast was engrossing.

My sister Nefertiti had clearly not been told of the death of the little princess, or else she was unaffected by it. She was dressed in a gauze gown so sheer that one could see her perfect body and rounded limbs through it. Her short Nubian wig was crowned with a cone of solid perfumed oil which would melt in the course of the evening, matching the one on my own head. I was worried about the state of Egypt, certainly, I would always be concerned about it while the Eunuch King sat on the throne, but one cannot always be concerned.

Sometimes one has to feast and forget. I did not like my chances of persuading my dear lord Ptah-hotep to do so, but I was going to try. The first thing I needed to do was to dose him with an reasonable amount of wine, and that would not be difficult.

He was sitting across the room with his scribes and their families, and I was already friends with his scribes. Khety, who had the eyes of a dreamer whose dreams have been fulfilled, had agreed to keep Ptah-hotep's cup filled with the strong wine of the south, a vintage as red as blood, which went down like honey and struck like a serpent.

Widow-Queen Tiye and Merope could not come to the feast, for they were still in mourning for Amenhotep-Osiris.

So now I thought of it, was Akhnaten, though he had shaved his chin and put on his jewellery again and showed no sign of missing his revered and wise father. I watched him across the room as he offered a bite of quail to Nefertiti and caressed her breast, pinching a nipple between thumb and forefinger while she purred like the once-sacred cat. The lord Akhnaten was undoubtedly incapable of generation, but he had learned a few things, it seemed, about pleasing women.

'Drink!' exclaimed the maiden who was pouring wine for me, quoting a saying of the wise Amenhotep-Osiris. 'For yesterday's wine will not quench today's thirst!'

Under the circumstances, I drank.

The wine was excellent and of the feast there seemed to be no end. A bewildering number of dishes were laid before us. There was roasted goose and boiled pigeon and roasted and boiled birds of every description, in dishes and on skewers; there was a whole great fish, previously forbidden to the palace, cooked with fennel and leeks. There was a soup of small fish, spices and onions, dishes of new cheese, fifteen types of bread, fruits of all types from the rare golden fruit of Libya to the plain peasant's fare of dates and figs. To refresh the palate, there were bunches of sour herbs, lettuce with its pearly juice for the lecherous, and brown beans and garlic to strengthen the weak-stomached.

The musicians of the Queen's palace were sitting on the floor in the middle of the room. I hoped that they had eaten before they came, as was the practice in the reign of Amenhotep-Osiris, who said that no person could play a pipe while empty bellies put him off his food. They began to play dancing music, and the acrobats came in turning somersaults.

I was covertly watching Ptah-hotep through the flashing limbs. They were beautiful, slim and muscular. How could a thick-bodied creature such as I hold his attention when sweat gleamed on fine flesh and the ear was charmed by the strings of little chimes they wore around their ankles? Each nipple was painted red, each mouth rouged, and their hands and feet were patterned with henna.

But he was looking at me, and smiling. I was suddenly hot, and a serving maiden noticed this and began to fan me with a palm-leaf fan.

The acrobats retreated, walking out of the room on their hands, and in came a singer. She was an old woman, a *heset*, one of the Singers of Hathor when Hathor had been worshipped. That meant that she had spent her whole life since childhood in the acquisition of erotic skills. These naturally included singing and dancing, for Hathor is—was—the Lady of Music. She carried a sistrum and sat down next to the woman with the small drum.

Silence fell. This was the famous Makhayib. Everyone in the Black Land had heard of her.

I wondered suddenly what had become of the dedicated women of Hathor. They had no other skills but copulation, singing and dancing, then I chided myself for an idiot. With such talents, they would never lack for a protector in Egypt.

Makhayib clapped her hands together several times, then started to sing. Her voice was not sweet like those of the Attis' priests I had heard in the ceremony of the Phoenix. It had a sharp edge to it which compelled attention, even though she was singing of love, the song of a maiden to her chosen man.

It is sweet, favoured boy,
To bathe in the river.
If you come this way
Down the green path
You may see me naked
Standing in the water.

Everyone was listening. The voice came from an old woman. Under the long Hathor-wig, with its curled-up ends, her hair was white; her breasts had fallen, her loins under their beaded belt and tassel must have been as dry as old leather. Even her hard-soled feet were wrinkled, with horny nails like the yellowed nails on her hands.

But what I could see, if I closed my eyes, was a slender maiden teasing a boy no older than herself with erotic visions.

I shall stand in the water
So you can see me;
I shall turn from you
So you shall see all of me.
Look at me, beloved,
I am worth your gaze.

I felt an emotion rising which was not mine, though I shared it. My lord was thinking the same as I; how sweet it would be to go down to the river and bathe, then lie together in the reeds. I had never done such a thing, but he had.

I shall swim down
And bring up a red fish.
I shall hold it between my fingers
It will be happy in my hands
I shall lay it between my breasts
Beloved, come and watch!

If anyone in that hall was in any doubt as to the variety of red fish which the singer wished to make happy in her hands, they must have been deaf. The Singer of Hathor allowed the musicians to play a bright dance tune while she drank some wine.

I smiled at my lord, and he left his scribes and came to me, sitting down at my feet. I was amazed that he would sit thus, a sign of submission, and I could not have it so I joined him on the floor and we sat shoulder to shoulder while maidens passed by us with more wine and the heset began to sing again. She sang sadly to a heartrending tune.

My love is on the other side,
My desired one is across the river
The water is deep and runs strongly
The water is the crocodiles' home.

The pipes joined in, playing a sad lament behind the harsh voice, which now sounded male. The heset was clearly a woman of power.

Ptah-hotep touched my side, just above my hip bone with the tip of one finger, and I gasped. Then I drew my nail very lightly across his shoulder where the collar bone leaves a hollow, and felt him react. Whatever power we had been given by the gods, we still had some of it.

I do not fear the river depths.
I do not fear the waiting teeth
I walk the riverbed as though it was land
I will come to you, my love.

The lament changed imperceptibly to a celebration. The voice swooned with pleasure as Hathor's singer finished the verse:

Wet, I will walk into your house.
Wet, I will lie down beside you.
Wet, you will embrace me
Wetter still shall we be.

The song shifted into more dancing music, and a troupe of Nubian women came in, wild dancers in body-paint and feathers. I could not get near Makhayib to congratulate her, nor did I have any little ornaments or beads with me to throw.

And Ptah-hotep was beside me and I did not want to move. He leaned closer to me in the salutation called 'the exchange of breath' and rubbed his cheek against mine. He smelt sweet, felt sweeter. I wanted to caress him, make love to him; my urgency astonished me, and I punched down my desire as a woman kneads prematurely-risen dough.

'We will have to stay until the last of the food is served. I am told that the King has ordered something special which he wants us all to taste,' he whispered. 'After that, lady, will you come to my bed?'

'Yes,' I said promptly, I had never learned the art of teasing and flirting and it was too late to start, now that I had given away my heart.

'More wine!' declared a woman near me. She was swaying on her chair and I moved aside in case she was about to throw up all over me—which had happened at these feasts often enough.

'You, Lady Mutnodjme, you have a lover with you! Let him declaim a poem to you. It is a night for love!'

I was about to demur—I was sure that Ptah-hotep, though an excellent person and the object of my profound desire, had had no training in love poetry—when he took my hand and said in his clear, precise voice:

Ask of the lotus, what say you?
My petals are her skin,
And my scent her scent.

This was a variant of a word game I had played as a child. It was a riddle game. "What says the wood? My arms are folded" for instance, meant a shut door. The drunken woman cheered and others leaned closer to hear what Ptah-hotep would say next.

Ask of the net, what say you?
I am my lady's hair; ensnaring her lover.

'Very good, very good!' enthused the audience. 'More wine and more words of love! Your turn, lady Mutnodjme.'

So I obliged:

Ask of the sycamore tree, what say you?
I am a young man's arms, strong and supple.

Ptah-hotep lifted a hand to my breast and cupped it very gently, yet I could feel the whorls on each finger's end, and said:

Ask of the pomegranate, what say you?
My pips are her teeth, my fruit her breasts.

The Nubian dancers had gone and the whole court was gathered around us, waiting to hear what Ptah-hotep and Mutnodjme would invent next. It was my turn again:

Ask of the night, what say you?
I am her beginning and her ending,
I am her musk and her mystery.

Ptah-hotep continued:

Nefertiti filled my wine cup again, and Ptah-hotep leaned on my shoulder, fatigued by love and poetry.

My lord Akhnaten dropped a golden arm ring into my lap and another into Ptah-hotep's hand. He smiled down on us, the vague and misty smile of a prophet.

'You are well-matched,' he told us.

I tasted the herb menhep in the wine. It was a known aphrodisiac, not that we needed it.

What was the King trying to do? Were we all to couple on the floor, as the peasants did at the festival of two gods in which he no longer believed?

I resolved at least to find a suitable corner for myself and my lover if we were overcome by lust.

When we were overcome by lust; there was no if. My blood was heated by the wine and the proximity of my lover and the music, which was now sinuous and erotic, the marriage music of the Black Land.

The heset raised her voice again, cutting through the babble of people calling for more wine or bread, to sing:

When I see your eyes shine
When I press close to look at you
Oh my beloved
Ruler of my heart!

The guests had begun to dance, not step dances but the marriage dances usually performed in private. The air in the hall was hot. My perfume cone had melted into my wig. Over my shoulders and down my breasts trickled cooling oil which tickled and made my skin shine. The same phenomenon emphasised all the muscles in the chest of Ptah-hotep the scribe.

The king and all the royal household were dancing. Pannefer and Huy were on their feet, mostly naked and smeared with oil, and their wives with them, giggling like children, as the Singer of Hathor continued.

This hour is happy
As you lie between my thighs
May this hour of bliss
Last forever, forever…

People were already seeking corners so that they could lie down with their chosen lovers. The drunken woman seized a passing servant and pulled his head down to her breast, spilling the ewer of wine which he had been carrying. I began to be afraid that I could not contain my lust much longer. The music was wild, shrilling over a grumble of fast-beating drums.

'Something is happening,' Ptah-hotep pulled away from my caress. 'My love, my heart, wait a little longer, I must see…'

I ground my teeth in frustration, dug my fingernails into the palm of my hand and saw that trays were being carried amongst the guests by clean kitchen servants. I saw roasted flesh laid out as always, but the source of the flesh turned me sick with revulsion instead of lust.

This is what it was; it was all the venerated animals of Egypt, cooked. Yet there was nothing wrong with the way they had been cooked, dog and ibis and cat and crocodile. They smelt appetising and everyone was eating, snatching pieces of holy flesh, tearing the carcasses apart.

'We will have to eat,' I whispered.

'Take a piece of the ibis for me,' he said, and we bit and swallowed the white cooked flesh of the avatar of Thoth, god of wisdom and writing, judge of the netherworld, Ptah-hotep's god.

The King, who had been drifting past, saw us and threw another load of gold at us in token of his pleasure.

Then I saw what beast had been served for the consumption of the royal family alone.

It was a beautifully-displayed roasted hawk, both Horus Avenger and Re-Harakhti, the most sacred of all creatures, symbol of Amen-Re at noon, the hawk in the horizon.

Ptah-hotep

As I ate a mouthful of the ibis flesh I dedicated myself again to Thoth, god of learning, and knew as my sister and spouse ate the same amount of holy beast that we would never be the same again, and neither would Egypt.

But we still burned. The feast was degenerating into such an orgy as Mentu my second in command had described as taking place in the more expensive brothels of the river-margin. Wine was spilled and rolled in, so that the floor was awash with it and trodden bread, broken pottery and the remains of shamefully slaughtered holy creatures.

I took Mutnodjme's hand and we crawled away through the tipped over chairs past the copulating lovers and the vomiting drunks until we came to the door, crept unobserved over the threshold, and ran.

We ran away from the sed festival feast as though we were running for our lives from a terrible foe. We slipped, leaving wine red smears on the floor from our tainted feet. We clutched each other in fear and kept running until we came to my own apartments, startling Anubis into a warning snarl before he recognised our scent.

We barred the doors successively behind us as we went in through the outer office, inner office, outer living quarters and finally the inner rooms, which only contained my bedroom, a small store for treasures, and my bathroom.

'Ptah-hotep,' gasped my lady, freeing her body from cloth and jewellery. 'I am horrified, I am revolted, but I am so sick with lust that I will not be able to think unless...'

I was in the same condition. Even when we had run—and why had we run like that? No one was chasing us, certainly no one would have missed us or noticed our going—I had been aroused almost to pain. I tore at the strings of my loincloth and threw it away and dropped the king's gifts on top of it.

No delicacies were between us this time, no more words, just raw need. I slid down onto the floor, lying on my back; she swooped down upon me like a heron, and we were joined so close and so hard that we reached a climax in what seemed like moments. Before my phallus had time to shrink, it was hard again, and this time our coupling lasted longer.

I had never mated like that, not with man or woman. It was so ferocious, straining to get closer, to bury myself in the female body which strove to swallow me into herself and suck an orgasm from me. Her muscles closed around my phallus like a fist. Our shared perception was gone. This was almost like battle, a struggle to wrench satisfaction from the other body, and when we climaxed again and collapsed, her body over mine, we were winded and shocked and unable to explain why we had been so rough with each other.

I was inside her heart again, and she in mine. Very carefully, we helped each other to our feet and stood on the cool marble of the washroom and bathed each other.

'Oh, my lord, my love,' she said, sluicing cool water over my body. She lathered my head and body with the soft herb-scented soap which Meryt made for me, and I felt oil and semen and wine wash off my skin and run down my body in runnels of filth. My lady used a whole huge well-jar of water on cleansing me, then she stood trembling as I did the same for her, soaping her hair and rinsing her until the water ran clear.

Then we were cold. We wrapped ourselves in several Nubian blankets made of softest goat's wool and lay down together and fell asleep as though we had been stunned.

I was woken in the dead of night by Meryt knocking on the outer door. It was her special knock and I climbed out of bed and went to let her in. She had brought the wives and children with her and Hani as bodyguard.

'Master, you shut me out!' she exclaimed. I must have looked at her strangely, for she did not chide me further, but bustled the little ones into their places and ordered Hani to take Anubis and mind the door. Hani was sleepy and drunk, but Anubis was alert. He was an old dog now, but his reflexes were as sharp as ever.

'I have heard strange things,' she said. 'But they can wait until morning, Master.'

I staggered back to the blankets, and wrapped myself so that I was lying as close to my lady as I could, and fell asleep again.

Morning brought Meryt with an infusion of bitter herbs and the news that most of the palace had gone mad the previous night.

'You were well out of that feast, Master,' she told me, watching to make sure that I drank her infusion and handing a pottery cup to my lady. I assumed that Meryt used pottery cups for her infusions because they would eat through bronze. While I was testing the inside of my mouth to see if all my teeth were there and trying to recollect the previous evening—which had ended agreeably, it seemed—Meryt continued.

'This morning the servants came to clear up and found three people dead of some sort of frenzy, Master. Dead among the broken wine cups and torn clothes and spilled beer. The floor was slippery with blood and man-seed, what happened at that feast? I have heard of such things in barbarian tribes such as the vile Kush, but never in the painted feasting-hall of an Egyptian King!'

'Oh, Lady Isis, I remember,' exclaimed Mutnodjme, and in a rush, so did I. We groaned. 'Did we...did the King...' she began, and I agreed.

'Yes, we did. We coupled like animals. And the King served up a special dessert. It was composed of all the sacred beasts of Egypt, and he made us eat it.'

I beat my lady by a whisker to the closet, where we vomited up all the holy flesh which we might have eaten, as well as a lot of wine. Meryt, understanding only that something terrible had occurred, made us a drink of beaten eggs and milk and cinnamon to settle our rebellious insides.

Then we washed again and clothed ourselves and sat down out of earshot to watch Meryt teaching Hani's youngest how to feed himself with a spoon—he was now three and had been newly weaned—and to consider what we had seen.

'There was an aphrodisiac herb in the wine the King poured for us,' Mutnodjme told me. 'It is possible that the whole feast was designed by the King to make us lose control. The wine was double strength, the food was excellent, and the music was exciting.'

'Someone designed this other than the King Akhnaten may he live,' I protested. 'He has little tact and has already presented us with the statement that there are no gods other than the Aten and we had better believe so, on pain of death. No, this is a dark plotting mind. This was to drag us all into dreadful sin, to turn us away from whatever we might have had left of devotion to the old gods. For now everyone at that feast, including me and even you, have committed an unforgivable sin.'

'So we cannot afford to believe in the old gods, because if we do believe in them, we condemn ourselves to everlasting torment?'

'As long as it takes for a heart to be eaten by Aphopis, yes.'

'And now we are accomplices, are we not? Co-offenders. We are all in the same prison wearing identical fetters having committed identical crimes.'

'That is the idea.'

'Huy,' she decided.

'Pannefer,' I argued.

'Possibly both,' she conceded. 'Do you feel burdened by a dreadful sin, Ptah-hotep, my beloved?'

'Not really. If I had been force-fed ibis flesh, I would have committed no sin, and that was close to force-feeding such as men do to geese. In the same fashion, watch the way Meryt distracts the child and then pops a spoonful of porridge into his mouth. It was like that. What could we do, with the King actually watching us?'

'We could say,' she observed, 'that by eating the flesh of our gods we have communed with them, taken them inside us.'

'That's a good thought, and it comforts me.'

I embraced her gently, my wise lady, careful of the bruises, and she kissed what she said was a bite on my throat.

I had another thought. 'Mark the ingenuity of it, my beloved lady. First they served fish, a forbidden creature, but every farmer in the Black Land eats fish so that did not seem sinful. Certainly not customary but not really sinful, and churlish to refuse in the middle of such a lavish feast.'

'Yes, I ate some of it, it was very good,' agreed my lady. 'But I have often eaten fish. Except for the one kind which consumed Osiris' phallus, it is not forbidden to Isis, just to the palace, and I always thought that that prohibition had something to do with making sure that the palace didn't eat all the fish and leave nothing for the common people.'

'To be sure, and many people at the feast would have eaten fish on their country estates. So it eased us into the greater transgression of the laws, do you see? By the time that grisly collation was being carried around, we had already broken one law so why not another? *Be exiled for a flock, not one single goat,* so says the maxim of the Divine Amenhotep-Osiris, how I wish that he had lived forever.'

'I, too,' she sighed.

'I still think it is Pannefer,' I stated.

'Huy. A career selling broken down asses to unwilling buyers teaches that sort of dirty skill,' she insisted.

'You may be right, my heart. Now, how do you feel? As though you are doomed to be eaten after death? As though your heart must sink against the feather?'

'We ate as little as we could,' she said slowly, curling one strand of night-black hair around her strong finger. 'We ran away as soon as we could. We coupled like beasts, but that was the night and the feast and the poisoned wine, and our own lust which it magnified, and lust is not a sin if the object is free and consenting.'

'You flung me to the floor, lady, I didn't have time to consent,' I protested.

And she said gravely, 'You were consenting in your heart. I could tell from the way you tore off your clothes.' Then she grinned and her eyes were much brighter than they had a right to be after the night we had spent and the wine we had consumed. I laughed at her reply and she continued.

'So therefore, no, although I will confess this to Maat and Thoth, I do not expect that one act to weight against my heart too badly. As long as I don't do it again.'

'The mating?' I objected.

'The blasphemy,' she reproved.

'Ah,' I was comforted.

'But what they will do to the author of this abomination,' she said slowly, 'Does not bear thinking about.'

We sat together companionably, both considering with vengeful pleasure the centuries it would take the serpent Apep to digest my lord Akhnaten in its boiling belly, and we laughed so much that Meryt released her prisoner, wiped porridge off her face, and asked us what the joke was. And we couldn't tell her.

Chapter Twenty

Mutnodjme

The decan which followed the abominable feast was very quiet. People avoided each other's eyes. Husbands and wives were careful of each other and servants walked on tip toe.

Widow-Queen Tiye had heard all about it by the time I came back to her apartments.

'Blasphemy,' she snorted. 'But tame enough, if one thinks about it. I am glad I was not there. I might have said something which even my son could not forgive. For what use has a eunuch for menhep herb? Ah, well, it is with the gods and they are not going to be very happy about this,' she warned.

It was no use asking Tiye may she live about whether she thought that, by eating the flesh of a sacred beast, Ptah-hotep and I had committed an unforgivable sin. Tiye the Queen had no patience with religion. Her view was that most things could be explained to the Divine Judges, and if they did not exist then they could be explained to the Aten, and she was prepared to berate either or both of them for creating her son Akhnaten.

'I was strong and loving and so was his father and we birthed and nurtured him as well as we could,' she argued. 'If he isn't the fault of the gods, then whose fault is he?'

It was a good question and I didn't have the answer.

Nefertiti mourned her dead child fittingly but briefly. Her putative father King Akhnaten cried for a day and then forgot about her. Now there were five royal children of Amarna and I did not like the look of the next little princess, Neferneferure. She was sitting on the floor with Tutankhaten, playing with blocks. The boy was thin but sturdy, taking after his mother like the child Smenkhare. His sidelock had a tinge of red and his complexion was pale rather than dark. The two children were building a city.

'The temple of the Aten is here,' declared Tutankhaten, placing a cornerstone and raising his hand. 'I declare that the Aten is the great god and there is no other.'

'Then the temple of the Phoenix is here,' said Neferneferure, placing a block on her side of the construction. 'Hail the Phoenix, firebird, sweet singer!'

Nefertiti often sent her children to play with the Widow-Queen Tiye's family. My sister was almost as vague as her husband now and declared that the shrill arguing of the royal children hurt her head. They did not quarrel when with Tiye may she live because the Widow-Queen's authority, which could command provinces, was just as strong as ever and it was very difficult to sustain an argument under the ironic and intelligent eyes of the Queen.

Also she was not afraid to clip ears or spank bottoms if the patient became really intransigent.

But with Tiye the children knew the rules, and played peaceably with each other. Ankhesenpaaten was engaged in her first attempts at spinning, an accomplishment which all women learn, and was doing creditably enough, spinning a thick thread full of knots. This did not please her and she grabbed the distaff in disgust, about to throw the offending tools across the room, when she caught Widow-Queen Tiye's dispassionate gaze and decided not to do that after all, but to pick up the distaff and spindle and try again. This time she spun a thread fully as long as her arm before the thread broke. Ankhesenpaaten measured out the spinning and chuckled.

'You see, little daughter, losing the temper does not help,' said Tiye quietly. I wished that she had had the teaching of me and my sister Merope. No one had been able to teach me true patience, not even the temple of Isis. I knew how to wait, of course, but I was not patient. Ankhesenpaaten took her thread to show Merope, who was looking better, relieved that her mourning had kept her from the unholy feast.

'Look, Lady Merope,' said the little princes, Merope admired the thread and began the spinning again, and for awhile there was no sound in the apartments of the Widow-Queen but the noise of building from the floor and the humming of Ankhesenpaaten as she spun a creditable thread. Most skills, I find, come suddenly. I remembered grubbing along trying to weave, dropping my shuttle, tangling my weft, starring too high so that I could hardly reach my first line and biting my lip so that I should not lose my temper with the irritating threads, until one day I found I could do it. The shuttle flew from one hand to the other, the woven material moved down the web like magic, and I was a weaver. Not that weaving was a female skill, of course, but the Temple of Isis instructed its daughters in all arts of making, never knowing what might be the most useful.

I missed the temple suddenly, the quiet and the learning and the freedom from surprise. That reminded me that I had a message to deliver and I beckoned Widow-Queen Tiye into an inner room.

'A letter has come from Tushratta,' I informed her, putting the clay tablet and the written translation into her lap. She read it carefully. Then she read it again.

'How many letters came before this?' she asked, her eyebrows rising.

'Three, and they seem to have gone unanswered,' I replied. 'This is bad. And my son has called in the army; the commanders are meeting with him tomorrow. Tushratta is an ally, moreover the Khatti are ambitious and fierce, and he could be overthrown. If so, where will the King of Khatti look for a new conquest? Why not the Black Land? Very rich, very big, and best of all, unguarded, because the King is a lunatic.'

Tiye combed her hair with her fingers, thinking deeply. Then she sat up straight and smiled.

'I have it. Your Ptah-hotep has a friend, Mutnodjme, a friend of his bosom from the days of the school of scribes. A very pretty young man—now what was his name? Kheperren, that's it. He's an army scribe with General Horemheb. This Kheperren always takes the opportunity to visit Amarna when he can, he is sure to have come with his General.

'Contrive to invite me to meet Ptah-hotep when he has Kheperren with him and the General happens to call as well. What could be more pleasant than a little dinner, perhaps, in the Great Royal Scribe's apartments? I cannot give orders about the army, now that my son has forbidden women to attend councils of state. I must do this by stealth, daughter— dear daughter. You are the daughter I would wish that I had borne, Mutnodjme. My Sitamen is an admirable woman but she is not here, and you are.'

Then she kissed me affectionately, as my own mother never had, and I went back to watch the children playing. I could not go to Ptah-hotep during the day, when he had work to do. And the task of women in the City of the Sun, it seemed, was to please their lords and mind their children; not to practice medicine or speak wise words, not to learn or advise or contrive. Just to be. It was very tedious.

Presently it grew hot. I do not know why my lord Akhnaten had decided to exclude women from all his councils. This had never been the case in the past. Wise Queens had advised their lords; Queen Tiye had always been with Amenhotep-Osiris, sitting beside him to receive ambassadors and discussing affairs of state with him every evening before he went to lie with one wife or another.

I was damp with sweat and there seemed to be no air in the room. I picked up the embroidery which Merope had half finished, threaded a needle and attached a few beads, then put it down again. I was restless. I wanted to do something, learn something, exercise my mind.

Though I was not allowed to attend councils, there was nothing wrong with the Lady Mutnodjme learning to read. Even the royal children were taught to read. Every woman was taught to read, I reasoned, and the fact that I was about to embark on learning to read cuneiform was not material. The principle, as Lady Duammerset had said, was sound.

I took the wrapped tablet and the translation from Widow-Queen Tiye and told them that I would be back before night. Then I walked quickly to the King's side of the palace. Of course, my desire for learning had nothing to do with the fact that it must take place in the office of my lover.

I did not want to disturb him. I just wanted to be able to see him, if I raised my eyes.

The office door was open. The Nubian Tani sat inside, leaning on a long spear with a wickedly barbed head. He grinned a big melon-wide grin and let me pass, saying something in Nubian about the insatiable desires of women to which I lacked sufficient vocabulary to reply. I bowed to Ptah-hotep and asked, 'Lord, I would learn to read the square writing. Can you spare either Menna or Harmose to instruct me?'

'I have some leisure, Master Ptah-hotep may you live,' said Menna, a split second ahead of Harmose, who subsided grumbling.

'You can have her tomorrow,' said Menna, giving his seatmate a nudge with a bony elbow. 'I saw her first,' he added, and Harmose nodded solemnly.

Ptah-hotep rose and came to where I was sitting, ensuring that I had a piece of soft clay to practice on and showing me how to hold the stylus which imprinted the letters into it.

Into my ear he whispered, 'Lady, I love you.'

And I said aloud, 'Indeed, Lord, such is also my opinion. I hope to be able to prove it soon. Oh, by the way, I took the liberty of inviting the Mistress of Egypt the Great Royal Widow Queen Tiye to your dinner tomorrow night with your friend the scribe and his protector—I don't recall his name.'

My tone was light and slightly bored. 'I really know nothing of military matters and the Royal Lady was kind enough to offer to keep me company.'

No one could ever call the great Royal Scribe Ptah-hotep slow on the uptake. After a moment's initial puzzlement when he tried to remember when he had invited me to meet Kheperren and the General Horemheb, he understood and replied easily.

'Certainly, lady, my friend Kheperren expressed a desire to meet you, but surely you would not find reminiscences of our days at the school of scribes interesting. And I am honoured by the condescension of the Widow-Queen Tiye may she live and will endeavour to amuse you both. Tell the Royal Lady, if you would, that it is just a small dinner, humble fare, but I can offer her good wine. The Tashery vintage of three years ago was superb.'

I saw Meryt, who had clearly been cooking—there was flour on both her cheeks and a wide smear on her haunches where she had wiped her hands—give my dearest love a sharp look. Clearly she did not think 'humble fare' a good description of the dishes she was presently preparing. But she allowed the moment to pass and went back to her pots.

Menna had been a royal scribe for thirty years. He was aware that the conversation which he had just heard was loaded with hidden references, but Menna was an old royal scribe and knew better than to comment. Royal scribes, even in the relaxed reign of Amenhotep-Osiris, were discreet, or they were re-employed as labourers on drainage ditches.

Menna laid out on the little table in front of him an inscribed clay tablet, a new clay tablet and a stylus.

'This is the alphabet, Lady. It is a syllabry, not one letter for each sound, as the cursive which you would have learned—you did learn cursive?'

'I did,' I assured him. 'I was taught first by Khons and then by Duammerset; and my dear friend Snefru allowed me to inspect many of his hoarded scrolls and copied inscriptions.'

I was relying on the spy in the office—Ptah-hotep had confidently identified him as Bakhenmut's scribe, a young man called Pashed—not knowing the names. They were all common. He would certainly not have heard of Duammerset, the Singer of Isis, and in any case the Lady Duammerset was in the Field of Reeds, probably with Snefru the Scribe, questioning the authors of the most intractable texts as to what they had really meant by them and having a wonderful time, which is what the Field of Reeds is for.

There was nothing that Huy or Pannefer could do to any of the persons I had named. They were all dead, though Duammerset was not the King Akhnaten's fault. Khons murdered and Snefru dead of shock, however, were.

Menna was a man of great self-control. He raised a papery-skinned hand to wipe tears from his face, but even a close observer would not have noticed that he was weeping, probably for Snefru the Scribe. Everyone knew Snefru and his eternal quest for more ancient writings, everyone liked him and everyone in the field of learning missed him.

'I was just saying to my colleague, I said, "This is a difficult passage, we'll have to ask Snefru, he'll know." I just said that. And here you are, another of Snefru's pupils. He has been much in my mind today,' he explained, very softly.

I said, 'Master, you have an insect in your eye, let me help you,' and made a great business of wiping his eyes with a piece of linen and re-drawing his kohl, and by the time I had finished he had recovered himself. He took my hand under the table and squeezed it gently. His grasp was dry, like papyrus. Then he remarked, 'See, daughter, this little picture which I am drawing is what?'

'A plough,' I said.

'A plough. Now this is the cuneiform sign for the word eppinu which means 'plough.' It also stands for the syllable or sound, of course. Can you see how the sign has developed from the picture? Good, here is another. What would you call this?'

I examined the pictograph. 'Trees, Master Menna?'

'Trees indeed, you are quick, daughter. That is the pictograph for kiru, orchard. This is sadu, mountain, and this is alpu, which means.'

'Ox, I see. How many signs are there?'

'Five hundred and thirty one,' Menna informed me with relish. Of course. He liked my company and this task was going to take a considerable time. 'Each mark has threads and bars; by these the syllable is qualified and this is the determinative and this marks the vowels.'

The system was alien to my mind, as strange as the signs which the Nubians carve on trees to warn wayfarers and mark boundaries. I was employed for two hours in attempting to grasp the syllabry, and I had made little progress when I had to return to the Widow-Queen Tiye's quarters, and I walked into what looked like a small and well-contained war.

Tiye the Queen may she live was standing in the middle of the room, absolutely beside herself with wrath. My sister Nefertiti was cowering by the door, her back against it, so that I nearly pushed her over when I came in.

The Widow-Queen was so angry that I was very tempted to turn around and go straight out again until she calmed down, but she gestured to me to come in and with Tiye may she live it was much better, in the long run, to do as one was told.

I joined Merope against the window. She was shaking. I took her in my arms and she leaned her forehead against my breast and whispered, 'I think we are all about to die.'

'Lady, sister, what is the matter?' I asked, holding onto Merope and turning her face away from the Widow-Queen's basilisk gaze.

'The Great Royal Spouse of Egypt,' spat Tiye, 'has come to inform your sister Merope and I that we must marry again and confer our authority and our bodies on a commoner.'

'Oh,' I said lamely. This was so totally unheard-of that I really did not know what to say. The widow of a pharaoh belongs to his successor, that was the practice. She could not marry again unless Pharaoh divorced her, and if he did she had a right to take with her two thirds of all that she owned, as did any woman in Egypt. And the widow of a Pharaoh could not marry a common man, because she held in her right of marriage some claim to the throne.

Nefertiti had not remembered that she could have us all beheaded if we crossed her, and I had no intention of reminding her. My sister was frightened and looked to me to explain matters to this intransigent Royal Lady.

'My lord Akhnaten has said, on our Divine Father's advice, that it is of no profit to support the whole house of women of his late father,' she quavered.

'Therefore he has given each woman the right to choose a husband and he will release them from their marriage, requiring them only to marry another man.'

'But, sister, that means that the Pharaoh Lord Akhnaten may he live will have to return to the Royal Women their property that is the law in Egypt,' I said carefully. I assumed that my Divine Father Ay had thought of that, and he had.

'No, no, sister, the priests of the Aten sole and only God will be happy to receive royal ladies into their houses, no dowry will be required.'

'Nefertiti my sister, you are telling a woman who has been queen that she will have to go and live with a priest of Aten, and you are proposing to turn her out of the palace naked,' I said, just to make sure that my sister got the point.

'I really don't think that the Lord of the Two Thrones could possibly have meant that. Are you sure?'

'My Lord has given orders,' she said mulishly, and there was never any reasoning with Nefertiti when she became stubborn.

'The Royal Women will go with the priests of the Aten where they will be happy, and they have the rest of the month to prepare.'

'Tell my son,' said Widow-Queen Tiye, 'that I will not marry again. If he wants me to die, I am willing to do that to please him and relieve that miser Ay of the burden of supplying my bread; but I will not marry. The others may do as they like, but not I. Is that clear, Great Royal Wife? I am staying here.'

Nefertiti nodded and made her escape.

I tried to release Merope but she clung. 'Sister,' she whispered, 'Oh, dearest sister, I think that I see an escape from this loathsome existence.'

I called for some wine. She was clearly overwrought.

Ptah-hotep

The King Akhnaten may he live called us all to the Window of Appearances to hear his announcement. The courtyard was filled with soldiers in ordered ranks. The Klashr archers and heavy infantry had the place of honour at the front. They lived nearest, in Thebes and all along the shores of the river down to Bubastis. The Hermotybies were behind, soldiers from Upper Egypt.

Each soldier had his land, awarded by the Pharaoh when he was accepted into the army and each tilled it as best he could, for he might be called into active service at any time. Each wore leather jerkins and battle-cloths provided by his own household and bore shield, sword, bow and arrows. Regiment, battalion and company, they all bore their own standards, a stout pole with a symbol on top, long enough so that when held by a mounted man it was visible to all fighters on the field

I considered them, the poles surmounted with a thousand images: hawks, crocodiles from Elephantine, the cat of Bubastis, the sun-boat of the discredited god Amen-Re. Some were simple like the flail of kingship, perhaps, or the leg-shaped symbol of the Goddess Isis; or simpler still like a huge bronze arrowhead, painted red. Some were complex and beautiful: a reed-boat with a fisherman catching Nile perch; a flight of flying ibis, legs trailing. All of them were decorated with ribbons and flowers.

This wasn't the whole army, of course. This was a representative selection of officers, come to hear what their King the lord Akhnaten wanted to say. They would relay his message to the armies camped outside on the hot plain surrounding Amarna.

My dearest love Kheperren was beside me, mostly hidden behind a massive bull's hide shield studded with metal rivets. I was pleased at being under the canopy which had been erected for the King to rest under during the sed festival, for we were waiting for noon and the sun was already hot.

I was also very pleased to see him again. He was very weary. I had promised him a real wash in real water, a massage from Meryt, a splendid feast and a night spent making love—all his requests—but still he was grim and distant. I was worried that he was concerned about the lady Mutnodjme, but it did not seem to be that.

I had told him about her and he had kissed me—he tasted of sweat and copper from his helmet-strap, a very male taste—and bade me not to fear, he was assured of my love. He had yet to meet my lady Mutnodjme but I was sure that they would be friends.

'Here is my General,' he said in relief, and I saw the strong figure of Horemheb appear under the balcony beneath the King.

'Why, where did you think he might be?' I asked.

'I thought he might be dead,' replied Kheperren.

Clearly there was more to tell and just as clearly I could not ask it, so I held my peace. The King stretched out both hands and called 'Soldiers of the Aten! I have a great task for you! The foes of Egypt are not inside her borders alone!'

The soldiers roared, 'Show us your enemies, lord!' and the King held out his arms again.

'They are here, in the Black Land!'

He paused, and I saw helmeted heads turn to each other. What did he mean?

I looked at Horemheb. I had never seen a face so set. The General had aged well. He was strong and heavily muscled, with a broad chest and legs like columns. The long wig mingled with his own harsh black hair, which still bore many locks tipped with blue beads. His arms were heavy with arm rings given to him by Pharaoh, and his breastplate was almost covered with the golden flies awarded rarely and only for extreme bravery. My lord Akhnaten cried out again.

'They are the followers of the name of the cursed so-called god, Amen-Re!'

The soldiers were silent. This did not seem to be something against which they could use sword or spear.

'I will send you out, brave warriors of the Aten, to remove the trace of the name of Amen-Re from this Black Land! I will reward you, my brave ones, for every inscription defaced, every name removed, every text burned! Let the foes of Egypt tremble on the borders, they will not attack us while the Aten rules us! Hail to the Aten!' he screamed, and stared straight up at the sun.

The soldiers roared approval.

'Why do they cheer? This is no task for a soldier,' I protested, very close to Kheperren's ear.

'This task is easier than fighting the vile Kush where every bush contains an enemy. This is more amusing than arriving, footsore and weary, at an oasis where the wells have been broken and the trees cut down by the shepherds, the Shasu. This is much less dangerous than crawling through the sand to attack the Apiru, where every dune has its asp,' he said bitterly.

'But who will guard the borders?' I gasped.

'The Aten, apparently,' he said very quietly. 'Let us hope that his god is heavily armed.'

Pharaoh Akhnaten lifted a huge basket and began to throw handfuls of small glittering objects into the mass of soldiers and they scrambled for them, breaking ranks. I flung up a hand and caught one.

'What is it?' asked the General, taking his eyes off the Window of Appearances. I opened my hand. I have never seen such a look of complete disgust on a human face. In my hand I had the highest award for bravery which the Pharaoh could give. I was holding a golden bee.

General Horemheb reassumed his place and his bland countenance very quickly. But when he came to dinner that night I noticed that he had removed from his breastplate every single award, and was as undecorated as any common soldier.

◇◇◇

But first I had to give my Kheperren all that I had promised. I stood him in my washing place and he emptied two well-jars of water and a dish of soap before he had removed all the dirt, grease and something which resembled tar, which he said was protective tree resin, applied to guard against the sun. He shaved his beard and lay down to be oiled and massaged by Meryt, who was the best massager I had ever encountered. She found every knot and pounded each one mercilessly, leaving her patient as completely softened as the meat which she flattened with a mallet before frying it in the Nubian fashion. Then I gave him a cup of wine and we made love, very gently, touching with wincing care. I had missed him like a crippled man misses his right hand, and clearly he had lacked me. We were slow, soft, stopping to exchange breath and to kiss, long kisses which turned languorous and then hot, so that we finished in a rush and a tangle of limbs.

Then we slept a little until the heat of the day was easing, for though it was Peret and the month of Mechir, the weather was unseasonable. I had not seen the records of the last harvest yet. Some of the Nomarchs were always late with their reports, but this year everyone was late.

I wondered if anyone was intercepting my correspondence and reading it, seeking heresy or conspiracy. If so, I wished them joy of the illiterate scribes of Elephantine and the extreme mendacity of the Delta. And if they could make any sense of the peculiar arithmetic of Thebes, which always seemed to come down rather heavily on the side of the Nomarch, then I hoped that they would tell me.

Horemheb was outside. We could hear him exchanging ritual insults with Mentu; who was with us for awhile, having been warned by his physician that a month's abstinence from wine and women might preserve his life a little longer.

When he felt inclined Mentu was an excellent scribe, wrote a beautiful flowing hand and could sum up a complex docu-ment in one sentence which, suitably censored, could be used as a briefing note for the Lord of the Two Lands who could usually be compelled to listen to one sentence. Mentu had just summarised a basketful of letters from three vassal states as, 'My neighbour is a liar. Send gold. Lots and lots and lots of gold!' which was an excellent summary; and Horemheb, laughing, also agreed.

He was escorted into my inner office by Tani and Hani, one on either side, and they did not leave until I ordered them to go. They didn't like anyone as big and warlike as the general anywhere near me.

The general slumped down into a chair, making the cords creak. Kheperren poured him a cup of the pale Nubian-style beer which he preferred and suggested that he would be more comfortable in the chair of state, which was built for such large limbs. Horemheb moved obediently, which was nice of him, because I was fond of the saddle-strung chair and I didn't think it would hold up his weight much longer.

He was huge. He was also very tired and very worried.

'How safe is it to talk?' he asked.

'There are two Nubians outside this door; the walls are thick and as long as we keep away from the windows no listener can hear; besides, we are on the third floor,' I told him.

'Apart from Hani and Tani and their equally huge brother Teti, there is Meryt; and apart from her there is Mentu, who will knock over a very large bronze pot which has carelessly been placed far too close to his chair, if he has to leap to his feet and prostrate himself before any Royal Personages. It makes a sound like a war-drum and can be easily heard from here,' I concluded.

The General passed one scarred hand over his ravaged face and said, 'You choose your lovers well, Kheperren. I can see that you are as careful and wise as your friend has been telling me these ten years, my Lord Ptah-hotep.'

He leaned forward and stared into my eyes. He had dark eyes in a broad face, much like the common people, a beaked nose and wide cheekbones. The eyes were very tired but shrewd and deep and they held my attention. 'This I must tell you, Great

Royal Scribe; unless we can contrive something, you and me and the Great Royal Wife Tiye, we are going to lose most of Egypt before the next Inundation.'

Chapter Twenty-one

Mutnodjme

Tani and Hani escorted me into the inner chamber of my lord Ptah-hotep's office. They were both carrying spears and were grave—no jokes about lust this night. The Widow-Queen Tiye and I had groomed ourselves very carefully for this meeting. She was wearing her greying hair loose, threaded through with garlands and ribbons, and the finest gauze draped her limbs. I had borrowed Merope's block-patterned cloth with indigo riders all over it and had tucked my own hair under a heavy court-wig, decorated with a lotus crown.

We wanted to look like we were going to a feast with no other thoughts but good wine and good company. The Widow-Queen had sung a little song as we paced the corridors. When I could hear what she was singing, it was not a feasting or a love song but a curse, sung to a light melody.

The Widow Queen Tiye says
The crocodile be against him in water
The snake be against him on land
He shall have no offering
No bread and no beer
No wine and no oil
The earth shall not be dug for him

The offerings shall not be made for him
When he dies, when he dies.

She was frightening me, this red-headed woman, and I began to wonder whether there might have been something in the old superstition that red hair is a sign of the children of Set the Destroyer.

The occupants of the room rose as we came in. There was my dear Ptah-hotep, and with him a young man equally slim and well made, with black eyes and dark, weathered skin. He smiled and bowed, as did the huge man hauling himself out of the chair of state.

General Horemheb still stood a cubit above me. His chest was massive, his hands were huge as he took mine very carefully, bowed, and then knelt to the Widow-Queen as was proper. She put her right palm on his head and told him to rise and we all sat down.

'Meryt has made a feast and we will have to eat it,' said Ptah-hotep with a trace of apology. 'Otherwise my domestic life will not be worth living.'

'That does not seem to be a heavy task,' said General Horemheb, smiling, and when Meryt and Teti came in escorting a train of children, all bearing dishes, he greeted the Nubians in very good Nubian.

'Hail, lady of the Village-between-two-trees!' he said, and Meryt was so surprised that she almost dropped her big platter of cooked meat. She replied in her own tongue, 'Hail, Great Warrior! You do my family honour by eating with us. When were you in the Village-between-two-trees, lord?'

'But last year. The children who were babes when the Egyptians came are grown now and your uncle is Chief. He sends you greetings, sister.'

It was a measure of the worth of the General Horemheb that he had remembered the slave Meryt, whom he had seen perhaps twice, and had enquired into the state of her home village. The Nubians all bowed to him.

Then I collected a piece of egg panbread and a slice of fennel cake and Meryt's speciality, flat fried goat, from a very self-important toddler. The food was exclusively Nubian and very tasty.

'How are you getting along in your study of cuneiform, lady Mutnodjme?' asked Kheperren. This was my lord's heart's love and I examined him closely, hoping that he was worthy of such regard.

'It is very difficult. I shall try learning a few new signs every day, practicing the previously-learned ones, and I may master it before I die of old age. I stand in awe of anyone who can decipher three languages from the same script. Babylonian is not too difficult to learn if you have someone to talk to, and there were three Babylonian ladies in the temple where I learned such things,' I replied, censoring the name of Isis may she forgive me. 'How is your Nubian? Your general is very fluent.'

'Not too bad, but I have had to learn it, lady, we have a large number of Nubian troops. It is not a particularly difficult dialect. But I can't speak Babylonian at all.'

He was far too thin for a scribe, who usually tended to fat due to the sedentary nature of their profession. He had a scar on his forehead, running up into his hair which was white over the track, giving him an appearance of being painted, like the Nubians warriors who had been known to dye their heads and beards red or blue. He looked like a child of the common people, his colouring much like my own. But I knew, because Tiye the Queen had told me, that his father was a nobleman and his connections were very high indeed. His hands were restless. He had them clasped so that they would not move or tap. I recognised my own method of restraining tension. The knuckles were pale under the tanned brown skin. He wore a scribe's long cloth, entirely plain, and a pectoral and earrings of stylised lotus blossoms, exceptionally beautiful and very valuable.

His general was wearing the same armour and cloth as any common soldier. I wondered that he had no medals of honour, because I had actually been there when Amenhotep-Osiris had given him a commendation for bravery, a golden fly, and the King had commented that he had a whole flock of flies already settled on his mail-shirt. That deed, I recalled, had been the rescue of a band of troops cut off and besieged under a mountain with no chance. Horemheb had sent his soldiers climbing down the cliff, going first himself, and had got all his soldiers out when the enemy's attention had been diverted by a line of bonfires on the opposite ridge.

Horemheb was relaxing. I knew that he was seldom in company and perhaps he was not used to the presence of ladies. He did not go to feasts, saying that he was merely a rough soldier and did not know how to behave at such things. There was a saying in the palace at Thebes, used when someone talked about an unlikely happening: *That will be when General Horemheb attends a feast*—meaning, never. But here he was at a feast, a small feast but a feast nonetheless, with garlands and wine and music.

The music was provided by Teti on double-pipe, his wife Hala on a drum and one of the other wives singing, all accompanied by any spare Nubian children clapping in time. Nubian children seem to absorb musical skill with their mother's milk. I had seen one of them sit down quietly with a little drum and play for hours, teaching himself how to produce a variety of sounds. Like Egyptian music, the Nubian 'day-long-song' consisted of one voice singing a verse and the rest singing the chorus. Most of the songs were about love. This one was no exception. I could not follow all of it and I asked Kheperren the scribe to translate.

'They are singing, *Oh, my love, my maiden, she who is as slender as the pine tree, as sweet as the melon, as faithful as the sun,*' he sang along gently in Egyptian.

'*Come to me, my maiden, when the moon rises, when the night is loud with frogs, and lie down under the tree of fragrance, take me in your arms, make the night fall in love with the day.*'

'It is a courtship song. A Nubian can keep singing it for months, until finally the object of his affection is seduced.'

'Or she cannot bear one more verse and complies,' I suggested.

He laughed and said, 'On the condition that he does not sing anymore.'

We were friends. This pleased me and would certainly please Ptah-hotep who had been worried about having two lovers. I did not see any difficulty and it did not seem that Kheperren did, either. This was a relief. The song continued—I could see how, after a decan or so, it would begin to irritate the nerves—and the general who never went to feasts made polite conversation with the Widow-Queen Tiye and even made her laugh.

He still had the blue beads which I remembered from my encounter with the Nile. He was still huge and I imagined that he was still as strong as he had been when he had been a youth with smooth shoulders. He felt me looking at him and turned very quickly, as if expecting an enemy at his back, and laughed when he saw that it was only me.

'Lady, I hope I did not startle you,' he said. 'I felt your eyes, and most eyes which have been fixed on my back have had an arrow trained along their gaze.'

'It is nothing, lord general, and I do not startle easily,' I replied. He examined me.

'No, you don't, do you? Tell me, lady Mutnodjme, where have you been since I last saw you?' I liked his voice, it was deep and a little harsh.

'In the temple, General, learning all I could learn, and then here, since Amenhotep-Osiris went to the Field of Reeds.'

'And what do you do here? Apart from feast and make love?'

'I learn, lord, one can learn anywhere. *Good speech is rare, but it can be found in the speech of common women at the mill-stone*, as was said in...'

'*The Maxims of Ptah-hotep!*' exclaimed General Horemheb. 'My scribe has been quoting him to me for years. A very wise man.'

'So is the present Ptah-hotep,' I told him.

'So I hear. You know, lady, I have been avoiding feasts for years. Do you know why?'

'No, lord. Perhaps you were shy?' I grinned at the huge, confident man.

'Because I have never been to a feast where I have not had to listen to hours of elaborate compliment about being a soldier, together which a lot of ill-informed curiosity about what it feels like to kill someone. Not that they really wanted to know, you understand, not enough to actually listen. I tired very quickly of bringing stay-at-home sluggards the thrill of action, so I just refused all invitations. This is the first time I can recall that I have actually enjoyed myself at a feast.'

'Perhaps because we know some of it, and would not think of asking the rest,' I said.

'Lady, I find it difficult to ascertain exactly what you know, but you are no palace ornament of the king, are you?'

'No, lord, I am merely, as you know, the base-born half-sister of Nefertiti the Great Royal Wife; and my father, I regret to say, is Divine Father Ay and my mother is Royal Nurse Tey; and I must ask you not to hold my parentage against me. And I would never qualify as Ornament of the King,' I said, making a play on the title of the Royal Women. General Horemheb was shaking his head.

'Certainly not. You are very beautiful,' he said consideringly, 'but you are far too intelligent to be a concubine. What is this I hear, by the way, about your father making the Royal Women marry? I never heard of such a thing.'

'Neither did I,' I agreed, signalling to him to keep his voice down. 'Not only is it shockingly unfair—some of the Royal Women have been here since they were small children, and they are old now—but what will the King tell the allies when they ask what has become of our sisters whom we sent you for espousal?

A lot of treaties were sealed with a marriage with Amenhotep-Osiris. The treaty with Kriti in the Great Green Sea was sealed with the gift of my dearest sister Merope, a princess of her island. If she is given away to a priest, what will King Minos of Kriti say about the insult?'

'And what will Merope say?' asked the Widow-Queen, who had caught some of this. 'He even had the audacity to tell me that I must marry again—I, his mother!'

Ptah-hotep, who had clearly not heard of this, looked startled. 'But, lady, are you sure that's…' he began, caught the Widow-Queen's eyes, and said hastily. 'I am sure that you are, of course, naturally, one would not make a mistake about such an outrageous proposal. But whoever thought of this must not have considered the foreign implications. One cannot give away the wives of a previous King as though they were a handful of festival ribbons!'

'Why can't he, if he does not care for the opinion of any but the Aten?' demanded Kheperren.

'Who are the priests of the Aten?' asked General Horemheb.

'Some of them are priests of Amen-Re who have seen the error of their previous ways,' said Ptah-hotep. 'Some are traders out of the market or commoners from the fields who do not even wash before they don their fine crowns and vestments. And some are boys, taken like I was taken, out of the schools. There is a school for scribes in the new temple of the Aten in Amarna now, and the children of the nobility go there. Some are aiming to repair their family's fortunes and all of them are aiming to amass as much treasure as possible as fast as they can.'

'Ah,' Horemheb put his chin in his hand.

'Shut up here in this city which the King says he will never leave,' I said, 'we know nothing of what is happening in the rest of the Black Land.'

'I will tell you all if you wish and have the heart to hear it, but it can be summed up in one word: ruin,' said Kheperren quietly. Horemheb nodded. Ptah-hotep sighed and Widow-Queen Tiye sighed with him.

'The festival of Opet did not take place this year, it was forbidden by the King Akhnaten, and the priests have been expelled from the temples of Amen-Re all over the country. The Nile did not flood and the people are saying that the country has been cursed for abandoning its old gods. The harvest last year was small and this year it will be less,' Kheperren said.

'The King takes more and more taxes for the building of his temples and this city, and the farmers will be on short rations this year. Without the central authority of the temple of Amen-Re, the local officials are cheating the people but not the King. The Watchers are being bribed and I even heard that Houses of Eternity are being robbed; the thieves' excuse being that they were made without acknowledgment of the Aten and are thus heretical. Some of the officials of the Necropolis are allowing this to happen provided that they get a percentage of the stolen treasure.

'Men are being taken for building labour even in the sowing season—even though this year all water for inner cultivation has to be lifted by hand from the river—so less land is being farmed and there will be less wheat.

'And since the loss of the Temple of Isis, lady...' Kheperren looked at me, 'superstition rages, fevers sweep villages and sorcerers have made their appearance. A whole Nome worshipped the birth of a two-headed calf last year. A wandering magician convinced three villages to slaughter all their cattle and have a great feast, because the world would end the next day. The people did as he said because there was no one to persuade them otherwise. They committed murders and various abominations because it was the end of the world, and then when they woke up the next morning the world was still there but...' he hesitated.

'But the magician had gone and so had all of their goods,' I concluded. 'There have always been people who see their chance for gain in a bad situation. And as Duammerset, Singer of Isis, used to say, *There is never a disaster but humans will make it worse*.'

Ptah-hotep

'There's worse,' said my dear Kheperren. 'Wise women are shunned now, and most children under five die because the mothers have no one to help and advise them. Many women die in childbirth because midwives are banned as witches.

'In one village in the Delta they burned an old woman in a fire, saying she was a sorceress and had put a curse on their cattle, and in Elephantine they are throwing offenders to the crocodiles.'

'The system of government is breaking down,' mused Widow-Queen Tiye, 'that means that all people will revert to whatever they believed before the wise lords of old introduced gods into Egypt. I would expect that fetishes and house gods will be venerated again, and that, as you say, human sacrifice and the long-forbidden cannibal feast will happen once more in places where there has been peace and stability for centuries. That would explain the crocodiles,' she said. 'Sobek was a local god before ever he was placed in the pantheon.'

'And the old woman,' Lady Mutnodjme agreed. 'Before Isis there was a female demon with her head turned backward who crept into houses and put the evil eye on children, gave cattle diseases and blighted crops.'

'And now,' I added to the general gloom, 'our lord is not only going to offend all of our allies by giving away their princesses like honey-cakes to beggars, but he is refusing to send aid to Tushratta of the Mittani; and if the Mittani fall we shall have Assyrians on the threshold.'

'There is something, at least, that can be done for Tushratta, evil old scoundrel that he is,' said Lady Tiye. 'General, you have your own honour guard, have you not?'

'Lady, I have,'

'And how many men are they?'

'Lady, one thousand. Three hundred mounted archers, three hundred light infantry, three hundred heavy cavalry and one hundred cooks, runners, scribes and others who count as light auxiliaries. They can fight if they need to, eh, Kheperren?'

My sweet love grinned at the general and touched the lock of white hair which covered the scar.

'Your men will not be sent on the Aten's business, my dear General, because they will be needed to guard your person, which is valuable and cannot be hazarded,' said Widow-Queen Tiye.

'There is nothing to stop you making a visit for me to Tushratta's court, is there, taking a present to the old ally of my husband?'

She drew off a very heavy and valuable arm ring, embossed with the discredited symbol of Sekmet, She Who Loves Silence, the blood-drinking lion-headed avenger. She tossed it to the general who caught it deftly and stared at it.

'I am ordering you, General, to take this arm ring to my old friend Tushratta with this message:

The Mistress of Egypt Tiye sends greetings to Tushratta of Mittani, and bids him remember that a lioness is more dangerous than a lion.

'Will you do this, General?'

'Lady,' the general left his chair and knelt down at the Queen's feet. 'I will deliver your message.'

'To Tushratta in person, mind, wherever he may be. You should try his border with Khatti. And try to kill Suppiluliumas if you can, he's very ambitious.'

The grin was now very broad but the general merely replied, 'Lady, I am your slave.'

'I know,' said the older woman dryly. 'I may ask you to carry further messages for me. In fact, the Great Royal Scribe here will draw up a document which will authorise you to be anywhere at all with your thousand men, on my personal business. While I am alive, no one will interfere with you. When I am dead you must manage as best you may.'

That was my cue, obviously, to rise and get papyrus and wax for a seal. Kheperren and I wrote a commission from the Widow-Queen Tiye in the broadest and vaguest of terms, added a translation into two other languages underneath and carried it to the lady Tiye with a little pot of warmed wax for her approval. She read it, demanded a translation of the other parts, sloshed wax over the bottom and rolled her personal seal along it. I had not realised that Sekmet Destroyer of Mankind was her deity, but that goddess had a very fitting devotee in the Widow-Queen. That seal said to everyone, down to the meanest peasant who could not read in any language, that this scroll had come from the Great Royal Spouse Mistress of the Two Lands Widow-Queen Tiye and it would be much better to obey the bearer.

Still on his knees, General Horemheb accepted his commission with both hands and kissed the Widow-Queen's feet.

'You may do another task for me, if you will lend me your scribe,' said the Widow-Queen, and Kheperren shot me an alarmed look. He was scared to death of the lady Tiye.

'You may have him for any task which does not compromise his honour or risk his life,' replied the General, replacing his gigantic frame in the chair of state.

'Take my daughter Mutnodjme and allow her to walk in Amarna with your escort,' the old queen smiled at my lady. 'I want her report on these Priests of Aten. I need to find a reliable one for my sister widow Merope. She is young and wishes to marry again,' said the Queen.

'Do not women walk alone in Amarna?' I asked in surprise.

'No, my dear scribe, they are constrained to stay at home, mind their children, be an ornament for their husband's house. A woman alone is hissed at as a whore, and may be attacked. A woman walking with a soldier, on the other hand, is safe. Wear subdued clothes, daughter, and do not stare any man in the face.'

'Why not?' objected Mutnodjme. 'How am I to judge if he is a good man or not if I cannot see his eyes?'

'Listen to his voice and watch his hands,' the Widow-Queen informed her. 'Discuss with your sister Merope as to what sort of man would meet her desires. It would be wise to do this quickly. When are you bidden to be gone, General Horemheb?'

'Two decans, lady, for I am required to wait until the first reports come back as to the progress of the work in destroying the cult of Amen-Re and advise Pannefer as to further action.'

'Good.'

'Lady,' said Mutnodjme, 'Why cannot Kheperren take my sister Merope out to find her own husband?'

'Because she cannot see him until the marriage is contracted; so said the King through his Queen Nefertiti.'

'Why in the name of all the gods…,' she began, and the Widow-Queen laid a finger on her lips.

'Because the King is afraid of everything; most of all he is afraid of the power of women. He gave the cult of the Phoenix to his wife to make her important and give her a position; a sop to satisfy her craving for adoration. She has not noticed that she has lost all her rights—the right to sit in council, the right to her own palace and her own guards, to her own general and army, to her own property, and even the rights over her own body, though that is not an issue. All women in the Black Land have lost these things, because the Queen has lost them. And he is marrying his eldest daughter, which is proper, but he is giving the mating of her to a priest of the Aten.'

'But she's only eleven, still a child. Which priest of the Aten?'

'The head priest of course, Mutnodjme. Nothing is too good for the head priest of the Aten. Not even a child princess of Egypt.'

'Divine Father Ay!' choked Mutnodjme, and I knelt down beside her, ready to support her head if she vomited. She mastered her disgust in a moment, but her hand remained on my shoulder.

'We can do nothing for the Princess Mekhetaten,' said the Great Royal Wife. 'But we can at least get one innocent out of this palace. Tomorrow, Mutnodjme, you will go looking for a husband for Merope.'

'As you will, Lady,' she said softly.

She sounded like the very pattern of humility, but I could feel her fury in my embrace, as though we were communicating skin to skin. I hoped that she was not angry with me. I hoped that she would not take her anger out on the innocent Kheperren. He knew very little of women, living almost his whole life as a man among men.

I remembered that the priestesses of Isis walked where they willed as did all women, and began to realise how terrible a prohibition this order might be to her. I was not only picking up anger from the lady. I was sensing despair.

I could not comfort her with words, though I could feel her side warming against mine and my touch might have soothed her. I had nothing, however, to say.

Kheperren had. He lifted his cup and said 'Few scribes receive such delightful orders! The last one I was given sent me into an ambush by the vile Kush, lady.'

'This one may be less perilous,' said my lady Mutnodjme, and smiled at him.

Chapter Twenty-two

Mutnodjme

I had never chosen a husband for anyone before. Merope had been unable to tell me anything particular, how could she? But she said she wanted a kind man, gentle and strong, with proven fertility and no vices, and we broke down giggling as we realised that what she was describing were the points of a good horse.

The stud market of Aten was open for business and Kheperren and I entered as worshippers. I knew that the Aten was a predominately male religion, but I was not prepared for the temple, which was beautiful beyond belief, decorated with friezes of rural scenes and golden images of the sun disc. All the walls of the inner chamber were carved with images of the royal family, worshipping the Aten together, with the sun's rays ending in little hands which came down to bless them; Nefertiti the Queen and Akhnaten the King and the little princesses.

I walked away from Kheperren to examine a particularly fine frieze, and at once I was surrounded by men. For the purposes of selecting a suitable man for another woman, I had donned an opaque cloth belonging to my days as a temple maiden and had covered my shoulders and breasts with a plain shawl. This did not preserve me from peering and whispering. I became very uncomfortable. I was behaving in the way which the lord Akhnaten required, I was modest, I was humble, I looked no man in the face, I kicked no man in the crotch for the vile things which they were suggesting to me, but it was not helping. Fingers slid inside my clothes and I was just about to forget this veil of humility and fight back when Kheperren came to my side and all the tweakers and whisperers fell silent. I looked up into his grave scarred face with a look of silent appeal.

He took my hand and said, 'Come, lady, this is no suitable place for you,' and I saw the feet shuffle aside as he passed, clearing a way for the soldier and his woman.

'There is no man in that temple whom I would allow to touch my sister's sandals,' I spat as we came out into the sun.

'I know. Things have become bad for women; the state of the country is very evil. "This land is in commotion and no one knows what the result will be, for it is hidden from speech, sight and hearing," but that is Neferti's old prophecy and has already come to pass,' he replied, leading me through the broad, flat, sanded avenue of sycamores to a square building marked like all others with the rayed disc of the sun god Aten. 'We may fare better here.'

'More priests?' I said, not quietly enough.

'Lady,' said a polite voice with a temple accent. 'How can we serve you?'

Heedless of this modesty taboo, I looked him in the face. He was a middle aged man, clearly a scribe. He did not seem to be horrified by either my person or my actions, which inclined me toward him.

'I am the Princess the Lady Mutnodjme on an errand of Widow-Queen Tiye, Ruler of the Double Crown, Mistress of Egypt,' I said, tired of anonymity and driven into using my conferred rank, which I usually forgot. I could not look around quietly for a suitable man, and all the whisperers and tweakers would not leave me alone.

'Lady Mutnodjme, I and all my men are servants of the Mistress of Egypt may she live,' he replied, bowing to a proper depth. 'Who are you and what is your position?' asked Kheperren.

'I am the servant of the Aten, the Lector of the Sole and Only God, my name is Dhutmose and I work here writing the stories and miracles of the Aten as they have yet been told. There are a hundred and twenty men under my command.'

'Are they all priests of the Aten?' I demanded

'Yes, Lady.'

'I need to find a husband for one whom the Widow-Queen loves. I need a man who has sufficient wealth to keep her, a lady of birth and position. I need a man who is gentle and kind and well spoken, one who will make her laugh.'

'One who is not already married?'

'Of course.'

His brow furrowed. He bowed us into a chamber which was clearly his; there were pictures on the walls of a dwarf and a dog driving a gazelle in harness, a cat's funeral procession celebrated by mice and some very athletic lovers in a variety of positions. A sexually-active man with a taste for satire, it seemed. I began to be interested in Dhutmose. He had a round face and fringed brown eyes like a cow, with a goat's wary gleam.

'Now, lady, let me send for some beer, it is disagreeably hot today, isn't it? And perhaps your escort would like some too. Soldiers drink beer.'

'He's a scribe,' I said shortly. The trip into the temple had ruffled my temper. 'But let us have beer, by all means.'

'He's a scribe? I beg your pardon, brother scribe, I did not recognise…' began Dhutmose, flustered. Then he peered closer at my escort and said, 'By the Aten, it's Kheperren, isn't it? My dear boy, don't you know me? I taught you demotic all those years ago. Where have you been, boy, to get so burned and scarred?'

'With the army, Master,' Kheperren broke into a huge smile. 'Master, I lost track of you ten years ago when I went with the army, and Ptah-hotep became Great Royal Scribe. I thought you dead,' said my escort.

'Beer!' Dhutmose called out the door. 'The best brew. Right away is not too soon, if you please, gentlemen.' This call brought an instant scurry of feet as someone raced off to get the best beer.

'No, no, dead, us? Not at all,' said Dhutmose. 'Our master Ammemmes bought himself a large house and estate with the present which he says Ptah-hotep gave him—that boy really did turn out well—and settled down with the scribes who were too old to start again. He's growing grapes. And making wine. And drinking it. But I was too young to rusticate so I came to the service of the Aten in Thebes. Then my wife died and I've been living in Amarna since we opened this house of books. Fine manuscripts we are producing, too. You've seen Ptah-hotep? Is he healthy?'

'Very well, master, he'll be delighted to learn that you are happy also.'

'Tell him I wish him very well, and refer him to line 37 in the Prophecies of Neferti,' said Dhutmose, his bright smile a little quenched. 'Now, lady, you are looking for a man?'

'Not for myself,' I said hastily, and Dhutmose laughed, a good rich hearty laugh.

'I can see for myself that you are suited,' he patted my knee. 'But for this protégé of the Widow-Queen Tiye may she live forever. A young woman?'

'Eighteen, as I am. Used to the old king.' I did not name him because I would have had to use the name of the forbidden god Osiris; and that did not strike me as a good plan in the temple school of the Aten.

'It is going to be very difficult to find a young man with the skill of the old king; especially it is going to be very difficult to find a young man who is unmarried who has those skills unless he has been taught by a very clever young woman. Now, let us see. Eighty-three of them are married. Twenty more are boys. Let me think. We have seventeen possibles. How would you like to proceed, lady?'

'Call each of them in and let me speak to them and touch them,' I said. 'We should be able to weed out the impossibles fairly quickly, I know the lady's tastes.'

Then we began a weary round of interviews. I had never seen such an unattractive collection of youths. The ones who were not unwashed were over-clean and over-decorated and at least three of them met Kheperren's eye and blushed or looked away; pretty boys who had been in the army camp, picking up soldiers as brief chance-met lovers. They, clearly, would not do. Not one had a spark of humour or imagination. I would not have lain down with any of them if I had been unmated for a year.

'Lady, they are all the young men I can show you,' apologised Dhutmose, reminding me irresistibly of a stock merchant regretting that he had no good horses this year. 'I agree that they are filthy and unlearned. I am thinking of ordering compulsory bathing before they enter the building. I can show you thirty nice young men with impeccable manners and learning, but they are all married and I can see that the Widow-Queen Tiye may she live would not want to give away her adoptive daughter to be a secondary wife.'

'Then, Master, in default of a pretty young man, I'm afraid it is going to have to be you,' I said, consulting Kheperren with a lifted eyebrow and getting a nod in response.

'Me?' Dhutmose sat down suddenly in his chair of state.

'I was sent to find a man of humour and intelligence, of kindness and gentleness, one without a wife who had sufficient wealth to support my sister,' I said firmly. 'Are you alone?'

'I am,' Dhutmose took a sip of beer and fanned himself.

'Have you sufficient property to take a woman without a dowry?'

'I have, but a royal lady...'

'Your wife, she taught to you make love well?'

'She was pleased with me after a couple of months,' he said, and then looked so sad that I wanted to hug him.

'Do you wish to please the Mistress of Egypt?'

'Of course. The question is, of course, will I please this daughter? What if she wants a strong young man? I am forty, getting a little thick around the middle and my hair is marching backwards across my scalp. I am not the figure of a lover in a song. If she had been the same age, well then, I would like some company, especially if she could read. My wife was a learned woman from the temple of Isis, and we used to read aloud by lamplight on the hot nights when no one can sleep.'

'She can read and write both cursive and hieroglyphics. She is slim and has light brown eyes and dark brown hair. She likes children and honeycakes and singing. She can dance all the Egyptian dances and Kritian too. She is....'

'By the Gods,' gasped Master Dhutmose, forgetting his lately-learned monotheism. 'Are you telling me that the King Akhnaten may he live is giving away the Royal Women?'

'Yes, without dowries, within the month and only to priests of the Aten, and the Widow-Queen Tiye is very anxious to make sure that her sister-queen goes to a good home,' I said angrily. 'She would do as much for any stray cat.'

'I speak a little Kritian,' mused Dhutmose.

'Good, then please put your seal here and here and you can come and fetch her as soon as the King divorces her.' Kheperren laid out a scroll on the table.

'That is outrageous,' he whispered. 'Those poor women!'

'Exactly so, master, now seal the document, if you please.'

'What is her name?'

'Merope. The Widow-Queen Merope of Kriti in the Great Green Sea.'

Even the shock he had just received could not induce a scribe to seal a document without reading it, and he spelled his way through the edict.

'This confers on me all rights over the lady, with or without her will,' he observed. 'I hope it is with her will. But if she is wishing to be out of the palace, she might like my house, the friezes are rather fine, and my little daughter needs a mother even if the lady does not want to undertake any more of the duties of a wife. I will understand. Poor woman!'

He sealed the papyrus and Kheperren rolled it up again. My private view was that of all the duties of a wife, the one which Dhutmose was prepared to forgo was the one which Merope was most eager to comply with. I only hoped that he was equal to the challenge.

We left the astonished and gratified Dhutmose calling for a Kritian grammar, and walked back through the wide airy streets to the palace.

I had not looked at it from this angle before. It was like a castle. All the walls were sheer and very high, crowned with square bevelled battlements. There were four gates into the palace, and we were taking the one which led to the Queen's palace.

'Tell me of Neferti and his prophecies,' I asked, remembering the message which Dhutmose had sent to Ptah-hotep.

'Not here,' said Kheperren.

Ptah-hotep

I was delighted to hear that my old teacher Dhutmose had found a place in the new regime, and thoroughly agreed with Mutnodjme's choice. He was, as I remember, a shrewd man, but gentle and kind. It was always Dhutmose who comforted the homesick and sat with the feverish. He loved only women. I recalled that one of the boys had tried to seduce him and totally failed. Dhutmose had lifted the boy's cloth, pointed at his phallus and said, 'You are very beautiful, boy, but that thing would get in the way.' He was just the man to soothe the wounded feelings of an ex-Great Royal Spouse.

But his message was worrying.

I did not have a copy of the prophecies, of course, because the work mentioned the name of Amen-Re and had been suppressed, but edicts cannot suppress memory. Their despairing tone had attracted me when I had been a boy, and I could recall many of the verses without racking my brains.

The line reference, however, meant that I had to reconstruct the whole poem, so I sat down after lunch when men usually sleep and wrote out, from memory, The Prophecies of Neferti on a plaster board which I could easily erase.

Kheperren was sitting at my feet, eating Nubian flat bread, roasted garlic and onions and filling in an occasional gap in my recollection. I am fairly sure that we had the whole of the poem after about an hour.

Line 37 began a verse. It said:

I show you a land in calamity.
Unimaginable happenings.
Men will take weapons of war
Confusion will live in the land.
Men will make arrows of bronze
Men will beg for bread of blood
Laugh with laughing at pain
None will weep at death
None will fast for the dead
Each heart will think only of itself.

'That sums it up, I think,' said Kheperren, kissing my knee. 'You are very cheerful for one reading news of disaster and prophecies of doom!' I objected. 'Don't drop onion juice on my clean cloth.'

'It's 12th dynasty, right? The prophecy of the coming of Ammenemes the First. In his time, look a bit further down, it says:

I show you a land in calamity
The weak-armed now are strong
I show you the lowly now as lord…

'You should have seen the priests at that temple school, 'Hotep, they were filthy and unlearned. Here, look at this next bit. Isn't all this happening?

The poor man will achieve wealth
The great lady will fornicate to exist…
A sentence is passed
And a hand wields a club
The land is diminished
The counsellors die…

'And here,' Kheperren continued:

There will be no Theban Nome
To be the birth-land of every god.

Kheperren dripped more onion juice on my cloth as he went back to his odorous repast, seeming to think that he had made his point.

'Well, what?' I twitched the cloth out from under his dripping repast.

'When Egypt got to that state last time,' he replied, speaking as though I was a very stupid schoolboy, 'then a great hero arose and saved everyone, fought off the invaders, brought back the gods and established his throne in might, correct?'

'Correct.'

'Then it will happen again. In Egypt, my dear Ptah-hotep, everything happens again and nothing ever happens for the first time, as Master Ammemmes used to say. I'm so glad that he's well and happy on his estate. What present did you give him, my heart?'

'All my bracelets and an electrum pectoral which could have purchased a small province. I hope you are right,' I told him.

'About what?'

'The rescuer.'

'So do I.'

We read the rest of the prophecy in silence. As we read, we drew closer together, until we finished it sitting in the same chair, hugging each other as though we were cold. His body was comforting, even in a fume of garlic.

I show you a son as an enemy
A brother as a foe.
Every mouth says 'love me'
all good things have passed away
A law is decreed for the state's ruin
men destroy what is made
Make desolation of what is found
What is made is unmade
Thieves plunder, lords steal.

In all it was something of a relief when the lady Mutnodjme arrived for her cuneiform lesson and we could stop considering the state of Egypt. Kheperren's general did not need him, so we sat down to sort the diplomatic correspondence and listen to her learning her day's quota of signs from Harmose, who had claimed his right.

'This is the sign for… Can you guess?'

'It looks like a field,' said my lady Mutnodjme. I observed her as she picked up the stylus to copy the sign. She moved decisively, as though she had always meant to do that which she was doing. It was very attractive, watching her do anything. She was deft. The Kritian princess had called her 'fat-handed' which I had taken for an affectionate insult, such as is common between sisters, like Kheperren calling me a commoner or my statement that the nobility were throwing undersized children if Kheperren was their best effort. But now I saw what the soon-to-be-divorced Great Royal Wife meant. The muscles of my lady Mutnodjme's hands, especially round the thumb and the wide part of the hand, were well developed and strong.

'It is se-u, which is grain. And this?'

The old scribe stabbed a number of wedges into the clay and my lady's brow wrinkled. 'It looks like a stack of building wood,' she confessed. 'What does it mean, Master?'

'It means nunu in Babylonian, which signifies 'fish.' See, here is the oldest sign for it.'

'Yes, I see. Something clearly happened to it in the translation.'

'Now we will look at compound words; phrases, in Egyptian. Yesterday you learned 'epinnu' the sign for plough. If I write that one, then this sign, what do we have?'

'Plough the field?' guessed Mutnodjme.

'Very good. Now there is a difference in these phrases is there not? Plough that field. Plough the field! He ploughs the field. The field was ploughed. The field will be ploughed. If the rains come, the field will be ploughed.'

'Yes, Master, you are talking about cases, such as nominative, accusative, imperative, dative and ablative, and tenses like future and past,' said Mutnodjme, disconcerting the scribe, for he had heard, but not really believed, that she was a learned woman.

'We will consider the grammar later. For the moment all you need to know is that the word order is important.'

'Master Harmose, I am sorry to interrupt, but I need some help with this Hittite inscription,' said Kheperren from the floor. Harmose, who was elderly, leaned down with some difficulty and peered, then objected,

'What's wrong with it? Just an honorific preface, all letters begin like that, 'To the lord of the Two Lands and the Mistress of Egypt Mayati in whom his heart delights...'

'It is Mayati, isn't it?' asked Kheperren softly.

'Who is Mayati?' asked the lady Mutnodjme.

'In Egyptian we would call her Mekhetaten,' said Harmose.

'You know, I'm getting tired of shocks,' Lady Mutnodjme complained after a pause.

'We all are,' agreed Harmose.

'What has happened to the position of my sister if foreign kings are referring to the little princess by her title?' she asked, and we did not have an answer.

The diplomatic correspondence was completed and we were casting about for more work when a slave slammed the door open and announced, 'The Great King's Chamberlain Whom He loves, Huy.'

And there was Huy's oily countenance and his scent of cassia, his usual perfume, offending my apartments. He wrinkled his nose at the smell of onions and garlic which Kheperren still exuded.

'My lord, what can a humble servant of the King do to honour your visit?' I asked in the accepted mode of address between superior and inferior, which I knew would annoy him.

'My lord has sent me to order you to come to his presence,' he said, using no words of ceremony at all.

'I come,' I said, climbing to my feet and brushing down my garment. This summons was unusual. I had not been called to the King's presence since he had dictated poetry to me. He seemed happy to know that the office of Great Royal Scribe went on efficiently—or perhaps he did not care what I was doing.

Now, however, something had attracted his attention, doubtless bought to him by either Pannefer or Huy, or perhaps the Divine Father Ay. It might have been a coincidence that this summons came after we had heard that something was going on to change the status of the Great Royal Spouse Nefertiti. I shot a look at Paneb, the boy whom I suspected of being the spy, but he looked blank.

I brushed Kheperren's neck with my hand as I stood up, and the lady Mutnodjme's knee. I straightened my cloth, which smelt of onions, and smiled reassuringly at my worried staff. I took up a papyrus roll and my writing board, ink and stylus, the tools of a scribe to which I was entitled.

Then I went out, flanked by soldiers, feeling like a prisoner.

They stopped in an antechamber to the great temple of the Aten and motioned to me to sit down, so I sat. Huy paused for a parting sneer at the door and left. Waiting has never worried me. I had a lot to think about.

The lady Mutnodjme and Kheperren appeared to be getting along well. This was excellent. I remembered the stab of jealousy I had felt when I realised that Kheperren was the general's lover, and his flash of rage when he knew that I had lain with Meryt so long ago. There had been nothing like that this time. Of all lucky men in the Black Land—and there were not many fortunate men in Egypt at this present time—I was probably the most blessed. I had position and wealth which had not made me proud like Pannefer, corrupt like Huy or a miser like Divine Father Ay. I had been able to benefit those whom I loved, my family and my Master Ammemmes. Those who loved me called me generous. I was healthy and over the age when field workers die of exhaustion and poverty, and I might live twenty years more. I had two lovers who both loved me and liked each other.

No one else could have made this boast, though I was not boasting. In spite of the advent of the Aten, I knew what I had to confess after I was dead, and I knew my Book of Coming

Forth by Day by heart. I would say: *Lord Osiris, I did no evil, except that under duress I ate the flesh of a sacred beast which I afterwards vomited forth. I gave food to the hungry and water to the thirsty and to those who could not cross the water I have boats. I lay with no woman when she was still a child. I took no bribes. I did not oppress the widow and the fatherless. No man cried to me for mercy that I did not hear.*

And in my mind's eye I could see my funeral, and I could hear the voices of the priestess of Isis and a scribe of the army, stretching out their arms to me, crying, *Ptah-hotep, dear love, come back to thy house!*

When the King's soldiers came for me, I was quite prepared to die.

Chapter Twenty-three

Mutnodjme

I had never been so frightened in my life.

Danger is all right if it's you. Not that I ever went seeking it. But if I am the threatened one, I am immersed in the action, and until it is over my attention is firmly engaged. In real peril one does not usually even have time to notice that one is afraid until it is all over.

But danger to another person is agonising. I could think of nothing to do after I saw my dearest love walk out between two soldiers to what Huy, at least, grinning through his rotten teeth, thought was a terrible fate.

Ptah-hotep walked calmly to whatever doom the mad king was going to put him.

'I'm going to the general,' gasped Kheperren, and was gone in a flash of limbs. I told Meryt to send for me as soon as any word came and ran to the Widow-Queen Tiye.

She was loading Merope with gold so that she would not go to her husband with nothing. Divine Father Ay had sent around a list of the jewellery and goods which had arrived with each princess, and he wanted it all back or accounted for before they left the palace.

'Oh, dearest sister,' Merope grabbed me as I whirled into the inner chamber. 'Tell me, is he young? Will he be a good lover?'

'I suspect he'll be an excellent lover, dear Merope, but he's forty. There was not a young man in the whole scribal school who was fit for you to wipe your feet on. I'll tell you more later. Great Royal Lady Tiye, what does the king want with Ptah-hotep?'

'There is nothing that you can do,' said Tiye slowly, 'Go on telling your sister about her new husband. Has this Dhutmose sealed the deed?'

'Yes, I saw him. The deal is made. What do you mean, lady, that there is nothing I can do?'

'I mean what I say, which is my habit,' snapped Tiye. 'We will see. If I can help your man, daughter, you know that I will. But he has to make his own destiny to live or die. We must await events. Now, tell us about Merope's new owner.'

'He's a cuddly forty, a scribe, a man of learning, with a small daughter who is motherless. He was a priest of the temple at Thebes before the present one, now a priest of the Aten so he qualifies,' I prattled.

What did she mean, the red-headed woman, that Ptah-hotep must make his own destiny? He had always done so, hadn't he? He had dealt with loss and pain and loneliness as best he could, suffered high office which was thrust upon him, lived within his own code in a palace with no rules.

I assumed that the Widow-Queen's calm meant that either his death had been decreed beyond doubt or that this was not a threatening situation. It didn't feel like the latter. I was distracted, but if she said there was nothing I could do then there really was nothing. Tiye would not have discounted any action; secret murder, treason, bribery, if the method would achieve her intended result. Widow-Queen Tiye alarmed me almost as much as the situation. She was a woman to whom literally nothing was, in itself, out of the question.

And she said that there was nothing I could do.

So I swallowed fear, digested anxiety, and gave such of my mind as I could locate to preparing my dear sister Merope for her new husband.

Merope was flushed with excitement. I had never seen her so beautiful. She had combed out her own ash bark coloured hair and garlanded it with lotus blossoms. Her cloth was gauze and draped her slim flanks and thighs as she inspected the growing pile of gold armrings and pectorals in her lap.

'This is too much,' she told the Widow-Queen.

'Are you not my sister, Great Royal Wife of my husband?' asked Tiye, adding a little pouch of the most precious of jewels, the blue rounded 'eye-stone' which came from deep in Nubia, eight dark-blue gems with a flash of white light in them.

'In case you are stripped of your adornment before you are allowed to leave, my dear, place these stones where they will not be found by any man except the one to whom you are pledging your future,' she said with a chuckle. Such a hiding place would only have occurred to that most ingenious of ladies. Merope blushed.

'I'll help you conceal them,' I promised, and she laughed and kissed me.

What was happening to Ptah-hotep? I could feel his calm, his acceptance. He was going to his death with perfect ease, perhaps even a tinge of relief. My whole mind and body rebelled against such an end to his life, to what might have been our shared life. Was this why he did not marry me? So that I would not share his downfall?

I wrenched my mind away. In mid afternoon the messenger from the office of the Master of the Household came to deliver to Merope the papyrus which decreed that she was no longer a Great Royal Wife and the order that she was to attend on the Queen in the courtyard an hour before night. There she would be given away to her new husband, the Aten.

'It appears that we are in the presence of sophistry,' commented the Widow-Queen Tiye. 'My son will say to all those Kings who ask for their daughters and sisters that they are all married to the Aten, and since the King is the Aten then they are all, in a way, still married to him and the alliances sealed with their bodies are still in force. I wonder who thought of that?'

'Probably my father,' I said. Was there no end to his meanness? I sent word to the temple school in the town that Dhutmose should come and collect his bargain after the ceremony.

The messenger came back breathless and reported, 'They are building the strangest fire in the courtyard!'

'Strangest? How do you mean?' I asked. Tiye gave me a look which bade me ask no more and I ignored her for the first time in my life.

'It's made of precious woods. Cinnamon wood, and cassia, and myrrh.'

It meant nothing to me. It did mean something to the Widow-Queen Tiye, however, for she immediately ordered the Royal Sculptor to attend on her. When he arrived—the best of the Amarna artists, a true genius with wood and stone—she drew him into her own bedchamber, leaving Merope and I to talk of her new husband.

I rapidly ran out of things to say about the worthy Dhutmose. Merope kissed me and drew me close, and we occupied a hour, perhaps, in pleasing her and inserting the eye stones into their treasure-chest. I brought her easily to a climax, but I was far too tense to take pleasure even in the breasts and the mouth of my most delightful sister, even though I was about to lose her.

Why was there no word of Ptah-hotep? I could not lie still even in Merope's embrace. I kissed her and said, 'Sister, I must go and discover what I can,' and with moist eyes, she released me.

I went to the office of the Great Royal Scribe and found it silent. Immense diligence was being exhibited by all of the scribes, even Mentu, who was translating Hittite letters into Egyptian. No one looked up and I was directed to the inner apartment by a wary wave of Khety's stylus.

When I reached the place where Meryt and her brothers lived, I found them packing. Bundles were being made of fine cloth and small children compulsorily fed and washed. Babies wailed. Teti, who was the calmest of the brothers, stubbed his foot on a table and swore explosively. Anubis was stalking stiffly from one group to another, whimpering.

'You have something heard?' Meryt's Egyptian was deserting her. I shook my head. She continued to fold cloth into a roll which would go over someone's shoulders, secured with leather straps.

'You're expecting the worst,' I commented. She finished the roll and grabbed my hand, leading me to one side, out of the way of Hala who was loading onto a small wriggling child all the bracelets which its little arm could carry, stiffening it from shoulder to elbow.

'All our lives together he has been living on the edge of a razor,' she whispered. 'We have orders as to what to do if he is summoned unexpectedly to the king. See, here I have all our freedoms, not written by him but by the old man Amenhotep-Osiris and sealed by the office.' She replaced the papyrus in the bosom of her cloth.

'We have title to all of our goods and we have a safe-conduct to the Village-between-two-trees sealed by the Pharaoh Akhnaten and countersealed by General Horemheb. As soon as any word comes, Kheperren's soldiers are waiting to take us to the river.'

'Kheperren is here?'

She waved at the bed chamber and I went that way, feeling superfluous. Meryt had the household in hand and would get it away safely at the earliest opportunity. I had not known my lover long enough to have received any instructions as to what I should do in this eventuality. I began to wonder whether I knew him at all.

But there was the emotion, which was not mine, on the edge of my feelings; calm acceptance. It was certainly not my mind. I stalked into the bed chamber and Kheperren demanded, 'What do you here, lady? Didn't he tell you to keep away if anything happened? He would not involved you in his ruin!'

'Oh, be silent,' I snarled. 'How can I not be involved in his ruin? The Pharaoh gave us to each other, put our hands together.

I am his and he is mine and he cannot repudiate me now. What is happening? Do you know?'

'No.' Kheperren did not seem to resent my tone. Actually it was a pity, as it would have been a great relief to my feelings to be able to scream at someone; but I suppose it was for the best.

'He was called and went, and he has been sitting outside the temple of the Aten for hours. The King is inside the temple. That monster Huy is walking about with a huge smirk on his filthy face—how I would like to hand him over to my Nubian irregulars! They can keep a prisoner alive for weeks, screaming in agony all the time.'

'Yes,' I agreed. 'They could abolish the screaming by cutting out his tongue, of course. We do not want to keep the children awake.'

I was keeping step with him as he paced from one side to the other of the large room. I was interested as he instructed me as to exactly what, and in what order, the Nubian irregulars do to their most precious enemies, and the recital pleased my heart. I got a truly evil pleasure out of imagining Huy suspended from a tree upside down with bone needles thrust into his phallus. But even the ingenious Nubians run out of tortures in the end. As time passed, Kheperren put an arm round my shoulders, and we walked more slowly.

Eventually we sat down in the Great Royal Scribe's chair together.

'You're afraid for him, aren't you?' he asked me. It was stupid question. But he was trying to communicate and I had walked out some of my bitter rage.

'Yes, and you?'

'Yes,' he agreed.

'Soldiers must be used to waiting for an attack,' I commented.

He snorted.

'That's the army. Hurry to get all prepared and every detail finished. Then wait. I have waited on the hills in Apiru country, lady, and in the jungles where the vile Kush lurk. I have sat all night and listened for any noise in the dead silence, a noise which might mean that the sentries have been surprised and killed and that an attack in force by the merciless shepherds is about to break upon the tents. I have waited three days together for rescue when Horemheb left us watching a border post and we were besieged. I have waited until my teeth hurt with gritting together and my body was exhausted just from the strain. But I have never sat in a cool delightful palace and waited, lady, and it is terrible beyond any battle. There at least I knew who the enemy were, and at the last I could fight for my life.'

'Terrible,' I agreed. 'For even the Widow-Queen Tiye says that there is nothing to be done, and that lady would have no compunction about any action if she thought that it would work.'

He was very like Ptah-hotep, if my love had been a soldier. His back felt the same under my hands, the long and beautifully arranged muscles. I had not been aroused when I had made love with my sister Merope. Now I was feeling an entirely inappropriate interest in Kheperren. I shook myself. The palace insanity was catching.

And we sat there for hours, and nothing happened, and no news came.

Ptah-hotep

I had been sitting for a long time, thinking about my life and putting it into order and perspective. Not many who die are given this time to think, and I was grateful for it. I knew that the King had arranged to dismiss the Royal Women before dark, and wondered if my summons had anything to do with that, though I could not see how it would. When the soldiers came at last to take me to the King, I gathered up my scribe's tools and walked between them into the immense temple of the Aten.

The pillars soared up beyond sight. The temple was lined with beaten gold, and the light of the westering sun struck such blinding brilliance from the walls and floor of the central hall that I was dazzled. I could still not really see when I was shoved to my knees before a throne and went down into the full 'kiss earth' before my lord, the Pharaoh Akhnaten, Sole and Only One of the Sun Disc Aten, Favoured Child of the Unknowable God, Aten.

It struck me as unfair that I was about to go to my death without once more seeing his face. I had served him to the best of my ability. He could at least look at me as he ordered my death.

'Ptah-hotep, great honour has come to you,' said the voice of the King. I saw through wet eyes and blinked, and my tears dropped upon gold.

'Lord, you have already conferred on me honours beyond my worth,' I replied in the correct form.

'I have yet another for you, favoured son of the Lord of the Two Lands,' he continued. His voice echoed in the great space. I beat down a surge of wild hope.

'Rise,' he ordered, and I got to my feet, leaving my palette on the golden floor.

My lord Akhnaten was standing on the dais, looking out into the courtyard.

'See!' he cried, flinging up an arm, and I saw men constructing what looked like a bonfire out of logs of sandalwood and acacia. More servants were approaching, carrying armloads of cinnamon bark. I could smell the sweetness of the spices.

'Lord, I see,' I replied cautiously. The strange face of the king was almost beautiful, disproportionate and odd but alight with divine purpose. 'Soon the royal women of my father will depart to their new husbands. Tomorrow the miracle will happen.'

'Miracle, lord?' I asked. The feeling of threat had eased a little but I still did not see what he wanted. However, that was often the case.

'The Phoenix will return,' he said. 'My astronomers have confirmed it.'

I bet they had. I seemed to recall that the period of renewal of the Phoenix was more than twelve hundred years, and I also seemed to recall that I had read a scroll no older than five hundred years which stated that the Phoenix had flown to Heliopolis, landing on the altar of the temple of the sun to leave the ball of myrrh and seed which would hatch into itself before it flew off to its palm tree or Bennu pillar to burn in its nest of spices…

My stomach dropped, my breath left me as though I had been speared in the solar plexus. I looked at the bonfire again. It was made of perfumed wood and in it I could discern the Phoenix's spices, cinnamon and cassia and acacia, sandalwood and cedarwood and whole branches of the frankincense tree. The pile of wood in the courtyard of the temple would have bought the whole produce of a Nome. It probably was the proceeds of the taxes of a Nome. Was this the reason why I had not received any reports? Were all the farmers in Egypt starving so that the King could commit human sacrifice, an unthinkable atrocity, a terrible return to the time before Egypt had gods?

And who was the sacrifice? Was it I?

I wondered how long it would take to burn to death. To destroy the body was to destroy the ka, the spirit-double. There would be no afterlife for me, no explanation of my life to the Divine Judges. I would not persist, I would not live, have flesh, speak again to my loved ones in the Field of Reeds and after they in their turn died they would never be able to find me. I would be nothing. I would burn like a candle and go out like a candle. There would be nothing left of me, Ptah-hotep, who had been diligent and loving, except a handful of ash which would blow away in the wind. The King was not just going to kill me. He was going to obliterate me, make me as nothing.

Made things are unmade, as Neferti had prophesied.

I was drenched in fear as if I had been in cold water. I had been prepared for death, resigned to it. If the King wished to kill me I could not stop him. But he was not only going to kill my life, but my soul as well.

I was craven, not brave. My bowels loosened and threatened to disgrace me. My knees weakened. I dared not speak, for my voice would quaver. If I unlocked my tongue I knew I would beg; yes, grovel and slaver and beg for my life; offer him my body, anything—as long as he did not slay my soul.

The King withdrew his gaze from the pyre and said, 'The Phoenix must die so that she may be renewed.'

I did not speak but nodded, dumbly. I slid down into my kneeling position again, the better to implore him for my life when he pronounced his sentence. Huy was beside him, Pannefer on the other side, and they both knew what was coming. They were smug with satisfaction at my downfall and would doubtless dance round my funeral pyre. They knew that he was taking my afterlife as well as my present life. A feeble flicker of hatred and pride kept me conscious, but that was all it could do.

'You have the honour,' said the King, beaming down on me, 'of lighting the fire for the Queen Phoenix Nefertiti, in which she will achieve translation.'

I almost collapsed with relief. He was not going to burn me on that fire of precious woods. He was going to burn the Queen. At that moment the idea seemed to be an excellent one. At least the sacrifice was not Ptah-hotep.

'Of course, if you refuse, you will take her place,' said Huy.

The soldiers drew me to my feet. I had to give an answer to the king, who was as pleased as if he were conferring a province on a deserving servant. If I refused I would die and all of me would be destroyed. But I did not assent or refuse. The temple swam before my eyes, the gold tarnished to dark green and then dark red like old blood. I fainted.

I woke in my own bed. For a delirious moment I wondered if I had dreamed the whole scene in the temple. But Mutnodjme and Kheperren were both holding me. I could feel their fear and concern. It was all true and I had to secure what I could before my choice could be made. I sat up.

'Bring Meryt,' I ordered, and she came to me, my dear Meryt who had loved me and protected me for many years. She was in tears and I kissed her and she hugged me. Her brothers crowded around the bed on which I lay.

'Go,' I ordered. 'Go now. Do not stop for rest or tears. Before night you should be on the river and on the way home. I cannot thank you, Meryt, for all you have done, not properly. If you want to honour me, Nubian, live well. Prosper. All the blessings I have I load upon your head.'

Meryt kissed my feet and Kheperren motioned to his two soldiers, not Nubians but Klashr, members of the general's own honour guard. The procession formed with Meryt at the head and her whole household walking behind, small children crying and Teti, Hani and Tani looking back to see the last of Ptah-hotep, who had done at least two good deeds for them. I had taken them out of slavery, and now I was sending them away.

I watched them as they marched out of my life, Meryt with Anubis by her side. He had already bitten Hani, and I had to order him to go. He was a good dog, so he obeyed and his obedi-ence snagged my heart. But they had gone. One group settled and safe, for I did not think that even the King would dare to outface General Horemheb, especially not on so unimportant an issue as a few Nubian ex-slaves.

I rose and walked into the outer office. All faces turned to me. I had no need to ask for silence. Menna and Harmose laid down their clay tablets and looked at me. Bakhenmut was terrified, patently anticipating his wife's reaction to his prob-able dismissal if my office came down with me. Khety looked shocked, Hanufer worried. Only Mentu was unconcerned. He even attempted to comfort me.

'Easy got, easy lost,' he quoted; always his philosophy. 'Do not be troubled, Ptah-hotep. You can always join the army, that's where I am going. Horemheb always needs skilled charioteers.'

So, my office did not know the terms of the demon's choice which the King had thrust upon me. I was glad. If I could manage it, no one would know. I said, 'There is no need to be concerned. There is no reason for the King to change this office in the slightest. He just wants me.

'So, tomorrow Bakhenmut, I will appoint you Great Royal Scribe, before I am summoned to the king again. Come to me at dawn for your jewels-of-office. You will, however, I trust, keep the office as it is. Menna and Harmose are here by the will of the old king, as well as the new, and their translations are vital in giving the throne the best advice. Your friends Khety and Hanufer are very skilled. I also remind you how valuable our friend Mentu is when he honours us with his presence. By the way, ask the king, when I am gone, what has become of this year's tax returns. I believe that giving you the position will preserve all of you from royal attention. Will you accept, Bakhenmut?'

For a long moment, fear warred with ambition in Bakhen-mut's face. The battle was so naked that I wanted to look away. Then he dropped to the floor and kissed my feet, murmuring, 'Lord, I am unworthy of this honour,' which meant yes.

'No more work is to be done today,' I announced. 'Go home, all of you. I thank you for your loyalty and your love,' I added. I did not know how much more I could stand, so it was good that they were mostly too afraid to approach their doomed master. Bakhenmut left at a run to carry to his wife the good news. The old men bowed and left. Mentu embraced me suddenly and hard, then left without looking back. Khety and Hanufer kissed my hands, murmuring long forgotten prayers which would have condemned them to death if they had been heard.

Then they were gone. The office was empty. I swallowed, thinking that my hearing was at fault, and realised that I was listening to utter silence. No noise of Meryt and her tribe, no babies crying, no sizzle of food cooking. No noise of rustling papyrus or thud of clay tablet into basket. No one left in the office of the Great Royal Scribe Ptah-hotep.

Except two people who would also have to be induced to leave. The lady Mutnodjme and Kheperren the scribe stood close together, considering me as I was considering them.

'I love you,' I said to them. 'I would not involve you in my ruin. I bid you depart.'

Neither of them moved a muscle.

'Must I order you?' I demanded. My control was slipping; I had a dreadful choice to make, such as no man in the Black Land had to make before, and they would not let me make it freely.

'Order away, 'Hotep,' said Kheperren. 'Anubis obeyed, but he's a dog. It won't make the slightest difference to us. We aren't leaving you. How could you think it?'

I knew I would not get anywhere with Kheperren, but I said despairingly to the lady, 'Mutnodjme, you have only lain with me twice, both times in strange states of mind, you could easily say that I or the night had overpowered you and be free of me.'

'So I could,' she replied, unmoved, fists on hips like a peasant. 'Do you think that I am likely to say that?'

'You could,' I encouraged. Her face shut in on itself like a box, concentrating into an expression of complete obstinacy.

'I won't,' she assured me.

'Now we've got that over with,' Kheperren said easily, 'Let us bar the doors, eat some of the food which Meryt has left for you, and we can talk about this. We cannot help you if you will not tell us anything, but if that is the case we are quite willing to drink your Tashery vintage and occupy your space. My lady Mutnodjme and I have nothing else to do today,' he added, and the lady nodded emphatically.

Kheperren knew me very well. He knew that in such company I could not keep silent forever. Forever, in my case, extended until the next morning, when I would have to officiate at…

They sat me down and held a wine cup to my lips and made me drink, and I told them all about it.

Then we began having the argument that I dreaded. I knew that they would not let me face the choice I had to make.

'It's simple, Ptah-hotep, we just get you away,' Kheperren urged for the one hundredth time. 'You need make no choice except the soldier's choice not to be there when the arrow lands. General Horemheb is leaving to take the Widow-Queen Tiye's message to the Mitanni soon. We can just go to the camp, hide there, and travel with him. I can teach you the ways of the army and we can be happy.'

'That seems sensible,' said Mutnodjme.

'But what about your sister the Queen?' I cried. 'If not I, then another will light that pyre. Do no evil deed in the service of the gods, that's what they taught me. If I do not die instead of her, then another will light the pyre, and the Royal Wife will die a terrible death!'

'Better her than you,' Mutnodjme flatly. She shocked me. Was she so willing to watch her sister immolated? She loved her sister. I said as much.

'Certainly I love her. But she is the king's accomplice in the evils of this reign. She rules the House of the Phoenix, and it may be fitting that she is the sacrifice, she may even be eagerly anticipating this end.' Mutnodjme was thinking, elbow on knee, chin on fist. She sat like a man, legs spread, and stroked where she would have had a beard, thumb moving across her chin.

'She knows what she is doing, she knows what the king is and what he has made of Egypt and of her. You know that such a death would condemn you to be nothing, to blow away. She may well be anticipating a happy afterlife, united with the Firebird. In any case, this choice which has been thrust upon you is not made for a religious reason.'

'I agree,' said Kheperren. 'The king perhaps has always worried about your loyalty. You have never asked to be made a priest of the Aten. This is his way of testing whether you are still wedded to the old beliefs, which of course you are. The person who should light this pyre is Divine Father Ay, curse him with many curses.'

'She is his daughter and he loved her once,' put in Mutnodjme. 'Perhaps he cannot bring himself to do it, so he has suggested this dreadful substitution to the king.'

'No, he may well have suggested finding someone else; but he approves of your love for me, as it relieves him of any responsibility for you,' I said, following her line of argument. 'Either or both of Pannefer and Huy have done this to me.'

'So they have. Now, we need to make plans for your escape,' said Mutnodjme as if it were all settled. My heart ached for my loves, my dears. But I could not let them do this.

'No, there will be no escape,' I said. 'I will appear tomorrow in the courtyard of the Phoenix, and on that I am not to be dissuaded. You see that it must be so,' I said.

They must have seen, for they stopped arguing.

Chapter Twenty-four

Mutnodjme

I left him only to see my sister Merope bestowed on her new husband. The courtyard was buzzing with women's voices, shrill and alarmed. Few of the women had been able to make choices such as I had made for my dearest sister, and most were afraid and all of them were talking. They had lived in palaces all their lives, I thought, looking at them with as much pity as I could summon.

What would they do, conferred on some unwashed commoner as secondary wife, dealing with the hatred and envy of his first wife and banished to the kitchen? Most of them were destined to be water-carriers or servants and few of them had the strength or the skill to even do that. The luckiest might find a kind man or a sex-starved youth who would appreciate them. But kind men were at a premium in Egypt, and I did not like their chances. They had been raised, trained and nurtured as the Ornaments of the King, and their fate was bitter.

So was mine. But if Ptah-hotep was to die on the morrow and there was still nothing that I could do, I could lie with him tonight, and I was resolved on that. If he tried to shut me out on my return I would break down his door.

Merope was scanning the crowd, greeting friends and searching for the sight of her new man. I wished her heartily well and said, 'Sister, may you bear many children and be happy,' as was customary.

'Sister, I am desolated to leave you,' she replied, which was true enough; she was in tears. But this fate was better than others which could come upon the king's women.

Great Royal Spouse Whom the King Loves Who Exudes Fragrance Ruler of the Ruler of the Double Crown Nefertiti was carried into the middle of the expostulating women and set on the dais above the pile of precious wood.

'Women, you are divorced of the King's person,' she yelled, and they fell silent. 'Now receive the Aten!'

I saw lights and smelt smoke. For a moment, I wondered if there was some trick, and we were all to be burned to death in one great sacrifice. But it was not the case. The fire I had seen had been a long line of men bearing torches. A hundred men in the robes of Aten-priest filed into the courtyard and began to line the walls. They were solemn and silent.

I caught sight of Dhutmose in the ranks. He had seen me, too, and edged his way along, elbowing a few of his fellows, until he was directly behind Merope. His eyes widened at the sight of her, most beautiful of sisters. I turned Merope to look at him. They were almost breast to breast. She said, 'Master Dhutmose?'

'*Adelphemou*,' replied the priest. This means 'my sister' in Kritian. Then he said *Philimou*, which means, 'my love' and Merope gasped, wept, and fell into his arms.

He had reason to hold her tight. The men with torches were given an order which I could not hear, and they just reached out and grabbed the nearest female. Fortunately, Dhutmose had Merope in a firm grip, and the man who mistook me for a Great Royal Divorcee retreated with a yelp as I kneed him in the groin. I slid behind Dhutmose as he and Merope edged their way out of a dreadful scene.

The Royal Women were not just being given away to the priests of Aten, politely and with order and precedence. The priests of that thrice-damned god were carrying them away, dragging them roughly from their friends without even time to say goodbye. The courtyard resounded with shrieks and slaps.

I saw my sister Nefertiti carried away on her litter, high above the chaos with a little smile on her perfect lips, and thought that it was much, much better that she should be burned rather than Ptah-hotep.

We were out of the courtyard of the Phoenix and into the broad approach to the palace before we stopped. I could not shut out the dreadful screams of ravishment and despair, and Merope kissed me quickly and said, 'Come with me, sister, we can live together, my lord Dhutmose will have us both, do not go back!'

'No, I have a task,' I told her. 'I will come and visit if I can. Farewell, dear sister.' I embraced her closely, smelling the scent of her hair for what might be the last time. I looked Master Dhutmose in the eye and said, 'Take care of her.'

He nodded. He was shaken by the events in the court of the Phoenix, but at no point had his hold on my sister's narrow waist loosened. He kissed my hand and hurried Merope away. They had not searched her. She was still loaded with the Widow-Queen's gold, and when Dhutmose lay down with her that night he would find that he had acquired a richer present than ever he had expected.

I went back into the palace through a side door. I did not want to see whatever else was happening in the court of the Phoenix.

I went to my own room to report to Widow-Queen Tiye on the disposition of her sister-queen Merope and found her gone and her servants with her. I scribbled a note on an ostracon which reported Merope safely bestowed and myself with Ptah-hotep; and went back to the quarters of the Great Royal Scribe, taking with me my own property, which was not much greater than it had been when I came to Amarna.

I and my bundle were halted at the door of the office by two soldiers wearing the bright feathers of the king's personal guard.

'You cannot pass!' one announced, the sort of bone-headed statement I might expect from one of the king's bodyguard.

'Yes, I can,' I explained. 'I just open the door and go in.'

'You cannot pass,' he repeated.

'Listen, you are stationed here to prevent the lord Ptah-hotep from leaving, aren't you?' I asked patiently, though I did not feel patient. The guards must have been sent after my departure for the Aten ceremony. They had not been there when I left.

'On the direct orders of the lord Akhnaten may he live!' agreed the soldier.

'Yes, but there are no orders about who should go in,' I told him, gambling on the fact that this would not have been covered. Who would be mad enough to join a doomed man on his last night? Mutnodjme, that's who. And if they did not let me in soon I might easily seize a spear and start a massacre.

'No,' agreed the soldier, slowly.

'And I am going in, not out,' I said, and opened the door. The soldier watched me with the bewildered expression of a man who has given his arm-ring to a conjurer at a fair. I slipped past him while he was still thinking about it and closed and barred the door from the inside. I might not be able to leave, but until someone lowered this plank, they would not be able to get in, either.

'I'm here, and I'm not leaving, because I can't leave,' I announced to Kheperren and Ptah-hotep, who were sitting at the same desk and puzzling over an inscription. 'I can't leave because there are two soldiers at your door to prevent it.'

Ptah-hotep looked resigned. Kheperren looked worried.

'We heard screaming,' he said. 'What happened in the court-yard of the Phoenix? We were about to go out and look for you.'

'Mass rape,' I said shortly, putting down my bundle. 'I went to tell the Widow-Queen about it but she was not there. I hope that nothing has happened to her!'

'She is more likely to have happened to someone else,' Kheperren soothed me. He was right. I doubted that there was anyone in the palace, even the dim soldiery, who would dare to threaten the lady Tiye.

'Well, Merope my sister has gone to her new husband, a nice man, Kheperren, he had even learned some Kritian to speak to her and she just fell into his arms. The others, well, the others are at least away from the palace.

'I saw my sister Nefertiti there, floating above the terror, serene as cream, the daughter of a dog! How is it with you?' I asked, looking at Ptah-hotep.

'We are consulting some old proverbs,' said Ptah-hotep. 'There is one which I am looking for, but the manuscripts have been so damaged by the King's insistence on removing the name of Amen-Re that they are hard to read.'

'Which one are you searching for? I might know where it is,' I said.

'Something about teaching a goat to talk,' Ptah-hotep said, and I laughed. I knew that one.

'Come and I will tell you about it,' I said, and they came to sit down with me in the empty inner apartments, far from any hearers, though we could speak any treason we wished, for doom had already come upon one we loved and Kheperren and I did not greatly care what happened to us if Ptah-hotep was to die. I knew he would die rather than set that pyre alight.

To push the thought away, I made a story of the proverb. Kheperren and Ptah-hotep sat down at my feet and listened.

Once there was an Eloquent Peasant, and his son who was a thief. His thieveries were many, and he was finally caught as part of a gang which robbed the treasuries of the Pharaoh, even the Lord of the Two Lands.

This is how he was caught; the Master of the Treasury knew that gold was vanishing, but not how. In fact there was a secret entrance, made by a king who was a miser and did not want his court to know how often he visited his treasury to croon over his gold. The thieves had discovered this entrance and the Master of the Treasury did not know where it lay. But he set a trap, such as we use for mice but very large, and when one of the thieves reached for a particularly fine golden vessel, the trap snapped shut and he was caught by the arm. The others fled but in the morning there was the peasant's son, caught fast.

The treasurer brought the thief before the king, who sent for the boy's father. He was allowed to speak to his son and advised him of what to say.

So just when Pharaoh was about to pronounce sentence of mutilation and exile, or even death, the boy said, 'Royal Lord, Master of the Two Thrones, give me a year, and I will teach a goat to talk!'

'Impossible,' said the King, but the boy repeated his statement, and the Pharaoh was interested. After all, he could still order the boy's execution after the year if he had not carried out his boast.

So the son of the Eloquent Peasant was released. As soon as they were out of earshot he turned on his father, angrily asking, 'Why did you tell me to say such a ridiculous thing? I cannot teach a goat to talk. No man can teach a goat to talk!'

'You're still alive. You've got a year,' said the Eloquent Peasant. 'A lot may happen in a year. You might die. The goat might die. The king might die. The goat might talk!'

'That is a heartening proverb, Ptah-hotep,' I added.

'It is,' he agreed.

It was getting dark. The sun was sinking. The ornaments of the king's house were all gone, and it must be truly cold and empty in the palace of women. I was glad I was not there.

Kheperren and I assembled a feast for the evening meal. Meryt as her last gift had left a lot of food prepared and waiting; a stack of flat bread, oiled meats, fine vegetables and fruits and a whole cheese in its web. I found myself hungry, which was surprising, and we dined well on Nubian food and Tashery wine, always the best in the Black Land. We had to find something to talk about, and Ptah-hotep was drawn like a fine wire.

'Do you remember, my heart, lying in the reeds with me, swimming in the sacred lake when we were boys, before the flail descended on your shoulders?' asked Kheperren.

Ptah-hotep looked at him over his wine cup and said, 'I remember. We were going to have a hut in the reeds and a dog called Wolf on guard. That will not happen now,' he said, and gulped more wine. Reminiscence was not going to assist us to while away the night.

'Do you remember lying with me on the night of Isis and Osiris?' I asked.

Ptah-hotep nodded and said, 'We were possessed by the gods, and that proves that they still exist. Isis was in you, lady, and Osiris in me. And tomorrow I will be burned to death, and there will be no meeting for us, never again.'

This sounded like settled despair and Kheperren knelt beside Ptah-hotep and took him by the shoulders.

'Who is to say that your belief is correct?' he said desperately in earnest. 'Who is to say that we do not all blow out like candle flame or all go into union with the Aten? It's just stories, 'Hotep, just tales that men make to ward off the dark.'

'No one has come back,' I added, joining Kheperren on the floor, 'to prove or disprove. No ghost has come to tell us that unless the body is preserved the soul is lost. How could Amen-Re allow such a good soul to be destroyed in such an act? You will live, you will live, you will live.'

'I am so afraid,' he confessed at last, and we carried him down into our arms, on the floor, on the Nubian blanket let fall by an overburdened child.

I had not known if they would exclude me, these two who had been lovers for years before I came into their life, but they did not. Both pairs of arms reached for me, both mouths touched mine. Kheperren stripped Ptah-hotep of his clothes and his jewels, and I stood up to remove all that I wore, then tugged at the soldier's loincloth. I undid the knots and it came free, revealing a phallus coming into erection slowly, still soft to my hand, hardening under my touch.

We stripped away even the wig which all men of any standing wore, freeing Ptah-hotep's own hair from its plait, scattering ribbons and feathers and mirrors. I found perfumed oil and sprinkled us all, so that we smelt of the divine fragrance, of frankincense which had once been the perfumed breath of Osiris and Isis and their son Horus, the Revenger.

If Ptah-hotep was Osiris, I was Isis, and Kheperren was Horus. I spoke and named us and consecrated us to the gods of the dead while I still had language, for this love-making quickly passed beyond speech. We sighed together, all on one note. I felt my body relaxing, anticipating pleasure, my emotions with my Ptah-hotep but also with Kheperren. I wanted it to last forever, in a charmed sphere such as magicians make to protect themselves from demons they have raised.

A mouth was on my breast, tonguing a nipple until it was hard. A hand was cupping my sisters, the two lips which guard the sheath of Hathor, cupping and then stroking between. I held and sucked, so slowly, a phallus such as that of Min who is fertility; while over my head I heard the slap of belly against buttocks as Horus lay inside Osiris and took pleasure of his flesh.

The fragrance of the gods was all about us.

I felt fire building inside me.

I took Osiris in my arms and as he penetrated me, I screamed.

Ptah-hotep

They were like gods and I was a god with them. My body was malleable, permeable, soaked in divine essences. I lost my thought and all my fear, poured out my loss in kisses on two mouths which meshed with mine, soft and silky and demanding. Time looked away from us. Khons god of moon and measurement overlooked us. Isis took me into her body and Horus slid inside me and I did not know who lay with whom, my name or where I was. I heard Isis cry out, felt her convulse, felt the throb of seed, mine or another's? I lay flat on my back, and someone rode me, I caressed skin warm with life and life poured into me, a vessel, a purified offering to the gods of death.

I turned on my side, supporting a head on my arm, while Horus knelt in homage between willing thighs and joined with Isis who received him eagerly, her mouth seeking mine, her hand caressing my phallus. Her legs were locked around his waist, her hips thrust upward to engulf the offered gift. She cried out and he thrust harder; she went limp and he came to me, our hands crossing the body of the goddess, and finally we climaxed together, spreading her belly with semen like a field is spread with seed.

We lay stunned until we grew chilled and stiff. Then we ran to my bed and lay down together, a warm body on each side of doomed Ptah-hotep, and I did not mean to sleep but I slept and they locked their hands over me. I slept so and I woke so, between my guardians, like a dead man between Nepthys and Neith.

I looked at them as the dawn light revealed their faces. Mutnodjme was half hidden by her hair, a tangled mass of ebony ringlets, her eyelids a fringed black line on her olive-coloured cheek, her mouth half-open against my arm. Kheperren lay heavily on my other arm. Even in sleep he seemed to be thinking, a line between his brows, his lips shut on some unwise declaration.

I was overcome with a wave of love and liking and I was suddenly and completely happy. I was about to leave them, but no man was loved as I was loved.

I woke them by trying to get up. I had to get to the wash-place. Kheperren watched me narrowly to make sure that I was not going anywhere else. He sat up, scratching his belly, and the lady woke and kissed the nearest flesh, which was Kheperren's thigh.

'All hail to Amen-Re,' I declared, coming back to see my two dearest people embracing each other, and they both repeated, 'Hail to the great god at his rising,' and I was carried back in time.

The years of Amarna and the new god fell away from me. I was Ptah-hotep, named after the Maker Ptah, worshipper of the only gods of Egypt. I was not Great Royal Scribe any more—or would not be after I surrendered my jewels-of-office to Bakhenmut. I need not watch my every word. I might be about to die, but at least I was free.

The others felt my happiness. We rose. I did not wash, as that would remove from me the perfumes of love. I donned a cloth which was no different from any scribe's, and packed up my palette and my styli, my ink pot and my papyrus. These things I had brought with me, and I would take them into the flames.

Perhaps I would have them, indeed, in an afterlife, if they went with my body into the fire.

Bakhenmut came as ordered and I invested him with the pectoral and arm ring of the Great Royal Scribe. He hesitated, shifting from foot to foot on my threshold, before he gave me an apologetic nod and walked quickly away. Then the soldiers came and they escorted all three of us into the court of the Phoenix.

We came into bright light and blinked. The courtyard had no worshippers. Only the King Akhnaten sat on his high throne, flanked with his advisors. I met the dreamy eyes of the king and the concentrated venom and triumph of his counsellors with no emotion at all. I walked in a dream and I stood in a dream. There was always a chance—it itched at the corner of my mind—that this was just a test, that indeed, at the end, the king would not order me to undergo this dreadful ordeal. I watched the flail of authority lying on his swollen belly.

It gave a twitch. At that signal, soldiers moved in around the pyre so that no one could escape from it. I took a step forward, then another step. The blind musicians of Attis began to sing and play sistra and, on the noise of high voices and jingling wires, a litter was carried into the court of the Phoenix on the shoulders of ten men.

I kissed Kheperren, then Mutnodjme. I caught sight of the Widow-Queen Tiye watching from the Window of Appearances.

Mutnodjme saw her too, and stared at the royal lady, who waved my followers back. Very reluctantly, they let me go, holding one another by the hand. They backed until they were standing in the archway of the king's palace. Neither of them looked away from me. Their faces were blank with pain.

I walked on, one step after another, as the men carried the litter around the pyre and the chant of the Phoenix stung my ears.

There was still a chance that the goat might talk. Widow-Queen Tiye was gone from the window. No friendly faces looked upon me except those of my lovers who were behind me. I hoped that they would comfort one another. All of the windows were filled with watchers. I waited in hope that the order would not be given in a rising cloud of spices strong enough to stifle me.

The drums beat, faster and faster, as the chorus of eerie voices cried on the Phoenix to return.

Come to thy perch, to thy resting
Come we have prepared a nest for you
Sweet mother of thyself
Self created, sweet bird of fire!

The men laid down the litter. The curtains opened to reveal the figure of a woman, perfectly still. I could see the profile of the Great Queen Nefertiti. She was the most beautiful woman in all of Amarna. There was no mistaking her, though she seemed to be unconscious or asleep.

The bearers, attended by the Widow-Queen Tiye, carried her into the heart of the pyre. Wood was piled all around her. I could only see her wig and the garland of cornflowers around her neck.

Come and renew thyself, Phoenix
Burn in the fire of your renewal
Give birth to thyself in a sacrifice
Thyself to thyself, a pure offering.

I looked desperately up into the exalted face of the King. The flail was raised. He was about to order me to light this abominable fire. In the nest of spices lay no immortal bird but mortal flesh, quivering and frail. I could not do it. I hoped that Kheperren and Mutnodjme would not watch my death, for it would be horrible. A soldier handed me a burning torch. The flames rose pale in the strengthening sunlight.

'Lord Akhnaten,' I cried. 'I am your slave.'

'You are,' said the King equably. 'We are all slaves of the Aten, Sole and Only God.'

'Lord, do not give this order,' I begged. 'This is an abomination, lord, a thing which cannot be done.'

'Yet you will do it,' he said.

'Do not order me to set this fire, lord,' I asked for the last time. The soldiers were closing around me.

Beside me, the Widow-Queen Tiye raked me with her eyes and hissed, 'In the name of the gods, Ptah-hotep, light the pyre!'

'Never,' I cried, 'I will burn instead!' but my words were vain, because holding my hand in a fierce grip, the Widow-Queen snatched the brand I was holding and forced it into the heart of the fire.

Spices burn with a thick smoke, and the Queen Nefertiti burned with them. I heard screams in the smoke and struggled to loose myself from the talons of the Widow-Queen, who had just forced me to commit murder.

'Stay still,' she hissed in the same tone. 'We cannot be seen but we can be felt. Hold my hand, Ptah-hotep. I will tell you all but you must not be seen here again, do you understand? Come with me. The King is about to find out that it is not possible to sit comfortably in a courtyard in which a king's ransom of spices are wastefully burning.'

'But the lady, the queen!' I protested.

'There is no woman in that pyre, boy, will you shut your mouth?' she snarled at me, reminding me that Sekmet the Destroyer was her patron.

I held my tongue. In any case the huge clouds of billowing burning spices made sight difficult and breathing almost impossible. A brief eddy in the smoke showed me that the throne was now empty and I heard soldiers coughing. A door in the palace slammed shut. Even the musicians of Artis had choked and fled.

I yielded to the tug of the Widow-Queen's hand and followed her, still carrying, I noticed, the bundle which contained the tools of my trade. If that hadn't been a real body, then what had it been? I knew Nefertiti's face, the most famous countenance in the Black Land, and it was her face. I began to be angry. I had been cheated of my death. I had given away all my goods, consecrated my lovers, given up my office, and now I was not to die after all. How could I go back? The king must have heard my defiance. If he saw me again, I was certainly dead.

I ran knee-first into what, on closer inspection, turned out to be a litter-carriage with heavy leather curtains, such as is used by ladies on journeys. Into this Widow-Queen Tiye shoved me, shouting through the smoke, 'The horsemen know where to go. Stay with her. Don't return until you have word from me, write no letter, send no word. I will tell them.'

Then, of all strange happenings in that most strange day, she took off her pectoral and put it around my neck and kissed me on the mouth, hard. She tasted of smoke and spices. 'You are a good man. Amenhotep would have been proud of you,' she told me. Then she stepped away and I was thrown back against a soft bundle as the horses were whipped into a gallop.

I was still alive, I was not burned. I rubbed my eyes. When I had cleared the smoke out of them, I found that the carriage was already through the gates of the City of the Sun and we were racing across the open plain toward the river. I pinched myself, hard, and watched a red weal come up on my skin. Yes, I was also awake.

The carriage bounced as the charioteer yelled to his horses to go faster. I clutched the bundle I was leaning against and found that I had my hand upon a breast.

I removed it hastily. I had been leaning on the most beautiful parcel in the world. In the carriage with me, stunned or asleep, was Nefertiti, Great Royal Spouse, Lady of the Two Lands, whom I had just sacrificed to the Phoenix.

Book Three

The Hawk
at Sunset

Chapter Twenty-five

Mutnodjme

I did not see his ending, for the clouds of smoke drove Kheper-ren and me back despite our longing to watch the unbearable, but we heard his defiance flung to the lord Akhnaten on his high seat. The fire had burned with a flame hot enough to melt bronze. There might not even be bones for us to bury fittingly.

We had nowhere to go to indulge our grief and horror. I could not take a man to the Widow-Queen's apartments so we trailed back to the office of the Great Royal Scribe. There Kheperren and I gathered all the personal belongings of our lover, weeping as we did so. I wept as I picked up a garment he had thrown aside to make love to us the night before, and Kheperren wept as he found Ptah-hotep's favourite stylus under a chair. We took his vials of Nubian oil, his store of copied papyri, his cloths and his sandals. We wrapped it all in the Nubian blanket on which we had made love together.

It was a burden for one man in the way such weights are measured. Not much for all those years of dedication. He had given away all his jewels—those of his office to the new Great Royal Scribe, those of his own to his slave Meryt and her household. We were not taking away anything that would be valuable to anyone but us.

Kheperren shouldered the burden. As I picked up my own, he said, 'Come with me, lady,' and drearily, I followed.

On the way out we passed a pop-eyed lady, very decorated, who was superintending the removal of her own furniture into the apartments. A line of servants carried beds and chairs and baskets. Bakhenmut, the new incumbent, gave us an apologetic look as we shouldered past the bearers.

The wife of the new Great Royal Scribe said nothing to us as we left, but her shrill orders to the servants: 'Mind that corner! By the Aten, what dreary decorations! Husband, we must have this all re-painted immediately!' followed us down the corridor.

Kheperren took me to the quarters of General Horemheb, who allowed us to come in, showed us to his bedchamber, closed the door and left us alone with our anger and fear. We lay and wept together as the day grew hotter and noon passed, and still the fire in the courtyard smouldered, a stench of spices.

'I knew he wouldn't do it,' choked Kheperren.

'I, too,' I wiped my face on my cloth.

'I go with my general to deliver the Widow-Queen's message to Tushratta,' he said to me, holding me close. 'You are the only woman I have ever lain with, the only woman I could ever love. Come with us. There is nothing for you here.'

'I still belong to the palace,' I responded automatically, then thought about it. Where was I to go, what was I to do? I had stayed in Amarna because of my sister Merope, but she was now gone. My sister Nefertiti was dead, sacrificed to the Phoenix; and my lover Ptah-hotep. He too was most horribly and gloriously dead, defying the Pharaoh, refusing to play Amarna games. He had died true to the old gods, but he had still died.

Why should Mutnodjme stay in the palace of the King Akhnaten? Not for the sake of her parents, to whom she was an embarrassment. There was only one person in the palace of the king who deserved my loyalty.

'I'll have to talk to the Widow-Queen,' I told Kheperren.

Then, worn out with grieving, we slept until the general woke us. He did not mean to, but he needed clean clothes for his audience with the Pharaoh, and he tripped over a chair in the half-light and swore and we woke.

Waking when one is mourning is hard. One wakes and for the first few moments one cannot recall grief; then it lands like a stone from above. I woke next to a male body, slim and young, and thought him Ptah-hotep. Then Kheperren rolled over and yawned and I recognised him and Ptah-hotep's death crashed down on me and I groaned.

'Waking is hard,' agreed the general, sitting down on his big chair and rubbing his stubbed toe. 'It is easier for soldiers, because they have an enemy and they may still die. Therefore rise, wash, you must face the world. There is a terrible task before you, and none but you can do it, Lady Mutnodjme, as men are forbidden to walk in the court of the Phoenix.'

I staggered to the wash-place and poured water over my head, wrung out my hair and mopped my tear-swollen face.

'What is the task, lord?' I asked. Even my voice seemed reluctant and words were slow in forming.

'The fire in the court of the Phoenix is, at last, out. You must sift the ashes for bones,' he said. Generals must often give orders which they know may result in the recipient's death and he gave this one calmly.

But this task was not as hard as he seemed to think. If I could find some bones—perhaps a skull, skulls do not readily burn—I could reassemble enough of Ptah-hotep for his voyage to the afterlife, and if ever man deserved to feast in the House of Osiris it was my dear love Ptah-hotep. It was the last service that I could do for him, and I was anxious to do it.

'I will go directly,' I said.

General Horemheb gave me that puzzled look again. Though I did not mean to, I kept surprising him. I tied my cloth close about me, grabbed another to put the bones in, and was starting for the door when Kheperren caught up with me.

'I will come with you,' he said.

'No, you are still too shocked and you are not used to handling the dead are you?' I demanded.

He was white as linen under the sun-darkened skin. He shook his head.

I was eager to keep my task, and did not want to have to support anyone else in doing it. I was just about sure that I could support myself, but I had no strength to spare.

'Stay, Kheperren, he would not want you to be further harrowed by his death. Besides, the general is correct. You are a man and cannot go into that cursed courtyard, whereas I—may all the gods forgive me—am an initiate of the Phoenix cult. Let me do Ptah-hotep this last service. We shall conduct the funeral together.'

The general patted me on the shoulder as he might do to a comrade, and I went out of the palace into the yard. There were no guards. No one challenged me.

The heap of ashes was not great. The spices had been tinder dry and had burned very bright, leaving little sign that a Nome's worth of precious wood had been destroyed there. The sweet scent was still extremely strong but in it I could detect no lingering scent of burned flesh, which was odd. But then no one had ever burned so many spices together before, so it was possible that any other reek had been entirely subsumed in the perfumes.

No one was there. No one watched me as I began at one side of the mound and spread the ashes, running them through my fingers, looking for bones. It was the second decan of Ephipi, very hot and dry, and the furnace wind rose, the breath of the Southern Snake. This usually blows all morning, and it was now long toward evening, but the wind blew harder. It seemed that the gods wished to assist me in my task. The hot wind was winnowing the ashes, blowing away the light bonfire fluff and stirring the heavier charcoal at the bottom.

I stood in the midst of a whirling cloud of ash. I covered my mouth and nose with the cloth I had brought with me and strove to see through watering eyes. Bone ash is white, and I saw no streaks of the right colour as the detritus blew around me, funnelled in the hollow of the courtyard. Two people had burned to death in this pyre, and they seemed to have burned away to nothing, so hot had the fire been. I saw the ghost of a garland of cornflowers as it flew past, dissolving even as I thought I saw it; the pins of a heavy court-wig; and some jewellery—possibly the ring I had given Ptah-hotep—were melted into little metallic globs puddled on the marble pavement which was cracked and discoloured by the heat of the fire. I gathered up the gold, two handfuls of charcoal and two handfuls of ash before it all blew away into the west where the dead journey to judgment.

Then, scoured by the heat, I entered the palace again and walked slowly toward General Horemheb's quarters. I carried, wrapped in his own cloth, all that remained of my sister and my lover, and it was a very light burden.

On the way I was stopped by two soldiers of the king's guard. They did not touch me—I must have presented a terrible spectacle, a reproach to those who had officiated over the blood-sacrifice. I knew that my hair was loose and filled with dust and I could feel ash stiffening into a mask on my face.

The taller of the two said, 'Lady, your mother would speak with you.' They were clearly not going to allow me past until I had spoken to Great Royal Nurse Tey, so I allowed them to usher me along a corridor painted with dancing gazelles.

'Mother,' I said as I came in. 'What do you want of me?'

'Daughter,' responded Tey, 'I am ill.'

This was a surprise. I had not seen my mother at the shameful sacrifice last night. I assumed that she had been there. I assumed also that the death of the Queen Nefertiti, his daughter, had been some part of Divine Father Ay's scheme to eventually own all Egypt. Though what he would do with it I had no idea. He could not sit and brood like a spider on a mountain of gold.

'Lady, what form does your illness take? And you are aware that I am forbidden to practice medicine? You told me so yourself. Tell one of your tame soldiers to bring you the palace physician.'

'I have done so,' said Tey. She was lying on a couch, picking at the straps with her restless fingers. 'He says that it is an illness which is not to be cured. He says that I have cancer of the womb.'

'Then that is the end of the matter, lady,' I said. I hated her with a remarkable depth of feeling, considering how exhausted I was.

Tey had warned me off trying to take Nefertiti away from the worship of the Firebird. Tey had watched over the sacrifice. Tey had seen the immemorial rights of every woman in the Black Land vanish into smoke and had applauded the loss. Tey had denied me my freedom and the use of my hard-earned skills. Also, I knew of no cure for such a cancer. She would die, and it could not be soon enough for me.

'You have sifted the ashes?' she changed the subject, seeing that I was not disposed to help her.

'As you see,' I sat down, placing the folded cloth in my lap.

'You found...traces?'

'Lady, I did.'

She glanced around as if someone might be listening and then said in a voice which was rich with pain, 'Give me something of my daughter Nefertiti.'

'No,' I said. Had she gone into that pile of ash and searched for the concubine's daughter as I had gone to seek my lover? Tey had no claim over what I carried.

'Cruel,' said Tey, very softly. 'Cruel, and it is I who raised you, educated you, unfitted you for a woman's life.'

'How, unfitted?' I demanded. The only reason that I was discussing this so calmly was that I was too shocked and grief-stricken to engage in petty arguments with my mother about her treatment of me. She had said this kind of thing before, mostly while gloating that I would not longer be able to use my talents.

'The little princess is sick.' She avoided the argument again.

'Then you must summon the palace physician,' I repeated.

'The King married her last night,' said Tey with something less than her usual ferocity. 'Ay lay with her though she is still a child. Now she is feverish and cannot sleep.'

'That is to be expected,' I said as calmly as I could, revolted by the idea. 'I'm sure that she will resign herself to the difficulties of a life in the palace, as I have had to do.'

'You will not help me, but you will help her,' said Tey with some of her old venom. 'You are a priestess of Isis!'

'I was a priestess of the lady whom I must not name, mother, but that worship has been discredited. Now I must go.' I said.

I did not look back as I went to the door. Tey rose on one elbow. She did not shriek curses at me. She only said one word, one which I had never heard from her mouth before.

'Please.'

So I turned back, hating myself. I took the lid off an alabaster dish which stood on the table, a beautiful thing carved in the shape of a bird breaking out of an egg. Into it I put a pinch of fine bonfire ash.

'Tell your soldiers to take me to the Great Royal Wife,' I said, and she clapped her hands to summon them.

But when I reached the room where the poor little princess Mekhetaten lay, they were already mourning her. I spoke to the women, but they could not tell me what killed her. She might have died of shock, of loss of blood, of horror or of suicidal or homicidal poisoning, and of course there was always disease. Any underlying condition would have flared up under such conditions, and it was Ephipi, the season of fevers. There was nothing for me to do and I no longer had an escort so I went back to the general's quarters, a ghostly woman, masked with death. I saw the women making the sign against the evil eye as I passed.

Ptah-hotep

The boat was not a royal barge, but a big fishing vessel, high-prowed and deep-keeled, able to take to the Great Green Sea. On the shrunken Nile it was wallowing, and the lady Nefertiti was sick.

I had found myself under hatches and wondered if I had been abducted or whether this was some strange dream from which I might wake to defy the Pharaoh and burn. But it felt very real. The sound of the water lapping against the side, the smell of the river, the noise of a queen vomiting into a bucket—not the stuff of a death dream. I might have had a queen in my last vision, but she would not have been so sea-sick.

In any case, my love was already given away. I wondered how my lovers had taken this escape. I hoped that they had not mourned me for too long. Doubtless they were even now receiving an explanation from the Widow-Queen. I could do with some explanation myself. I examined my surroundings.

I was in the hold of the boat. I shared it with a queen and a large collection of baskets, which to judge by the way a cat was staring fixedly at one corner, contained grain and a few attendant rats. Sitting composedly in the middle of the hold was a soldier, the golden feathers of his headdress marking him as one of the Widow-Queen's personal guard.

'Good morning,' I said to him.

'Good morning, lord,' he replied. 'Are you feeling better?'

'Better than the lady,' I replied. 'Where am I, where am I going, and what is happening?' I asked, three good questions.

'Lord, you are on the boat *Thousand Fishes In A Net*. You are safe, you are going to a place owned by one of the Widow-Queen Tiye's daughters, and you have been saved from certain death,' he replied. Three good answers.

'Have we anything to drink?' I asked. I was coated with ash from head to foot and some of it had dried out my throat. The young man gave me a flask of mixed wine and water and I swilled, spat, and then drank thirstily.

'Can I go up on deck?'

'No, lord, I have orders to make sure that you are not seen by anyone. We will put ashore as soon as it gets dark. Then you may go up and breathe the air,' he responded.

'This seems to have been a very well-conducted rescue.'

'Lord, the Widow-Queen planned it, and there is no better strategist. I am her chief of the guard, Lord Ptah-hotep. My name is Aapahte.' He bowed slightly from where he sat and I nodded.

Then he went on in a worried tone, despite his crisp military delivery, 'I have been with her for years, the red-headed woman. I and my men are the Sekmet guard. I have never known her to make a major tactical error. Though I am worried about her now. If the king or his two sliny ministers saw her in the court-yard of the Phoenix, she may be in danger. She never agreed to initiation into that cult.'

'But what about the body of the queen? I saw it myself, it was definitely Nefertiti may she live.'

'No, lord, it was...'

'Yes, what was it?' asked the queen, her nausea abated. 'He meant to kill me, to burn me to death, my husband meant to kill me! I have done all he wished, comforted him and soothed him, given him children, even watched over dreadful things done in his name and the name of his god. And then he tried to kill me; he really meant to kill me!' Her voice rose to a tearful wail. I did not know if it was in the least proper, but I accepted her as she flung herself into my arms and held her close.

She wept for some minutes, racked with pain, then demanded of Aapahte, 'Who went into the flame instead of me? Not Mut-nodjme, not my sister—tell me that it was not her!'

'No, lady, it was a model, a huge puppet such as the danc-ers for Osiris used to make and carry around the streets,' said Aapahte. 'The best sculptor in Amarna made it. He has the measurements of your face, lady, and he made a carving, a mask which fitted over the puppet's head. It wore your jewellery and your wig, lady. It looked just like you.

'Meanwhile you had been drugged and smuggled out of the palace. I myself had the honour of carrying you. The Widow-Queen did not know whether you might be consenting to that sacrifice, lady, perhaps out of love for your husband. She could not afford to chance asking you.'

'I see that,' said Nefertiti slowly. 'Yes, if my lord Akhnaten had put it to me that I would rise again as myself, I might have consented; but he did not. He just sent Huy to tell me to ready myself for death, because I was old and no longer fertile and he was marrying my daughter Mekhetaten that night. I suppose he must have married her by now. No, the Lady Tiye acted rightly, though not in accord with my royal dignity,' decided Nefertiti.

I began to think that perhaps she was not very intelligent.

'Lady, why did you ask Aapahte here to tell you that it was not Mutnodjme who died in your place?' I asked.

'Oh, that odious Huy told me that if I would not die, then Mutnodjme would have to die in my place. I told him that it could not be her. She was initiated, of course, but I was the avatar of the Phoenix so it would have to be me. The very idea!'

Nefertiti had clearly been shocked by the notion. She put back a lock of intrusive hair and sighed. She was terribly beautiful and very stupid, but she had at least not offered up her sister to the fire in her place. Any other woman may have leapt at that chance to save her own life. Or at the next offer which she proceeded to disclose.

'Huy then laid a hand on my thigh and told me that if I mated with him he would save me. He smirked at me, the animal! The Great Royal Nurse Tey urged me to accept, but I had the soldiers throw him out. I was so shocked by my husband's perfidy that I resigned myself to die. Then the soldier from the Widow-Queen Tiye came and offered me a potion to deaden the pain. I thought that it might be poison, to cheat my husband of his sacrifice—the Widow-Queen Tiye has never liked me—but I took it anyway, and woke up here. It is very strange and I suppose I should be grateful, but how could he? How could he?' She wept again.

I met Aapahte's eyes over the bowed royal head. He shrugged. I allowed my burden to cry for a little longer, then shook her gently. I needed more information.

'What then of Mutnodjme, lady? Is she safe?'

'Yes, I suppose so.' That wasn't enough and she saw or felt that. 'Yes, the Widow-Queen said that she would look after her. Besides, Mutnodjme is strong and clever. She should have been a man. And your friend is the scribe of the general, of Horemheb Cunning in Battle, isn't he? He won't let any harm come to her. But what will become of me? Not queen anymore, my children abandoned to the care of their father who does not love them, what will become of Nefertiti?' she lamented, and this time I let her weep unmolested.

What would become of all of us? I still felt that mysterious connection to Mutnodjme, and all I felt was sorrow. Deep, aching sorrow, which lay on the stomach like lead.

I slept with sorrow and woke with mourning. I was perhaps mourning my own life, Meryt and the Nubians lost, my office and titles stripped from me by my own hands, the loss of all that I once owned. My wealth would now go to satisfy the greed of Bakhenmut's wife. Henutmire would enjoy my lands and my estates, probably converting them into jewels to decorate her already overdecorated person.

Fortunately, she could not retrieve what I had rightfully given away in my lifetime. My parents would still own their estate, my Master Ammemmes his house full of old scribes and his vineyard. Both those gifts had been from my private fortune, the salary and presents which the lord Akhnaten—may the breath of life be removed from his nostrils—had given me freehold. Once they had changed hands not even Ay the miser could get them back.

So here I was. Free of all burdens. Possessed still of my scribal tools. Possessed also of a despondent queen of Egypt, a pectoral of eye stones belonging to the Widow-Queen Tiye, a monumental headache and with all I loved lost and gone.

For the moment, just for the moment. The red-headed woman would inform Kheperren and Mutnodjme of my safety and whereabouts, and even though I might not see them, perhaps for years, I would know they were there. And surely Kheperren would pass the palace of Sitamen, which was where I surmised that we were going, and perhaps if Mutnodjme tired of Amarna she could come and live with me.

That thought was comforting, and I slept until I woke in the morning loaded with misery, and wondered if both of them were imprisoned or worse, for they had seen my 'death,' and the mad king might have taken revenge upon them. If they were dead I thought I would have known, but this twin-feeling was too new and untried to rely upon.

Morning bought brisk activity on deck. Feet thudded over our heads. The vessel rocked and swayed as they pushed her into midstream. The doleful queen Nefertiti and I ate bread and salt fish and drank sour beer. She could not eat much, saying that the food was coarse, which it was. I was weighted down with a dread for which I could not account. I was in little danger here, under guard in a boat on the Nile, and in any case known to be dead. Anyone who saw me would assume that their eyes had deceived them. I should have been elated. I had defied the Pharaoh, I had not done a vile deed in the name of his god, and I had escaped, moreover in the company of the most beautiful woman in Egypt.

But I was close to tears. I shook myself. *Thousand Fishes in a Net* heeled a little then the current caught her; we were going towards the Delta. I curled up on my fish-scented boards and watched the ship's cat, who was still staring at the same corner of the same basket.

She did not move for hours, and I found my attention entirely engaged by the hunter. She was a slim stripy cat, very like Basht, the cat belonging to the little princesses Merope and Mutnodjme in the days before terror and madness had ruled Egypt. The cat was resting easily on all four paws, her tail out behind her to act as a balance for any swift movement. I concentrated on her, the alert ears, the spread whiskers, the eyes never moving from the place where her prey must, eventually, emerge. The cat had immense patience. She would stay where she was until she caught that rat. Its doom was already written in the book of life.

My lady Nefertiti, finding me disinclined for conversation, took herself to a corner and began to comb out her hair with a crude bone comb which must have belonged to a sailor. Her head must have been shaved recently, for the hair was no more than a span long, but it was gummed to her head with sweat and dust. I heard her exclaim every time she found a knot, and after a while I heard her weeping.

I was too tired to rise and comfort her. I lay on the decking and watched the intent face of the cat.

We had sailed all day. I had been interrupted once by Aapahte coming to see that all was well with his prisoners, and several times by sailors bringing food or loading split fresh fish into the salt-baskets which lay on the other side of the hold.

Their advent did not disturb the cat, or me. I thought it sensible that the vessel *Thousand Fishes in a Net* was behaving as it usually would. We did not want to attract any attention. By the number of fish which were being deposited, she was also living up to her name.

I wondered how the queen—clad only in the gauze cloth suitable for the City of the Sun—was feeling about having naked sailors carry burdens past her as she lay in her corner. But they were extremely well behaved, passing her as though they did not see her. They ignored me, too, except for the one who apologised for treading on my foot.

We had turned and I heard the order for oars. We were rowed into a harbour, perhaps, or the jetty of a city. Aapahte came down to tell us that we had arrived. He had just set foot on the boards when the striped cat sat back on her tail and batted something with a skilled deadly paw. It flew through the air and landed beside my hand, and she was on it in a flash. It was, however, quite dead. Its neck had been broken by that ferocious blow. A huge rat, almost as big as she was. The cat hoisted her prey proudly in her mouth and carried it away to show her captain, its tail trailing on the ground behind her.

A good omen, perhaps, to mark the arrival of Ptah-hotep and Nefertiti at the palace of the Widow-Queen's daughter— the Great Royal Lady of Amenhotep-Osiris, Daughter of the King's Body Whom He Loves, Sitamen, devotee of the goddess of hunters, Lady of the Arrow, Neith.

I was so weary that it was all I could do to drag myself across the landing-plank, up the steps, and fall into a 'kiss-earth' at the Princess Sitamen's bare, calloused feet.

Chapter Twenty-six

Mutnodjme

We wailed for the little princess, and for a wonder I saw the King Akhnaten—may he perish—weeping. He was now completely isolated, I realised. No one still lived who might have told him the truth. He had disposed of his wife, who although foolish and ambitious had loved him; and his Great Royal Scribe, who would always have been truthful because it was his nature. His most blasphemous and horrible ceremony in the courtyard had lost him the most beautiful woman in the Black Land and his new little Great Royal Wife had died the next day. He would have to wait some time before the next princess, Meritaten, suffered under the phallus of the Divine Father, though she was ten and youth had not given her sister any immunity.

Things had changed a great deal in a few years. When he had established the city of Amarna, Akhnaten may he die had a wife and six daughters. Now the king had lost his wife, three of his daughters—for little Neferneferure had died of the summer fever a week after her sister Setepenre—and he had to endure growing unpopularity. The dispersal of the Royal Women had been seen as disgraceful. The sacrifice to the Phoenix would not increase his reputation. Even in an Egypt grown corrupt and cynical, such things were not done in the courts of the Pharaoh.

I looked at the royal family at the Window of Appearances. Standing next to the king was the boy Smenkhare, a slim youth with a very new wig-of-state. Before my eyes, the King Akhnaten kissed the boy on the mouth, pinching between his thumb and forefinger the nipple on the flat chest.

Standing next to his brother in this strange gathering was Tutankhaten, the last remaining child of Amenhotep-Osiris. Both Meritaten and Tutankhaten were dusted with the ash of mourning and I could see tears on their cheeks. Ankhesenpaaten had her arms around her brother's shoulders and he was leaning back into her embrace. I reflected that of all those present the princess Ankhesenpaaten was the only one who appeared to be finding something useful to do.

The rest just stood there, the ministers of state with their mouths open. Huy looked even more like an unsuccessful ass-seller than ever, and Pannefer appeared to have been struck dumb. Mekhetaten's untimely death had surprised them all and disarranged their plans.

The only person who had maintained their demeanour was my father Ay. He was not smiling, but he looked full-fed and satis-fied. Whatever befell the royal family, Ay's position was secure. He was, in a way, a pure man. He had no human ties, though he was perhaps a little fond of Nefertiti and my mother Tey in his way. But he was devoted, body and soul, to gain. There was only one thought in his mind, how to own more and more of everything; not to do anything with it, but to own it. His rape of the little princess would have had no lust in it. The likelihood that he would have to lie with possibly all of the remaining Amarna princesses in blood and against all propriety did not concern him either, if it meant that by committing any foul action he could increase his wealth. He did not even want power. Just wealth.

I repeated the Widow-Queen Tiye's little curse on him as I watched the bearers bring out the litter. Mekhetaten was going to the House of Life, and after forty days her embalmed body would lie in the new rock-cut tombs to the east of the city. I had no more tears.

When the litter had gone and the wailing had died away, I went back inside. I needed to speak to the Widow-Queen Tiye.

But when I came to her door, I found my way barred by the king's guard.

'The lady is in mourning for the Princess Mekhetaten,' they told me. 'She has given orders that she is not to be disturbed for forty days, until the child is buried.'

'Can you tell her that I am here and I will share her mourning?' I asked.

'The lord Akhnaten may he live has ordered us to let no one in or out,' he said solemnly. 'The lady is in mourning.'

'Surely she will see me?' I persisted. 'Ask her, if you please, captain.'

For the first time he met my eyes. In his face I saw the stolid inflexibility, the puff-faced righteousness, of a man doing something which he knows is wrong because he has been ordered. The captain was taking refuge in his orders, and against that I had no argument which would succeed in getting the door open.

'If she should ask for me, I will be with General Horemheb.'

'If she should ask,' he said, 'I will tell her.'

I knew, just from the way he said it, that she would not ask. I hurried away to find Kheperren. The Widow-Queen was imprisoned. I did not know if she were dead or alive, though she was probably alive; she had said that her son would not dare to kill her and she was probably right. But now I had no one to advise me. What to do? Ptah-hotep would know, I thought. But he would not be able to advise me, because he was dead. I missed him suddenly with an almost unbearable pang. My dearest love, my sweet scribe.

I gathered my strength. I could not expend the rest of my life in weeping for him. He was gone. If I was lucky and managed the remainder of my days well, I might meet him again in the Field of Reeds, for I was sure that he would be there. After all, he knew all of the Book of Coming Forth By Day and if the judges would not hear him because his body was ash then there was no justice. I felt weary beyond belief. I stopped and looked out of a window, leaning both palms on the sill, trying to focus. For some reason, I could smell the river, the dock smell of water and fish and tarred ropes. I sniffed again and it was gone. All I could smell was the stench of spices and the usual palace smells, perfumed oil and people. Grief was making me hallucinate.

Kheperren was with his general and they both looked grave.

'Lady Mutnodjme, I have done a thing which you may not like,' began the general.

'Tell me,' I said, sinking down onto the floor at his feet. My head ached. He leaned down from his chair. His big hands took my shoulders and began to massage them. He was very strong but he did not hurt me, and some of the pain began to ease.

'I am anxious to protect you, lady. You are at the mercy of your father and mother if you remain unmarried. I do not trust the motives of either.'

'Neither do I.' I closed my eyes as the wise fingers found knots and kneaded them.

'And now your sister is dead, your mother is ill and the Widow-Queen Tiye has been put under house arrest by her son, if it is no worse,' continued Kheperren, taking my hands in his.

'This is all true,' I agreed.

'So we thought to find a way to give you an unassailable place, Lady Mutnodjme,' rumbled Horemheb. 'A position which even the king may think twice about violating. You need an establishment of your own. And failing that, you need a line of retreat. A good general always secures a line of retreat for his soldiers. One must never assume that one is going to win a battle, even if the omens are excellent.'

'Indeed,' I murmured. Who would have thought that those big spade-like hands had this much sensitivity?

'Kheperren, who might be an acceptable husband, is not of sufficiently high rank to offer for the dead Queen Nefertiti's sister and the daughter of Divine Father Ay,' said the general, still holding my shoulders. 'So I have asked for you in marriage, and I have been accepted.'

This news did not sink in immediately. Then instead of pulling away from him, I considered as the clever hands took away some of my pain. The general's position was, indeed, very high. As long as he commanded the Klashr he had ten thousand soldiers and a possible levy of thirty thousand more to back any decision he might make. If Divine Father Ay tried to have him dismissed, there was a good chance that his faithful Klashr might rebel and stay with their general, and that would leave him in possession of the throne, if he wanted it. I would survive as the wife of Horemheb against anything which my parents or the mad king might want to do to me.

And I did not greatly care what happened to my body now that Ptah-hotep was gone. If the general wanted Mutnodjme, then he should have her. That, too, I could survive.

'Lord, I am unworthy,' I said. I felt their astonishment. Clearly, they had anticipated disagreement, and had marshalled all their arguments in favour of their action. I did not need to hear them. I knelt and laid my hands on the general's feet in token of submission, though he knew that I was not submitting and so did Kheperren.

'Lord, it is very kind of you to take me, knowing that I loved another man and am devastated by my loss. It is very kind of you to want to protect me and the action you have taken will do so. I will serve you faithfully.'

'I accept your service.' Horemheb put his hand on my head. 'I will reward your fidelity with love and your loyalty with gold. You are a remarkable woman, Lady Mutnodjme. I do not require your body if you do not wish to give it, and if you wish to lie with my scribe Kheperren then it shall be consummation of this contract as if you were lying with me.'

This was doubly gentle of my husband Horemheb. He knew that marriages have to be consummated or they can be annulled. He knew that I could not have borne the touch of a new lover with anything but cold jaw-clenching endurance.

But Ptah-hotep had loved Kheperren and they were sufficiently similar that I could lie with the scribe almost as though

I was lying once again with my heart's love. I hoped that Ptah-hotep, who should have got past the various doorkeepers by now, would understand. I was sure that he would.

'Tonight, husband, we have a ceremony to perform, and I cannot eat or make love before that is done,' I told General Horemheb. 'But tomorrow, if it pleases you, I will consummate this marriage with your scribe in your place.'

'That will please me,' he said. 'In four days we will be gone and I will not trouble your household or your manner of ruling it. This marriage does me honour, Mistress of the House. Now sit down again, if you will. There is a knot in those neck muscles which I still have not smoothed out.'

◇◇◇

Kheperren and I laid the pitiful collection of dust and charcoal which had been our lover Ptah-hotep in a niche in the tomb which would one day contain a royal body. The ashes were in a mummiform case. We poured the libations and made the sacrifice, a lamb made out of pastry for we dared not risk a bleat being heard, and a vessel of the best wine. Four soldiers stood impassively on guard as we whispered all the prayers, consecrating our lover to the trial of the weighing of the heart in the name of the abandoned gods, Osiris and Isis and Maat who is truth. Then, because blood was required, we cut our wrists and sprinkled our blood over the tiny casket as we bade farewell to Ptah-hotep and wailed for him as Isis and Nepthys had called to Osiris, 'Come to thy house!'

Then the soldiers escorted us back to the City of the Sun. I tightened a bandage around my wounded flesh and stemmed Kheperren's bleeding with another. We could not die yet.

'He will wait for us,' I comforted my scribe and brother. 'He will build for us a little hut amongst the reeds.'

'He will miss us, even in the Field of Offerings,' he responded. That was true. The sand crunched beneath our feet. The stars blazed.

'You are the only woman I have ever lain with,' he told me

as we came close to the city. 'I had thought myself impotent with women.'

'You are not,' I assured him. 'Let doubters ask Mutnodjme, if you need references.'

'This consummation will not be against your will, then?' I took his hand. If I had to lie with a man again, better it should be with this my brother, who loved the same man as I loved.

'It is with my will,' I said.

And the next day I lay down against Horemheb's thigh in the general's bed, in the manner required of any substitute consummation. In such a way had the King Akhnaten watched the violation of his daughter by Divine Father Ay.

I dismissed the thought from my mind. This was a willing sacrifice. If I closed my eyes, Kheperren felt like Ptah-hotep; the same long muscles, slim body, hard hip-bones, the same scent of cinnamon oil, the same soft hair tickling my face. Washed clean of the ashes and thirst of our mourning, slaked of our fasting and half-drunk on the last of the wine, I caressed Kheperren and he caressed me. I tasted tears on his lips. With a sudden, almost desperate movement, his phallus was inside me, eased in its passage by the oil with which I had been anointed. Horemheb stroked my breasts which were pressed against his body; pinching the nipples which were engorged and hard. I had not expected a climax, but when I felt seed spring inside me, it came. Fast and hard, a joy close to pain, instantly extinguished in remembered grief.

Thus I was married to General Horemheb, and no one could take me away from him.

Ptah-hotep

I was worried. I could not account for my sense of dread. I was in the palace of the Great Royal lady Siamen—not even an edict of the king could make her change her name to delete the forbidden god and turn her into Siraten—and I could not have been more safe. The daughters of Neith—warrior women and well-armed—guarded every entrance.

The lady Nefertiti had been handed over to a clutch of doting ladies who had obviously been longing for someone to look after.

I had tired of her continual wailing about how her husband could do this to her—'how could he?'—for it was beyond me that she could ask such a thing when she had seen there was nothing he would not do to honour his foul god; when she had been his active accomplice in, for instance, the suppression of learning in Egypt.

She was very beautiful, but only if she was out of earshot.

I concluded that my nerves were obviously out of order and left the room I had been allotted—a cool shaded one, under a vine—to go and find someone to talk to. Preferably, I wanted the Princess the Lady Sitamen. I needed some task.

I found her watching archery practice. She did not seem to have taken her eyes off the field, but she greeted me by name.

'Lord Ptah-hotep, blessed be Amen-Re in his rising.'

'Praise to the good god,' I answered, after a moment's fumbling in my memory. I had used this only once since the Aten had been established, and that was when Mutnodjme and Kheperren had bidden me farewell and I had walked out to my death.

'It was a close thing,' she said, motioning me to sit beside her. 'My mother had only time to send me word that you were coming an hour before you came. If you had arrived unannounced, the guards would have kept you in the boat until daylight, and that might have been dangerous.'

'Indeed, though I doubt that we were pursued.'

'If the king finds out that his wife is here, I may have to stand a siege,' she answered, then clapped her appreciation as a stalwart woman drew back a full-sized bow to her ear and the arrow thudded into the exact centre of the cloth and straw target.

'Lady, that is true. Princess, what would you have me do here? For I would not exchange one prison for another, and I am used to working.'

'Hmm,' I had caught her attention. 'You wish to leave?'

'Not precisely, lady. I am delighted to be alive, or I would be if a cloud of misery had not settled on me. Give me something to do.'

'That is easily found,' she said. The Princess had aged like a soldier, as Kheperren had aged. Here were the helmet galls, the crows' feet, the harsh lines on throat and forehead from staring across the plain and from the weather. But she was vigorous and strong still, this daughter of Amenhotep-Osiris. Her eyes were bright and their gaze was level.

'When the temple of Amen-Re was closed we rescued a huge bundle of documents,' she said. 'Some of the citizens had found them, dug them up and were using them to light fires. No one has looked at them yet. Some of my women are literate, but none have a taste for learning or they would have gone to the temple of Isis. I would esteem it a favour if you could catalogue the writings.

'Come every evening and read something to me, Ptah-hotep. It is not safe for you to be abroad, not yet, and in any case it is too hot for journeys. When inundation comes with Akhet and the days are cooler, men will have ceased to search for Ptah-hotep.'

'If they are searching at all. No one was near when the pyre blazed up but the Widow-Queen Tiye.'

'Who would never forgive me if anything happened to you after she has gone to such a lot of trouble and put herself in such danger to rescue you. You still wear her pectoral, lord. She must have commended you highly.'

'She said that Amenhotep-Osiris would have been proud of me.'

We paused to watch the archers. They were very skilful. I made up my mind. Learning had always served me well. As that very same Amenhotep-Osiris had said: *The one comfort which will not fail is learning.*

I took the Princess Sitamen's calloused hand. Her nails were cut short and her knuckles had recently been rubbed raw. 'Lady, I will do as you wish.'

She punched me lightly in the chest and sent me away to look at the manuscripts while the warrior women shot arrows into targets in the courtyard of her palace.

◇◇◇

I found that the days were slipping past without anything to mark them. I found that I could sleep, though I had vivid dreams. I dreamed one night that Kheperren was lying beside me and the disappointment when I woke alone was so acute that I burst into tears. I dreamed strange little pictures which had no connection with anything I had ever seen. I saw Mutnodjme cleaning a soldier's armour, humming as she often did, under her breath, and I had certainly not seen that in waking life. I saw Kheperren throwing a spear, though I could not see his enemy, but woke with the sensation of dust in my eyes and war-shouts echoing in my ears. I heard the sound of wailing and saw the funeral of a royal princess through eyes which were quite dry.

I also wondered that they sent no word to me, and so, after Inundation had failed again, did the Princess Sitamen.

'I have had no word from my mother,' she announced, walking into the house of books. I was sitting easily on the floor, reading a full copy of the Prophecies of Neferti, pleased that my reconstruction had been, as far as I could remember, accurate to the word.

'You are worried, lady?'

'Very worried.' She bit her knuckle. 'Never has such a long period gone past without some greeting from her, even if she had nothing in particular to say she would not fail to write to me. I have written four letters to her and received no reply. My messengers have handed over the correspondence to the right people, I have questioned them. Something has happened in that cursed city.'

'Nothing more probable,' I assured her, putting down the prophecy and allowing the scroll to roll up under its own weight.

'Could he have killed her?' she asked with a soldier's bluntness.

I thought about it. I shook my head.

'I really don't think so, lady, I cannot imagine him having the courage even to order such an execution. What do your messengers say? Is there gossip about the Widow-Queen's fate?'

'No, there is nothing. You are accounted dead, Ptah-hotep; and so is the queen Nefertiti. You both perished in the fire of spices. The daughter of the king who was married to him that night, Mekhetaten, is dead, died the next morning, and the townspeople are whispering that Tey poisoned her.'

'That does not seem likely,' I said.

'No, she would want the royal daughter alive, though there are more royal daughters. Meritaten is the next in age. Bitter will be her fate and that of my brothers. Smenkhare is already invested as Great Royal Wife and is being used, they say, by Divine Father Ay as though he was a woman. And there is still Tutankhaten and Ankhesenpaaten to play with. Poor children, to be so abused.'

'But the Widow-Queen, what does gossip say of her?'

The Princess scowled at me. 'Nothing, I told you, scribe. There is no word of her at all. Not alive, not dead. I came to you to ask if there was someone to whom we could write who might know more.'

'Mutnodjme,' I said, delighted by the idea of communicating with my loves again. 'Or Kheperren. One is Tey's daughter, one is the scribe of General Horemheb.'

'Horemheb has gone, taking his personal guard to the borders where Mitanni wars with Assyria. It will have to be the lady. Very well, you may write, but you must use such words as cannot be attributed to you,' she warned.

'We do not know what is happening in Amarna while the rest of the country goes to ruin and destruction. The message may be intercepted. I wish I knew what was happening in that cursed place!'

She began to pace and I began to think.

What could I send to Mutnodjme which would tell her where I was? A terrible thought occurred to me.

'Lady, when did the Widow-Queen go into seclusion? Do you know when?'

'She has not been seen or heard from since the night of the sacrifice to the Phoenix, why?'

'Because my lovers have been thinking me dead unless she has managed to get some word to them,' I knew now where the load of despair which had descended on me had come from. They mourned me. They thought me gone. If they had not been able to speak to Tiye the Queen then they did not know that I was alive. Nor did they know the fate of the complaining woman who had shared my boat. This was awful.

But the Princess was right. All correspondence was probably intercepted. I had to find a way of conveying to Mutnodjme—for Kheperren would surely have left with the general to assist Tushratta—that she could write to Sitamen and would find both her sister and me. I racked my brains.

'I will consider this, lady. I will not do anything which would bring your palace or the lady Nefertiti into peril. I must speak with her. She might know something, some shared incident of their childhood which would convey the message to her sister.'

'Rather you than me,' snarled Sitamen, and stalked out.

The lady Nefertiti, who had been Great Royal Wife and Queen of Egypt, was sitting by a pool when I found her. She was staring listlessly into the water, where silver fish swam under the lotus flowers. It was a beautiful place, a courtyard shaded by a great vine which had grown across the space, supported by trellises. She looked up as I came through the gate, sighed, and returned her gaze to the water.

'Lady, we need to speak,' I began sitting down next to her on the broad marble rim.

'Once you would not have dared to approach me except on your knees,' she commented.

'Lady, that is true, though as the husband of your sister I might have been allowed some familiarities,' I agreed.

'You were never her husband, only her lover,' snapped Nefertiti. I began to see why the Princess Sitamen had avoided this interview. Clearly loss and fear had not improved the lady's temper.

'Do not quarrel with me, most beautiful of women,' I said. I needed her cooperation, and I have always found flattery very reliable. 'Look kindly on a fellow fugitive, jewel of the Black Land, peerless daughter of the Aten.'

To charm this sulky woman into helping me, I was even willing to speak the name of the Aten, a god whose worship I had utterly abandoned.

'I am old and cast aside,' she said bitterly; but her expression, which had been that of a stone image, had softened.

'Lady, no man could cast you aside. Your husband is mad,' I said truthfully. 'For who could plot the murder of beauty? Shed the light of your smile upon me, lady,' I pleaded and sank to my knees, embracing her shins.

She did smile then; and she was still beautiful, once the lines of discontent had been smoothed away. Even abandonment and betrayal could not take away the pure lines of her brow and throat, the delicate line of her mouth. She was designed to be sculpted.

Not entirely without some truth then, I said, 'Lady, your beauty dazzles me.'

She ordered me to rise with a graceful wave of her pale hand and I resumed my seat.

'What do you want of me?' she asked with a flirtatious lilt. That was more than I had bargained for, and was certainly not my desire.

'I would never aspire to any more grace than the touch of your hand, Great Royal Lady. The Princess Sitamen is worried about her mother, the Widow-Queen Tiye, to whom we owe our deliverance. Nothing has been heard from the Widow-Queen for two months. She may be captive or dead. Therefore I need to write to your sister Mutnodjme to assure her that I, that we, are alive and well, and I need to do this without words. I want you to cast your mind back to your childhood, and find me an incident which will convey this news.'

She looked a little disappointed—I may have been flattering myself—but obliged me by thinking.

'We did not really share a childhood,' she said slowly. 'I was with my step-mother and she was with her nurse. Her mother, my step-mother Great Nurse Tey, nurtured me very carefully, considering that, although I was not the daughter of her own body, I was the most valuable of the children of Father Ay. As I was. He sold me to the Pharaoh for a mountain of gold.

'Mutnodjme was never beautiful. She was wilful and far too sharp for Mother Tey's liking. The only thing I can think of which would convey me to her is a flask of my perfume. It was mixed from the finest oils, precious and distinctive.'

'If the ingredients can be found, daughter of the sun, can you make some of this perfume for me to send to your sister?'

'If the ingredients are here,' she said carelessly, 'I can probably make some for her.'

I kissed her feet and left the courtyard. I knew what shared incident I could use to convey my existence to Mutnodjme. And if the two items, a little carved potsherd and a flask of perfume, were delivered to Mutnodjme, my most beautiful lady—far more beautiful to me than the lady now honouring the lotus with her attention—then she would understand in a matter of seconds that she was not alone, that I was not dead, and that I still loved her.

And if they were delivered with their origin-mark as a shield and crossed arrows—the symbol of the city of Sais but also of the goddess Neith—then she would know where I was.

Chapter Twenty-seven

Mutnodjme

I had been a month the wife of the General Horemheb and I was not accustomed to being Mistress of the House.

It was intensely frustrating. The general had had no household to speak of, only a few servants to keep him clean and fed, after a fashion. Their idea of dinner appeared to be bread and a dish of beans, and their idea of a large festival dinner was bread, beans, and a piece of dried salted goat.

This had to change. After a few days of sulking and a few more days of outright defiance, the three original servants settled down with the seven new ones and began to form alliances and foster feuds. I did little to discourage this, while doing nothing to encourage it. While they were vying for my favour, I thought, they were probably not plotting mutiny. The general had given me a free hand, stating that the household was my concern and he would never question my governance of it, but that meant that I had to rule it as mistress or I would never be able to take some time away to pursue my studies in cuneiform. I did not mean to tolerate a group of servants who could not be relied on to manage the house from one moment to the next, and that is what I had.

So I listened to hours of complaint from my new cook, about the old cook who had been relieved of burning roasts and boiling beans to pursue his natural talents—which were complaining, and a remarkable skill at carving wood where he had shown no flair for carving meat. None of them had to do lowly work like carrying water; and all of them were well-fed and well-housed. After a week spent being served grudgingly by the household, who resented my advent and were taking advantage of their master's absence, I gathered them together for a conference.

There were my four house-women, my own choice and therefore my own fault. Ankherhau and Ii had been priestesses of Isis, though one would never guess it from the way they had reverted to the Amarna ideal of women—brainless and promiscuous. Takhar the cook was a young woman who had just been cheated of marriage by a manservant and who had become despondent. Wab was a little girl who had been mistreated in the kitchen, whom I had personally rescued.

There were my six manservants, ranging from Ipuy, a surly old soldier whom I had inherited from Horemheb—he had been in his first campaign and I assumed that he had sentimental value —to Kasa, a pouting boy of about ten who had a vague connection to the cook.

They all came in and knelt before me. I sat in the chair of state, missing Horemheb and especially missing Ptah-hotep. He was always in my mind, my sweet scribe. What would Ptah-hotep have done with this collection of grumblers? He would have found a weak point in all of them, and used it.

I considered, allowing them to shift from knee to knee, awaiting my pleasure. *Every man has a lever, and he who governs men must find it*, the Divine Amenhotep-Osiris had said, and he was famed for his wisdom.

What did this crowd have in common? Naught but General Horemheb and me. Horemheb was fighting Tushratta's war on the border; therefore they would have to contend with me. 'I have listened to you all for a decan, and I cannot judge between you in your quarrels. I am willing to dismiss anyone who wants to leave, though I will make no presents-of-parting.

'None of you have served me well and you deserve nothing of me. However, anyone who does not wish to continue in my service can leave now, with no penalty. You,' I pointed to the sulky maiden Wab, 'can go back and be beaten in the kitchen.

'You,' I pointed to Ipuy the old soldier, who had caused most of the trouble, 'may be pensioned off to go to your acres which Pharaoh awarded you so long ago, as you keep reminding us all.

'You and you,' I indicated the servants who were brothers, 'may go back to your father and take your sister with you. The same applies, one for all. I see no reason why I should not dismiss all of you and begin afresh with some people who wish to serve a very powerful general and to live in his well-conducted household.

'I do not have time to adjudicate small quarrels between people who should know better. And if, as you may think, the state of the kingdom means that you may skimp and laze and complain endlessly, I am here to tell you that you are wrong. I want a household that can rule itself, and I mean to have it. The next things I have to say will relate to the internal workings of the General's household, so anyone who wishes to leave will please leave now.'

I waited. No one moved. I stared from face to face, and each one nodded, even the old man Ipuy. Kasa burst into tears.

'Do you all wish to stay?' I asked, and ran my gaze along the faces again. Each person said, 'I wish to stay.'

'Very well. Here are the orders, and they come from the general, as well as me. But the general is not my source of power, my household. The source of power in this house is me. I am the Mistress of the House and I will be obeyed, and any repetition of behaviour such as I have endured this last decan will earn you instant dismissal. Do you all understand? You no longer have the luxury of serving me a slopped-over bowl of cold soup in place of dinner. You will not tear my cloths or burn holes in them because you are distracted when carrying a full lamp by a flirtatious comment from another servant. And you will not behave like children if I give you an order.

'If we all do our part we will be comfortable and eventually we may even be friends. But for the moment we will strive for comfort. This is the way this household will conduct itself, beginning tomorrow. The cook Takhar will rise and make breakfast for all of us when the sun rises; no later and no earlier. Her cooking stove is to be kept supplied by Kasa; always supplied, with no excuses and no loud quarrels as he is slapped and sent for more fuel. If Takhar needs more fuel, she will ask for it the night before, not make a riot at daybreak.

'Then my own maids will help me rise and care for me as I require, which is not much. My butler Bukentef will draw the household allowance of wine and other things as required. He must keep a list of what is expended so he can draw more ahead of time, not rush around borrowing from our neighbours at the last moment. Think ahead.

'We are still going to eat tomorrow, so draw enough for tomorrow as well. *Today's wine will not quench tomorrow's thirst*, to paraphrase Amenhotep-Osiris the wise.

'There is not much to do. You are not being worked to the bone. I must be able to leave you and not come back, as I came today, to find Kasa snuffling in a corner, Bukentef drunk, Ipuy snarling insults and Takhar beside herself because she has nothing to cook and nothing to cook with. Four of my guards had gone to a dice game out of earshot. I find Ii mating with a soldier who should be on guard and the other two women quarrelling about who burned a hole in a fine linen cloth. Is that the behaviour expected of grown people?'

They hung their heads. Their knees must have been getting sore, as well. I kept them there a little longer.

'The next quarrel which comes to my ears, I will dismiss both of the contestants. Instantly. Now, consider for yourselves if you want to defy me. I mean what I say and I am a woman of my word.'

My household inspected me for signs of weakness or bluff. They must not have found any. I was not bluffing. My mother had many evil ways and weak points, but she knew how to be obeyed and that, I suspect, I must have inherited from her. After this little intimate talk I had no further trouble with my household.

Bukentef began to write notes on an ostracon which was always kept by the kitchen door, and stopped running out just before dinner because he had forgotten to draw enough wine for dinner. Takhar, who was a good cook, began to exhibit her talents. Kasa gained confidence from not being slapped and began to adopt a lordly air with the other boys. My maidservants remembered what they had learned in the service of the Unnamed Lady and began to talk of other things than clothes, jewels, and who was lying with whom. The old man Ipuy softened after being threatened with banishment. He and his wood-carving tools were ensconced in a cool corner of the outer apartment, where he could talk to the soldiers on guard.

More than anything, I now had leisure to miss everyone; Kheperren, the general, Ptah-hotep. But I could not scold my household for laziness and sit musing over my broken heart all day while they were working. I helped wherever I was needed, folding linen with the maids or cleaning armour with the soldiers. Nebnakht, the soldier whom I had surprised in mating with Ii, taught me how to sharpen a spear, and the old man Ipuy listened to the sliding gritting noise with pleasure.

'That takes me back,' he said in his gruff voice, poising his knife over the spine of a horse he was carving for Kasa. 'I was beside the general when he fought his first battle. Ay, I was there with him, climbing along a ridge with a scared boy—what was his name?—beside me.'

'I haven't heard of this battle,' I said. 'Go on, Ipuy.'

'They were aiming to take us in ambush, but he out-foxed them, my general. No one can outmanoeuvre Horemheb. That's why they call him Cunning in Battle. He had authority, Mistress, like you have. He made his charioteers dismount and climb the mountains in case the enemy were lurking; and he was right and they were, and we came down on them like falling boulders and killed them all, and the boy fought like a lion, saved Horemheb's life, and then was sick as a lizard. Kheperren, the general's scribe, that's the name. Brave and faithful, lady. A good boy.

'But that's where I got a spear through the leg, and it never healed right. It got so I couldn't march any more, and the general said I could live here and mind his household, and that's what I'm doing.'

'And I am glad to have you,' I said truthfully, for he was faithful and valiant and that, said Horemheb, is what one wants in soldiers and in dogs. I quoted the saying to Ipuy and he laughed aloud, a strange sound from his old throat, and said 'He chose well in choosing you, Mistress. The general, he chose well.'

I was beginning to think that he had chosen well for me, as well as, perhaps, for himself. His household was showing distinct signs of domestication. I felt sanguine enough about them after another decan to go back to the House of The Great Royal Scribe to ask Bakhenmut whether I could resume my lessons in cuneiform.

The old men, Menna and Harmose, were still there, with a basket of clay tablets at their feet. Khety and Hanufer leapt up to greet me. Bakhenmut remained seated in his chair of state and inclined his head nervously to my bow, which was to a carefully calculated depth. I had brought a maiden with me, in case proprieties were to be observed. It was Ankherhau, who could once read and write. Ii of the roving eye would not be a safe person to introduce into an office full of men.

'Wife of General Horemheb,' said Bakhenmut. 'Greeting.'

'Great Royal Scribe, greeting,' I replied, 'Lord, I was once allowed to learn the mysteries of the square writing from one of your scribes. I have the general's permission to ask of the Great Royal Scribe that he allows me to continue this acquisition.'

'Lady, the general spoke to me about this before he left. I am honoured by your presence. Menna, I entrust this task to Harmose and you. The lady Mutnodjme is to learn as much as she wishes.'

Bakhenmut returned to the tax return he was reading and I sat down on the bench between the two old men.

'Lady, we are rejoiced to see you,' said Menna, and Harmose patted my knee with his dry hand. I was pleased to see them, as well, and pleased that Bakhenmut had retained Ptah-hotep's staff. At least the office of Great Royal Scribe would continue, and that must cheer my love's heart as he watched us from the Field of Reeds.

I knew that Ptah-hotep was watching us. I could feel his presence, sometimes so close that I could almost touch him. And I dreamed odd dreams. The most vivid had been of women shooting arrows. I had never seen such a thing in my waking life.

Menna resumed our lesson where we had left off. Thereafter I spent two hours every day in the office of the Great Royal Scribe and improved my knowledge of cuneiform. I had learned more signs within the next decan and was beginning to get an inkling about the way that the writer arranged his sentences, when Nebnakht came to the office door and summoned me from my lesson.

'Mistress, please come,' he said, and I went with him, wondering what domestic disaster had overtaken my household.

I walked into the outer apartment and saw a snivelling boy, naked and very wet, who had evidently just been punitively washed.

'He came in through the drains,' said Ipuy. 'I told the women to wash him clean so that we shouldn't choke on the stench. I never smelt such a smell. Made my nose want to lie down and cry. But that Ii is an impulsive woman. She's scrubbed the child almost to extinction. Poor scrap's never been that clean before, I'll wager.'

I would have said the same. Ii brought in a linen towel, with which she rubbed and polished the boy, trussed him into a clean loincloth and sat him down in the general's chair. I judged that Ii had been in charge of at least three little brothers. She had such sisterly jurisdiction that the boy had surrendered immediately.

'Now, what are you?' I asked the child. 'A burglar?'

He shook his head emphatically. 'Are you Mutnodjme daughter of Ay?' he asked, as if repeating a lesson.

'I am Mutnodjme, daughter of Ay,' I told him.

He grabbed the remains of his cloth, which had been wrapped around a small parcel, which had escaped the worst of the excrement with which this now-immaculate child must have been coated. Ii carried the cloth away to be washed, for weaving is valuable and cannot be wasted unless it is completely worn out or irreparably stained.

I examined the parcel. It was covered with oil cloth, sewn together, the stitches coated with beeswax. Someone had gone to a lot of trouble to render it waterproof. Ipuy gave me his knife and I cut the stitches, wondering what could be so valuable and so secret to require sending a child in through the sewer.

When opened, it merely contained a carved potsherd and a vial of common glass, such as is used to contain perfumes. I examined the wrapping, which was sealed with a clay seal marked with the shield and crossed arrows of the city of Sais.

It all meant nothing to me, thought it was clearly supposed to convey a message. Well-wishers with gifts of perfume did not usually send them anonymously through the drains.

'Where did you come from, child?' I asked the boy.

'Docks,' he said, shining with pride. 'Man said he'd give me a pair of gold earrings if I could get this parcel to the lady Mutnodjme daughter of Ay without being seen.'

'What did the man look like?' I persisted. The child shrugged.

'Just a man,' he said. 'An old man,' he added. "Same age as him.'

He pointed out Nebnakht, a youthful nineteen.

'Feed him, Ii, will you?' I instructed my maid. 'Then get him out of the palace by a side door. He's deserved his gold earrings. Just in case you miss your man,' I told the boy, 'Here is a piece of copper.'

'Return,' said the boy, struggling with an unfamiliar word or concept. 'You got to send a return message.'

'How very mysterious,' I said, turning the strange presents over in my hands. I opened the vial.

'Even so, it is but a minor mystery. Doubtless someone is playing some sort of joke on me—those soldiers have a crude sense of humour,' I said, returning the knife to Ipuy.

I was smiling, though—and could not help it—for I had just realised what the carving on the potsherd meant; and I had inhaled the perfume.

'I'm going to find something to write on. Everyone can go back to work,' I hinted, walking into my bedchamber and rummaging for a stylus and some papyrus under the general's bed. I found them and then sat on the floor, knees drawn up, clutching the potsherd to my breast.

Who else would have sent me a drawing of a goat with the cuneiform for 'I talk' scratched over its head? Who else would have sent me a phial of the perfume which only Nefrititi knew how to mix? And where else would Ptah-hotep be but in the palace of Sitamen, the daughter of Widow Queen Tiye, who had sworn friendship to him when he was a young man? The daughter who was a devotee of the goddess Neith, whose symbol was crossed arrows on a shield, identical with the city of Sais?

Nefertiti was alive, which was more than she deserved; but most importantly, Ptah-hotep was alive, and I felt as though someone had removed a sack of rocks from the back of my neck.

But I was married to the general; and I could never marry Ptah-hotep now.

No wonder I had sensed him close. We were still twinned, he was still feeling as I felt. No wonder that I had not found any bones in the ashes. There had been no bones to find. He was alive, alive! I almost laughed aloud.

And what did it matter if I never lay with him again? It was pure selfishness to question the ways of fate. I had married the general, well, that had been a kind gesture of the general's and it had preserved me from being given away or banished or possibly even sacrificed to something.

All things can be cured but death, as Amenhotep-Osiris the Wise had said. What mattered was that I was alive and in the world and so was Ptah-hotep. I thought that I felt an answering rush of gladness from him, as though he had leaned down and kissed my mouth.

Now what could I reply which would not give me away in my turn? The precious potsherd looked like any old ostracon on which an artist had scrawled a satirical cartoon, like the cat's funeral on the wall of Merope's husband Dhutmose's living room. I could do the same. I found a piece of broken pottery under the bed and blew dust off it, reminding myself that I must speak to Ii about her sweeping.

I scribbled a double-crowned goat, that would tell him that I recognised that both he and Nefertiti were alive. I gave the goat breasts and a bow and arrow—altering the symbol to that of a woman warrior that would mean that I had worked out that he was not in Sais, but with Sitamen. At the bottom I carved a heart, which would tell him that I still loved him.

Then I gave it to the boy, who was now stuffed full of honey-bread and figs, and watched Ii lead him out of the room by the hand, the picture of an obedient palace child. I knew that she would get through the gates without trouble. Ii knew most of the soldiers in the king's guard intimately.

Ptah-hotep was alive. I returned to the office of the Great Royal Scribe, outwardly placid, inwardly vibrating with joy.

Ptah-hotep

I knew the moment when she opened the parcel and understood; or I thought I did, for out of nowhere came a great wave of joy and relief. I was reading the *Instructions of Amenemope To His Son*, which was not likely to have produced such a response, though it was a worthy text. I was convinced that at that day and hour my dearest Mutnodjme discovered that I was alive, having thought me dead. I wondered how she would contrive to get word to Kheperren, though I knew she would.

Life in the palace of Sitamen was peaceful, though the season had been bad, the Nile had not risen, and if it did not rise the next year the farmers would be looking famine in the face.

This should not have been so. Amenhotep-Osiris in his wisdom had retained enough grain to provide seed for seven years of failure; but his son had poured out our grain like water before the feet of merchants who fetched him precious woods from Nubia and jewels and gazelles and strange foods. I doubted that there was another year's grain in the stores. And of course the king would not abate the taxes because there was less grain this year. I cursed him daily for his sole and only god.

Not that the Aten was to blame. It was a venerable concept which had its roots in the oldest known ennead, the group of nine gods at Karnak. But the king's monomania had blinded him to every other consideration. He had broken the power of the priests of Amen-Re, which his wise father had not done.

Amenhotep-Osiris had known that the temple of Amen-Re was too powerful and had striven to reduce its influence by taking some of its functions away and giving them to other temples. But he had known that without the priests of Amen-Re there were no tax inspectors, no keepers of weights and measures, no record keepers, no river watchers.

The temple of Amen-Re was essential for the smooth government of Egypt. It balanced its power against the throne and the army, and as long as all three were in the hands of reasonably competent men then the country would work. In fact it worked even if the throne was occupied by a child or a drooling idiot as it had been before.

It had taken a poet, a dreamer, a devoutly religious man, to attack the temple and destroy it, along with most of the historians, scholars and learned men in Egypt. And we still did not know what had happened to the Widow-Queen Tiye.

◇◇◇

Mutnodjme's reply arrived in at the same time as my beloved Kheperren, who threw himself at me, held me away so that he could look at me, then hugged me so tight that he left fingermarks in my shoulders.

'Oh, praise to all the gods, I wondered if I had misinterpreted

Mutnodjme's message so I came straight here as soon as I got it. How did you survive, dearest?' he asked.

'I was kidnapped. What message did Mutnodjme send you?'

'Here,' he shoved a piece of papyrus at me. It bore a crowned goat sitting on crossed arrows. Its mouth was gaping and in the space between upper and lower teeth was the character in cuneiform for 'talk.'

'And her cuneiform lessons are obviously coming along,' I said, impressed as always by this learned lady. 'Have you seen her? She is well?'

'No I have not; I came straight here to find you—alive, you scoundrel! We wept for you and buried your ashes in a rock tomb above Amarna in the strictest secrecy, 'Hotep. How can you possibly be alive? The lady went and sifted through that pile of ashes for your bones.'

'That must have been a terrible task,' I stopped laughing with joy at my reunion with my dear Kheperren.

'She has a lot of courage—more than me. I was afraid of what I might find, but she wasn't. Come and lie down under this vine and talk to me, kiss me; gods, I don't know what to say to you. I feel like you've been to the Field of Reeds, and I ought to ask you what it was like.'

A man and a woman lying down in love might have attracted comment in the palace of the lady Sitamen, but not a man and another man. I laid Kheperren down and put my head on his chest, listening to his heart, which beat wildly under my cheek.

The sun shone hot above the vine, making dazzling patterns through the leaves, outlines in gold against the plain marble tiles. We lay so quietly that I heard fish splash in the pool and dragonflies zooming amongst the lotus flowers.

Then he began to kiss me and to laugh, and to kiss me again, and although I had never thought him dead I had thought him lost, and I had missed him. So we made love under the vine to the apparent approbation of a few of Sitamen's women who wandered past, not averting their eyes.

'So, will you stay here?' he asked me, as the cool air dried the sweat on our skin.

I kissed his neck. The skin was wet against my lips. 'I don't know. I cannot go back to the City of the Sun. I don't want to go back. I don't want any office. By the way, have you any news of the Widow-Queen Tiye?'

'The king has not released her from seclusion. He had her locked up for forty days, supposedly mourning the death of Mekhetaten, and since has just forgotten to let her out. She is reported to be well, though her temper will not have improved if she has heard the rumours about what the King is requiring Divine Father Ay to do to Smenkhare.

'Mutnodjme's mother Great Royal Nurse Tey is ill, perhaps fatally ill. I would have thought that she would be forever preserved by the vinegar that runs in her veins. And... General Horemheb has married.'

'Oh? That is a surprise. I thought him forever devoted only to you,' I said idly. 'Who has he married? Not some shrinking maiden, surely?'

'No 'Hotep, he has married the lady Mutnodjme. It was the only way he could protect her.' Kheperren held me down with one hand on my chest.

'You could have brought her to me,' I said slowly.

Now I could not marry the woman I loved. I should have married her when I had the chance, but she would not agree.

Now she had married the general instead of me. He was, perhaps, a better choice—certainly stronger and bigger and probably more of a man.

But I had thought that she loved me. Surely I had not deluded myself when I felt her relief and joy at knowing that I was, after all, alive?

'She would not leave the Widow-Queen, even though Tiye the redheaded woman is locked up, unable to communicate with us,' Kheperren said. 'We thought that you were dead; and her father was suggesting that she be married to any of the priests of Aten as long as he would take her away.

'And did I say we thought you were dead? The general will not keep her from you, 'Hotep,' he said gently.

'Has the marriage been consummated?' I asked, forcing the words out through reluctant lips.

'Yes, but she lay with me, 'Hotep, because she knows that I love you, too. I felt her as she imagined that I was you, I felt her body open, melt with longing; and I felt her shock when she realised again that you were dead.

'It was on the general's order that she lay with me to seal the contract, not with him. He is a kind and just man. He likes her. He would never keep her from her lover. Be comforted,' he told me, kissing my mouth again.

I could not go to Amarna and see the lady Mutnodjme again, and now she could not come to me, since she was the wife of the general.

But I was comforted. Kheperren lay in my embrace. And I had a potsherd carved with a heart which told me that Mutnodjme still loved me, and it was as precious to me as any jewel.

Chapter Twenty-eight

Mutnodjme

The general returned. Everyone was pleased to see him, including me. Even the elegant cat Mou, lord of the household, descended from the high shelf in the kitchen on which he slept and condescended to wrap his body around the general's feet. Horemheb tripped and I steadied him. He smiled at me.

'Mistress of the House Lady Mutnodjme, I can see that you have been busy in my absence.'

He was right. I had. The apartments were scoured clean, everything that could be polished was polished, and I had bought Nubian blankets and felted carpets from Upper Egypt. I did not know the general's taste, and when asked no one could tell me. So I had consulted my own.

I had not spent his gold like water. The rooms, like all rooms in the palace of Amarna, were decorated with friezes. The outer chamber had duck hunters all round the walls, delicate papyrus-reed craft floating over impossibly clear water teeming with fish. In that room I had blue fabrics. The inner rooms were lined with flying birds, a masterpiece, and all I had added to that was a tall lamp in the shape of an ibis, which reminded me of Ptah-hotep and Thoth god of wisdom, and furnishings in white and pale yellow.

Horemheb kissed me and sat down to have his sandals removed and his feet washed by Ipuy. This was his privilege and I would not think of taking it away from him. While the old soldier knelt down, I introduced my maidens and men. They all behaved well. I had even induced Kasa to wipe his nose.

'Tell me,' he said to Ii, who giggled. 'Does the Mistress of the House treat you well?'

'Yes, Master,' she replied. 'She makes us work hard, but she works hard herself. Your woman is a good woman, Master.'

'My opinion also,' he said gravely.

Ipuy dried his feet. Horemheb reached into a little bag and handed out a thin gold bracelet to each servant. They had not been expecting this and gathered around Horemheb, thanking him, until he waved an arm and bellowed, 'Food and drink, especially drink! I must wash. Go and prepare a feast!' and they scattered like birds.

'Who is coming to the feast, lord?' I asked. His broad face split with a large grin.

'You shall see, Mistress. Four persons, apart from us.'

'Where is Kheperren?' I asked gently, hoping that I did not have to hear bad news. 'Has something...'

'No, he's gone to see the scribe of Sais.'

My heart leapt up and the general patted me. 'Yes, the scribe is well, the woman is well, all is very well, and I need a real wash. Ipuy, where is the old scoundrel? I need a scrub.'

Ipuy had slipped out to talk to the guard who had come with Horemheb and I did not want to get him into trouble by noticing this. So I said to Horemheb, 'If you will allow me, Master, I have washed a lot of people in my time.'

'Come along then,' he strode into the washing place, stripping off his armoured shirt and his breechclout. I had already ordered well-jars of warmed water and I knew that Ankherhau had assembled the pumice and brushes and soft soap which the general favoured. I stripped also, because I considered that I was going to get very wet before the general was clean.

He stood under the falling water until he was soaked, and I began to groom General Horemheb as though he were a horse. He was almost as big as a horse. His thighs were as broad as my waist, I could not get both arms around him, and none of this girth was fat. Scrubbing at the stubborn marks which the shirt left on his shoulders and neck felt like scouring a leather-covered rock. He sat down on a stool so that I could reach his back, and I lathered the expanse of scarred skin and muscle. He was very different from my Ptah-hotep or the scribe Kheperren.

He was relaxing under my attentions, though I was scrubbing him with a hard bristled brush as vigorously as I would scrub a floor. I leaned his head into my breast so I could get at the back of his neck when his mouth found my nipple. I kept scrubbing, though I was becoming aroused. One strong arm went around my hips, moving me until I was straddling his lap. One hand caressed between my legs.

He was not going to force me, though he could have; he was the strongest man I had ever seen. A finger slid inside me. My body was reacting. After all, he was a soldier, a man who risked his life for Egypt. After all, I had been a long time without a man.

After all, he was my husband.

Feeling down to position the phallus correctly, I lowered myself onto a hard spike, carefully so as not to hurt the delicate tissue. Horemheb gasped and threw back his head, so that I could kiss him, the scarred face, the broad cheekbones, the hard mouth, which sucked at my lips. His phallus fitted inside me, just fitted. I had never been so filled and the sensation was strange. I sat awhile joined to him, savouring the feeling.

Then I began to move. I had seen the dancers of Nubia revolve their hips, and Meryt had told me that her success in lovemaking was entirely due to this skill. She had taught it to me. A sideways flick, a return, then a rotation like the upper grindstone. I had seen the effect this had on susceptible Egyptian audiences, who often had recourse to putting plates over their rising laps. This had always amused the dancers, and this is what all those men were thinking of. A woman in the Isis position, rising and falling like a rider.

This had advantages. If Horemheb had descended to lie on me, I might have been crushed flatter than a frieze. This way I could control the depth of the phallus and its angle and something that was itching for attention; some place in my vessel of Hathor which did not ordinarily react. I leaned away from my lover to contrive that this itch should be rubbed, and I began to gasp, almost to sob, as a flood of sensation washed over me.

He seized my buttocks in both hands and I clutched his neck and the mating grew strong. I was not going to hurt Horemheb no matter what I did, not without a weapon. The phallus twitched and he began to seed me, and at the same time I shoved myself down on the spike and wrapped my legs around his waist. He was deeper inside me than anyone had ever been. I shuddered. He held me tight.

'Mistress,' he said into my neck, as I disentangled myself and stood up on weak legs. 'My Mistress of the House Mutnodjme. Lady, you honour me.'

'Lord,' I agreed. I kissed his mouth again and picked up my brush, which I had let fall in an excess of passion. We were both covered in lather. 'We are certainly the cleanest lovers in the palace of Amarna,' I commented, wiping soap off my belly.

'It reflects the purity of my passion for you,' he said, and I laughed and resumed scrubbing.

My household had exerted themselves and I was very pleased with them. When I had eventually emerged from the washing-place with a very clean general, Ipuy and Kasa offered to massage him with perfumed oils and Ankherhau had found his best cloth. She had, without being ordered, shaken out the folds and mended a little tear in one corner.

Takhar was laying out plates for the feast on the low long table which the general had ordered especially built for his house. He often had secret conferences and preferred to serve himself and his guests from a selection of dishes on the table rather than have servants filling cups and supplying food who were also attending to his secrets.

'Willing hands have listening ears attached,' he remarked, a truly strange image, but I saw what he meant. Ears did come along with the usual human package.

Apart from Mou, who did us the honour of attending on the preparations, approving of the cuisine and making off with a large piece of roasted beef, I did not know who was attending the feast. Wab had made garlands for seven, as the general had said that there would be six and it was always the custom to make one extra. They were very good garlands, collars of little flowers which I had not seen before put together with skill and I commended her. She put one finger in her mouth and wriggled with pleasure at my praise. I supposed that she would grow out of this, for she was a good child, mostly.

'Mistress, I had to use small flowers, because the lotus are scarce this year.'

'But it's Khoiak, Wab, there should be unnumbered lotus in the pools.'

'No, Mistress, hardly any. The season has been bad and the flood failed again and now there are few lotus. The farmers are eating the lotus roots and making bread of the seeds.'

I parted Wab and gave her a honeycake, but this was bad news. I saw no need to tell the general—he undoubtedly already knew—and surveyed the table.

There were stewed pigeons and roasted quail, a huge roasted fish, and a dish of garlic, leeks and onions cooked with beans. The general had always liked beans. Bukentef was standing guard over his jars of beer and wine. He gave a jug to Ii, who was to greet the guests with wine while Kasa and Wab draped them in flowers and anointed them with oil. I had bought a set of wine cups, light pottery decorated with cornflowers, and they stood ready on a tray.

General Horemheb, the picture of a cared-for man, clean, satisfied, massaged and clad in an indigo-printed cloth, threw himself down in his chair of state and accepted a cup, tasted, and grinned.

'I like having a household,' he announced. Wab trotted over and put a garland around his neck and he patted her on the buttocks as she did so. She giggled.

Then Nebnakht opened the main door and announced, 'Widow-Queen the lady Tiye, Mistress of Egypt, Menna and Harmose Scribes of the Pharaoh, General Khaemdua Ruler of the Hermotybies.'

Wab and Kasa distributed garlands, Ii presented filled cups, and the guests came in and were seated around the long table.

'Lady,' I said a little breathlessly, 'I am so glad to see you.'

I knelt next to the red-headed woman Mistress of Egypt, and she cupped a hand under my chin.

'I know that you came every day of my captivity and tried to get in, Mutnodjme,' she said softly. 'I know that of all of my friends you never forgot me. I know that you have married the general and he never forgot me either. If it had not been for you, lady, I would still be shut in my rooms, well fed and well cared for but utterly unable to communicate with the outside world. I am so sorry about the scribe. I would have told you if I could, but my son chose that moment to lock me up. I hope that you forgive me.'

'Lady, I have nothing to forgive,' I said truthfully. 'If you had not acted as you did, that scribe of my heart would be dead. I and the general agree very well.'

'So I see,' she commented, taking in the room, the servants, the feast and the terribly clean general in one comprehensive glance. 'You have done well, Mistress of the House.'

I bowed. Ii poured wine for the Widow-Queen and she went on. 'Tell me, how well do you know your servants?'

'Not at all well, lady, they are almost all new except for the guards and the old man Ipuy. He is the only one I would trust, for he loves Horemheb like his own brother. In due course they may come to trust me, but it will take another season. But in any case they will be sent away as soon as the feast is laid out and our wants supplied. Horemheb always conducts his gatherings in this manner—it will cause no comment, Lady, when did they release you?'

'Just now,' said the Widow-Queen, curling a tress of grey-streaked red hair around one finger in the way I remembered.

'Horemheb's men came and relieved my guards. Then I was bidden to come to a feast. The times are very odd at the moment, so I saw nothing particularly strange about being taken out of prison to a feast. I put on my gown and here I am. I may, of course, be dreaming.'

I took up her hand and kissed it. 'No, Lady of Egypt, you are not dreaming.'

The feast was laid, the wine flowing, and the servants were all dismissed in Horemheb's usual fashion. Sitting around the table were my two tutors in the cuneiform script, Horemheb and me, the Mistress of the Two Lands and General Khaemdua.

I had heard of him. He was the ruler of the other division of the army. A very powerful person, with a reputation for courage and cold skill. He was not loved, as Horemheb was loved. He would not, for instance, have climbed down a cliff as Horemheb had, ahead of all the others, to show his soldiers that it could be done. But he had never lost an engagement in the whole time he had ruled his army, and he was very careful of his men. It was Khaemdua, however, who had been caught in a blazing fortress with no way out over the fire which the enemy had set about the walls. He had called for volunteers to die for Egypt, killed them swiftly and painlessly, and laid out their bodies across the coals. On this bridge they had walked to safety, eighty-three men and General Khaemdua last of all, treading the roasting bodies of their comrades.

In person he was slim, elegant and very well dressed. He wore no gold-of-valour. His cloth was the short kilt of the Hermotybies. Over it they wore a red cloth which came almost to the calves and a very long and heavily decorated belt which hung down at the front into two tails hung with metal beads. The General's belt was, of course, sewn with electrum sequins, and his tassels were silver, tagged with Nubian stones. He was married,

I had been told, to a very cool and aloof lady who was some connection of the scribe Khety. Khety had often remarked that it was no wonder that the General had no children. Engendering would mean that he had to get close to someone.

But he was sipping wine and eating roast quail with some enjoyment. It was only when he looked on the Widow-Queen that his austere, high-nosed face changed expression at all, and then he looked startlingly like a boy devoted to a goddess.

The food had been tasted and praised, everyone's health had been asked after, the general's marriage with me had been toasted and both the Widow-Queen and General Khaemdua had approved of my decorative work. Then the lady Tiye put her elbows on her knees and said, 'Well, what of Egypt?'

'Bad, lady. The flood has failed again. The farmers are hungry. The soldiers sent out to obliterate the name of the old god are behaving badly. The inspectors sent out from the temple of Aten are too few to properly administer the cultivation and they are also accepting bribes,' said General Khaemdua with distaste.

'I hanged four scoundrels for terrorising a village, and the air is full of denunciations. My own scoundrels are under control, of course,' he added, though no one would suppose he would tolerate an army that was not under control.

'Bad, lady,' agreed Menna, having consulted with Harmose as to who should speak. 'Letters for the Pharaoh Akhnaten are not being dealt with, and our own chief is accepting gold to pass incorrect tax returns. Some of the Nomarchs are growing rich and some are reduced to beggary. The Watchers are overworked and are falling victim to corruption; some are even extorting money from their villages.'

'Bad, lady,' said Horemheb slowly. 'I rescued Tushratta and put him back on his throne, but the watch on the borders has slept and my soldiers and those of my comrade Khaemdua's are constantly being diverted to this mad work of destroying the Aten.'

'The King is totally isolated,' I said. 'There is no honest Councillor left. Huy and Pannefer between them make sure that he hears nothing that does not please him. Divine Father

Ay plots to own the whole world. His wife plots with him. The children know nothing, are not even literate, and no one sees them but their own court. Great Royal Wife Smenkhare is flirting with the king, using his body to excite whatever it is that can be excited in a eunuch. I fear that the atmosphere has completely corrupted him. The Great Royal Lady Meritaten is trying to seduce Smenkhare, to whom I am told she is also married, and the little ones have no chance, as far as I can see, of growing up sane. Though Ankhesenpaaten at least appears to have some maternal instincts, she looks after Tutankhaten.'

'In a word, then,' said Tiye heavily, 'bad.'

'The country is lurching along,' said Horemheb. 'Egypt has got used to being governed and many officials still hold to their truth which is in Maat. The situation is not good, but if the Nile floods next year then we will all eat, at least. Surely this utterly and uniquely-corrupt royal family cannot last long. Their own way of life, one would think, will kill them.'

'Possibly,' said Tiye. 'We will see. Meet me regularly, my lords, if you please. Menna and Harmose will keep an eye on foreign affairs. The lady Mutnodjme will hear them if they have anything to say, for they are still teaching her the square letters and that is a task for a lifetime. Now I am freed from captivity there may be some words I can say to my sons which will moderate their behaviour. Off hand I cannot think of any rule of virtue which they have not broken, but there may still be some. We will take no action. Yet.'

This was agreed. Then we called in the musicians, and the feast became merry.

I was pouring beer through a strainer for my husband when I realised that I was happy.

Ptah-hotep

I was sitting in a shady spot on a wall with the three volumes of *Imhotep's House of Ascent: Building the Pyramids* in my lap. I was not reading the puzzling and difficult script. I was looking at the horizon, where the pale line of dew was burning off the desert, and thinking about nothing at all. Kheperren had gone back to his army, Mutnodjme had married the general, and I was at a loose end.

Sitamen's steward came to me and dropped to one knee at my feet.

'Rise,' I said lazily.

'Lord, a man who was a priest of Amen-Re has come and wishes to speak to you urgently. He is unarmed.' She didn't need to tell me that. The guards would never have allowed an armed man into Sitamen's palace.

'Bring him here, with some of the light beer and some bread,' I ordered, and the steward went away, returning after an interval with a small girl carrying a tray and a young man whom I thought I recognised, though I could not place him. I had seen him a long time ago, that was plain. The face was associated with fear and darkness. I rubbed my eyes.

'Lord Ptah-hotep, who was Great Royal Scribe, now scribe of the Royal Lady Sitamen, one who was once a priest of the god Amen-Re kneels to your honour,' he said.

I still could not work out where I had seen him before. A thin face, a thin body, long limbs. I clad him in my mind in a priests' gown, added a decade or so, and now I knew him.

The last time I had seen this man, he had been a priest in the temple on the night that the terrifying old man Userkhepesh, Chief Priest of the Good God Amen-Re, had attempted to frighten me out of my wits and then decided not to poison me.

I had played many games of senet with Userkhepesh in the palace of Amen-Re in Karnak before the mad king moved the court to Amarna. We had almost become friends. He always won. I had enquired after his fate when the temple was disestablished, but no one could tell me where he had gone and I had assumed that he was dead. Perhaps he was.

'Rise and sit next to me,' I told the young man. 'Have some beer and a bite of this good bread, then tell me what brings you to me, face out of my past.'

He drank a mouthful and ate a token crumb of bread which was required of him by courtesy. Then he said, 'Lord, I have a request from a dying man.'

'Speak,' I said. I guessed who this dying man might be. So the old man had not moved from Karnak after all—I should have known that he would not go far from his temple.

'It is the man who was once Chief Servant of Amen-Re,' whispered the priest.

I thought that it might be. What else could bring you into this dangerous place, and who else would be bound to know where I could be found?'

'Lord, he is very old now, and dying, but he always knows where people are and what is happening in the Black Land.'

'Yes,' I agreed. 'I will come.'

'Then you must come now, Lord Ptah-hotep, and secretly.'

What had I to lose? If this was some trap devised by the palace, it was so clever that it deserved to succeed. And what could Pharaoh do to me now that I had not done to myself? I had been stripped of all titles and wealth. I was just Ptah-hotep. I was completely without influence and valueless.

'Very well. I will leave my refuge and come with you. But you will tell the Princess Sitamen's guard where we are going and when I will be back—I will not listen—and if I am not returned by my hour, they will tear Thebes apart looking for me. If you are wishing to encompass my death, you can kill me now with a lot less trouble by just pushing me off this wall.'

He said gravely, 'Lord, that is not my intention or the intention of my master,' and I believed him well enough.

We went through the alleys and lanes of Thebes. The condition of the people was parlous. By the rubbish through which I had to wade, they were living mostly on dried fish, which is not good for humans. Their beehive ovens were cool. No one had enough grain to bake bread every day and the palace was no longer handing out rations of grain when the season was poor.

It was not lightly that the gods who invented writing, Isis and Thoth, made the same character for 'bread' and 'life.' For what was the Black Land without bread?

Swollen-bellied children played in the detritus, throwing fish-spines at each other and quarrelling over scraps. I was almost bowled over by a foraging pig which snapped at me, its jaws clumping shut just short of my shin as I hit it a sharp blow on the snout. It snorted and ploughed on through the stinking midden.

'The animals are growing bolder,' commented the priest. 'In the country the desert wolves are creeping into the villages and taking children, now that the Watchers and the army have been diverted to carve out the name of Amen-Re from monuments made a thousand years ago. Masons make scaffolds to climb up and deface our history instead of repairing what we have.'

'Truly the state of Egypt is bitter,' I agreed. He led me into a space between two houses just wide enough for me to traverse and knocked at a door.

It opened inwards, which was a mercy, and I bent under the lintel. Lying on a pallet in a small room whitewashed all over like the inside of a clam-shell, was indeed the old man Userkhepesh, wrapped in a linen sheet.

The only light came from a small oil-lamp. He had aged far beyond age. He was so old that his hands trembled on his breast. His skin was like vellum which has been left in the sun, a multitude of fine lines. His black eyes had filmed over. Time had struck him down and stripped him of his sight, but his voice was clear and he recognised my greeting.

'Ptah-hotep,' he said, 'Greeting, I fear that I cannot offer you anything—not even a game of senet,' he chuckled. 'Though I shall soon be playing Passing-Through-The-Underworld in earnest.'

'I am glad to see you, lord,' I said, sitting down on the edge of the pallet. It was the usual peasant's mud-brick shelf-bed, which was usually padded with a straw mattress. 'I have come as you asked.'

'You always had courage,' he remarked. 'Even when a terrible old man did his best to overawe you. Ah, well, I am dying,' he said, taking my hand in both of his fleshless claws.

'Yes, lord,' it would have been discourteous to argue with him.

'And I wished to tell you something before I die and have to confess my sins to the judges in the underworld. My heart will weigh heavily against the feather, for all of this is my fault, my fault,' he began to cry. Tears trickled down the old face and I wiped them gently away.

'Lord, how can this be all your fault? The state of the Black Land is too terrible for it to be any one man's fault. It is not your doing that the river did not rise, is it, lord?'

'Don't humour me, boy, I am old but I am not senile,' he snapped, sounding much more like himself. 'Do you remember the temple of Amen-Re in its splendour?'

'Certainly, lord. As I recall Amenhotep-Osiris thought that the temple had too much power; for there were two rulers of Egypt, you and the Pharaoh. The lord Amenhotep-Osiris tried to reduce your influence; and it was played like a game, in the sunlit courts, in the golden halls of Amen-Re.

'When I came to see you, lord, for the first time, a boy just taken from the school of scribes, I was left waiting in your inner apartment. There was a wall painted with doors and a floor made of inlaid turquoise, a ceiling all webbed with golden images of Amen-Re, and your throne made of electrum with a footstool of silver. I had never seen such wealth. And you, my lord, came in through an unexpected door like a spider, attended by two naked women more lovely than any I had ever seen.'

'You were no fly, Ptah-hotep. I did not realise then what an honourable creature had flown into my web. Though I did realise it after. I heard how you surrendered your office, boy, gave away your goods, set your slaves free, in order not to obey a dreadful order from the vile king. I wished that I had shared your courage.'

'Userkhepesh, what are you trying to say?' I asked gently, wishing I had at least bought some wine to moisten the old man's dry throat. I had not thought to find him so unprovided with basic comforts. I had not imagined that the Chief Servant of Amen-Re could really be poor. I summoned the attendant.

'Priest, here is maybe a twentieth of a deben. Go and buy some wine and bread, if some can be found. I gave all the copper shavings that I had in my pouch to the attendant. He vanished without a word, closing the door behind him.

'Once a twentieth of a deben would have brought you more than bread and wine,' commented Userkhepesh.

'I could have given him a couple of gold beads, but that might have got him murdered,' I replied. 'The streets of Thebes are very unsafe now for anyone carrying anything of value.'

'Indeed. Do you recall the son of the Wise King Amenhotep-Osiris?'

'Lord, he rules all Egypt now, and a worse king has never sat on the Throne of the Two Lands,' I replied, wondering if he was indeed senile.

'There was a parley between all the chief priests, before you were born,' he went on. 'It was held in my apartments in the great temple of Amen-Re. The priests of Ptah were there, and Khnum, the strange cosmogeny of Hermopolis. We drank wine and watched Nubian dancers and indulged our flesh with women, with hair the colour of ripe corn, who had been bought in slave-markets beyond the Great Green Sea. The feast cost me a basket of gold.'

'Yes, lord.' I could understand why he wanted to live in the past. There was no glory to be got from a tiny room in a mud-brick house in the back streets of Thebes.

'But the real reason for the gathering was to consider the Great Royal Heir Thutmose. You never saw him, did you?'

'Never,' I told him. Prince Thutmose had been bitten by a snake and had died long before I had anything to do with the palace.

'He was a bold young man, strong, healthy, and the King greatly loved him. He had been trained in diplomacy and could speak three languages and read five. His favourite occupation was chariot-racing, and soldiers said that he would make a good commander. But he had no love for our temple. He had absorbed his father's views on the balance of power in Egypt. He meant to devote some of his funds to the temples of the lesser gods, Sobek and Bes, Neith and Maat who is truth.'

A horror was growing on me, in the lamplight, in that small bare room.

'In our arrogance and foolishness we thought that his brother would be more malleable. We thought that Akhnamen would eat out of our hands, once his noble father had gone into the otherworld. Should I ever get there, if my heart is not immediately eaten as I deserve, I do not know what I will say to him.'

'Master, please,' I begged, unable to bear the suspense.

'When I say to you it was my fault, that all this is my fault, Ptah-hotep, I am not mad or deluded. It was the agreement of the meeting—they all agreed—and I myself administered the venom through a hollow needle placed in a chair-leg. It took him two days to die, but he died.

'I killed Prince Thutmose, and ruined Egypt,' confessed Userkhepesh, once Great Servant of Amen-Re.

He closed his eyes and did not speak again. I sat and held his hand. I heard the rattle which is death beginning in his throat. At the last, he opened his eyes and stared into mine, pleading perhaps, begging for forgiveness.

It was not for me to judge him. I said, 'You are absolved,' and the lashes of the blind eyes closed over them, and he was dead.

When the attendant came back, we arranged the body fittingly and carried it out into the street. We delivered him to the House of Life to be properly embalmed at the expense of the Princess Sitamen. The body was very light.

Then we gave away his wine and bread to the street-children, as the only funeral feast we could make for the high priest who had almost destroyed the land and the god he had sworn to serve.

Chapter Twenty-nine

Mutnodjme

Widow-Queen Tiye was henceforth free. I do not know how she explained her release to her sons, co-regents now and rulers of Egypt, but they did not attempt to lock her up again. Not even in Pharmuthi two years later, when Great Royal Wife Meritaten died of the sweating fever and Ankhhesenpaaten was married to her brother Smenkhkare. The little princess had borne one child, a pale and sickly creature which only survived for three hours.

In this she only lasted a little longer than her mother and grandmother, for I had news from the palace of Sitamen that my sister Nefertiti had fallen into a despondency and thus into a fever, and had died peacefully.

Ptah-hotep wrote me letters of love and I replied with love. I visited my sister Merope in her house by the square, where she quickly bore two sons for Dhutmose. They were very pretty children and her husband doted on them and on her.

Otherwise I ruled my household, learned cuneiform, lay with the general, conceived and miscarried. I had no one to consult about my state of health; and I had no suitable prayers. The only learned women left in Egypt did not dare show their learning. Although after the first few years midwives had been allowed to practice again to stem the rising mortality amongst mothers.

Someone must have told those stupid men that if the mothers died in childbirth they would have no sons.

No sooner was seed settled in my womb and my purifying blood had ceased for half a season, then would come the grinding ache which meant that the child had loosed hold on the flesh, and I would shortly bleed another baby.

My mother, who had recovered miraculously from cancer of the womb, told me that I would never bear, because learning had unsettled my female parts. I ignored her. For the first time in my life, I had Mother Tey in a vice.

On my advice, she had gone to Thebes and prayed for healing in the disestablished temple of Hathor, lady of music, and then in the remains of the temple of Isis. She reported that there were still some priestesses there, living in what had been the servant's quarters at the back of the compound, and they had given her a potion and told her to pray to Isis nine nights in succession. She had done that and had been healed. Either the physicians had been mistaken in their diagnosis, and nothing was more likely, or Isis had healed her. Presumably Isis had some use for her, though I could not think of one, except to assist in punishing Egypt for its apostasy.

So now she was alive, which was something of a pity as she encouraged Divine Father Ay in his greed, but I held her life in my hand, knowing that she had appealed to forbidden gods.

She was probably right about my ability to carry children. I seemed to conceive easily, but the child would not stay with me. I could have visited the temple of Isis myself, and seen Ptah-hotep, but somehow there were always things in the house to be done, and somehow the general was always away when I thought of going, and somehow I never got there, and the years passed.

I never loved the general like I loved Ptah-hotep, never felt that strange feeling of being twinned by the night and the gods, but he was a good man, fair and just and kind, and I liked him well. I was putting ointment on Kasa's skinned knee—the clumsy child had become a clumsy man—when I heard trumpets blowing. I walked to the window. I had not heard such a clamour for years. The general woke up, sitting up in mid snore.

'Those are battle trumpets,' remarked Ipuy, picking up his wood-carving knife. Our soldiers had sprung to attention and grabbed their weapons. Horemheb summoned them to form a guard around us as we went out into the court of the Aten. Either an army was attacking or some amazing announcement was to be made. All the people in the palace had poured into the great court.

All eyes were on the Window of Appearances. The royal family filed out.

There was Akhnaten may he die in his most extravagant cloth, a parody of an army uniform. Long contemplation of his god, the Aten, had damaged his eyes and now he had to squint to see a hand's span in front of him.

There was Smenkhare in the wig and jewellery of Great Royal Wife; worried and maternal Ankhesenpaaten with her little brother Tutankhaten holding her hand; and Divine Father Ay, along with Pannefer and Huy, all smirking.

'People of the Aten' announced the King. 'I have called you together to hear my words.'

'Hail sweet child of brightness,' called the crowd, hoping for their usual ration of gold trinkets. "Hail to the Aten!'

'Misery is upon the land,' said the King.

I was astounded that he knew anything about what was happening in Egypt. He never left the city and he did not listen to anyone but his own dishonest ministers.

'In my own household, three of my daughters are dead and the Beautiful-One-Who-Is-Come is gone into flame. The Phoenix has not risen.'

This was true. However, the sacrifice which he had designed to bring the Phoenix had not been properly made, though I had no intention of telling anyone that. After a year of watching on the walls to sight the first flock of birds escorting the Firebird, the cult had fallen into disfavour.

'Hail to the Phoenix!' cried a few voices, and were hushed.

'Therefore I consulted with my priests.' The king looked on Divine Father Ay.

'Why is the Aten angry with us? Why does the river Nile not flood? Why has the Aten punished us?' the king asked.

He was even untrue to his own theology, I thought with disgust. His Aten had no compassion, no justice, no mercy, no personality. He had constructed it as pure life-force, creating and created. It had no incarnation, unknowable and unknown, a primeval thing—which-is-all. Therefore the Aten could neither punish nor reward. As well ask the sun not to burn skin, or the water not to wet it.

'I have communed with godhead,' the King yelled, blinking at the crowd. 'We have been lazy, accepting all the gifts of the Aten without trying to spread the knowledge of it to foreign lands. Therefore I have decided. Now that the name of the old god is obliterated from Egypt, now that we are pure, then we must purify the barbarians. We must go forth not as soldiers but as instructors. All of my army will be used to take presents to foreign kings, to foreign places, even as far as the Great Green Sea and the nests of the vile Kush. And the most valuable present they will carry will be knowledge of the Aten!'

I looked at Horemheb. His mouth had fallen open. I struggled to work out the implications of what the King Akhnaten had just ordered. His soldiers were to go forth to foreign kings to preach the cult of the Aten. That did not seem perilous. Someone asked the king a question.

'What shall we do, child of the Aten before all stand in awe, if these foreigners do not accept the teachings?'

'Why, kill them,' said the king calmly. 'If they will not accept, we must kill them.'

This, on the other hand, made the situation disastrous. Egypt was surrounded by desert nomads who had their own form of monotheism for which they were perfectly willing, even eager, to kill or be killed; and by kingdoms who had their own long-established gods who were just as precious to them as the Aten was to the mad king.

I could not see Babylon surrendering Nun, or Ishtar being abandoned in Assyria. Even if the rulers wished to do so—and an army on the threshold can be very persuasive in religious matters—they would not dare, for their people would rise up and slaughter them.

'What's the king doing?' I whispered to my husband.

'He's declaring war on the world,' said the general.

◇◇◇

It being Mechir, which in the old days was the month to celebrate the story of Sekmet and the destruction of mankind—averted by the gods pouring her a lake of red beer—the Widow-Queen Tiye decreed a feast.

Sekmet was her goddess, She Who Loves Silence, the lioness in the peak. The Widow-Queen invited the whole royal family; excluding Ankhesenpaaten and Tutankhaten as too young to take part in the special celebration which she had in mind.

She did not invite me—and I was rather hurt—but she summoned me to her rooms as the finishing touches were being made to what looked like a very lavish feast. She saw my slightly downcast face and kissed me.

'Come and open this door tomorrow morning, daughter Mutnodjme,' she said gently. Her red hair was concealed under a full court wig, and she was wearing her own weight in gems. She was old. She was, now I calculated, over fifty.

'Make me a promise, daughter,' she said, sounding so serious.

I responded instantly, 'I am your slave, lady,'

'Help the little royal ones,' she added, and I swore to do so.

Then she put around my neck a very precious necklace, loaded my arm with bracelets and placed a lotus wreath on my head.

'Remember me,' she said, and then ushered me out, for her guests were arriving.

I stood by the door in the corridor of gazelles and watched them come in. Pannefer and Huy, greasy with expensive scents. Smenkhare walking in a parody of femaleness, hand on hip. His eyes were glazed. I had been told that he had become habituated to opium in larger and larger quantities, to kill misery and help him to sleep. And of course the king and his guards—he never moved without guards. Akhnaten had not aged well. The body which had been strange was now grotesque. His belly swayed as he walked, his breasts bounced. He did not notice me. The Widow-Queen welcomed them all in and shut the door.

I did not sleep well. I could not explain why I tossed and turned and eventually got up, so as not to wake the general; though nothing short of a battle alarm woke Horemheb. I lit a small lamp and sat down in the empty outer apartment and waited for the sun to rise. In the silence I heard sounds of merrymaking from the right direction, screams of mirth and the smash of dropped pottery.

I walked about. The night was not cold. The painted walls grew too close. I walked out of the general's rooms and out to the battlements, where I would see the whole City of the Sun laid out beneath me as soon as Khephri pushed the ball of light over the horizon.

The night, of course, was not completely silent. I heard a woman giggle, a man whisper, then the noise of kisses as someone made love just behind the wall against which I leaned. Down in the kitchen courtyard, someone was making dung and straw fuel-bricks. I heard the clamp and thud as the bricks were pressed into their moulds and then released, to be laid out to dry in the sun. A soldier paused when he saw me standing by the wall, identified me and went away.

Light grew. I could not wait for full sunrise, and I did not want to be on the wall when the mad king again came forth to hail his Aten at its rising.

I hurried to the quarters of the Widow-Queen Tiye and I found her; still alive—though the others were all dead.

Both guards were lying across the threshold with not a mark on them, even the feathers in their helmets undisturbed. Akhnaten had fallen at Tiye's feet. His eyes were open, still strange and dreamy, though the personality behind them had fled to its maker. Tiye cradled Smenkhare in her arms. His wig had fallen off, revealing his vulnerable boy's scalp and nape of the neck, which the red-headed woman kissed.

Master of the Household Pannefer lay in his place, Chamberlain Huy on the other side, bundles of fallen garlands and wigs and jewels.

'I gave them life,' the Widow-Queen said with an effort, trying to smile. 'Now I have taken it away. Tell your father Ay that I am sorry he missed my festival—I wanted to take him with me as well. The deed is mine,' she said with immense dignity.

Then she drained the cup in her hand. The poison was fast acting, and in moments she had joined her sons on their journey to the Otherworld.

I knelt down and sprinkled some of the poisoned wine over my lady the Widow-Queen Tiye, and offered up long-forgotten prayers for her soul, saying to the judges:

She was a great Queen, and by her actions she has saved
Egypt. She lived in Maat and died in Maat, and truth was
*   in her.*
She will live, she will live, she will live!
For Isis has her hand and Nepthys her arm.
For Neith is her guardian and Sekmet her defender.
The lioness of the peak is her lady, She Who Loves Silence,
and she has died in carrying out her desperate strategy like
*   any general who dies in battle.*

I could not bear to look on the scene any more. The air was heavy with death. But now there was another chance for the Black Land, for the intelligent boy Tutankhaten was now Pharaoh, and the maternal and well-disciplined Ankhesenpaaten his Great Royal Wife.

Widow-Queen Tiye had paid for the salvation for Egypt with her life, and I could not condemn her. My principal feeling as I looked on the dead face of King Akhnaten was great relief that the nightmare in which we had all been enmeshed was now abolished.

When I came back with Horemheb the sunlight was falling full on Tiye's face, and she looked like the young girl she had been when she had been married to Amenhotep-Osiris the Wise, who would by now be aware that she was coming to dwell with him in the Field of Reeds, and who would welcome her back into his embrace.

Ptah-hotep

The news came to Thebes with a thudding of drums. Sitamen caught me as I went through the gate and told me that she was coming with me to inter her mother as befitted a Great Royal Wife. My captivity had ended and I was free in the world again, for both the Pharaohs were dead, though I did not know until I saw Mutnodjme again what the manner of their deaths had been.

She came to the landing dock and embraced me, pressing close. She was older and heavier and the trials of the Amarna household had aged her, but she was still very beautiful to my eyes. She took my hand and led me to a waiting litter, preceded me inside and sat down to embrace me and tell me everything that had happened, very rapidly and very clearly, which had always been her practice.

Perhaps in getting older I had outlived the nervous shocks of my youth, but her account of the deaths of the two ministers and the Pharaoh and his brother did not strike me aghast. I was moved because Tiye had died so well and for such a good cause, when the king was on the verge of committing Egypt to a path which could only have led immediately to invasion by one or other of the outraged powers.

Now there would be an interval of seventy days when a large number of diplomatic relationships could be resumed and most of the problems ironed out, before we laid to rest a Widow-Queen, two Pharaohs and two ministers.

'I think it very charming that the Widow-Queen took her sons with her; and Pannefer and Huy along to do the dirty work, to which they were accustomed as no others could be,' I told Mutnodjme. 'It's a great pity that your father had to miss the feast of Sekmet.'

'He had a bellyache, unfortunately,' she replied. 'And I do not believe that he is to be unseated from his position as High Priest of the Aten, either.'

'No need,' I said. 'We can just allow the old worship to re-emerge. The Aten can be allowed to fade away quietly. Once the court moves back to Thebes this city also will just be reduced to a provincial capital. A Nomarch should be put in charge.'

'And you, Ptah-hotep? What will you do?'

'Since I cannot have you, lady, I shall find some employment which uses my learning.'

'You can have me,' she said quietly. 'The general knows all about us, about you and Kheperren and me.'

'You still love me?' I asked.

'Have I not said so?' she replied sharply.

And she embraced me, there in the litter, and I lay down on her breast and breathed in the scent of her skin.

◇◇◇

Forty days are long enough to embalm commoners—in fact forty days are long enough to embalm anyone—but the seventy days required for a Pharaoh are to synchronise with the Sothic cycle; magic, not science.

I went to the funerals for Huy and Pannefer, not entirely, as Mutnodjme accused, to make sure that they were dead, but that sureness did play some part in my attendance. They were both buried in the ritual of the Aten, which made no mention of the other gods and would, I hoped, ensure them a good hungry reception from Aphophis. The beast's only difficulty would be to locate a heart to eat and I feared that he would gain not even a toothful from both of them.

We buried the Widow-Queen Tiye with great ceremony in the language and ritual in which she had been born, married and reigned. The little King Tutankhaten had given orders that his mother should be laid to rest in a way which she would have ordered for herself. Even so, it was strange to see the priests of

Osiris looking over their shoulders in case the inspectors of the Aten should appear from the ground and arrest them for heresy.

Sitamen and the priestess of Isis, Mutnodjme, acted as Isis and Neith, crying over the body and trying to hold it back as the priests of Osiris came to fetch Tiye away from them.

Mutnodjme's once jet-black hair had streaks of white in it. We were getting old, I more than my lady, and soon I would go away from the City of the Sun to Thebes, where the priests of Amen-Re had come out of hiding and begun to repair their buildings. Snefru was long dead, I needed something to do, and I did not want to stay with Mutnodjme if she belonged to the general. Half measures were not enough for me. I was tired of intrigue, of courts, of danger. I might even have been tired of love.

Seventy days took us into the heat and dust of Mesore. I walked along behind the coffin of the boy Smenkhare, who had been hastily interred in a sarcophagus made for his mother Tiye. The embalmers had been at a loss as to how to classify him. He had been born male and was still male, though dead, but his title had been Great Royal Wife. They compromised, in the end, folding one arm across his breast as a woman is embalmed, but bandaging his phallus into erection just in case.

Smenkhare—who was in my view a blameless victim—and the heretic Pharaoh himself were hurried to a scanty burial in the same tomb.

A great change had already come over Amarna. Now that no one handed out free grain every decan, now that no one flung golden bracelets to the commoners every festival, there were many murmurings against the Pharaoh who was less than three months dead. The signs of the Aten began to be torn down. The priests of the Aten were being attacked in the street by hungry people flinging dung. In the beginning it was dung; later it was stones. They needed the dung for fuel.

So the royal funeral was hurried and secret. I saw Akhnaten's sarcophagus packed away with Smenkhare's in a tomb originally intended for their great mother.

We had buried the Widow-Queen Tiye in a splendid tomb decorated with the most beautiful frieze of fishermen, and she had her eyes on the Book of Coming Forth By Day which was inscribed on her walls. She was supplied with everything we could think of, including an army of shabti, the answerers, little model people who would do her bidding in the Field of Reeds.

By contrast we spared only the basic funeral furniture for Akhnaten. He had not believed in an afterlife, so why should we impoverish the people by providing him with goods for which he would have no use?

The people were impoverished enough.

The state of Egypt was evil, but as Horemheb said, they were used to being governed. Tutankhaten had changed his name to Tutankhamen, and his sister-wife was now called Ankhesenamen. The priests of Amen-Re would doubtless enjoy resuming their own power, their old temples, and their old position, and here was a chance to make sure that the power of the three arms of government—the temple, the crown and the army—were in balance again.

The people would enjoy having their old festivals back, which had given shape to their lives and their father's fathers back to the reign of Khufu. Preparations were already in train for Opet next month, when Amen-Re would go back to his wife Mut, having been away from her for so long. I expected that the gods would be very pleased to see each other again. The temple of Isis was gathering its lost priestesses and digging up its buried manuscripts. Isis would wail for Osiris again, and time-honoured Horus contend with ever-evil Set.

I visited my old office in the palace. There I saw soldiers leading Bakhenmut away in fetters. General Horemheb was watching with grim satisfaction, stroking his ceremonial jewel-of-office with his broad, blunt fingers.

'What is happening?' I asked the soldiers.

'He's under arrest for taking bribes,' they told me, and one look at Bakhenmut's hanging head told me that it was true. The General drew me aside.

'Ten judges and thirty-six scribes,' the General told me. 'All guilty of peculation and theft and extortion. We shall have no judges left, soon. The Pharaoh gave me the power, Ptah-hotep. Do you want your old title back?'

'I? No, I resigned it, I am just Ptah-hotep now. If you want my advice, though, General, might I suggest that you split the office? My scribes Khety and Hanufer have worked here for many years. If they have not taken bribes during the reign of the heretic then they never will. I cannot choose between them. Khety is still, I guess, rather impulsive and Hanufer rather stolid. Together they will make one very good Great Royal Scribe.'

'Done,' said the General, towering over me. 'Scribe Khety?' he bellowed into the office. 'Scribe Hanufer?'

Both of them jumped, but I saw no signs of guilt on their faces, just the wary countenances of anyone who lived through the Amarna regime where an unwise word could be fatal.

'Are you willing to jointly accept the position of Great Royal Scribe?' yelled General Horemheb into the room.

They both said, 'yes' in stunned voices.

'Good. Commence immediately. Report to the Pharaoh tomorrow morning for your orders.'

'General,' I ventured, 'you put great trust in my advice.'

He gave me a big grin from his wide face and clapped me on the shoulder so that I staggered.

'First thing a commander learns, Ptah-hotep,' he said. 'Find out who you can trust, and trust them. Widow-Queen Tiye-Osiris, the red-headed woman, she trusted you. Mutnodjme is a remarkable woman. I trust her. She trusts you. That's sufficient for a simple soldier. Come along with me, if you will,' he added. I fell in beside him. It was very hard to disobey Horemheb; he had the habit of command.

We walked together through a palace humming with activity. The households of several high officials were being evicted with bag and baggage into the court of the Phoenix, to await transport to their Nomes of origin. There were soldiers everywhere, not just the red feathers of the Pharaoh's guard but the blue of

Horemheb's men and the green of the Hermotybies. I had never seen so many soldiers. I said so.

'Pharaoh has called all the commanders in. They will be dispatched, if he takes my advice, to settle the borders. But I will need fully half of mine just to begin the task of distributing grain to the starving.

'We will see if Opet this year will bring on a proper inundation. If so, we shall be able to distribute seed grain early and see if we can get two crops, which will avert immediate famine—if we can find enough measurers and inspectors who aren't entirely corrupted by their devotion to the Aten. Ah, here we are.'

'Where?' I asked.

'As a special favour to the throne,' said Horemheb, leading me up a set of stairs. 'For a short time.'

I had a growing feeling of unease, but somehow I could not stop following Horemheb up the steps. He opened the door into a small room where various regalia of state was laid out on benches, and three servants were combing and dressing wigs. They smiled and ushered me to a chair, where my head was measured, a suitable court wig found, and before it was placed on my head, General Horemheb dropped a necklace of office around my neck.

I stared at the pendant: a vulture, holding the eye of Horus, over the scarab beetle Khephri. I knew that set of symbols.

'General, I'm not a judge!' I protested, trying to get up and being pressed firmly but respectfully back into my seat by the servant who was draping an assortment of gowns over my shoulders.

'Just for the moment,' the general assured me. 'You are the only man of unassailable virtue in the whole of the Black Land. You are the only one the people will accept to judge the corrupt officials who have been amassing fortunes at the expense of the people.

'Amen-Re is obviously with you and the new Chief Priest Dhutmose has approved you. He will be here directly to bless you in the name of the Great God and remove any lingering stain of Atenism. He has already renounced the Aten himself.'

'Why do the people approve of me?' I asked, bewildered. General Horemheb, seeing that he was not going to have to restrain me bodily, sat down and accepted a cup of beer from one of the servants. I drank some too, bewildered.

'The story went all over Egypt,' he said slowly. 'Children on the borders of Nubia tell it around campfires; boys in the service of the border fortresses hear the tale from soldiers; the children of commoners dip into the bean-pot and listen to it. Everyone knows the thrilling story of how Ptah-hotep—born a commoner like them but risen to Great Royal Scribe—stripped himself of all his wealth and titles, freed his slaves, and dismissed his household and walked out naked to defy the Pharaoh to his face, when he was offered a choice of doing a vile deed which would have saved his life.'

'It was simple,' I told him. 'There was nothing else I could do.'

'When it was thought that you had perished in your brave deed,' the general said, watching me closely, 'your parents wept until you wrote to tell them that you were alive and safe. Being sensible people, they did not allow this to be known.

'But ever since you "died" in the pyre of the Phoenix, your parents received small gifts from the people. They were not formal gifts-of-offering—which have the name of the giver attached—but were loaves and jugs left anonymously on the threshold. People who were hungry, when there was so little grain, gave them bread and beer to honour and commemorate the scribe Ptah-hotep who was the only one of all that vast horde of courtiers who dared to defy Pharaoh. Do you see now why you must be a judge?'

A servant gave me a linen cloth to wipe my eyes. I had never thought that what I had done, which had seemed utterly inevitable at the time, would have been seen as courage.

'Very well,' I said. 'I will be a judge. But I will be a just judge, ruling on the cases I have before me. I will not have any persecution of those who believed in the Aten if they have done no other wrong.'

'That is also the will of Tutankhamen may he live!' agreed General Horemheb.

Chapter Thirty

Mutnodjme

I reflected, when I looked across the feasting multitude, how well the boy who had been born Tutankhaten and was now Tutankhamen had managed. He was slim and bronzed and good looking, greatly resembling his brother Smenkhare whose fate had been so bitter. He was soft-spoken, serious, ready to take advice, but decided in his own mind.

I wondered how many scars the Amarna regime had left on his mind and soul. He showed no signs of them, except that he paused occasionally if the name of the god Amen-Re was mentioned, as though he was still not altogether sure that he could mention the god, or as if he had been mispronounced.

He was sitting with the Great Royal Wife Ankhesenamen on chairs of state, decorated with gold and silver and lapis lazuli. They made a pretty picture and I rested my eyes on them.

Ptah-hotep was lounging at my right, Horemheb at my left, and I was comfortably full and slightly merry, when the Pharaoh Tutankhnamen called to me, 'Come, Aunt, and play the song game!'

'Ask of the scented rush, what say you?' I replied. 'I am the scent of his hair.'

'Ask of the lotus-pod, what say you?' responded the Lord of the Two Thrones, looking at his sister and wife. 'My curve is her breast.'

Ankhesenamen stroked the smooth shoulder of her little brother and husband and replied readily, 'Ask of the palm tree, what say you? I am his strong back.'

'Ask of the lion, what say you?' Ptah-hotep put in, pouring more wine for Kheperren and leaning over to kiss his wrist,' I am the strength of his love.'

Ankhesenamen kissed Tutankhamen full on the mouth. I realised suddenly that this was no mere mating for dynastic reasons, but a true, if sisterly, love. She was always fussing over the boy-king, massaging him with scented oil and making him take strengthening potions. He was a little abashed still by his royalty, but he was growing into majesty just as his father Amenhotep-Osiris had done. The realm was in safe hands.

Horemheb growled into his cup, 'I wish he'd allow me to give him more guards.'

His train of thought was similar to mine. So much hung on this life, and although the boy was strong and healthy, he had been frail as a child and a lot depended on one human life. Humans were so very fragile, mortal, and easily snuffed out.

'There is no one here who wishes him ill,' I whispered into the general's ear.

He shook his head like an annoyed bull so that the blue beads clicked together. 'There is always someone who wishes Pharaoh, may he live, ill,' he objected.

And of course he was right. But they looked so beautiful and so secure, the older sister and the younger brother, now abandoning the song game for simpler riddles. Ankhesenamen never displayed what I suspected was superior wit and learning in front of his majesty. She also must have spent her childhood in terror. I was delighted to see them, after such suffering, so happy with each other.

And Egypt was flourishing.

'Aunt, Aunt,' called Tutankhamen. 'What says the wood? My arms are folded.'

'I can't guess,' I said, and he beamed.

'A shut door,' he announced.

◇◇◇

Another feast, another meeting found Horemheb and General Khaemdua, Ptah-hotep, Kheperren and me, and Divine Father Ay all sitting in the outer room of the Pharaoh's audience chamber. We were anxious about news from the borders, and Divine Father Ay was anxious, though with an air of strange complacency, about Ptah-hotep's allegations—backed by a pile of scrolls—of his thefts from various temples.

'Daughter,' Ay beckoned to me and I went to stand next to him. I knew that the protocol required me to kneel when speaking to a parent but Ay had long ago forfeited any respect, at least from me.

'Father?' I disliked him even more than usual when he was exuding this greasy benevolence.

'Are you happy with your husband?'

'Yes, Father,' I said warily.

'Then you would grieve if he should put you away?'

'That will not happen, Father.'

'You have not borne a child for him,' insinuated Ay, sliding a hand up to my thigh. His fingers curled inwards and might have touched my inner parts if I had not stepped aside.

I could not believe that he was suggesting what I thought he was suggesting.

'He is content, Father,' I said firmly. 'Ask him yourself if you do not believe me.'

I moved away from him to Horemheb's chair. His big hand dropped to my shoulder, caressing my neck under the long court wig.

'Tell me later,' he grunted, though I doubted that I would.

We were ordered inside and Tutankhamen came in with his Great Royal Wife. I listened as he dealt efficiently with the requisitions for the army, the call up of some thousand soldiers, the pleas of Rib-Adda, who was destined to remain unsupplied because Horemheb said he couldn't get men through to the vassal without fighting most of the Canaanite states.

'And there are these,' said Ptah-hotep softly, laying the pile of papyri on the King's lap.

The boy-king examined them carefully. All his actions were considered.

'These are all accusations against Divine Father Ay,' he commented in his soft sure voice.

'They are,' agreed Ptah-hotep.

'I cannot deal with them now,' said Tutankhamen. Beside him, Ankhesenamen pulled at his shoulder and hissed into his ear. I could not hear what she was saying but some of Ay's full-fed assurance departed from him and he began to look almost haggard.

'He was kind to me when no one else was,' said Tutankhamen, almost pleading. 'He was with me when all others deserted me. I cannot hear these matters now,' he said, giving them back to the Great Royal Judge. 'Claim whatever has been lost from the Throne and replace the lost goods from my treasury.'

'Lord, you will eventually have to hear me on this matter,' said Ptah-hotep gently. 'Justice requires...'

'I know,' said Tutankhamen, almost in tears. It was a pity to oppress the poor boy so. Ankhesenamen slid an arm around his waist but continued to whisper to him, directing occasional glances at Divine Father Ay which should have left little smoking holes in his body and probably set fire to the curtain behind him.

'Not yet,' said Tutankhamen. 'Lord Ptah-hotep, come to me again with this if...if it is repeated.'

As the Lord of the Two Thrones commands,' said Ptah-hotep, and kissed the slim fingered boy's hand, loaded with rings.

'I have decreed a feast, for Horus goes to Hathor this year,' said Tutankhamen, drawing a deep breath of relief. 'And next year...' he exchanged a conspiratorial glance with his sister-wife, who giggled, 'we may have the birth of a new Pharaoh to celebrate.'

'May the Lord of the Two Lands live forever,' said Ay. I hated him more than ever. I didn't know how much loathing one human soul could contain until I looked on my own father.

'You remember Amenhotep-Osiris, Aunt Mutnodjme?' the young Pharaoh said to me as we filed out of the audience chamber.

'I remember him very well, lord.'

'Do you think, do you think that…' he struggled with words. 'For all his sixteen years, he was very young. 'Do you think that he might be pleased with me? I saw him in a dream, that old man. He was smiling.'

My heart caught. To dream of the dead was an omen of death. I hugged the King and Pharaoh of the Black Land to my bosom and he rested his forehead on my shoulder. He felt lithe and smelt young, like a puppy.

'I'm positive that he is very pleased with you,' I whispered into the beautifully-shaped ear.

The years had been busy. Seven years spent caring for the general, caring for my household, which kept growing, caring for Kheperren and Ptah-hotep when I housed them.

Seven years since Widow-Queen Tiye had brought the Amarna nightmare to a conclusion. I never forgot her, the barbarian woman who had begun and then finished the reigns of her sons. When the court moved back to Thebes, General Khaemdua and the Pharaoh arranged that Tiye's body should be moved also, where she could receive regular offerings. We left Akhnaten to his rock-cut tomb on the wrong side of his city. I later heard that tomb robbers had broken in and destroyed the corpse in their search for the gold amulets which should have been there, and weren't. It struck me as fitting; but then I have never had a forgiving nature.

People drifted away from Amarna, which was a foolish place to put a city anyway, as they drifted away from the cult of the Aten; though it still had its die-hard enthusiasts. They were tolerated by the priests of Amen-Re, still too new in their authority to start a religious purge. In fact, as the general remarked, the reign of the Aten had had one advantage. It had subdued the priests of Amen-Re and would probably keep them subdued for a generation.

The years slipped by. Everything seemed hopeful. Gratified perhaps by the celebration of Opet again, inundation had come every year and the granaries were full. The people were still complaining of oppression in the country, and the borders were never really calm, but that, Horemheb told me, was what borders were like—centres of instability.

Invested by the solemn boy-king's own hands, Great Royal Judge, He Who is Pure of Heart, in Whose Hand is Maat Which is Truth Ptah-hotep, who was also my friend and sometimes, my lover, was ruling his courts with his usual meticulous equity. I was a little surprised when he ordered a beating for one who had brought a false claim and looked on with outward calm as this was done. He had the scales of life and death in his hands, he told me later, and could not afford any false charges. There were enough real ones to occupy him for the rest of his life and beyond, and the courts were always busy.

In the combined household which contained Kheperren, Ptah-hotep, the general and me, and all our servants—we occupied a whole wing of the palace of Thebes—Ptah-hotep often came home bone-weary and needed to be fed soup, massaged with oil, and put to bed. Horemheb returned filthy and occasionally injured from his forays into the disputed lands. Kheperren, always with the general, once brought home a putrid fever which had to be nursed in isolation and which may have brought on my third miscarriage, because I caught it as well.

The Great Royal Wife Ankhesenamen had the same problem, miscarrying twice of six-month children, and wise women attributed this to her being abused when young. But this was certainly not the case with me. The priestesses of Isis consulted their hoarded writings and took counsel, and told me that it was the wisdom of Maat that I could not carry a child, because doing so might result in my death. I tried to be philosophical about it, but it was difficult, when my servants seemed to engender at the flick of a loincloth and bring forth bouncing fat babies with perfect ease.

I suggested to the general that he might take a secondary wife, but he always refused, saying there were enough women in his household as it was and that he was comfortable with my ways.

The only real insect in the ointment was my father Ay and his wife Tey, who were still very powerful. Tutankhamen cherished them as the only stable people in his erratic, fearful childhood. Of course they were stable. Ay wanted only gold, Tey wanted only what Ay wanted, which was more and more gold. He was appointed Great Royal Chamberlain over heated objections from Ptah-hotep and both generals, but the king Tutankhamen may he live liked him and there was nothing to be done about it.

Ay particularly hated Ptah-hotep. Ptah-hotep, being a honourable person, was puzzled by Ay because he was so devious and so greedy, even when he had all that he could possibly use.

'Why does he want to divert the temple offerings to his own pocket?' he asked me, as he slashed a line through the order and sent it back to the office of record. 'Why, especially, does he want to steal, when Tutankhamen is a nice boy and will give him all he wants?'

'Great Royal Wife Ankhesenamen doesn't like Ay at all,' I replied. 'He was the one who raped her, lying on her father's belly, when she was a child, and that may be reason why she cannot give Egypt an heir now. She won't let the young king give Ay all that he wants, and in any case even if the Pharaoh could give Ay most of Egypt it would not be enough. He is as rapacious as a crocodile; he is *the mouth that can never be filled* of the old riddle.'

'*These have never been filled, can never be filled,*' repeated Ptah-hotep slowly. '*The hands of the ape, the claws of the vulture, the mouth of the crocodile and the eyes of man.*'

'I suppose that you are right. I could wish that Widow Queen Tiye-Osiris had taken him with her. Ay would have made a good footstool for the journey. Or a chamber-pot. He demands tribute from foreign kings, and the crown never sees a deben of it. I can't accuse him of profiting from his office again—the little king threw the latest charge out when Ay begged him to remember how he had carried him on his back to the festivals of the Aten when he was three.

'Ay is a centre for the remaining corrupt officials, though I am weeding them out. But he is protecting some and while he does that I cannot get rid of them. Ah, well,' he said, and looked so sad that I ordered musicians to attend at dinner and Ii to attend on him while he was washed and massaged.

In all, I expected that my life would continue in its pleasant path until I died and went to the Field of Reeds. I had mastered cuneiform and was consulted by the scribes on any difficult passages, as I could read it easily in Babylonian or Hittite. I walked down to the temple of Amen-Re now and again for a refreshing argument with the keeper of cuneiform, or to talk to the priestesses of Isis about medicinal plants or to swap stories. When the court went on journeys, I went too, to feast on fried fish at New Year or eat hippopotamus cakes in Tybi.

I was getting old for a woman—nearly thirty. Horemheb had already purchased a suitable tomb for us, painted with his favourite scenes of marching soldiers and war, and I had a sub-chapel there with Isis looking down on me. Ptah-hotep and Kheperren would lie there as well in their time, and I expected that after such a strenuous youth, this was my time of peace.

Horemheb was away, Ptah-hotep was in the south on the usual circuit, when a maid came running. Little Wab, who had grown into a fine woman, threw herself at my feet and wailed, tearing off her wig and scratching her breasts with her nails.

'What has happened?' I dropped the tablet I was translating and it smashed on the floor. Whatever the spy at the King of Hatti's court had to report was now in a thousand pieces.

'Someone is dead? Is it Ptah-hotep? Kheperren? The general?'

She shook her head, gulping down tears, and finally managed to cry: 'The Lord of the Two Lands Tutankhamen is dead, Mistress, the Great Son of Amen-Re is dead!'

I shook her by the shoulders. 'Don't be ridiculous, girl, he's only seventeen, he's healthy, he can't be dead!'

She went on crying. I left her there in a heap on the floor and went to the door.

I heard the noise of wailing, close and loud. Women were screaming and tearing their hair. Men were weeping as they stood. I saw a soldier crying on guard, which I had never seen before. But the source of the grief seemed to be outside the walls, and I went to find out what had happened.

I did not need an escort. Women walked alone in Egypt again. All our ancient rights had been restored by this same king. I was jostled by court ladies as we jammed in the main doorway and then saw a sight which beat most of them to their knees.

Four priests were carrying a body. It was the young king. I saw his face. His pelvis seemed to have been broken and one leg and one arm dangled at acute angles. I looked because I could not take my eyes away. The boy's wig had fallen off. His skull was fractured. Also his spine. No living spine would allow a neck to drop like that. I had only seen such injuries once before, in a man who had slid off the roof of the temple of Isis.

Tutankhamen had fallen from a height onto hard ground, for there were smudges of the sand that servants use to cleanse marble on his face and body. Pitiful, broken, dead. From whence had he fallen?

I looked up at the walls, and there was Divine Father Ay, his face a mask, no emotion at all, watching them carry the body of the Pharaoh Tutankhamen-Osiris to the House of Life to be embalmed.

I gathered my wits and went back inside and told my household the news. I bade them send an urgent message to the general and to call Ptah-hotep back from Memphis. I said nothing of my dreadful suspicion. I might be able to gather some proof, though surely not even Divine Father Ay would have dared to murder a Pharaoh?

Not when it would not advantage him.

Though I had heard from Ptah-hotep that he believed that his urgings had finally borne fruit, and that the intelligent and far-seeing Pharaoh was about to dismiss Divine Father Ay.

I let my hair down from its pins and cast a handful of ash on my head while I thought. Assume Ay had murdered the King. Why would he do that? How did this fit in with his all-encompassing greed?

A thought occurred to me. There was no heir. The Great Royal Wife had never borne a living child. The Princess Sitamen had died in a chariot accident three years before, a fitting end for such a warrior. Mentu the Scribe had died with her.

And now, the last living child of the Pharaoh Amenhotep-Osiris had just died. Therefore the only persons with any rights to the throne were Ankhesenamen, who had been Great Royal Wife twice and was a Great Royal Heiress; and possibly me, Mutnodjme who, as child of Divine Father Ay and Great Royal Nurse Tey, and sister of Queen Nefertiti, had been awarded the rank of Royal Princess; though I had never used it. .

Resolving to die rather than marry my father, no matter what happened, I went to find the Great Royal Wife and warn her of her fate.

Ptah-hotep

I heard of the death of the Pharaoh Tutankhamen from many sources, and the question of the safety of my household was uppermost in my mind as I ordered my crew to re-load the vessel *Glory of Thoth* and set out at once for the capital. I had been complacent. I had not expected anything more to happen in what had been, by any measure, a very active life.

The hawser was freed and dragged back into *Glory of Thoth* and we were loosed into the current. The rowing-master ordered the sweeps out. I accepted a bite of bread and a cup of wine and sipped and thought as the cultivation slipped past, date palms and men ploughing with oxen, someone driving a light carriage between two villages, women coming down to the river for water.

I looked into my cup, swilled and tasted with pleasure. I still liked the Tashery vintage best, though that produced by the Ammemmes vineyard was very promising. I had expected to spend the night at the house of my father, who was very old and ill. I had expected to spend tomorrow judging a complicated land tenure case. My mind was full of the laws of measurement and taxes, not the matters of state which I now had to consider.

I had grown sure of my place, and that is not a good thing for a man or a judge. I lived in the combined household which contained all that I loved; Kheperren and his general and Mutnodjme. It also contained all that I needed, a place to lay my head, someone to help me wash and dress and take care of my garments, and a table laid with good food. Unlike some of my contemporaries, I had not become dyspeptic over the years, and I could even join the general in his favourite dish of leeks, garlic and onions, though such an indulgence meant that we would sleep together, because both Kheperren and Mutnodjme were sensitive to garlic breath. My mind was dwelling on these domestic matters because I did not want to think about the death of the Pharaoh Tutankhamen-Osiris.

There was the question of the succession.

Now that the boy was dead, it was up to Ankhesenamen to choose the new Pharaoh. Whoever she married, within limits, would be king. I did not know her well, she seemed a pleasant young woman, though remarkably unlearned like all the Amarna princesses.

Suddenly I recalled Khons, dead many years, and the fate of learning under Akhnaten, and the pull-along clay horse in a pool of blood.

I found myself praying as the *Glory of Thoth* sped along towards the capital to whatever fate waited for me there.

I found the palace in an uproar, all of the furnishings of the dead king being carried to the docks to be placed in his tomb.

My household was going about its business as usual. Ipuy, very old and gnarled now, challenged me at the door and then let me in. I found Mutnodjme sitting quite still. I spoke to her, but she did not seem to hear me. When I came closer, I saw that she had a knife in her lap and was looking at it.

'Ptah-hotep, I have a terrible suspicion,' she said, as though I had just been at court and come home as usual instead of being summoned from Memphis and exhausting my rowers in getting to Thebes in record time.

'Tell me,' I said, sitting down. I did not touch the knife.

I saw the body of the young king,' she said slowly, choosing her words. 'He had various broken bones: a fractured skull, a broken arm and leg. He fell from a height, Ptah-hotep, that is the only way he could have sustained such injuries. They picked him up from the courtyard. The walls are very high there.'

'Yes?' I prompted her gently, as one encourages a reluctant witness.

'When I looked up to see where he fell from,' she said, making herself speak, 'I saw Divine Father Ay looking down on me.'

'And?'

'He wasn't shocked,' she said.

Though this was not evidence, it was evidential. I still didn't understand the knife. I touched it and raised an eyebrow.

'I have been trying to summon the courage to go and confront my father about this death,' she said. I took the knife away.

'If this terrible thing did take place,' I told her, 'we must wait. If he means to take power, he will show his hand.'

'He already has,' she said tonelessly. 'He sent to Ankhesena-men and told her to prepare to marry him, when her husband is buried. You can hear her,' she said.

Indeed; a long, sobbing shriek in a female voice had been noticeable from the moment I walked into the palace.

'Then we must tell the general,' I said.

'I have sent a message to him, but he is on the border, deal-ing with the Canaanite incursion. I have tried to call him, but we were never close like you and I are close. He will not be able to feel my fear. He might, however, get my message. But it will take him a long time to get here,' she said.

I worried about her. She did not seem angry. She was not reacting at all. It seemed that this dreadful murderous act of Ay, her father, might be the last straw which broke the ass' back for Mutnodjme.

'Come, woman, where is your hospitality?' I demanded. 'Here I am, your husband, newly returned from a long journey, and are there garlands? Is there wine? Must I kiss your feet, Mistress of the House, for a wash and some oil?'

'You may kiss my feet if you wish,' she said with a return of some spirit. 'And you shall certainly be tended. Come, my dear.'

If I felt her emotions, she felt mine. And I was not afraid.

If Ay took power, then things might not go so badly for Egypt, though they might not go so badly for me. There were worse persons than misers for Pharaoh. If Ay proved incompetent, then returning Horemheb might have another solution. In any case, we could do nothing on our own, and just for my own sense of justice, I would investigate who had been where when the young king fell from the wall.

It did not take me long, just by walking around and asking idle questions, to locate the king on the wall. He had gone up there shortly before noon, without any guards. I could not speak to the Great Royal Wife because she was still wailing. She had been doing this for days. I understood how bitter her fate was, but I wished that she would mourn it in silence. The sobbing wail was hurting my ears.

But I did speak to one of the servants of the Pharaoh Tutankhamen-Osiris; the son of that Khety who was Half Great Royal Scribe. The boy had known me since he had been a small child. Khety-Tashery, which means Little Khety—for an imaginative man Khety was surprisingly unimaginative at naming children—was willing to be taken on a walk by someone whom he looked on as an uncle, and willingly accompanied me on the king's last journey.

'He came here to look at the river,' said Khety-Tashery. 'You get the best view of it from here, because the temple of the Aten isn't in the way.'

I could see a long way down the Nile in one direction, and several shoeni up the river the other way; I could see the docks where the fishing boats came in, and the front door of the palace. Yes, it was a charming place to stand and look out over one's domain.

'And from here he fell,' I said quietly; I could see no marks on the stone. Khety-Tashery began to weep.

'He wouldn't let us come with him,' he sobbed. 'But he came up here with someone.'

'So he wasn't alone?' I asked.

'No, lord. He said he had something to say to the person that he didn't want anyone else to hear; so they wouldn't be shamed.'

'And you don't know who it was, Khety-Tashery?'

'No, lord.' He paused, as though he might have been going to say something more. I did not speak but raised an eyebrow and motioned for him to continue.

'It's nothing, lord. Nothing much, anyway. He talked about dismissing some officials, lord, because they had been stealing from the crown. He'd been about to summon two of them to come to him, then he countermanded the orders.'

'Whom did he summon? It's all right, child, no one is angry with you. I am as grieved as you are that the young king is now with Osiris. It's all right to talk to me.'

'Of course, lord,' Khety-Tashery looked shocked. 'You are the just judge, lord, and anyway my father says that you were never unjust even when you and he were boys together.'

'Ask your father about the night that Hanufer, Ptah-hotep, Kheperren and Khety stole four sesame-seed cakes from the Master of Scribes' kitchen.' I smiled at the boy and the memory.

'I'll ask him. Oh, the names of the persons he summoned? It was Nakhtamin, lord; and Divine Father Ay. But then he called the messenger back.'

'Thank you, Khety-Tashery.'

I took a small constitutional to the office of Nakhtamin, Fan Bearer on the King's Right Hand, about whom I had always had doubts. He was responsible for the conduct of the king's entertainments and feasts, and for a long time I had heard rumours, though nothing I could substantiate, that he was being given presents by troupes of dancers so that he would employ them. Performing at the palace was a way of ensuring success and many subsequent engagements.

The office was silent; as it should be. No business was supposed to be conducted in the seventy days in which the kingdom prepared for the burial of a king and the accession of a new Pharaoh. I knocked at the door, and heard a flurry of movement and then a smothered giggle.

'Nakhtamin, it is Ptah-hotep,' I said, and the door was flung open and I was ushered inside by three entirely naked women. They were shining with oil. They looked like tumblers with their long hair tied into tassels and the dancer's muscular, long-limbed build. They were all avoiding my eyes, though their nakedness was part of their trade.

Nakhtamin was disclosed, also entirely naked—which was not proper for his trade—lying on a pallet bed with a young woman astride him. He saw me, lost firmness in the part in which the girl was most interested, detached her and waved his hands at the women to go away. They dived for the door but I ordered them to halt.

'Sit down, most beautiful of women,' I said. Do not tear our eyes from the contemplation of your beauty. Greetings, Nakhtamin, I am sorry to have disturbed your mourning. I was wondering if you had spoken to the Pharaoh Tutankhamen-Osiris just before he died? I seem to have no note of the conversation in the records.'

'He wanted to see me,' agreed Nakhtamin. 'About some of these scandalous rumours about bribery which are, of course, not true.'

'Indeed, I can see that,' I said politely. The girls giggled again, covering their mouths with their hands. They really were very attractive, and may have thought that mating with Nakhtamin, who was presentable enough, was a reasonable fee for an engagement at the palace.

'And what did the Divine King have to say to you?' I asked. Nakhtamin scowled. 'I was to see him at one o'clock in the afternoon,' he said. 'See, I wrote it down.'

I had before me an ostracon with the day and 'Lord of T.T. T.M.H.I.' scrawled on it.

'Lord of the Two Thrones Tutankhamen may he live, at one o'clock,' I translated.

'Yes,' Nakhtamin said. 'But he was dead before then.'

'You keep no permanent household here?' I asked.

'No, lord, but the maidens were with me just before, I asked them to audition at noon for the feast, and then just when we were getting friendly, the wailing started.'

'Your acquaintance seems doomed,' I agreed, 'for today in walked a judge just when you were getting friendly again. Is this the case, young ladies? Tell me the truth. I am a Royal Judge, and you will have your engagement whether or not you please this man. Did you come here just before that time on that dreadful day?'

They consulted each other and then one was elbowed into a 'kiss earth' from which I raised her. Her hands were very strong. 'Lord, it is as he says. We came to show him our tumbling, and we were just showing him our other skills—we were trained by a priestess of Hathor, Lord Judge—when we heard the screaming that the poor Pharaoh had died.'

'Thank you. Where was he going to meet you, Nakhtamin?' I asked as I was leaving, wondering if the Fan Bearer would recover his potency and at least have enough sense to lock the door. From the way his parts were twitching, I assumed that he would.

'On the wall, lord. He liked to stand on that part of the wall and watch the ships.'

I walked a little further to the quarters of Divine Father Ay. A maiden in correct mourning opened the door, scurried away to find her mistress, and returned with Great Royal Nurse Tey. She had not aged well. The ashes and dishevelment of mourning does not improve the appearance, of course, but she was thin and acidulated and her voice was meagre, as though she would not even release a word from its cage until it had been drained of juice.

'Ptah-hotep,' she acknowledged awarding me no titles at all.

'What do you want? The Divine Father is in mourning, as are we all.'

'I just wondered if he could clear up a little point which is worrying me,' I said.

She raked my face with a hard stare. Well?'

'I have no note of his conversation with Tutankhamen-Osiris on the morning of his death. I believe that Divine Father Ay had an appointment with him?'

'No,' she snapped.

'No? But I am quite sure that he had an appointment with the king. To discuss the dismissal of corrupt officials?'

'No,' she snarled, and closed the door in my face.

I walked away quite convinced, though I still had no proof, that the Pharaoh Tutankhamen-Osiris had been murdered by Divine Father Ay.

Chapter Thirty-one

Mutnodjme

I agreed with my lord Ptah-hotep that no action should be taken about Ay until Horemheb came home, so I went to visit Ankhesenamen to try and calm her. The Great Royal Wife had been screaming for two days and two nights with pauses of a couple of minutes, presumably to take a breath. No one was getting any sleep and I wondered that her throat had held out as long as it had. I was forbidden the door by her little maidens, but I smiled at them and refused to move until the Mistress of the Queen's Household came out to see what the trouble was.

'Let me in,' I said. 'I need to speak to the Royal Lady Ankhesenamen.'

'You are the daughter of Ay,' she said suspiciously.

'I am also the wife of General Horemheb and the friend of Ptah-hotep the Just Judge,' I rejoined.

She seemed to feel that I had jumped her pieces and signalled to the small girls to let me in.

When the door was safely shut and barred, she conducted me into the inner chamber, where three young women were sitting in a group with the Queen. A fourth maiden was wailing at the top of her voice. When she saw me, she broke off and another immediately took up the cry.

'What are you doing, Ankhesenamen?' I asked, for in neither case was the voice that of the Great Royal Spouse.

'Providing music for your father's ears,' she snapped.

'He is your grandfather,' I pointed out, joining the maidens on the floor.

'I know, and I am not going to marry him.'

'Well, there are ways and ways,' I said. Her intelligent face lit up and she descended from her chair to join me.

'You have a plan? I can't think of anything but to try and find a husband out of Egypt. I am not going to marry Ay,' she said with unshakeable determination.

'You can't marry out of Egypt; in you resides the right to the throne,' I objected.

She looked instantly guilty, but I could not see how she could have contacted anyone who might be able to bring her a foreign prince so I forgot about it and returned to the matter at hand.

'Do you remember deciding not to throw your spindle at the wall in the apartments of the Widow-Queen Tiye-Osiris, lady?' I asked.

She smiled. 'Yes, and just after I got the knack of spinning. I recall it, Aunt. What's your point? I mean, here I am, I've been a plaything for the royal house since I was born. I had to marry Smenkhare who was utterly corrupt, then I had to marry Tutankhamen-Osiris. I really did like him but now he's dead, and I'm sick of it. I won't marry again, I won't be Great Royal Wife again, and I will die rather than marry my grandfather. He's a cold cruel miser. He hurt me when I was a child and he'd hurt me again, too.' She shuddered with loathing. 'He doesn't even want me. Not me, myself. He just wants the throne.'

'Well, you could give it to him,' I suggested.

There was a silence which could be felt. The young woman who had been wailing had stopped and the next one had been so astounded that she had missed her cue.

'Aunt, Aunt, you're dreaming!' Ankhesenamen shook her head at me. 'He has to have me to have the throne.'

'He doesn't have to have your body, your person, he just has to have your consent to marriage,' I pointed out.

I had asked Ptah-hotep about the law of marriage, and he had agreed that perfectly valid marriages could be made without one party being there. They could be repudiated later, of course, but that would not matter. It all depended on whether Ankhesenamen really meant to give up power.

'Wonderful,' she said. 'Wonderful. I'll do it. I don't actually have to be here to marry him, do I? Just to agree, or at least never to disagree. Yes, yes, I'll do it, find me a scribe, where's my seal?'

'But you must leave the palace, leave all your wealth, for he will not let you take anything with you. You must leave everything,' I said.

'I don't care,' said the Great Royal Wife flatly. 'I want to learn. I want to be able to read and write. I can't bear a living child and I don't like men; I never want to be fumbled by sweating hands again. They can keep their love. It's all false. It's not important. I have seen you, Aunt, reading cursive and even Hittite. I've got a good mind. I can learn. Let me out of this palace or I'll go mad. If I leave, there must be somewhere I can go! I'm tired of pregnancy and pain.'

'There is the temple of Isis,' I suggested.

'Would they take me? With nothing?'

'Yes,' I agreed, for I knew that the Singer of Isis the lady Peri was back in charge. I also thought that Ankhesenamen would make a good scholar, and Isis appreciates dedication.

'Here's a papyrus roll, write my consent to the marriage with my revolting grandfather. Then all I need to do is stay for the funeral—poor Tutankhamen, he was a nice boy—and then I'm free.' She clapped both hands together with joy.

'But once gone, you cannot pine for your pretty fabrics and your jewels and return,' I warned. 'Ay is not scrupulous; you know that. I would not make any optimistic predictions about the length of your life if you come back and challenge his right to reign.'

'My dearest Takha is coming with me,' she said firmly. 'She has already taught me the beginnings of my letters. See?'

She exhibited a child's writing board with exercises in black ink, corrected in red. The maiden who had been wailing smiled shyly at me. This was the studious and learned young woman Takha. She could not have been more than eighteen. I looked at her hands. Yes, there was the flattened middle finger with the permanent ink-mark. This was a scholar.

'Ptah-hotep the Just Judge shall write it, you will seal it, and I will deliver it to Divine Father Ay after you have safely gone. You must go to the funeral, as you say, poor Tutankhamen deserves that of you and he is to be buried in the full Osirian ritual, which requires your presence. Then, niece, we shall slip you out of the palace, and your grandfather need never come near you again. I will go now to the temple of Isis and arrange your admittance. If you are sure, Ankhesenamen? This is your last chance to change your future and be queen again.'

'I am sure,' she assured me, and she had always known her own mind, even as a child.

'Give me a pectoral and a few pairs of earrings. You should not go to the temple unprovided-for and Ay has not done an inventory of your jewels yet.'

She handed over the gems. On my way out, I turned and said, 'Don't resume the wailing. It has served its purpose,' and walked straight out of the room and into Divine Father Ay.

He was pot-bellied and double-chinned and hung about with gold. There was a greasy mark down his chest where he had spilled something sticky.

'Daughter,' he said. 'You have been with the Great Royal Wife?'

'I have,' I said, instinctively stepping back a pace. His black eyes scanned me and focused on the bag I held in my hands. It was uncanny, I believe that he could smell the gold through the fabric.

'What is in there?'

'Father, I have just, I believe, talked the Great Royal Wife into marrying you,' I exclaimed in disgust. 'I have even made her stop screaming. She has given me a few presents in token of her affection and soon you will have everything she owns.'

'She will agree?' he asked, eagerly.

'I think so, if you leave her alone. Don't try to see her and especially don't remind her of the good old days at Amarna. That will not work on this royal child of Akhnaten.'

'You have been of some use after all, daughter,' he admitted. Then he extracted a pair of earrings from my bag—commission, perhaps, or because he could not help himself—and let me go on my way.

I commended the Great Royal Wife's decision in my heart as I went unmolested out of the palace and into the street, to talk to the Singer of Isis about two new pupils.

The next visitor who graced my house was General Khaemdua. I found him sitting in the chair of state, condescending to sip a little of the very best wine and eat a few crumbs of Wab's special date bread. He was immaculate, as ever; very bored, as ever; and elaborately simple in his clothes, as ever.

I bowed to him and he waved a distracted hand.

'Mistress of the House, I am trespassing on your hospitality. I need a translation of a clay tablet, and there are no scribes free in the house of archives.'

'General, I and my household are at your service as always,' I responded correctly, and found my basket of scribe's tools. He gave me a tablet and I sat down to construe it.

'This is in Assyrian,' I noted. 'My knowledge of that language is not perfect, but this is what I believe it says. It is from Suppiluliumas for an Egyptian woman called Ankhati, and he says:

Why should I send you my son? Never has it been heard of that an Egyptian princess married out of her own land."

Isis protect us!' I added, staring at the square writing. I read it again. That is certainly what it said.

'Have you any idea who the traitor Ankhati might be?' he asked with his affected laziness, allowing Wab to pour him some more wine.

'Oh, I know who it is, and I have just solved this problem! I thought she looked guilty when I mentioned that she could not marry out of Egypt.' I explained what was to become of the Great Royal Wife of Tutankhamen-Osiris, and General Khaemdua almost smiled.

'Well, then, as long as someone intercepts Suppiluliumas' son—the king has one hundred and seventeen sons, so he will probably send one—then no harm is done. That's the trouble with young women, they are impulsive.

'And since I now do not have to rush off and invade Assyria, I will have some more of that very pleasant date cake,' he said, and Wab cut him another slice.

Ptah-hotep

The late king was on his funeral trip, and the new King Ay had been crowned, though without the actual presence of the Queen Ankhesenamen. She and one of her maidens had slipped undetected out of the palace on the night of the funeral, dressed in servant's clothes. No one could find the Great Royal Wife but her written consent to the marriage was on record and I was forced to suffer the sight of Divine Father Ay crowned Lord of the Two Lands. His Great Royal Spouse was the crone Tey. They both looked indescribable in the pomp of state, but such sights need not be remembered.

The trouble began when Pharaoh Ay found out how much he was spending on the army.

'It costs a fortune to keep all these soldiers in the field,' he protested, and would not be dissuaded from sending most of the standing army home.

Without gifts-of-valour or severance allowances to which they were entitled, he disbanded regiment after regiment. They laid their standards in the hall of warriors and went home to the land which the government had given them.

Reports soon came in from all of the borders, crying for help. The combined Great Royal Scribe Khety and Hanufer came to me almost in tears, relating letters received from garrisons who were going under, besieged villages which would shortly be destroyed—and there was nothing that I could advise. Though I was interested in a letter from the King of Assyria, demanding to know the fate of his son. It had been sent to a lady called Ankhati, but there was no one in the palace of that name and I replied to that effect.

I was still, to my astonishment, Great Royal Judge Ptah-hotep, possibly because I was too well guarded to poison and too well-regarded to dismiss.

Apart from his meanness, which was legendary—it was said that Ay would skin a louse for its hide—the new Pharaoh spent most of his time ordering an exceptionally grand tomb, in which we all hoped that he would soon lie.

And General Horemheb still did not come home. He and his thousand men were the only effective force left on the borders of Canaan and he could not leave. Mutnodjme and I worried about him and Kheperren, and kept the household going and advised the king when he would take advice, and we waited.

No one expected the manner of the general's return.

Late one night, I was out keeping watch on the high walls. I quite often had trouble sleeping, and I liked to walk where the little king had walked and remember that the present Pharaoh was his murderer. The night was still—it was Ephipi, still and hot, before the Southern Snake's breath scorches Egypt, crisping every leaf.

A lone horseman came galloping straight across the plain. I heard the hoofbeats. A soldier, perhaps. Another warning from the edges of mismanaged Egypt that another fortress was about to fall. Another spokesman from some small town ringed with bandits. And nothing I could do because all of the soldiers were home on their farms, waiting for harvest.

I heard the sentry's challenge, saw them fall back and salute as the horse passed into the courtyard. So, an officer of some sort, and one whom the sentries recognised.

Idle and uncomfortable, the heat pearling my skin with sweat, I marked the horseman's progress as he dismounted in the yard.

He grunted as his feet hit the ground, and the horse staggered and almost fell. A servant led it away to be groomed and watered, and the soldier strode into the king's side of the palace.

For no good reason, I followed him. I had been hoping for some major invasion, in a way, something which would force a few debens of silver out of Ay's fist. I did not know the news which the soldier brought, but it was probably dire.

I passed the guards on the king's door and came into the outer apartment, which had no guards and no attendants. Divine Father the Pharaoh Ay had dismissed most of the servants to save their board. A sleepy Master of the House was standing by the door to the inner apartment, obviously listening. He clutched at my wrist.

'Lord Judge, go in, I fear that the Pharaoh Ay may he live is in danger.'

I went.

Under a huge painting of Maat who is truth, Pharaoh Ay was backed up against the wall and General Horemheb was confronting him. I had never heard the general talk in the voice he was using this night. It was low, clear, and almost toneless. It was the voice of one tried beyond endurance and weary almost to death.

'I have come from the Canaan border, Pharaoh Ay. You left me my one thousand men, with which I have been attempting to hold a stretch of land almost as long as the Nile.'

'Soldiers are expensive. You did not need all those men.'

'So you say,' said General Horemheb, 'but you have not seen what I have seen. Villages raided, smoking ruins with weeping, dazed children lying on the bodies of their dead mothers. Violated women swallowing hemlock rather than live a moment longer with their pain. The Shasu have crossed the border at twenty points, all of them little raiding parties, and I am like a man who is trying to put out a hundred little fires with only one bucket.'

'You are the Chief of the Army,' sneered Ay. 'It is your job to hold the border.'

'I have held it, for the moment,' he replied. 'I left ten men at each little post, you see, to hold it against the raiders. They do not want to stay. The Shasu, they just whip across the border, slay a few men, rape a few women, steal the flocks and drive them back. In a well-run country they would only be a pest. But we cannot hold them off.'

'Then we shall appoint another general, one who can manage his post,' said Ay. He seemed to feel no fear, even though Horemheb stood over him, a cubit taller and strong as an ox.

'The Assyrians are coming,' said Horemheb, quietly. 'You will not be able to ignore them. The King of Khatti is a persuasive man. I have just fought a battle; I have just met Assyria,' he said. 'Shall I tell you how I won?'

'If you must,' Ay yawned.

'I took the shepherds and the goatherds of the threatened village,' Horemheb's voice had never risen above an ordinary speaking tone. 'I gave them no weapons because I had none, and in any case they were used to pruning hooks and mattocks.

'I am a soldier, I have always been a soldier, and they might have made good troops if I had had time to train them, but I had no time. You gave me no time, Ay. It was a small village but they were proud of it and wished to save it and they had courage, those shepherds.

'I could see no way of keeping the Assyrians back but by encircling them in a narrow place and blocking the ends of the pass. It was a reasonable strategy and it worked. But they are all dead, Ay. Every one of those goatherds has died, cut to pieces by the Assyrians, calling for their mothers as they bled. If they had had real weapons they might have survived. My own ten men are dead, except for one whom I left in the village to live or die under the care of the women. They had been with me for years. But they are soldiers and soldiers face death willingly, it is part of their service,' he said.

'But the goatherds of Palm Tree Village are yours, Ay; the deaths of seventy men and boys almost too young to hold a stick are your fault.'

Even then, perhaps, Ay might have retrieved the situation if he had demonstrated some remorse. But instead he sneered.

'What are goatherds?' he asked. 'We have plenty of goatherds in the Black Land. And what are armies? Open mouths and open hands. I care nothing for the deaths of a thousand such. I will not have to feed them.'

Horemheb's great hands were around his throat in a second, crushing the life out of him. And in the doorway the crone Tey shrieked, ran and clawed at Horemheb and was shoved backward with such force that her head impacted against a table and she fell to the floor.

I said, 'Let him go, he is dead,' and Horemheb dropped the body of the Pharaoh Ay-Osiris and wiped his hands on his shirt.

I bent and inspected the body of the woman. 'She is also dead,' I told the general. He sank into a chair and passed his hand across his forehead. It came away black with dirt. He stared at it, as though he wondered whether he had turned into a Nubian overnight.

'He murdered Tutankhamen, you know,' I commented. 'Maat has been done.'

I pointed to the picture on the wall. The Goddess of Truth, crowned with her feather, had not altered her expression.

Ay-Osiris lay where he had fallen, a broken doll. I reflected that we had better get him to the House of Life immediately. Bruises putrefy faster than other flesh.

I sat the old Master of Household down and gave him some wine.

'They're both dead?' he quavered.

'Yes, do you want to join them?'

'No. He was as bad as she and they were both as mean as rats,' he said frankly. 'I'm glad they are dead.'

'Good. Summon the priests of Osiris. We are about to have another royal funeral. Ay-Osiris is going to his tomb before his decorations are complete,' I observed.

Then I went into the inner room, where Horemheb still sat

slumped in his chair. I knelt down and slid into a full 'kiss earth' and nearly kissed his feet. They were filthy.

'Why are you kneeling to me, Ptah-hotep?' he asked with unutterable weariness.

'Because you are now Pharaoh,' I told him. 'Come along. You need a wash, and Mutnodjme has been worried about you. General.'

Then I asked the question which was making my heart as cold as ice, 'What of Kheperren?'

'I left him in the Village of the Palm Tree,' said Horemheb, still bemused. 'He's got a broken arm, which means that his scribing days may be finished. I'll ask… no, I'll send, by all the gods, I can send a whole regiment to get him. For he fought like a lion, and only fell at the last.'

Relieved, I dragged the corpse of Ay-Osiris into his room and laid him on his bed, his wife beside him. I looked for the last time on the face of greed, then closed his eyes and left him to judgment.

Chapter Thirty-two

Mutnodjme

On the night that Ay joined Osiris, I received into my arms a stunned, filthy, blood-stained general, and woke my household to care for him. It took three jars of well-water to scour him clean, and I found five arrow wounds on his chest which had pierced his armour. None of them were deep but they must have been very painful. On his wrist was the mark of a bite and he had ridden for so long that the skin on the insides of his thighs was raw and weeping. I had to cut off his cloth.

Ii ran for the strongest wine and Wab for bread to be soaked in it, and Ipuy talked to the general as we cared for him. The old soldier said that he had seen this before, this unresponsive state. 'This is battle-shock. You leave it to me, Mistress,' he said. And so he sat down at the general's head while I and the others worked on his body.

For a long time he said nothing. Just when I was about to shake him, he spoke in the most casual manner.

'A nasty business, soldier,' Ipuy said, and for the first time Horemheb reacted. He began to talk.

'There were more than a hundred of them, escorting one of the sons of Suppiluliumas,' he said, not even wincing as I peeled the blood-soaked inner shirt away from the wounds.

'Only the gods know what they were doing in Egypt! I had them hemmed in and the children poured rocks down on them, and we shot our arrows until there were no more arrows. Then they began to break out. The goatherds were afraid, of course, not battle-hardened, and the Assyrians bold and well armed. All I had were hoes, Ipuy, hoes and reaping hooks. It was a massacre. But they didn't flee. They died where they stood, and they all died. But so did the Assyrians.'

'How did that happen, general?' asked Ipuy.

'I think I killed them,' said Horemheb. 'Yes, Kheperren and I were back to back, I saw how they killed the children, I charged them. Then I fought them all, and they all died. At least, when I could see again, there were no more enemies, not alive.

'Then I helped my brave scribe to the village where the women said that they would set his arm; but it's a bad break. I'm sorry, Ptah-hotep, I don't think he can be a scribe any more unless he can learn to write with his left hand. And he had at least one arrow in him.'

'General, rest easy,' said Ptah-hotep. 'As long as he's alive, it doesn't matter.'

I patched the wounds with bandages and it took all of us to carry the general to his bed, administer wine and poppy, and watch until he slept.

'He killed them all by himself,' commented Ptah-hotep.

'That's the general,' agreed Ipuy.

Ptah-hotep told me that Ay was with Osiris and Tey was dead; and the manner of their deaths, which I felt that they had deserved. However, they were my parents. I searched for a reaction, but could not find one. They had never loved or wanted me, and lately they had done their best to ruin Egypt.

So though I played Isis for their funerals, I did not weep.

I was to be the Pharaoh Horemheb's Great Royal Wife, because I was the only remaining royal princess of the whole Amarna dynasty.

Ankhesenamen was in the temple of Isis and proud of her learning, and in any case by marrying me, Horemheb became

Ay's son-in-law and therefore had a double claim, though not a strong one if there had been a living son.

On the day we laid Tey and Ay-Osiris in their tomb—and hoped that they might reform in the otherworld, though I had little hope of it—Ptah-hotep came to me. Kheperren was with him. Horemheb had sent a whole regiment to fetch him and the women of the village had cared for him as best they could.

Horemheb had sent two good masons to make the Shepherd's Stone, and had exempted their village from taxation for ever after, though he could not bring back their men.

The frontier forts were reinforced. Horemheb did not have to call his soldiers from their farms. At Opet they flooded in, their harvests done, ready to follow the general and to share in his triumph. He had been very moved by that.

Kheperren's arm had healed cleanly enough, but it would never be serviceable again. He had been honourably discharged from the army.

'Lady, I am resigning my post,' said Ptah-hotep. I had more than half expected this, ever since Kheperren had been discharged. But it was a shock, anyway.

'But you're Great Royal Judge!' I protested.

'I was. For eight years I have been a judge, and I am getting old. I am very tired. I wish to enjoy the remainder of my life, lady, and I want your permission to leave your palace.'

'You have my permission,' I said, though he must have seen my disappointment in my face. I was looking forward to an expanded household, a whole palace of my own, in which both of my dear ones could have beautiful quarters. And, selfishly, I wanted him with me. I still loved him. But I could see that he was in earnest.

I was to be Great Royal Wife, the Lady Mutnodjme in Whom the Pharaoh Delights, and she must lie only with her husband. And Horemheb would need my help in re-ordering Egypt. He was a good man, and I could not leave him.

I put my necklace around Ptah-hotep's neck, looked for the last time as a lover into his beautiful eyes still fringed with jet black lashes. He still wore my thin gold ring. My heart was wrung, but it would not repay him for his love if I was to weep on his breast, so I did not weep.

Ptah-hotep kissed my hand, and Kheperren kissed my feet. I watched them go away, hand in hand. I had not noticed that they were aging, but now they were both old men, forty at least, and they deserved their peaceful end.

And I would still see them. Sometimes.

◇ ◇ ◇

The general was drafting a document when I came into the inner apartment. He looked up and smiled at me.

'I am making an edict,' he said. 'I need your help with the wording. How shall I put it that all bad judges shall be dismissed, that all lawless acts by the soldiery shall be suppressed, that all bandits are to be hunted down, that all tomb robbers shall be exiled?'

'Begin at the beginning,' I suggested. 'With your reign name.'

It was going to be a long edict, the statute of abuses which Horemheb was pledging himself to abolish. He lifted a strand of my hair and put it to his lips. I leaned over and kissed his neck where the blue beads still dangled.

'Are you content, lady?' he asked.

'I am content,' I replied.

My husband, the general and Pharaoh wrote:

Horus Mighty Bull: Ready in Plans: Golden Horus: Satisfied with Truth: Creator of the Two Lands: Favourite of the Two Ladies: Great in Marvels at Karnak: King of Upper and Lower Egypt, Djeser-kheperu-re, Ruler of Truth, He-whom-Re-has-chosen, the Son of Re, Horemheb.

Wab bought me wine and beer for the Mighty Bull of Horus, and he began with his claim to the throne, which was through me.

Behold, this fortunate Son of Re proceeded to the palace, and he brought before him the revered eldest daughter

Mutnodjme. She embraced his beauty, she placed herself before him.

I nodded. 'That is probably better than saying: *I fished her up out of the Nile.*'

King Horemheb laughed. 'Now for the reformation of Egypt,' he said with relish, and wrote again:

His majesty took counsel with his heart as to how to destroy evil and suppress untruth. Behold, his majesty spent his time seeking for ways to remove oppression and to deliver the Egyptians from violence.

Then he took palette and brush and wrote:

Lo, my majesty commands, concerning all instances of oppression in this land.

If a poor man has made for himself a boat in order to be able to serve the Pharaoh, and he is robbed of his craft and his taxes, then my majesty commands that every officer who seizes the boat and the taxes of any citizen, the law shall be executed against him, and his nose shall be cut off, and he shall be exiled to Sinai...

It was going to be a very useful reign, and I was happy.

Ptah-hotep

Honourably discharged ex-scribe, my heart's brother Kheperren led me by the hand down the steps of the palace of Thebes and onto the docks. He was being very mysterious about where we were going, but I was so pleased to be with him that I didn't mind.

I had come to my decision to retire when I had felt ice in my heart when I thought that Kheperren was dead.

Now, fortunately, he could leave his general and I could leave my Mutnodjme whom I still loved, because I did not know how many days I had left and I wanted to spend them all with Kheperren.

The servant loaded my basket of belongings into a boat. It was not a large craft like Glory of Thoth, which I had left for the next Great Royal Judge. It was a middle-sized and well-built wooden vessel and its name, according to the writing around its prow, was Rider of the Reeds which was a nice name for a flat-bottomed craft, which would indeed ride the reeds.

Kheperren loaded another basket in beside me and jumped in, casting off and grabbing the tiller.

'Come along, Ptah-hotep,' he urged. 'Have you forgotten how to row?'

I had not, and it was not really rowing anyway; just steering. The current carried us gently. The early morning mist was burning off the river. Later it would be hot. I asked how far we were travelling.

'Not a long way,' Kheperren smiled. 'We will be there long before noon. I hope you like it,' 'Hotep. It's not a grand place. I've lived all my life in army camps, so any place is good enough for a soldier. But you've lived in palaces. This is...'

I bade him to stop worrying and mind his steering. We were in the middle of the river, the current was running quickly, and I had already seen one hippopotamus. Hippopotamuses, like troubles, seldom come singly.

I wasn't worried about where we were going. I was free of all loves but this, my first. Free of all learning except a few curious scrolls which I meant to spend a few years puzzling out. Free of all command, all responsibility, all allegiance.

I was a little intoxicated by being loosed from captivity. I began to sing, and soon Kheperren joined in.

Rise thou, my glad heart,

With thy diadem in the horizon of the sky

Grant thee glory in heaven

Power on earth

That I may go forth with gladness

That I may lie down in peace.

That my heart may be satisfied

That my journey be at an end.

I woke late at night. Kheperren was asleep beside me. He had bought me to a small well-made house by the river, surrounded with a vineyard. I had been introduced to the three men and two women who were to care for us.

I had admired the fish pool and approved of the vintage. It was a very pleasant place. We had eaten a peasant's supper, of beans, bread, roasted fish and melons.

We had lain down in love and slept, and now I was awake. I could hear the rustling of the reeds, but there was something else, animal feet moving, a sniffing, and then a sharp thief-scaring bark.

'Kheperren,' I shook him by the shoulder and he drowsed awake and kissed my neck. A wave of delight was sweeping over me, but there was something I had to know.

'Kheperren, what is the name of our dog?'

He pulled me down into his arms on the reed-mat bed.

'Wolf,' he said.

Afterword

On the State of Egyptology

A scholar, says poet A. E. Housman, is in the position of a donkey between two bales of hay who starves to death because it cannot make up its mind which bale to eat. Even though my friend Dennis Pryor says the natural position of a scholar is between two mutually antagonistic theories, I find the state of Egyptology unduly contradictory.

Consider the following, which confronted me just before I lost my temper with the whole thing. I am considering the position of scribes in the 18th Dynasty.

Barbara Metz, author of *Red Land, Black Land* and a notable authority, says on p 134: 'there were no little mud-brick school-houses in Egypt.'

Strouhal, also a notable authority and author of *Life In Ancient Egypt*, says on p 36 that there is evidence: of whole classes run for trainees…scribes…in the capital city of Thebes…(and) at the Ramasseum…and in later times…at other centres too.'

Now, although they may not have been made of mud-brick, they sound like schools to me.

Metz adds, 'girls were not taught.' Strouhal retorts, 'we know the princesses joined in (the classes) because one is portrayed with a writing tablet in her hand.' Metz says: 'there were no schoolbooks;' to which Strouhal replies: 'the textbook was called Kemyt'.

Metz says: 'arithmetic was not taught'; but Strouhal states that: 'the teaching (of mathematics) was limited to simple arithmetic and algebra which scribes might need…there were textbooks.'

Metz says: 'we do not know what age education began'; while Strouhal says without any qualification that: 'schooling was from the age of five to eleven, though there was one scribe who was there when he was thirty.'

All this disagreement is on a relatively minor point. Both go on to quote extensively from the *Satire of Trades*, where a scribe urges his son to be a scribe and get a job where he can sit down. Both scholars agree on the palette, the pens, and the habit of learning to write on ostraca or on a plastered board which could be wiped clean—because these objects have been found in tombs. What, I ask, is one to make of this? Strouhal and Metz both sound authoritative, which is the habit of scholars. Both clearly have read widely and know their subject. But they can't even agree on what age Egyptian scribes began their training; and this is repeated across the whole spectrum, from analysis of various hieroglyphics to the names of Gods and the outcome of wars and the dates of reigns.

To say that Egyptology is in a state which my mother would call 'a dog's breakfast' is, in my view, to understate the case. I studied this area for some years. Then I travelled to Egypt to see it for myself. After a week of hard reading on my return, I was on the point of homicide; and if an Egyptian scholar had asked for my aid in extracting him/her from a deep pit it would have gone hard with them.

The other problem is that, much more than Greece or Rome, Egypt has been an ideal *tabula scripta* for each person to overwrite their particular religious—particularly religious—views upon.

Thus James Henry Breasted, the learned translator of every document in Ancient Egypt, except the ones I want—and who trained for the priesthood before being captured by

Egypt—insists that Akhnaten was a secular pre-Christian saint because the cult of the Aten was an attempt at monotheism, and [unsaid] monotheism is good, solid and worthy; a real religion, while polytheism is crude, primitive and superstitious.

The utterly worthy and very learned Wallis-Budge, Keeper of Egyptian Antiquities at the British Museum and translator of hieroglyphics, wrote a long monograph on the subject, also insisting that the whole Egyptian culture was monotheist. This argument, though fascinating if that's what interests you, has taken up an awful lot of scholarly capacity which could have been directed to finding out, for instance, what the calendar of festivals looked like; something which six month's work could not do for me.

The Akhnaten/Neferiti marriage has also attracted more past-life regressions and reincarnations than any other; and the general reader could easily sink into a wallow composed of new age air-headedness and 19th century religious intolerance if some sort of sceptical lifebelt was not available.

The prejudices of the writers seem much more to the fore than in, say Greek scholarship, which even so certainly had its debates. The arguments over Orphism, for instance, should not be attempted by the infirm or those susceptible to sudden shocks.

But most Greek scholars seem to have admitted that there was a strong homosexual element to life in ancient Greece, and have not been unbearably shocked by it. After all, it was Greece, and it was a long time ago, and chaps don't have to behave like that now.

But when Akhnaten is suddenly seen without Nefertiti and in the company of his brother Smenkhare, who has been given the title of Great Royal Wife, and is pictured playing kitchy-coo on the Berlin Stele, it provokes indignation.

The 'saint' who made a brave attempt at a real religion could not possibly have been perverted! says a shocked and horrified Metz. He couldn't have had an endocrine disorder, impossible! He had six children! (I have an explanation for this) and in any case it is out of the question. Breasted and Strouhal agree with her.

I have never seen such a parlous state of scholarship. Surely there is nothing which is, per se, out of the question? What have these people been doing with their remarkable learning? What is wrong with Egyptology? The scholars can't consider an ordinary case of transferred parenthood, and the wild edge are convinced that the pyramids came here from Mars.

Attitudes like these must have driven some fine fresh minds right out of their heads and into the latest discoveries in Anatolia, rather than take on Egyptian Scholarship. The rest belong to the Velikovsky/Ahmed Osman lunatic fringe. There doesn't seem to be anything in between.

So, gentle reader, I have been forced to make Executive Decisions. I have based them not on anyone's theories but on the papyri and the tomb inscriptions. As far as I can manage, the Egyptians speak in their own words. Where they were silent, I have supplied my own and if I have four contending theories as to what something means, I have picked the one I liked best.

I am quite probably wrong in some cases, but with the state of learning in this field, who could possibly prove me so?

On the Pathology of Akhnaten and Related Subjects

I don't know what some historians think with (see previous remarks on the state of Egyptology) and I do not exempt myself from this criticism. Much study can send one mad, and much study on a small bit of a complex subject can render one bonkers faster than an indulgence in white crystalline powders of unknown origin.

The pathology of Akhnaten is a case in point. The depiction of the King grew progressively more grotesque with every passing year, as can be seen by comparing the early shabti of a plump boy with drooping breasts and a belly which overflows his cloth, with the full blown freak on the colossi in the Cairo museum. This is not a normal person. He has an exaggerated jaw, sloping, bulging eyes, a receding forehead, breasts, no visible penis or scrotum, and the fat distribution seen in such women as the author. He had classic childbearing hips, a belly which bulges and folds, and thick, heavy thighs.

There are some signs that this physique was adopted by courtiers for their own portraits—and this is not uncommon. There was, for example, a short-lived period in China where all the court ladies were fat, because the Dowager was fat (and they were very attractive, too) but this reverted to the Chinese ideal of a willowy beauty as soon as the Dowager departed the scene—but there are no 'Akhnatens' after Akhnaten is gone.

Two theories are extant: the general freedom of Amarna art produced mannerism; or the king had Fröhlich's syndrome, or some other endocrine disease, possibly caused by a pituitary tumour. The second has the advantage of combining with the first—the realism of Amarna art meant that the king was depicted as he was, i.e., deeply strange.

There is, as far as my untrained eye can discern, no mannerism in Amarna art beyond the freeing of the figure to be depicted face-onwards, the addition of many subjects which were not drawn before (like the lady throwing up at a party), and a certain fluency of drawing. Egyptian art was never realistic—consider the unpleasantness of meeting a man with two visible sideways shoulders and one leg perpetually advanced—but Akhnaten's reign certainly loosened the style considerably.

I therefore was immediately drawn to the second theory—that there was something wrong with the king which was not wrong with other members of his immediate family, as evidenced by the examination of their mummified bodies. There was nothing awry Akhnaten's brothers, Smenkhare or Tutankhamen; or with his father Amenhotep III, afflicted with toothache as the poor man must have been.

We do not have Akhnaten's body, so all this must be speculation.

However, the learned Cyril Aldred, author of *Akhenaten Pharaoh of Egypt*, has considered that Frohlich's syndrome is the most reasonable explanation.

On p 104 he says: 'Until recently it was possible to speculate that though the daughters of Nefert-iti were described as begotten of a King, it is by no means certain that the king was Akhnaten, particularly when Amenhotep III was alive two years after the youngest had been born...'

This entirely agrees with the theory at which I had independently arrived; and I was astonished to read Mr Aldred's conclusion:

The discovery of damaged texts at Hermopolis... has made it reasonably clear that Akhnaten claimed responsibility at least for begetting the eldest daughter Meryt-Aten; and the presumption is that he is also the father of the other five daughters of Nefert-iti. If he is not, he cannot also be the father of the daughters of Meryt-Aten and Ankhes-en-pa-aten.... [it might be argued that they are the children of Smenh-ka-re]... but it seems that both princesses bore children before Smenh-ka-Re could marry either of them. In that case the royal father of their children can only have been Akhnaten.

In that case the father can *only* be Akhnaten?

Historians are bound by the mores of their own time (as am I) but all of them assume that there must be some betrayal or deception if children are not fathered by the husband of the mother, because *they* lived in a biologically-limited society, when marital fidelity was fidelity and adultery was adultery.

In my time, when surrogate motherhood, reproductive technology and sperm banks exist, there need be no breach of marital faith if children are fathered or even mothered by someone other than the person who claims parenthood.

Akhnaten's lack of ability to father children was dynastically disastrous and his own father—who had proved his fertility—might have considered it his duty to impregnate the Queen.

In a more squeamish century, the Queen might have taken a secret lover to ensure the succession—as Queens have done in historical time.

In the Amarna dynasty, when all beliefs were up for grabs and the King believed in an immortal unknowable God, when Amenhotep III himself was the product of a divine birth, when the King believed that he was personally and by virtue of his deformities, growing into a God himself, would he not have claimed fatherhood of any child his wife and daughters bore? The daughters' children would have been sired by someone in the Royal line, probably Smenkhare, but possibly a priest of the Aten. The child would be seen as a child of Aten, fountain of all fertility as Hapi, the God of the Nile whom Akhnaten strangely resembled.

Also, I have always been suspicious of anyone who proclaims so consistently that he is a family man.

Anyway, the fathering of her children by her father-in-law need not have interrupted Nefertiti's relationship with her husband, any more than it destroys the amity of the couples who presently resort to IVF or sperm donation. The use of a donor does not mean that these children are any less their parent's, or that they are loved any less than those born by the conventional method. Akhnaten and Nefertiti could have been blissfully happy together. By the pictures, they were.

Transliteration of Egyptian

This is really difficult. Ancient Egyptian is not the father of modern Arabic, so few useful comparisons can be drawn, unlike modern and ancient Greek or Latin and Italian. Like Hebrew, written Egyptian did not have vowels. Intelligent guesses can be made about vocalisation, but no one knows how it really would have sounded (though the Copts still speak an extensively modified version). It had also interesting dialectic points, like three versions of h. Much as I appreciate authenticity, I contemplated a few names in their direct transliterated form Smnk'r' for

Smenkhare, Nfrtyt3 for Nefertiti, Akhnaten is Gm.(t) p3-itn, for instance and decided that I would stick to a uniform spelling, using the system which employs an 'e' as a default vowel, even though this may occasionally be erroneous. I have thus used Amen instead of Amun. I have also used Maat for the Goddess of Truth rather than M'3t or Mut on purely euphonic grounds and to avoid confusing her with Mut the Mother of the Gods, wife of Amen-Re.

I have also not used the personal names of the Pharaohs but their reign names, simplifying the number of people the reader has to remember. Otherwise this would have borne a startling resemblance to one of those Russian epics where you encounter a character three times under different names and you can't recall what a patronymic is, anyway.

Times

This is another problem, but I am boldly and with some justification assuming that the reign of Amenhotep III was about 1450 BC.

In the rest of the world at that time: Troy dominated the entrance to the Black Sea; cities were beginning to form in Greece, centring on Mycenae; Minos ruled the Aegean from Crete or Kriti; China went into the Bronze Age; and my ancestors in Wales were working on the perfect bronze arrowhead and trading in tin with Achaean adventurers. The Trojan war had not yet happened, nor any of the events from the *Iliad* or the *Odyssey*, but they were imminent. The world was about to change.

The Measurement of Time

The Ancient Egyptians divided the year into three seasons of four months each. They were *Akhet*—inundation; *Peret*—sprouting; and *Shemu*—harvest. Each month was composed of three ten-day weeks. One worked eight days and rested two (and from the Deir-el-Medina records, frequently made it a three day weekend). Lacking the right word, I have called these ten-day periods a *decan*, from the Greek.

Of course, this adds up, as alert mathematicians will have noticed, to 360 days. The extra five intercalary days—the *epagomenae*—were part of a rather large festival, the days on which one celebrated the birth of certain Gods: Osiris, Isis, Set, Nepthys, Neith.

The Egyptians loved a good festival and there seems to have been no lack of days of rejoicing, feasting and getting seriously drunk.

It was common for the calendar to get out of synch with the real world, but no one seems to have worried much, as long as the many festivals and the free beer arrived.

They were an admirably relaxed people in most matters. Like the Roman hours, the day was divided into 12 hours of light and the night into 12 hours of darkness, measured by water clocks. In winter, of course, the night hours were longer than day hours, and vice versa in summer. The klepsydrae used to measure time were almost as accurate as the Chinese ones of the same date.

The hours seem to have had more of a religious or ritual use than an everyday one. Priests need to know when to change the God's attendants and soldiers when to change guard. Peasants know when they can stop working and go home by the sun.

The Calendar

The year begins at Summer Solstice—the rising of Sothis/Isis/ Sirius from 70 days absence in the underworld—and it is the occasion of the New Year Feast. It ends with the epagomenae.

AHKET   *inundation/food*
22 June–July *Thoth* New Year.
The Nile begins to rise.
Sothis rises 9th day; ' eat fried fish at your door' *Festival of Hapi.*

19th day *Festival of Thoth.*

July-August Paophi 19th day *Opet Festival* of Amen Re at Karnak & Luxor (at least a seven days festival, later extended to 22 days).

22nd day *Festival of the Nativity of the Staff of the Sun.*

The Nile is red.

August-September *Hathor* Amenhotep III's Accession was the second day of Hathor.

The Nile becomes green and poisonous for a week, and drinking-water is stored until it becomes red again.

17th *Festival of the Death of Osiris.*

September-October *Khoiak* equinox

Birth of Osiris

18th to 30th *Festival of the Opening of the Ways* (sluices opened to flood inland plain)

PERET   *spring/sprouting*

October-November *Tybi heb-sed* (jubilee)

11th day *Festival of the return of Isis* from Phoenicia with the body of Osiris.

Ritual mating mystic marriage and, on the 19th day, hippo cakes for Horus' victory over Set.

November-December Mechir *Festival of Sekhet* destroyer, the lioness in the mountains. Everyone drinks red beer in memory of salvation of humanity.

December-January *Phamenoth*

Sowing of seed in tears and mourning for the *Feast of Dead Osiris* Lamentation 'come to thy house,' branches of wormwood are carried, dogs lead the procession.

January-February *Pharmuthi, Feast of Khons*

Moonlight feasts, entry of Osiris into the moon.

SHEMU   *harvest*

February-March *Pakhons, Festival of Rennutet* (cobra lady) 19th Osiris is found.

March–April *Paoni*, *Festival of Isis* equinox 25th day feast of lights Fires in the streets because Sothis has sunk below horizon. Osiris in Field of Reeds.

April–May *Ephipi* Horus goes to Hathor, *Feast of Apis* (Osiris as bull) 7 days in Memphis; birthday of Horus' eyes. Hot dry weather, khamsin.

May–June *Mesor festivals* first fruits (harvest) Grapes ripen; everyone gets thoroughly drunk. Very hot and dry.

EPAGOMENAE   *the intercalary days*

The five extra days of the calendar, are the birthdays of:

1. **Osiris**

2. **Anubis/Horus**

3. **Set**

This day is terribly unlucky and no one does anything on it, no contracts are signed and no work is done, especially by creators. A red-headed male child born on this day might well be killed. It was kept as a fast.

4. **Isis**

A very lucky day for weddings and births.

5. **Nepthys**

Also a lucky day for weddings.

The Gods

There are several trinities of gods, reflecting the thrifty way that the Egyptians never wasted a good deity but just incorporated them into the existing pantheon; a custom which the Romans later found useful.

When Upper (south) and Lower (north) Egypt joined, their gods were also combined; although the most important was always some form of the sun, **Re** (or Ra) or **Amen**; and, of course, briefly the **Aten**. **Re** could manifest in the form of a ram, a hawk or a dung-beetle.

Note also that *nefer*, the word for god, has no levels of importance; unlike the Hebrew scale of angels or the Christian's 'thrones dominations and powers.' This makes it difficult to judge, just from the name, whether a *nefer* or *nefert* was a small local deity or a star in the state religion.

Iwnw or Heliopolitan Cosmogeny

Amen-Re began as **Aten** who emerged self-created from the primeval ocean **Nun**, took the form of the **Bnbn**—or the phoenix, a bi-sexual creature. It flew to the top of the Bennu stone, masturbated and from his swallowed sperm created **Shu**, god of air, and **Tefnut**, goddess of water/moisture/rain; who then produced **Geb**, the earth, and **Nut**, the sky; who in turn gave birth to the sun or **Amen-Re**. This was the cosmogony adopted at Thebes and Karnak and was as close as Egypt got to an official religion.

Heliopolitan/Theban Trinity

Amen Re   God of the sun (aka Amen Ra) is **Khephri** when a scarab beetle, and **Harahkti** when a hawk

Mut   Mother Goddess, vulture-headed wife of Amen

Khons   God of the moon and time, son of Amen and Mut

Children of Amen-Re and Mut

Tefnut   Goddess of water/wetness

Geb   God of the earth (only the Egyptians had a male earth god)

Nut   Goddess of the sky. Nut mates with Geb every night and gives birth to the sun.

Shu   God of air, he prises Geb and Nut apart and allows for day.

Children of Geb and Nut

Osiris   God of the dead and King of the Field of Reeds

Isis   Goddess of magic, women and fertility, wife of Osiris

Horus   The Hawk, the revenging son of Osiris and Isis

Set	The Destroyer, brother of Osiris and his murderer
Nepthys	Guardian lady, sister of Isis
Neith	Guardian of the dead, sister of Isis
Hathor	Goddess of beauty and love, sister of Isis, lover of Horus, depicted as a cow.

Lesser Gods

Thoth	The Scribe, ibis-headed God of wisdom and healing
Maat	Justice and Truth, who weighs all hearts against her feather
Opet	Hippopotamus-headed mother of Osiris
Ptah	The Creator who formed the world with words
Sekhmet	Warrior Goddess, lioness-headed wife of Ptah, mistress of epidemics, 'spreader of terror'
Sobek	The crocodile god
Basht	Cat Goddess, mistress of erotic love (especially in Bubastis in the Nile Delta)
Edjo	The Cobra. She appears on the crown as a uraeus and protects the King.
Min	God of fertility, depicted with an erect phallus.
Wepwawet	The Wolf, avenger of Osiris
Anubis	God of embalmers, jackal-headed protector of the dead
Apep	The Great Serpent, foe of Amen-Re
Apis	The Bull, an aspect of Osiris
Hapi	grotesque male-female God of the Nile
Bes	God of childbirth and fun, a grinning ithyphallic dwarf

Memphis Cosmogeny

Ptah is identified as **Nun**, the primeval ocean, which produced **Amen-Re** and acted through thought and word to create the whole world and everything in it.

Ptah was called Lord of Truth but Memphis was less powerful than Thebes and so he only achieved a local popularity.

Memphite Trinity

Khnum   God of the Nile, the Potter who made humans on his wheel

Satis   Goddess of the Nile Floods, gazelle-headed wife of Khnum

Anukis   Goddess of the Nile, Daughter of Khnum and Satis

Hermopolitan Cosmogeny

This never caught on as a royal religion but involves a group of eight gods, or Ogdoad: **Nun**; **Kuk**, the god of darkness; **Amen**, 'that which is hidden'; **Huh**, eternity.

Their female consorts have feminine versions of their names: **Naunet, Hauhet, Kauket** and **Amaunet**. The male gods had frog's heads and the females had serpents; possibly reflecting the soggy nature of Hermopolis.

In the beginning the eight deities created and ruled the world; or in an alternative version it was laid as a world egg by an ibis, representing **Thoth** (though Thoth is usually male) and hatched to reveal the child **Re**, whose tears became humans.

◇◇◇

This is only a partial list of the gods worshipped in Ancient Egypt. A full list can be found in any study of ancient Egyptian religion, though you must retain an open mind about how popular they were and where they originated.

I favour the accretion theory—that they were all local gods who remained known because they were written down, and remained in worship because they had temples which were perpetually endowed with taxes and staffed by priests and priestesses who were useful to their supporters, by being also doctors and scribes. There are a lot of other theories.

A survey of the number of religious beliefs which the average Egyptian could hold simultaneously will explain how King Akhnaten was able to grab hold of one aspect of Amen-Re and turn it into a solar cult with himself at the head of it.

It also explains why this was so desperately unpopular that no one mentioned his name for the next thousand years without calling him 'The Traitor' or 'The Villain'.. Akhnaten had tried to steal their gods and their afterlife from the common people, and this was unforgivable.

On Egyptian Customs

Herodotus—my favourite ancient historian—was wandering around Egypt in about 450 BC and had this to say about Egypt, in Book 2 of *The Histories:* (translation Aubrey de Selincourt)

I travelled to Memphis, Thebes and Heliopolis...and about Egypt I shall have a great deal more to relate because of the number of remarkable things which the country contains...

Not only is the Egyptian climate peculiar to that country, and the Nile different in behaviour from all other rivers, but the Egyptians themselves in their manners and customs seem to have reversed the ordinary practices of mankind. For instance, women attend market and are employed in trade, while men stay at home and do the weaving. In weaving the normal way is to work the threads of the weft upwards, but the Egyptians work them downwards.

Men in Egypt carry loads on their heads, and women on their shoulders; women pass water standing up, men sitting down. To ease themselves they go indoors, but eat outside in the streets, on the theory that what is unseemly but necessary should be done in private, and what is not unseemly should be done openly.

No woman holds priestly office...Elsewhere priests grow their hair long, in Egypt they shave their heads. In other nations people...mark mourning by cutting their hair, but the Egyptians mark a death by letting hair grow on head and chin.

Other men live on barley, but...in Egypt they make bread from spelt (wheat). Dough they knead with their feet, but clay with their hands.

They practice circumcision...Men in Egypt have two garments, women only one. The ordinary practice at sea is to fasten the sheets to ring-bolts fitted outboard; the Egyptians fit them inboard.

In writing or calculating instead of going, like the Greeks, from left to right, the Egyptians go from right to left and obstinately maintain that theirs is the dextrous method, ours being left-handed and awkward. They have two sorts of writing, the sacred and the common. They are religious to excess...

They wear linen clothes which they make a special point of continually washing. They bathe in cold water twice a day...they never eat cows, for they are sacred [to Hathor]... this is the reason why no Egyptian, man or woman, will kiss a Greek, or use a Greek knife, spit or cauldron, or even eat the flesh of a bull known to be clean, if it has been cut with a Greek knife.

I always felt that there was a sense of personal affront in his account of the Egyptians' refusal to kiss Greeks, but otherwise the Father of History is pretty much spot on about Egypt.

Herodotus was an excellent observer, and many of the things he said, which have been discounted for centuries, turn out to be true.

Consider, for example, the recent discoveries of ancient graves in Northern Kazakhstan—made by the Centre for the Study of

Eurasian Nomads—in which several women were buried with well-used weapons made to fit their hands, and some men were buried with cooking pots and children. They are quite likely to be Herodotus' Amazons and he may have been right all along.

One can see from the tomb paintings that he was right about the way people carried loads; we know that each house of any pretension contained a lavatory, so they would have gone inside to excrete. I have myself seen present-day women pee quite respectably while standing up—so that too is possible. I have no information about men, however, because no Ancient Egyptian drew this act (possibly because it was 'unseemly').

Herodotus is right about barley being food for animals and wheat for humans, about kneading with the feet, and about men weaving—for the *Satire of Trades* is clear on this point.

As he was also correct about linen clothes, about circumcision and about writing, I am assuming that he was right about women attending market and trading; though all modern commentators reject this out of hand based on observations of both Copts and Arabs in present-day Egypt. Although even in modern Egypt, I might add, the people in any given souk are mostly women, though few of the traders are.

Herodotus was accurate about the process of mummification; but he was wrong about no women being priests. There have been many priestly offices held by women, including, for instance, the Chantress (Singer) of Amen at Thebes, who was ruler of her own kingdom at some times.

Based on similar ancient practice in other nearby lands, I have assumed that the priests of Isis were women, and that there were sacred prostitutes in the temple of Hathor. I might be wrong; but see my previous comments on the state of Egyptology. I am more likely to trust ancient practice in other places than a modern interpreter drawing parallels from their own entirely different culture, race and religion.

Sexuality & Marriage

There are few references to sexual sins in the confessions. One is required to say 'I lay with no woman when she was a child'; and in one of the *Maxims of Ptah-Hotep* he tells his son not to 'lie with a boy-priest (or boy-lover) because to satisfy his heart one must do such things as are not done.' But the latter can be read as requiring his son not to get involved with the dangerous cult of Astarte, which could lose him his testicles.

Sodomy is depicted in paintings as something which occasionally happens at feasts and in the fields. So is ordinary sex. I am not even talking about the *Turin Erotic Papyrus*, where the 'raise high the roofbeams' massive phallus of the bald man would have qualified him for a great future in porn movies, out-doing Long Dong Silver of recent fame.

Before they married, Egyptians seem to have been able to mate as they liked, and this is borne out by shocked comments from all the ancient visitors. They were already shocked by the way the Egyptian women could go where they liked and lie with whoever they fancied. There is a considerable body of erotic verse by women, and I cannot dismiss all of it (as one writer has done) by assuming it was written by wishful-thinking men. It has a strong female feel to it; unlike, say, *The Wife's Lament* in Anglo Saxon which was almost certainly written by a man. It is more like the verses of the troubarits in Provencal.

The only absolute duty one had in ancient Egypt was to marry and beget. After marriage both parties were supposed to be faithful to each other. No one has found a marriage ceremony, which in most cultures is a transference of property from father to husband; but the woman seems to have left her own home to live in her husband's house.

Commonly she would have had a pre-nuptial agreement on which she could sue if the marriage broke down. Egyptian women had rights to two thirds of their property, a right to divorce, a right to own and run her own business and to will her property to whomever she pleased. She did not belong either to her husband or her father, but to herself, and what else can one require of a sensible system? No other ancient woman, except perhaps in Troy, had such freedom.

Burial Customs

One of the multitudinous problems which confronted me when considering the reign of Akhnaten was, if we have a king who believes in the 'unknowable immortal' Aten—who denies the worship of, and actively suppresses the worship of all other gods—what are we to make of the fact that all the royal personages buried during his reign, even at Amarna, were mummified in the usual way and laid in painted tombs with their furniture to await the afterlife?

The worship of the Aten precludes any other gods and also precludes an afterlife, because all that the spirit can hope for is union with godhead after a brief flirtation with reincarnation. That means no judgment, no weighing of the heart, no confession, no magic, and indeed, no Osiris, no Isis, and no Field of Reeds.

There are no intact royal burials from Akhnaten's time, but we have the mummy of his brother Smenkhare who was certainly embalmed in the proper way. The burials of his father, his mother, his daughter and the officials from this time—though sacked by Horemheb and relocated and robbed—appear to have been done in the time-honoured fashion. Akhnaten may have modified the ritual and omitted portraits of the gods, but the bodies were still preserved as usual.

My friend Mark Deasey mentioned that in the North of England people who have been converted to Methodism for four generations still bury their dead by Quaker rites; and in Afro-American ritual, traces can be found of the African customs, remembered from the time before slavery. I suggest that burial is the most traditional of all rites, the one where most old religion and superstition attaches, because doing it wrongly may mean that the dead come back and tell you about it.

That means, logically, that the temples of Isis and Osiris must have remained and that the large funeral industry must have continued during the time of Akhnaten.

Watchers

I have translated these as Watchers, rather than Guardians, and they were the world's first police force. They were responsible for the maintenance of public order; for the care of the vital dykes, walls and canals; and for any other duties, like guarding tombs and settling domestic disputes. They reported to the Mayor or Headman of the village, who in turn reported to a District Court, which reported to the Nomarch and thence, if it was a really hairy issue, to the Pharaoh's judges.

In this it is remarkably similar to the Chinese system of District Magistrates who had their own staff for investigation, who reported to a District Court and thence to the Emperor's High Court.

The Watchers, as an institution, lasted into Roman rule.

Nomes

These were the equivalent of states and everyone disagrees about how many there were. There were probably forty-two, although by Strabo's time there seem to have been twenty-seven. My favourite source, Herodotus, writes of Nomes but does not say how many there were, which would indicate that he didn't know. I find it hard to believe that he didn't ask. He does say that the Labyrinth of Government contained twelve halls so there may have been twelve major divisions and sub-nomes as well.

Each Nome had its ruler, or Nomarch, who was usually the biggest landholder. All land in Egypt belonged to the king however; ever since the Age of Chaos when a number of warring Nomarchs reduced Egypt to ruin. After that, no man could own any land—but was allotted it by the king, who owned everything; although this modified freehold could be given, sold or willed.

Every Nome also had its attendant god. For instance, the Nome of Uast—which is Thebes—had, as its capital, Thebes (or Uast); its symbol, the Ram; and its God, Amen-Re.

The Nome of Set had as its capital, Shas-hetep; its symbol, the Black Dog; and its God, Khnem (Amen the father, a phallus).

A full list can be found in Strabo, though he is late; or Pliny, who is later. In the 18th Dynasty, there appear to have been ten Nomes in Upper Egypt, ten in the Delta, and seven in the Heptanomis in Nubia.

Tax & Labour Systems

All land belonged to the Pharaoh; the land title system was a lesser form of freehold (see above); and taxes were assessed on variable factors—the rise of the Nile flood, the fertility of a given field, and the previous history of the land.

The harvest was assessed by inspectors, the seed allotted on that basis, and the farmer left to get on with it. When the grain was harvested the tax was collected. If the farmer had not worked diligently, he owed labour to the state; unless he had a good reason—which included death of a son or parent and climatic factors.

Egyptians used few slaves; those they had were all captives of war; and the child of a slave was not necessarily a slave. Therefore, during the reigns of the belligerent kings, say Rameses II, Egypt had a lot of slaves; and in the reigns of the politically ingenious pharaohs, such as Amenhotep III, there were correspondingly fewer slaves.

Indentured labour—farmers who had not paid their tax and labour levied in something similar to the feudal corvee in Europe—had to be fed and cared for; and their services could not be either demanded during the farming season or kept beyond the dry season.

All those monuments which astound the beholder were built either by indentured or by hired labour, and not by slaves. The Romans also used soldiers, not slaves, to build all those roads which led to Rome and all those remarkable water systems. As the 20th Century has shown, slaves do not make good labour.

On Meteorites, Heliopolis & the Bnbn Bird

Have I mentioned that much study on Egyptology drives people insane? Nowhere is this more clear than in the subject of pyramids. One look at the astounding symmetry and telemetry of the pyramids has fine scientific minds talking about a pre-existing and possibly alien race which must have existed before 10,500 BC; because how otherwise could such simple people align these monuments perfectly on 30 degrees of latitude.

You see what I mean? I don't know how they did it either; except that assuming ancient people were stupider than we are (because we are so terribly modern and have computers and technology) is foolish.

For this reason—but more so because they were built long before the time I am considering—I shall say no more at all about pyramids.

But the bnbn bird, on the other hand, is fascinating.

Every visitor to Egypt in the ancient times was told about the long-awaited bnbn—or benben—bird. The Greeks called this self-created, self-generating creature the Phoenix. It was later adopted into Christian iconography as a symbol of Christ and his resurrection.

The temple of the Phoenix at Karnak is an open space surrounded by massive walls. In it is the Bennu pillar—a pillar with a rounded top, later a stele with a rounded top,—on which the bnbn bird will perch when it returns to Karnak. Escorted by all the birds of the air, it will deliver its 'parent'—a ball of myrrh and semen which produces the new Phoenix. (Squeamish later writers made the bird female and the 'parent' an egg, which is much more sanitary).

Then the bird will betake itself to its favourite date palm, make a nest of cinnamon, cassia and frankincense and sing its last song; after which it will summon fire, by cupping its wings, and burn away to ash. The new Phoenix, or the same one, will then fly from Karnak returning only to die, in the same way, after an interval variously described as anything between 500 to 12,000 years.

Tacitus, in his *Annals*, and agreeing with Herodotus, suggests that it came back to Karnak in AD 34 after 500 years; while Pliny, in *Natural History* says 1200 years. The best poem about it is by Lactantius, who describes, in gentle elegaics, its escort by the birds, its red and gold colouring and its final and glorious death: *ipse quidem, sed non eadem quia et ipsa nec ipsa est, aeternam vitam mortis adepta bono*— 'Because she is herself and not herself, gaining eternal life by the boon of death'.

I am, by the way, entirely convinced by Bauval and Gilbert's thesis of *The Orion Mystery* that the pyramids were aligned to the rising of Isis/Sothis/Sirius; and that the Egyptians were aware of the precession of the equinoxes.

This also solved a problem for me. In the remarkable book, *Akhenaten: The Heretic King*, Redford has shown that Nefertiti was repeatedly depicted as priestess to the Bennu/Benben/Phoenix bird in the form of a black stone—like the pyramid-capping stone in the Cairo museum. This is explained by the hypothesis that this was—like the *ka'aba* in Mecca—a meteorite, which flew like a firebird and left just a black iron egg behind; from which it would doubtless again arise.

The connection of the Queen to the cult is not obvious, but may be as I have hypothesised—that she signified the divine or cosmic womb, the womb of Isis seeded by Osiris/Orion, who gave birth to the Aten, the mystic unknowable God whose avatar was the disc of the Sun.

I am fairly sure that the Phoenix can be identified with Isis/Sothis/Sirius; and that possibly the interval of 1260 years—a Sothic cycle or Sirius year—regulates the return of the Phoenix.

However, the fact that the iconoclast monotheist Akhenaten has a whole wall and chamber at his new Aten In Splendour temple at Karnak devoted to Nefertiti as the head priestess of the bnbn cult is strange and to my mind must signify more than a desire to confer honour upon his wife. I have suggested some reasons why the King did this.

The Fate of...

Ankhesenamen

No one knows what happened to the sister/wife of Tutankhamen. If she was alive or present at the accession of Horemheb, he would certainly have married her. She did attempt to bring a prince of Assyria to marry her, and he met with a fatal termination of his matrimonial hopes somewhere on the border. Several writers have sentimentalised about her sad fate, notably Desroches-Noblecourt, who thinks that Ay is a good guy and Horemheb a cruel and brutal dictator. It occurred to me, however, that she might have decided to take some hand in her own fate before she expired of acute nomenclature.

Tutankhamen

The young Pharaoh's mummified body has extensive damage, but it is now hard to tell if it is post or antemortem. If it was postmortem, then someone dropped the Divine Corpse down a lot of stairs.

Ay, who took over the rule of the Black Land, is the obvious suspect.

Mutnodjme

The accidental Queen of Egypt died in childbirth some years after the accession of Horemheb. He never remarried and had no children. After his death, the kingdom went to an old army commander, and thence to a new dynasty.

Horemheb

The warrior Pharaoh died peacefully after reigning for twenty-seven years. He had the temple of the Aten pulled down, and even the tombs of Huy and Ay looted of their treasures (though their bodies were not touched). Despite his bad press, I do see his point.

Horemheb was certainly not a tyrant and his reign smoothed away most of the problems created by the Amarna experiment. However, the kinglist puts him directly after Amenhotep III, giving him a reign of fifty years, and making the discovery of Tutankhamen's tomb a real surprise because no one could identify him. Horemheb decided—or the later writers decided it for him—that the Amarna dynasty had been a mistake and that the Pharaoh who *should* have followed Amenhotep the Wise, was Horemheb; and therefore deleted all references to all of them.

I don't think, as some writers have suggested, that Horemheb was a miser who robbed all the Amarna tombs for gold and who only missed Tutankhamen's tomb because he couldn't find it. He was at the funeral; he knew where it was. He merely pillaged the tombs of the pillagers; and since he spent most of his reign attempting to mend the damage they did to Egypt, one can see his point.

◇◇◇

Ptah-hotep

The scribe was actually called Amenhopis but, for story I had to tell, I decided this would cause too many identification problems as I already had two Amenhoteps.

Ptah-hotep died at an advanced age and in honour. His tomb paintings—which rather stress Thoth god of scribes and the making and drinking of wine—also include a hut by the river with a dog on guard, and two men making love in the reeds.

◇◇◇

The amount of research which this book entailed was much heavier than I expected, due to the aforementioned state of Egyptology.

I was surprised by the change in my attitude to the Egyptians. I began by thinking that they worshipped death, and ended by realising that they worshipped life.

Kerry Greenwood

Bibliography

Original Sources

Egyptian Rituals and Incantations translated by John A Wilson in ed James B Pritchard Ancient and Near Eastern Texts Relating to the New Testament 3rd Edition Princeton UP 1969

From *The Literature of Ancient Egypt* ed W.K. Simpson (New Haven) Yale University Press 1997

    The Maxims of Ptah-hotep

    The Prophecies of Neferti

    The Instruction of Dua-Khety (The Satire on the Trades)

    The Man Who Was Tired of Life

    The Instruction of a Man for his Son

    The Instruction of Amunnakhte

Medinet Habu Temple Calendar

Documents relating to the Amarna Dynasty and the accession of Horemheb

From Breasted James H *Ancient Records of Egypt Histories and Mysteries of Man* Ltd London 1988

From the *Papyrus of the Scribe Ani* in The Book of the Dead translated by E.A. Wallis-Budge, Bell Publishing Company New York 1962

    The Pyramid Text

    The Book of Coming Forth By Day

    The Book of Gates

The Amarna Letters translated by William L. Morgan from The Amarna Letters John Hopkins University Press Maryland 1992

Secondary Sources

Aldred, Cyril *Akhenaten Pharaoh of Egypt* Abacus Thames and Hudson London 1968

Andrews, Carol *Egyptian Mummies* British Museum London 1984

Bierbrier, Morris *Tomb Builders of the Pharaoh* British Museum London 1982

R. Bauvel and A. Gilbert *The Orion Mystery* Mandarin London 1995

Cott, Jonathan *The Search For Omm Sety* Arrow London 1989

Cottrell, L. *The Secret of Tutankhamen's Tomb* Mayflower New York 1964

Cottrell, L. *The Warrior Pharaohs* Evans Bros. London 1968

David, Rosalie A. *The Ancient Egyptians, Religions Belief and Practices* Routledge and Kegan Paul London 1982

Desroches-Noblecourt, C. *Tutankhamen* Penguin London 1965

Desroches-Noblecourt, C. *Life and Death of a Pharaoh* Rainbird London 1963

Desroches-Noblecourt, C *Temples de Nubie Des Tresors Menacés* UNESCO Paris 1961

Duff, J. Wright and Arnold *Minor Latin Poets* (Lactantius) Heinemann London 1961

Edwards, I.E.S. *The Pyramids of Egypt* Pelican London 1947

Freed, Rita A. *Egypt's Golden Age* Museum of Fine Arts Boston 1982

Grant, Joan *Eyes of Horus* Corgi London 1942

Gurney, O.R. *The Hittites* Pelican London 1966

James, T.G.H. *Egyptian Painting* British Museum London 1985

James, T.G.H. and Davies W.V. *Egyptian Sculpture* British Museum London 1983

Jenkins, Nancy *The Boat Beneath The Pyramid* Thames & Hudson London 1980

Kamil, Jill *The Ancient Egyptians* Wren Publishing London 1976

Lamy, Lucie *New Light on Ancient Knowledge: Egyptian Mysteries* Thames and Hudson London 1981

Laver, James *Costume in Antiquity* Thames & Hudson London 1964

Leavesley, J.H. *Medical By-ways* A.B.B. Books Sydney 1984

Malek, J. and Forman W. *Echoes of the Ancient World* Orbis Books London 1986

Metz, Barbara *Red Land, Black Land* Hodder & Stoughton London 1966

Neubert, Otto *Tutankhamun and the Valley of the Kings* Mayflower London 1972

Norton, Andre *Shadowhawk* Harcourt Brace New York 1960

Oates, Joan *Babylon* Thames & Hudson London 1979

Osman, Ahmed *Stranger in the Valley of the Kings* Grafton London 1993

Redford, Donald B. *Akhenaten: The Heretic King* Princeton University Press published in Egypt by The American University Cairo Press Cairo 1992

Simpkins (series title, no authors given) *The Temple of Queen Hatshepsut* and *The Temple of Karnak* (guides bought in Egypt at site)

Strouhal, Eugen *Life in Ancient Egypt* Cambridge University Press Cambridge 1992

Tyldesley, Joyce *Daughters of Isis: Women of Ancient Egypt* Viking London 1994

Velikovsky, I. *Oedipus and Akhnaton* Sidgwick and Jackson London 1978

Wallis-Budge, E.A. *Egyptian Religion* Routledge and Kegan Paul London (reprint) 1975

Wallis-Budge, E.A. *The Gods of the Egyptians: Studies in Egyptian Mythology* Dover New York 1969

Journal Articles

Aldred, Cyril 'The Tomb of Akhenaten at Thebes' in *Journal of Egyptian Archaeology* 1957 p41

Botermans, Jack and ors Le Monde des Jeux Société nouvelle des editions du chine, Amsterdam 1987

Gardiner, Sir Alan 'The Coronation of King Haremhab' *Journal of Egyptian Archaeology* 1953 13-31

Sandison, Dr A.T 'Analysis of Frolichs Syndrome and Akhenaten' in Aldred, JEA op cit

Tair, John 'Senet' *New Scientist* 22/29 December 1990

Thibault, Daniel U. 'Senet: The Game of Passing Through the Underworld' in *Tournaments Illuminated* Autumn 1996 Issue 120 p16

Music

Music in the World of Islam 2. Lutes 4. Flutes and Trumpets and 5. Reeds and Bagpipes.

Tapes and recordings done by Jean Jenkins and Paul Olsen Tangent Records London 1972.

To receive a free catalog of Poisoned Pen Press titles, please contact us in one of the following ways:

Phone: 1-800-421-3976
Facsimile: 1-480-949-1707
Email: info@poisonedpenpress.com
Website: www.poisonedpenpress.com

Poisoned Pen Press
6962 E. First Ave. Ste 103
Scottsdale, AZ 85251